BEWITCHED BY A VAMPIRE
ETERNAL MATES BOOK 21

∽∾

FELICITY HEATON

Copyright © 2022 Felicity Heaton

All rights reserved. No part of this publication may be reproduced, stored in a retrieval system, or transmitted, in any form or by any means mechanical, electronic, photocopying, recording or otherwise without the prior written consent of the publisher, nor be otherwise circulated in any form of binding or cover other than that in which it is published and without a similar condition being imposed on the subsequent purchaser.

The right of Felicity Heaton to be identified as the Author of the Work has been asserted by her in accordance with the Copyright, Designs and Patents Act 1988.

First printed June 2022

First Edition

Layout and design by Felicity Heaton

All characters in this publication are purely fictitious and any resemblance to real persons, living or dead, is purely coincidental.

THE ETERNAL MATES SERIES

Book 1: Kissed by a Dark Prince
Book 2: Claimed by a Demon King
Book 3: Tempted by a Rogue Prince
Book 4: Hunted by a Jaguar
Book 5: Craved by an Alpha
Book 6: Bitten by a Hellcat
Book 7: Taken by a Dragon
Book 8: Marked by an Assassin
Book 9: Possessed by a Dark Warrior
Book 10: Awakened by a Demoness
Book 11: Haunted by the King of Death
Book 12: Turned by a Tiger
Book 13: Tamed by a Tiger
Book 14: Treasured by a Tiger
Book 15: Unchained by a Forbidden Love
Book 16: Avenged by an Angel
Book 17: Seduced by a Demon King
Book 18: Scorched by Darkness
Book 19: Inflamed by an Incubus
Book 20: Craved by a Wolf
Book 21: Bewitched by a Vampire

**Discover more available paranormal romance books at:
http://www.felicityheaton.com**

Or sign up to my mailing list to receive a FREE vampire romance ebook, learn about new titles, be eligible for special subscriber-only giveaways, and read exclusive content including short stories:
http://ml.felicityheaton.com/mailinglist

With great thanks to my awesome husband for constantly buoying me up, my beloved cat for constantly distracting me, making my husband have to work even harder to keep me on the tracks, and my editor and beta for their hard work.

Also, a huge shout out to my awesome Sapphire Dragons at my Patreon, Tracy Meighan (bonus thank you for all you've done for me over the years) and Amanda Abney, for being so incredibly supportive of me and helping me continue to do the thing I love most: writing!

CHAPTER 1

It was safest to live on bagged blood. But where was the fun in that?

After fourteen hundred years, a vampire craved a little excitement. A change to the normal pace of life. Something to distinguish one day from the next and stop them all from blurring into a monotonous existence.

When you had eternity ahead of you, you needed to find a reason to keep plodding forwards.

Night had found excitement in a multitude of ways over the centuries. Chasing females in his youth. Courting princesses and queens in his adulthood. Fighting against the odds on a battlefield. Slinking through the shadows as an assassin for the Preux Chevaliers, serving his older brother, Grave.

None of it could compare to the hunt, though.

The hunt was delicious. Something to be savoured.

Picking prey wasn't like a human going to a supermarket and grabbing the first pack of meat from the chiller. Not if the vampire had any pride or finesse, anyway.

It required patience.

Placing himself in the most strategic position so he could survey all in the room and study them in turn. Seeking a suitable host that would have just the right flavour he desired or strength he needed. It could take hours for the perfect donor to appear. Tantalising hours in which his hunger would build to an excruciating level and he would know that first sip of blood from the vein would be like manna from heaven.

And once he had found his prey?

Night shivered.

Once he found his prey, centuries of experience kicked into action and the real hunt began.

He sighed. The hunt was all that made him feel alive these days. His fingers brushed his throat, feeling the ridge of scar tissue that ringed it, and his mood darkened. Maybe he had died that night. He felt as if he had. He had never really recovered from that vile witch's attack, or from the emotional blow her comrade had delivered him.

And he had led a dark existence since then.

Night dropped his hand back to the steering wheel of his sleek all-black Jaguar F-Type and glared at the narrow road the headlights illuminated ahead of him.

He should have been in the city, hunting as planned. If he had walked out of the door a second sooner, he might have missed his phone buzzing and he might not have checked it, and might not have grimaced at the reminder that he was due at his eldest brother, Bastian's, house tonight.

But he had, and there was no changing it.

There was only bearing it.

He growled, his top lip peeling back off his emerging fangs, and cursed Bastian for denying him the one thing that made him feel alive. He didn't want to spend a week leading a pampered existence, subjected to Bastian's dull parties where only other vampires attended and blood was handed to him on a silver platter. Bastian loved hosting elegant soirees designed to remind the other aristocrat vampires in the area that they lived in close proximity to a Van der Garde, as if others of their kind should feel blessed to be in their presence.

Night hit a hard left turn and gunned the engine, his mood darkening further at the prospect of Bastian showing him off as if he was some kind of prized possession rather than his own flesh and blood. Sometimes his brother irritated the hell out of him. But—he huffed—Bastian was right. They were Van der Gardes, and that meant they had a reputation to uphold, and he would end up doing his part to impress whatever guests Bastian threw at him and endure their gushing and compliments. His bloodline had clawed their way to the top and made a name for themselves as the most powerful and vicious pureblood family, one many in this world feared, and not only the vampires.

Grave had carved out a dark and bloody reputation for them during his tenure as the leader of the Preux Chevaliers, a mercenary corps for aristocrat vampires. Anyone who knew of his brother trembled in fear.

Night found it all rather dull. Maybe it had excited him once.

Before a witch had tried to remove his head.

He slowed and swung the sports car to the right, through the gap between two impressive sandstone columns that supported the black iron gate of Bastian's mansion. He slowed further, drawing out the approach, prowling along the drive. Moonlight cut through the slender cypresses that lined the road, making it flash over the bonnet.

The temptation to turn the car around and make up an excuse was strong, but Bastian would only be angry with him if he did. Which would only make things worse. Bastian would guilt him into a longer visit, and possibly a damned ball in which Night would be expected to dance with every pureblood female vampire in the vicinity. It was better to put up with this short stay than risk subjecting himself to that torment.

Still, it was about time Grave subjected himself to the horror of spending a week with their brother. He blamed Grave for the torture he was about to suffer. If Grave didn't ignore the yearly summons without fail, Night wouldn't feel obligated to obey it in some pathetic attempt to keep their family together. It didn't help that Night lived in the mortal realm, making it far easier for Bastian to reach him. He didn't have the excuses Grave did. He didn't live in Hell, where pen and paper or a physical messenger were the only real way to get in touch with someone, and he didn't run a busy mercenary corps.

Yes, there had been a few years where Night had managed to skip the ritual torment, but thanks to the advent of modern technology, otherwise known as mobile phones and the internet, he could no longer easily escape it. Not only that, but if he missed a year, Bastian more than made up for it the next.

He wasn't talking about balls now. He was talking about Bastian's tendency to make every moment they weren't in the presence of other vampires, putting on a show so they appeared perfect to their guests, a living nightmare for him. Night had grown tired of hearing his brother regale him with his failings as a Van der Garde.

It wasn't exactly fun to have them pointed out to him.

For once, he would like his brother to notice the great things he did, not the mistakes he made. He chuckled at that. Hell would freeze over long before Bastian praised him for anything. His brother didn't have it in him.

He stared at the elegant Georgian sandstone mansion as it came into view ahead of him.

A golden glow emanated from most of the sash windows on the two levels, especially those closest to the double-height portico in the centre of the long building. Lights set into the ground illuminated the façade, including the Grecian columns that supported a triangular pediment with a beautiful carved frieze set into it. He stared at the figures and blew out his breath.

It looked more like a prison than a home to him as dread pooled in his stomach.

A whole week of putting up with Bastian and whatever fawning vampires his brother invited over.

Sometimes he wished Grave had succumbed to bloodlust and gone as nuclear as their cousin had, finishing the job Snow had started that dark night by murdering the rest of his family. Except for him, of course. Snow had spared his brother, Antoine. Night was sure Grave would do the same for him, clawing his sanity back in time to save him.

Or maybe he should just let his brother finish the job the witch had started on him.

Grave would never do it, though. His brother was cold and ruthless, but Night wasn't as blind to his feelings as others were. His brother loved him too much to let him die. Proof of that was the fact Grave had reassigned him to the mortal world soon after the incident, using some excuse about him commanding a new black-ops type team that would be responsible for carrying out covert missions. His brother had wanted him out of Hell and away from danger. He wanted to keep Night safe.

Maybe his brother's desperate desire to keep him alive was the reason Night had been seeing less and less of him over the decades. Night wanted things between them to reach a point where Grave wouldn't stop him.

He tightened his grip on the steering wheel and crushed those dark thoughts, putting them out of his head. He had important missions to complete for Grave. He was vital to Grave's plans to become the most powerful man in Hell. Someone had to watch his brother's back.

And who better to do it than his shadow?

Night frowned as the door of the mansion opened and Bastian hurried out of it, one of his owned humans following him.

With a lot of bags.

Night parked his car and stepped out, the golden gravel crunching under his black leather shoes. "What's this?"

Bastian spared him a glance and then pointed at the boot of his enormous black Bentley. "Put the luggage in there. Hurry."

The young man dipped his head and rushed to comply with his master's orders, and Night strode towards his brother. Something was wrong. It wasn't like Bastian to be flustered and his brother looked close to doing something terribly undignified, like running his hand through his neat dark brown hair.

Or losing his temper.

"I asked, what's this?" Night stopped close to him, but Bastian moved away and did something very unlike him.

He opened the rear door of the car himself.

"Things must be dire if you're not waiting for a servant to do that for you. I'm a patient man, Bastian, but it looks a lot like you're leaving and I would like to know why." Night steeled his nerves when Bastian paused and his head swivelled towards him. It wasn't wise to demand anything of his eldest brother, but he was tired and had come all this way to see him, sacrificing a hunt to be here.

"I have business I need to deal with." Bastian's baritone was as smooth and calm as ever, but it didn't fool Night. His brother was harried and the crimson ringing his pale blue irises told Night that the business in question had angered him, or maybe something else had.

Night's own impertinence, perhaps.

He couldn't be sure.

Bastian went to get into the car and Night gripped the top of the door, stopping him and earning himself another look that warned him he was treading on thin ice.

"I shall be back before the end of the week, Night. Make yourself at home." Bastian looked over his shoulder as the servant shut the boot and the driver started the engine. "Stay here and look after the house."

It wasn't a request. It was an order.

While Night felt he should be aggravated by the fact his brother was demanding he stay in his home for the week despite the fact he wouldn't even be there, he actually felt as if he had hit the jackpot. By the time Bastian returned, his week of torture would almost be up, and he had the huge mansion to himself.

He was already planning parties in his head. Not elegant balls, but debauched gatherings. Lavish affairs at his brother's expense. Bastian could afford it. He was a shark. Bastian had a head for business that was more terrifying than Grave's head for bloody mass murder on the battlefield. He had made billions since the mortal world had begun advancing, and the bastard kept it all to himself.

Bastian was a firm believer in making your own mark, which Night knew really meant he was a frugal son of a bitch who wanted to keep all his money to himself. Night couldn't really hold it against him, because he knew where this side of his brother had come from. Their father had always been absent, far more concerned with his business dealings than his own family, leaving their mother to raise them.

In response to that, Bastian had started pushing Night and his siblings to make their mark on the world and live up to the Van der Garde name, foolishly believing that if he made a big enough impression that their father would take notice of him.

It had never happened.

Bastian slipped into the back seat of the car and Night rounded the vehicle, moving to the side of it nearest the house and giving it room to leave. His brother popped out again and looked over the roof of the car at him.

"Watch the female."

Watch the female? What kind of cryptic request was that? While Night was trying to figure out the meaning of that demand, the car pulled away and he was left standing in the driveway, frowning at the gravel and wondering what Bastian had meant.

There were so many choices.

The female was a lover. The female needed protection from something. The female was an enemy and was incarcerated in the house, something which wouldn't surprise him since many people had tried to claim the honour of killing one of the Van der Gardes over the years.

All had failed, of course.

His senses sharpened and he looked over his right shoulder at the butler, one of Bastian's owned humans.

The dark-haired man bowed his head, pressing his gloved hand to the breast of his formal black and white attire. "Shall I retrieve your luggage, sir?"

Night nodded and shunned the uneasy feeling that went through him as the servant moved to carry out his request. He was never getting used to someone waiting on him, not again. His family had owned human servants when he had been living at the chateau in Switzerland, but since moving away, he had only been around them at Bastian's house.

Bastian had a horde of owned humans, each with the scar of his bite on their neck. His brother was traditional that way. It was an aristocrat thing. A show of power. A simple exchange of blood made the human docile, a slave to the vampire. He supposed it was one way of staffing such a large house.

It wasn't to Night's tastes. He didn't really care that humans were used as slaves for work, sex and blood, but he didn't own any himself, despite how many times Bastian had extolled the virtues of having servants. Night's apartment was small in comparison to this country house. He didn't need someone to tend to his home for him, or for blood and sex. He preferred to get those things from a different female each time.

Speaking of which.

He smiled slowly and walked towards the steps up to the entrance, intending to go to his quarters and kick back on the four-poster bed and start planning his first soiree.

Only he hit an obstacle.

Night stopped in the doorway.

Standing in the middle of the elegant double-height foyer, her back to the twin wooden staircases that led up to the first floor and her head bent, her eyes fixed on the Italian marble floor, was a woman.

The female?

Her dark chocolate hair tumbled around her shoulders, brushing the black material of her short dress, and her hands were twisted in front of her white apron.

Night studied her. She wasn't tall. Had to stand a good nine inches shorter than his six-three. She was dressed as a maid, which meant she was one of Bastian's servants. She was rigid despite her deferential appearance. Afraid.

He drew down a breath as Bastian's butler moved past him, carrying his luggage towards the right staircase, and several other servants milled around the room, going about their business. As the foyer cleared, he caught her scent and almost gasped.

She was mortal.

And she wasn't owned.

He knew because while he could look at the other females in the house and had no desire to do anything with them, he couldn't stop the flood of hunger that made his fangs itch as she slowly lifted her head, her caramel-coloured eyes inching up to meet his. Desire struck like a thunderbolt, zinging through his bones and burning up his blood, and it only worsened as her dark hair fell away from her neck.

Revealing the smooth pale curves of it to his eyes.

Eyes that zeroed in on the fact she wore no marks.

The knowledge that Bastian didn't own her, that no vampire had marked her, had his fangs lengthening and his mouth watering.

Gods.

What new hell had his brother thrown him into this time?

CHAPTER 2

Night ignored the voice at the back of his mind that whispered to seduce the beautiful human standing before him. As much as he desired her, he couldn't act on it. Bastian might not have placed his mark on her yet, but she was to be his. That was the reason his brother had asked him to watch her. She had agreed to become his servant in exchange for the benefits it would grant her, like a longer life and immunity to disease, and this mansion as her home. Night couldn't break that contract.

He would do as his brother had asked and watch her.

In his own fashion.

"Where is your room?" Because he intended to lock her in it and have a servant bring her three meals a day until he was gone or Bastian had returned. When her lips parted, he spoke before she could, not sure he would be able to handle the sound of her voice if it was as beautiful as the rest of her. "Do not speak. Show me."

He grabbed her arm.

Surprising her.

And stupidly himself too.

She wasn't owned. Touching her without Bastian's consent wouldn't hurt him or her. But part of him had been ready for a blast of white-hot pain and prepared to see her crumple in a heap as Bastian's ownership of her took effect and punished her.

Night drew down a deep breath, catching her scent, and followed it up the stairs. He tracked it along the cream corridor, his shoes loud on the wooden floor, punctuating the heavy silence as the female followed him.

Her eyes on his profile.

Gods, she had to stop looking at him. His control was threadbare, and he feared it wasn't because he had been due to feed tonight and had worked himself up for a hunt. Had he thought himself dead? He was no longer sure that was the case as his heart thundered, blood rushing in his veins.

He would be dead if he touched her though.

If he surrendered to the wicked urges she roused in him.

Night groaned inwardly as he passed the door of his own quarters and discovered her scent ended at the next one along on the opposite side of the wide corridor. Too close for comfort. He would be able to smell her in his room. He would know whenever she moved, would be fixated on her, tracking her with his senses and unable to stop himself. Maybe he could move. Bastian's quarters were at the other end of the house.

He shook that thought away. Bastian wanted him to keep an eye on her, and what better room was there to be in than one close to hers in order to fulfil that mission? He could easily keep track of her without ever having to see her.

Night opened the white wooden door and pushed her inside. She gasped, the sound delighting his ears, triggering a war within him. He wanted to hear her gasp like that again as he gathered her into his arms and sank his fangs into her throat.

Marking her.

He shoved her away from him, perhaps a little rougher than he should have been treating her given she belonged to his brother and Bastian wanted him to take care of her.

Watch the female.

Night wasn't sure that was a good idea.

Watching her would only lead to wanting her.

She moved away from him, walking deeper into the pale green room, and as she veered left towards the dressing table, he caught sight of the dress laid out on the end of her four-poster bed.

It was crimson.

Ceremonial.

His gut clenched.

Bastian had meant to place his claim on her tonight and business had pulled him away.

Night wasn't sure what to make of that.

What sweet fucking fate had intervened to leave her free of Bastian's rule?

His gaze shifted to her, tracking her as she paced the room, her eyes downcast. He looked from her to the dress and back again, a question bubbling up inside him.

Did she want to be owned?

It was taboo to claim a human against their will these days, and she had been waiting in the foyer, watching his brother leave. He ran a hand over his short dark hair and down the shorn back of it to his nape. It was probable that she was entering into this contract willingly, wanting the life it could give her.

She glanced at him.

A violent flash of heat went through him, had him lurching a step towards her before he reclaimed control of his body.

"Stay in the room," he growled as he pivoted and stepped into the corridor.

He slammed the door behind him and strode along the hall. Straight past his room. Back down the stairs. Right out into the night.

He didn't stop until he was on the lawn. He paced across the grass, breathing deep of the cool air, letting it fill his lungs to bring his temperature back down. Whoever the female was, she was dangerous. It had been a long time since he had felt so close to breaking so quickly. A simple look from her had his hunger roaring to the fore, his bloodlust surging to the surface with it. He scrubbed a hand down his face and pulled down another breath, trying to calm his racing heart.

His hand dropped from his face.

He needed to leave.

The other humans would keep her safe until Bastian's return and she had no reason to go anywhere.

Night paused and looked back at the house, at the floor where her room was.

Right at her window.

The golden light emanating from it silhouetted her where she stood before it, watching him pace like a madman. He was tempted to wonder what she made of him, but was too occupied with figuring out the answer to the question that had risen into his mind.

What if she did have a reason to leave?

Bastian had a short temper. He did his best to hide it, but his brother was quick to anger if he felt slighted or disobeyed. Not only that, but he had specifically asked Night to watch the female, which meant she was important to him. He had entrusted Night with this task and would expect him to carry it out. Night had never gone against his brother's wishes in the past when he had asked him to do something. He wasn't sure he wanted to find out what Bastian would do to him if he failed.

He imagined it might involve ripping out his heart and feeding it to the dogs.

He stared at her.

He wasn't sure he could stay, though. His brother was asking too much of him. Guarding the house he could do, but guarding an unclaimed female—a beautiful unclaimed female who didn't look as if she was enjoying the thought of becoming his brother's property—was beyond him.

He couldn't leave.

Night growled and clenched his fists, his arms flexing beneath his black suit jacket, causing the material to tighten over his muscles. He had a duty to stay now and watch the female as his brother had asked. What he felt was of no consequence. He would master his attraction to her, or at least put together a big enough distraction to keep his mind off her.

He pulled his phone from his trouser pocket.

Woke the screen.

And called the cavalry.

They answered on the first ring.

"Well, if it isn't Lord Van der Garde," Laurent drawled, his French accent lending a softness to his light voice that Night knew the male lacked in every other aspect of his person.

"Shut up," Night muttered, the same response he always gave his ex-subordinate whenever the vampire dared to use his title rather than his given name.

Laurent had served under him for four hundred years, the standard term for a male aristocrat vampire, and for every single one of them, the blond had amused himself with driving Night mad. Whether it was asking him idiotic questions about what life was like as a member of one of the most illustrious vampire families, abusing his title to irritate him, or flat out bowing and scraping before him, Laurent had savoured pushing his buttons.

And in a way, Night had enjoyed it.

He almost missed it in fact.

There were far too few vampires in the Preux Chevaliers with the balls to treat a Van der Garde in the way Laurent had.

As if they were just another vampire.

"I need a favour." Night stared at the female. She hadn't moved. She still stood in the window, watching him, the feel of her gaze on him drawing all of his focus to her. He resisted the urge to sharpen that focus and dragged his gaze away instead. It would be a mistake. He wanted to hunt her as it was. Wanted to seduce her out of his brother's grasp. Dangerous. He needed a distraction to get his mind off her. "I need a party put together for tomorrow night. All the usual suspects."

"You called the right vampire." Laurent sounded amused, or possibly proud, but then his tone sobered. "Any special requests?"

Night swallowed. Was this a good idea? Or a terrible one? He looked at the female and settled on it being a good idea. It wasn't like him. It wasn't his style. But if he didn't satisfy the needs building inside him, he was liable to do something that might get him killed, and strangely, he didn't want to die right now. He refused to look too closely at that.

"Night?" Laurent prompted.

Night closed his eyes and turned away from the female, sure this was a good idea for another reason, too. She would hear about it, might even witness it, and it would give her a good reason to stay the hell away from him.

Might even go as far as destroying any shred of attraction she felt towards him.

Because it would paint him as the monster he was.

"A hunt." He let those words tumble from his lips.

Laurent was silent for a moment, in which Night was sure the male was going to question why he wanted the vampire equivalent of a fox hunt, where humans would be turned loose within the grounds to run for their lives while Night and his guests tracked them down, or maybe even point out this wasn't like him, but then Laurent said, "I can do that. Renard has some contacts who can get him the humans on short notice."

"The party will be at Bastian's house. I'll send you the address. Invite some of your friends too. And the most beautiful women you can find." Night resisted the urge to look at the window to see if she was still there. Still watching. "He's away for a few days and I plan to turn every damned one of them into a party."

"Wrecking your brother's home? Sounds like fun." Laurent chuckled. "Just make sure what you do doesn't come back to bite you."

That was what Night was trying to do.

He looked at the window.

But it was empty.

CHAPTER 3

For the first time since accepting her mission, Lilian felt she was in danger.

When Bastian had declared he had urgent business to attend to in London and that he would return in a week, she had been thankful for the reprieve, but as she stood in the grand entrance hall of his home, staring at the vampire who was to be her guard for the next few days, she was starting to wish he would come back.

Night resembled his older brother in many ways. Same neat rich brown hair. Same ice-cold pale blue eyes. Same ridiculously good bone structure. One thing was different about him though.

While Bastian was handsome, Night was *seductively* handsome. It was as if fate had taken Bastian as the blueprint and turned the dials up to eleven when they had made his younger brother.

The tall, lithe and elegant vampire before her cut an all too alluring figure in his tailored black suit, with his equally dark shirt unbuttoned just enough to reveal a hint of the honed body it concealed.

His aquamarine eyes pierced her soul as she dared to look into them and the corners of his profane lips tilted into the ghost of a smile, one that had her pulse quickening.

Mother earth, she was in trouble.

If Bastian's sudden disappearance hadn't thrown a spanner in the works, Night's sudden appearance might. Need threatened to burn up her blood and she had to fight her own body to keep her reaction hidden from him, fearing what he might do if he realised the effect he had on her.

The other servants left them alone and she told herself to move, to follow the mortals and escape this vampire, but her feet refused to cooperate, remaining rooted to the marble floor.

Something crossed his face, darkening his eyes for a moment, ringing them with crimson.

"Where is your room?" His deep voice rolled over her. Rocked her. Shook her to her core. She opened her mouth, but he didn't give her the chance to tell him. He barked, "Do not speak. Show me."

Before she could do that, he was before her, his hand locked around her arm.

Skin on skin with her.

She tensed at the sudden hot wave that rolled up her arm, electric tingles chasing in its wake, and stared up at him. His eyes widened and for a heartbeat he looked as if he might release her, and then he was dragging her towards the stairs and up them. She struggled to keep up with his long strides as he tugged her along the corridor, fought to tear her eyes away from his profile even as she drank her fill of him, caught up in the hurricane of feelings he had caused inside her with only an innocent touch.

Lilian stumbled along the cream hallway behind him, trying to rouse herself because she needed to remain in control. If she lost control, she would ruin everything. She wasn't surprised when he paused before her door. Vampires had acute senses. Her intel said that Night was over a thousand years old. At his age, his senses would be incredible. He could probably sniff her out over a vast distance.

Like a shark detecting a drop of blood in a large body of water.

He pushed her into the room and released her.

Lilian was quick to move away from him, placing some much-needed distance between them. She secretly rubbed her wrist and looked at it, unsure whether she was trying to ease the pain of his bruising grip or work the heat of his touch into her skin so it would remain forever. She was deeply aware of his gaze on her as she crossed the wooden floor of the pale green room, heading for her dresser and pretending she meant to do something there.

When she felt his eyes leave her, she glanced back at him.

He was staring at the scarlet dress on the dark green covers of her bed.

His irises ringed with that bloody colour.

Lilian couldn't bring herself to look at it. She stared at the floor instead, fighting the same battle she had waged with herself since she had stepped into this house. Duty warred with her sense of self-preservation. Her coven meant everything to her, and she knew she should be honoured to carry out this mission given how important it was to her family, but whenever she thought about what she was going to have to do—how much it would cost her—she wanted to run.

She closed her eyes. She had to be here, though. It had to be her. Only she could get the proof her coven needed. Only she had that power. Bastian was lucky that her coven hadn't decided to kill him based on the rumour that placed him at the scene of the crime. He was being given a chance to prove his innocence.

She was being given the chance to prove it.

To do that, she had to go through with the ceremony that would bind them. Didn't she?

She glanced at Night.

Their eyes clashed and heat swept through her, igniting her blood. His eyes darkened, but not from anger. The desire that shone in them was unmistakable.

It scorched her.

"Stay in the room," he growled as he pivoted and stepped out into the corridor, and before she could ask why, he had slammed the door behind him.

She listened to his footsteps as they receded, waiting until she could no longer hear them before daring to move. Her legs were unsteady as she went to the bed, grabbed the dress, and stormed to her wardrobe. The hangers rattled as she grabbed one, and she slipped the dress onto it and shoved it onto the railing, and then slammed both the doors. She pressed her palms to them and leaned forwards, so her forehead came into contact with the cool mahogany. It did nothing to lower her temperature or tame the fire in her veins.

Lilian sagged against the wardrobe doors and turned her head to her left, towards the sash window that was one of a pair that framed her four-poster bed. She stared out into the darkness, seeking a sliver of strength, enough to get her through the next few days.

Enough to stop her courage from failing her.

A door slammed below her.

She frowned and drifted to the window, pausing there as she caught sight of Night. He strode across the gravel and she was sure he was going to his car and intended to leave, but then he went straight past it, out onto the lawn. He paced across the grass, moonlight caressing his shoulders and his hair as he ran a hand through it. He looked as worked up as she felt.

When he pulled out his phone, she canted her head. Who was he calling? His brother? She wasn't a fool. He had made it perfectly clear he wasn't happy about having to deal with her. Maybe that would work in her favour. She could happily spend the next few days in this room, avoiding him.

She needed to keep her mind on her mission.

She would use the time she had been given to find the courage to keep moving forwards with it, crushing the side of her that wanted to run.

Lilian pressed her hand to her chest. It was going to be easier said than done. Her heart had been wavering for a while now, ever since she had set foot in this mansion. She clenched her fingers into a tight fist. She could do this. *Only* she could do this. If she didn't carry out her duty, then her sisters would have no choice but to kill Bastian. Her coven needed revenge for what had happened. They wouldn't care whether he was guilty or not. They needed someone to pay.

She had killed in the past—her coven regularly took on jobs as mercenaries after all—but something about walking away and sentencing Bastian to death had guilt stirring inside her. She wasn't sure she could live with herself if her courage failed her and she didn't carry out her mission.

But then, she wasn't sure she could live with the alternative.

If Bastian was innocent, her coven would have no reason to execute him.

Meaning, she would be his servant forever.

Her coven swore they were working on a way to break the bond that would tie her to Bastian, but she didn't believe them. They had only mentioned it after she had asked about it, and they hadn't been convincing. Deep in her heart, she knew that by exchanging blood with Bastian in order to prove his innocence or guilt, there was a fifty percent chance she was dooming herself.

Night looked away from her and she dragged herself away from him, turned to her bed and flopped face-first onto the dark green covers. She exhaled and stared at the pillows to her right.

What was she going to do?

Her eyelids grew heavy as she pondered that and she fought sleep, desperate to seek an answer to her question.

Only sleep took her anyway, denying her the time to think.

The bastard.

Lilian frowned when a loud banging stirred her. She groaned and reached for the pillow to cover her ears, but there was no pillow beneath her. She cracked her eyes open and frowned, squinting against the bright light that invaded her room. That was right. She had fallen asleep lying across the bed.

The banging came again.

She turned her head to her left and watched the white door shudder with the force of the knocking. Was it Night? She almost laughed at that. It was daylight. The vampire would be safely tucked away in his quarters, sleeping until dusk.

Meaning, she was free of him for a few hours.

"Miss Lilian," a woman snapped and knocked again.

The housekeeper.

What had possessed Bastian to form a master-servant bond with the grouchy old bag, Lilian would never know. She huffed and pushed off the bed, and plodded to the door, opening it a crack.

"The vampire across the hall will be very angry if you wake him with your attempts to knock my door down." She gasped when the white-haired woman shoved the flat of her right hand against the door and forced it open.

"Everyone is to work today. You are no exception." Ellen reached for her arm.

Lilian snatched it away from her. "The vampire across the hall will also be very angry if you take me from this room. He made it painfully clear last night that I'm to stay in it."

Ellen frowned at her.

Lilian was about to chalk up a victory for herself when the woman seized her arm.

"The vampire has a name, and Lord Van der Garde has requested the entire mansion be prepared for a large party who are arriving tonight." Ellen dragged her from the room.

Lilian glared at the back of her head, itching to pull the slender pin from her tight bun and stab her with it. She got caught on what the woman had said, though. That was what Night had been doing on the phone while pacing the lawn. He had been putting together a party. He didn't strike her as the partying type, but then what did she know? Her intel was sketchy at best. She knew his rough age and his bloodline, but other than that, she didn't have much to go on to help her form a better picture of her new guard.

Which had her wary of him.

Grave and Bastian had reputations that preceded them, a long and bloody history recorded for everyone to see. Night on the other hand. So little was known about him that it unsettled her.

She had the feeling he took great pains to make sure no one was left alive to record the things he did.

"He really will be angry if he finds out you let me out of my room." She looked back over her shoulder at it as they reached the stairs.

"I have too many rooms to clean and prepare, and refreshments to arrange, to listen to your idle talk and lies. You can return to lazing around your room once your work is done. You can start in the guest rooms. I've assigned the dozen on this floor to you." Ellen's tone brooked no argument.

Lilian twisted her arm free of Ellen's grip. "I'm not lying. He really did order me to stay in my room."

The thought that this interfering old woman believed she was making up excuses so she didn't have to work made Lilian want to curse. She settled for glaring at her instead, which had zero effect. The housekeeper just left her at the top of the stairs, next to a cart that had cleaning products stuffed into one of the caddies and a huge empty linen basket at the front.

"Not a speck of dust, Miss Lilian. Those rooms must be spotless!"

Lilian flipped her off, grabbed the handles of the cart and stormed along the hallway, heading for the guest quarters that occupied the front rooms of the house in the west wing. At least she was further away from Night. She reached the first room, shoved the door open, and wheeled the cart inside. It was pitch black thanks to the thick metal shutters that covered the windows. She left the cart near the door and carefully crossed the wooden floor to the windows and punched the button on the wall beside one. The shutters whirred and clanked, and slowly rose, allowing sunlight to stream into the room.

Just in case a vampire had any ideas about coming to mete out justice for disobeying him.

It wasn't her fault.

And it really wasn't as if she wanted to clean rooms.

Menial work had never really been her thing. Although she had done her fair share of it at the coven over the years. Everything from cooking and cleaning, to decorating and gardening. Everyone in her family participated in daily chores until they were old enough to take on missions or teach the younger witches.

Lilian opened the sash windows to let the air in and then set about cleaning the room, pulling the dust covers off the furniture and shoving them into the linen basket on the cart. Once everything was uncovered, she took a cloth and polish and made every surface shine. She followed that with the vacuum, going as far as running it under the bed and using the attachments on the curtains and skirting boards. Miserable old Ellen wouldn't have a reason to come banging down her door and complaining to her.

When she was done with the first room, she closed the shutters and moved on to the next, falling into a rhythm. She was on the seventh room by the time Night popped into her head again. She pushed him out and focused on her work, and on her predicament. She wanted to curse again, but held it back. What she really needed to do was get in touch with her contact and get a pep talk that would boost her courage and help her go through with becoming Bastian's servant.

It was too risky.

By the ninth room, she had started wondering what kind of party Night was holding. Would it be an elegant soiree, where the men would be wearing suits and the women fine gowns? An image popped into her head and she found herself almost dancing with the vacuum cleaner. Period dramas had a lot to answer for. Or maybe it was the house. It looked like something out of *Pride and Prejudice*. She doubted the vampires were going to dance in a beautiful candlelit ballroom and flirt with each other in a very coded manner that most would mistake for idle talk though.

Vampires probably had very different gatherings.

The urge to contact Gillian and ask if she knew what kind of parties vampires held blasted through her, and she denied it, because she was just looking for an excuse to reach out to her contact.

Her friend.

She had known Gillian all her life, and when she had taken on this mission, Gillian had told her she would be there with her every step of the way. But she wasn't. Lilian was alone, and she had never felt it as much as she did at that moment, when she couldn't get her mind off a certain vampire or calm her fears about what she was doing here.

What if Bastian returned and wanted to carry out the ceremony with Night still here?

Mother earth, Night would kill her.

She could see it now. Her blood splattered up the walls. Night's fangs ripping out her throat.

The inevitable harm that would befall Bastian when he claimed her as his servant would no doubt send Night into a killing rage.

And could she blame him?

If someone hurt Gillian, she would kill them too.

The last few rooms passed in a blur as thoughts crowded her mind, and they continued to weigh her down as she pushed the cart to the top of the stairs, where one of the men who served Bastian was waiting. She left it with him and drifted down the stairs rather than heading back to her room, and found herself walking out into the evening light.

Lilian breathed deep of the warm air, savouring the space that surrounded her as she wandered towards the grass. She rubbed her arms as she went in circles, trying to figure out what to do. The coven needed to know that the situation at Bastian's house had changed and things had become more dangerous for her. She was meant to be giving regular reports, and she hadn't checked in for a few days, not since she had worked her way into Bastian's home.

If she could call it working her way in.

She hadn't even needed to approach Bastian about becoming one of his servants. The vampire had taken one look at her at that fancy bar he frequented when he was in London and had decided she was going to be his. Which was irritating in a way. It was almost as if he believed all humans had been born to serve him anyway, so adding her to his ranks was only natural.

And he hadn't given her a choice in the matter.

He had tried to place her under thrall, a power to control humans that all vampires possessed, one that allowed them to manipulate their minds and make them do as they pleased, and even control what they felt. She supposed it probably helped them when they were hunting. They used their thrall to make their prey compliant, to make their bite feel good, and, if they were the sort to leave the human alive after taking their fill of their blood, to make the human feel a warm haze akin to pleasure. Humans mistook it for sexual release and thought they'd had a wild night with a stranger.

Which in a way, they had.

Bastian's thrall hadn't worked on her, of course, so she had been forced to pretend she was under his spell.

And he had carted her off to his mansion.

It wasn't quite how Lilian had expected things to go. The plan had been that she would discover he was a vampire and press him to make her an owned human, playing the desperate mortal who had heard rumours they would gain a longer life and wouldn't get sick if they served a vampire. He was meant to have agreed and then vetted her, like most vampires did when a mortal wanted to be their servant.

She had worked hard setting up a backstory and putting together a paper trail that would tie her to her new identity. Fake bank accounts. Education. Doctors' records that placed her as a cancer risk because of her family history. Loans. Employment. She had spent weeks expending time and magic to get all the information in place and make sure there weren't any holes that would give her away, sure that he would run a background check on her.

All the information her coven had painted Bastian as a cautious vampire, one who thoroughly researched things before making an informed decision. Apparently, his business practices didn't extend to his personal life.

Or at least they didn't extend to choosing who would serve him.

He saw someone he liked the look of and just added them to his staff whether they wanted it or not.

Entitled much?

Sure, he was an aristocrat, something the pureblood vampires called themselves, those whose family hadn't been tainted by adding turned humans to their ranks. And sure, she had been warned his breed were haughty and elitist. But some part of her hadn't believed it until she had witnessed it with her own eyes.

Bastian clearly viewed himself as the very peak of aristocrat society, someone who stood far above other vampires, let alone the mortals he felt should be bowing and scraping at his feet.

Lilian had lost count of the number of times she had wanted to box his ears. Or curse him.

Did Night own humans?

A shiver bolted down her spine and she turned towards the house, and froze as she spotted the familiar silhouette in the doorway.

"Crap," she muttered.

She was in for it now.

Night lifted his hand and crooked a finger, and she didn't want to go to him, not because she was afraid of him and the fact he was no doubt angry she had disobeyed him, but because she was afraid of this heat he stirred inside her.

The wildfire licking through her veins only grew hotter as she stared at him, becoming an inferno that scorched her reserve and had her taking a step towards him, as if she was under his thrall and powerless to resist him.

Forget messaging Gillian. She needed to speak to her face to face about this problem. Before she did something reckless.

She drew down subtle breaths as she went to Night, trying to calm her nerves and settle her heart. A foolish endeavour. He was a vampire. He would have detected the effect he had on her the second she had turned to see him standing in the golden glow of the doorway, watching her.

Maybe she wasn't only afraid of the heat he stirred in her.

As she drew closer to him, she could make out his face—and his eyes.

There was no anger in their pale blue depths. No. They were sharp and intense, and made her feel he was studying her, putting her under the microscope and trying to figure her out. This vampire was shrewd. He was intelligent. Calculating.

Her heart drummed a little faster.

She feared that he could see right through her and that if she stayed here, he would figure out what she was up to and she would end up dead.

Lilian tried to hold his gaze, but his aquamarine eyes were so penetrating that she couldn't manage it. Her gaze fell towards his chest.

Snagged on his throat.

A silvery scar ran from beneath one earlobe all the way to the other and was thickest over his Adam's apple.

What had happened to him?

It looked as if someone had tried to cleave his head off and had almost succeeded. How had he survived such a wound? She knew the answer to that question. He was a fighter. That scar told her as much. He wasn't one to lie down and accept his fate.

The intensity of his gaze grew and she tried to look away, but the scar bewitched her, had her caught in its snare.

She tensed as he growled, the sound vicious and commanding and enough to propel her into action at last. Her gaze dropped to his shoes, but it wasn't enough for him. He stepped closer to her, narrowing the distance down to a few inches, until she could feel his heat and smell his expensive aftershave. Her heart shot into her throat when he lowered his head and growled again, his fangs dangerously close to her forehead, and her fingertips tingled as her magic rose to the fore.

Prickles swept down her spine as she desperately fought to hold it back, wrestling for control. He wasn't a threat to her. He wasn't a danger. She told herself that on repeat in an attempt to calm her magic, even when part of her knew he was both of those things.

Because she had stared at his scar and he didn't like it.

"Go to your room and stay there until you hear otherwise," he snarled, his deep voice a rumble of thunder as he eased closer to her and then suddenly stepped back, clearing the way.

Lilian nodded and stepped past him.

He caught her wrist and she stopped, a fiery ache sweeping through her to reignite the embers of the inferno he caused in her. She looked back at his hand where it gripped her, his long fingers curled tightly around her flesh, and then up into his eyes, sure he meant to snap and growl some more, maybe even tell her outright never to look at his scar again.

He didn't take his gaze off his hand.

She waited, unsure what to do. Try to free herself or remain where she was? How would Night react if she did either of those things? His expression slowly softened as he stared at his hand on her arm, the darkness swift to leave his eyes as his features relaxed, and then his brow furrowed and he swallowed hard.

And she swore he was torn about something.

His grip loosened and his hand fell from her wrist, fingers brushing her and sending another bolt of lightning zinging up her arm to strike her soul.

He turned away from her and a feeling bloomed inside her, powerful and overwhelming, driving her to talk to him and discover what was wrong.

He exhaled, not quite a sigh. "Bastian will return soon. Remain in your room where you are safe."

She lowered her gaze to his hand, the one that had been on her, watching as he flexed his fingers. He was shutting her in her room because she wasn't owned, meaning the vampires coming to the party could mistake her for a snack or a companion. He wanted to protect her, and something deep in her soul said it wasn't because she was meant for his brother. The compulsion to say something became too strong to deny and she opened her mouth.

"Go," he barked and she tensed as his head swivelled towards her and his crimson gaze clashed with hers. Lilian stared into his eyes, at the fiery corona that surrounded his elliptical pupils, her heart thundering and blood rushing as his face darkened. His lips peeled back off his fangs, white daggers that sent both a thrill and ice-cold fear through her. "Now!"

She stumbled backwards into the middle of the foyer and turned, hurrying for the stairs and not slowing until she reached her room.

Lilian closed the door behind her and locked it.

But she had no intention of staying.

She went to the window and lingered in the shadows, peering down at the drive as the first car arrived, the tinted windows so dark it was impossible to see who was inside.

As soon as the party was in full swing, she was sneaking out to meet Gillian.

She was going to do something reckless.

Night appeared in view, stirring fire in her heart and bewitching her as he smiled and greeted his guest as the male climbed out of the rear of the car.

Before she did something even more reckless.

CHAPTER 4

Bastian would never approve of his home being used like this.

Night swirled the blood in his fine crystal goblet, watching the lavish affair that Laurent had put together unfold. The blond vampire had made good on his promise. All of Night's finest friends were present, together with a few of Laurent's that he didn't recognise, and the quality of humans Laurent had managed to get on such short notice was impressive. His fangs itched as a black-haired vampire seated near the fireplace opened the vein of one of the females, a stunning brunette on his lap, and the scent of blood in the air thickened.

Gods, he wanted to find a female to sink his fangs into and feed from.

The human moaned, her pleasure rippling through the room, drawing the gazes of several vampires to her. A fair-haired male approached and she reached for him, her gaze drowsy as the vampire at her neck sucked harder. The newcomer dropped to his knees beside her and sank his fangs into her wrist, eliciting another loud moan from her.

In the corner of the room, one of the female vampires Laurent had brought with him was working her charms on a human male, reinforcing the thrall he was under so he would feel only pleasure when she took his vein.

And more than that, judging by the heat in her dark eyes.

Night roamed the room, making sure all his guests were comfortable and satisfied, dipping his head to any vampire who greeted him.

He arched an eyebrow as one of the female vampires decided she didn't want to wait to get somewhere more private before taking her fill of the human she had under her control. The human groaned as he thrust between her legs, pinning her to the wall near the door, and she tore another from him as she licked his throat. The sight probably would have shocked Bastian, might have even given his older brother a coronary if he could have one. Openly fucking your host wasn't the done thing in fine society. It wasn't respectable.

Bastian acted as if they didn't have cousins who ran an erotic theatre that catered to the aristocrat and elite vampires.

The male grunted and pumped her harder. No doubt the female was exerting more of her will on him, pushing him past his usual limits and unleashing him. Thrall could be a beautiful thing. Thanks to it, the humans Laurent had brought would shed their inhibitions and experience a night of sensual indulgence. They would enjoy what pleasure they were given and they would all be alive come the morning. A little sore and weak, but otherwise unharmed.

He set his empty glass down on the tray one of Bastian's owned humans was carrying around the room and picked up a full one. The young male stared wide-eyed at the couple, a blush staining his cheeks. Night almost pitied him. As an owned human, he was off-limits—safe from the vampires thanks to his bond with Bastian.

As much as the owned human wanted to take the female in the way the other mortal was, he couldn't. Any touch born of desire would pain them both.

Night wandered away from him, into the adjoining drawing room, where Laurent was busy seducing not one but two females. One of them was a vampire. He shook his head and smiled at that, not surprised that Laurent was being greedy. Whenever they had held parties in the past, Laurent had always ended up in bed with at least two females and often one male.

"Lord Van der Garde." The soft female voice, laced with a faint French accent, snagged his attention, drawing it away from Laurent, and he looked to his right, towards the door to the foyer.

"Elspeth." Night dipped his head.

The pretty brunette ran her finger around the rim of his glass as she pressed closer, angling her head up so he got a good view of her cleavage in her black corseted dress. Her grey eyes glittered at him as her red lips tilted into a semblance of a smile.

"Are you not enjoying the humans?" She dipped her finger into the blood, withdrew it and brought it to her lips.

Lips she wrapped around it as she gazed up at him.

He had known Elspeth for centuries and wasn't surprised she had convinced her older brother, Laurent, to bring her with him. Laurent had often joked over the years that Elspeth was saving her heart for Night. Night didn't think it was something to joke about. At every opportunity, Elspeth tried to seduce him.

Only she didn't really want to claim him.

She wanted to claim his title.

"Does the host ever really get to enjoy their own party?" Night set the glass of blood down on a small side table, leaning away from her for a moment.

Apparently giving her the perfect excuse to run her hands over his arm and help him straighten up again. He frowned and resisted the desire to sigh, turned to her and plastered on a smile.

Playing the good host.

"Shall we sit awhile?" She gestured to the black velvet couch as someone stood and left it vacant.

As little as he enjoyed the idea of sitting pressed close to Elspeth on the small two-seater sofa, he didn't want to be rude to her. Mostly because he would never hear the end of it from Laurent. The last time Night had flatly turned her down and told her to leave him alone, Laurent had plagued him for close to a year, constantly sending him messages about how upset his sister was and that he needed to apologise to her.

Night was starting to get the idea that Elspeth wasn't the only one who wanted him to marry her.

He eased onto the seat, as far from her as he could get, and she chose to sit right beside him, her thigh pressed against his. He was tempted to point out that there was plenty of room for her to sit further away, but decided against it. This party was supposed to be a distraction, a way of keeping his mind off Lilian, and what better distraction was there than a beautiful female?

When he rested his arm along the back of the couch, almost placing it around her shoulders, Elspeth got a look in her eyes that made him want to run for the hills. Or Hell. Maybe Hell. She had told him many times that she would never set foot in such a dangerous, wretched place. He would be safe there.

"Lord Van der Garde," she murmured, her voice going low, and the desire that always shone in her eyes whenever she was near him deepened.

He gestured to one of the owned humans, beckoning them. The male hurried to him and dipped low, presenting the tray of goblets to him. Night took two and handed one to Elspeth.

An attempt to get her to stop gazing at his throat.

The tips of her fangs showed between her red lips as she smiled and took the glass, brushing her fingers over his.

Gods, maybe this was a bad idea.

Indulging Elspeth would probably lead to her thinking they were engaged or something just as ridiculous, and then Laurent would be on his case for a decade or more.

So he summoned another of the female vampires, a petite raven-haired one with large green eyes who had been watching him all night. He wasn't familiar with her and had been curious about her from the moment he had seen her, wondering whether she was one of Laurent's friends or someone Renard had brought with him.

The pretty little thing was quick to hurry towards him, almost tripping over her long crimson dress in an effort to reach him in less than a second, as if it was a criminal offence to keep him waiting. She had to be young and relatively new to vampire society. Many aristocrat families kept their daughters away from society until they had matured and then they would host a grand ball for their coming out.

They were antiquated like that.

Night shunned thoughts of his own dear sister's ball, the pain of losing her still too raw after close to two centuries, and focused on the newcomer instead.

Elspeth hissed low as the delicate creature reached him.

"Come. Sit." Night stood and offered his seat to her and she blinked at him.

Elspeth looked ready to commit bloody murder.

He took hold of the black-haired female's arm with his free hand and guided her onto the seat, and then turned and pulled one of the armchairs close to them. He settled himself on it and surveyed the two females. They were a pretty picture, one all bright-eyed innocence and excitement, and the other all darkness and determination.

The perfect distraction.

"I'm not sure I know you, but you are a pretty petite thing," Night started and ignored the way Elspeth scowled at him now, a corona of crimson around her grey irises. "Are you a friend of Renard's?"

"His sister," Elspeth said before the young vampire could answer him. "And Renard will not be pleased to see you talking to her."

Night scoffed. "If that was the case, Renard would not have brought her to such a party."

Her lips flattened.

"Come now, Elspeth. There is more than enough of me to go around. A beauty such as you cannot feel threatened by this female, surely?" He smiled at her.

She fluttered her eyelashes and lowered her gaze to her lap for a moment before slowly bringing it back up to meet his. Now that he had her wrapped around his little finger again, he could question the young vampire.

"Your name?" He shifted his gaze to her, holding his smile in place.

"Annalisa." She toyed nervously with one of her raven curls.

Her French accent was barely noticeable, a sign that she hadn't been in her native country for a long time. Renard had lived in London for centuries and had mentioned once that he had lost his parents around a hundred years ago. Was it possible that he had been given custody of his younger sister upon their death? Her lack of accent would point towards her having been in this country for most of her life.

"You look thirsty, Annalisa." He offered her his goblet of blood, and she cast her gaze down at her knees and then looked up at him.

She leaned forwards and took the glass from him, and fidgeted with it as she settled back in her seat. "Thank you."

"How old are you?" He sat back to admire her and Elspeth.

Someone growled in the foyer to his left and several people murmured comments.

Annalisa tensed, her green eyes leaping towards the source of the commotion.

"Nothing to worry about," Night said. "I'm sure it's just a scuffle between males over a female. They do not know I have the two most beautiful ones with me."

He started to smile.

"Leave me alone. Unhand me!"

That familiar feminine voice was a stark reminder that he didn't have the most beautiful female with him.

Lilian.

Night vaulted from his seat and used all of his preternatural speed to reach the foyer in under a heartbeat. His eyes widened as a big male dragged Lilian towards him, her stricken expression hitting Night hard in the chest as she fought the vampire, clawing at his hand and stumbling.

Her fear an acrid note in the air.

Night had an infinite well of patience, had trained himself well so he could be the best assassin there was, and he would have dealt with this male in a calm manner under normal circumstances.

But the sight of Lilian frantically fighting to escape a male who meant her harm had him feeling like a beast on a very short leash, and he couldn't hold himself back.

Couldn't be calm and collected.

Not even close to reasonable.

On a low snarl, he stepped into the vampire's path, a male who was twice his build and looked as if he knew how to handle himself. The male suddenly stopped and glared at him.

Night kept his focus on the vampire, denying the urge to look at Lilian. "Unhand the female. She is the property of my brother."

The older vampire growled, "She's unclaimed."

"My brother was called away before the process was complete." Night didn't miss a beat. "Unhand her."

The male tightened his grip on her instead, tearing a pained cry from her that had Night's bloodlust roaring to the fore, veiling everything in red as it goaded him into tearing this male apart, into feasting on his blood as payment for what he had done to Lilian.

"She was attempting to leave," the vampire grunted.

That gave him pause and had him looking at Lilian.

He expected her to make up a reasonable but flimsy excuse, such as she had only wanted some fresh air and had decided to walk the grounds despite his order to stay in her room and the danger of so many vampires being present.

But she averted her gaze and refused to look at him, confirming what the vampire had said. Night scowled at her. Bastian was right. He did have to watch her.

"Maybe you just want her for yourself. Maybe you're lying about your brother so I'll leave her alone."

Night bared his fangs at the vampire for that one.

"I do not want her." The lie tasted bitter on his tongue, because gods, he wanted her. He wanted her so badly that he had thrown a debauched party in some vain attempt to get his mind off her, and look where it had gotten him. He had ended up placing her in danger instead. Bastian was going to kill him. He snarled, "My brother will end you—*I* will end you—if you do not unhand her. I will not ask again."

Seeing the vampire had no intention of being reasonable, and unable to blame him given how beautiful Lilian was, Night looked around the foyer, seeking a suitable exchange to avoid this conflict coming down to a bloody fight that would ruin the party.

Two human females stood among the crowd that had gathered.

Night focused on them, easily placing them under his thrall, and they obediently came to him, pushing through the crowd and earning a few growls along the way.

"Surely two compliant females are better than one unruly one?" Night swept his hand out towards the two humans, drawing the focus of the vampire to them.

If someone had asked him that question, he would have gone with the unruly one who was fast becoming a pain in his arse. He resisted the urge to look at her, keeping his focus on the vampire, unwilling to give him an opening.

"I recommend you take the offer," Laurent drawled from off to Night's left, beneath the stairs and close to the entrance to the main drawing room. "Upsetting our gracious host is quite the faux pas."

Night stared the big vampire down, haemorrhaging patience.

He was on the verge of forcing the male to release Lilian when the vampire cast her away from him and grabbed the two human females instead. Lilian hit the wall near the door with a grunt and Night growled at the vampire and took a sharp step towards him, intending to rip him apart anyway.

And then Lilian hissed in a pained breath.

His gaze was instantly on her, the world narrowing down to only her as she rubbed at her wrist.

The feel of everyone staring at him had him casting a glance around him, and his mood soured again as he caught the look in Laurent's eyes that said he could see straight through his lie. His friend knew he wanted her. Several other vampires were giving him the same look.

He growled at them all and stormed to Lilian, seized her wrist and pulled her onto her feet. She gasped and he snarled at her, flashing fangs in her direction now, and tried to shut out the way everyone's gazes followed him as he dragged her up the stairs.

And the whispered comments about him punishing her.

Wanting her.

He sharply turned right at the top of the staircase and flinched when Lilian struck the cream wall and grunted before stumbling into the middle of the hallway behind him. He quickened his pace, his blood burning now, ears twitching as he couldn't stop himself from listening to the rumours that were rapidly spreading.

He was going to be doing some damage control when he had finished dealing with Lilian.

Aristocrats affected an air of sophistication, acting as if they didn't have any bad qualities, but Night knew better. They loved to gossip. A vampire wanting a human who was earmarked for his brother would be the talk of the town for the next few years if he didn't put an end to it before it got out.

A Van der Garde wanting a human who was earmarked by his brother?

Society would feast on that one for decades.

Longer than Night would be alive once Bastian got wind of it.

His fingers flexed around Lilian's wrist and she let out another pained gasp. Sure, he was being rough with her, but she deserved it for almost wrecking his party and potentially getting his heart ripped out by Bastian.

He reached her room and tossed her into it as he barked, "I made it very clear you were to stay in this room… but apparently you do not know how to follow orders."

She turned on him, her caramel-coloured eyes flashing with anger and stirring a dangerous response in him.

He wanted to grab her and make her submit to him.

It was dangerous to provoke a vampire.

Especially when they had bloodlust.

The ravenous beast stirred within him, spreading darkness through his soul, always ready to rise and seize control when he was at his weakest, when his hunger for blood or sex was strong.

And gods, he wanted both of those things from this female.

"I'm not your property," she spat and stood her ground when he advanced a step into her room, her fists clenched and trembling at her sides.

"No. You belong to my brother," he countered, wishing she didn't.

She stepped right up to him, her eyes darkening as she tilted her head back and her gaze clashed with his.

Her voice lowered to a snarl. "I belong to no one."

Night stared at her, his eyes slowly widening as he saw the truth in hers, confirming his worst fears.

Lilian smiled victoriously, anger flowing from her in palpable waves that rocked him as much as her words had, but there was hurt and fear laced within it.

"You didn't know your brother was into taking humans against their will?" she barked and he held his tongue, not wanting to damn his brother, even when the proof of Bastian's crime was right before him. She shook her head, causing the glossy dark waves of her hair to brush across the shoulders of her plain black dress. "I can see it, Night. You didn't know. If you had—"

"It's none of my business," he growled and turned to leave.

Her hand on his arm stopped him.

Despite the sleeve of his jacket and his shirt that separated them, his skin burned where she held him, the thrill of her touch ripping at his fragile control and flooding him with a need to turn and gather her into his arms.

His bloodlust rose, pushing to the fore as his focus narrowed to the point where she gripped him, to how close she was behind him. He dragged down a sharp breath, catching her scent. A torment. His face twisted as he screwed his eyes shut, trying to shut out the urges running rampant through him, denying the one that pushed to the front, shoving all the others aside.

It wouldn't be wrong of him to kiss her.

Bastian didn't have any claim on her. She didn't want to belong to his brother. Would she want to belong to him?

Not in the way Bastian had wanted to claim her, but in another way.

He swallowed hard and fought back against his feelings, refusing to let them control him. It was lust. That was all. Lilian was beautiful and spirited, and he wanted to break her and claim her as his prize. It was just another hunt.

So why did it feel as if his entire life hinged on the next few seconds?

If he turned and looked at her, would he see desire or disgust in her eyes? He cracked his eyes open and looked at her hand, at her delicate fingers where they clutched at the black material of his jacket, gripping it fiercely. A silent command to look at her. He couldn't. He feared what he would do if he did.

He had never felt so out of control.

It was as if he was spiralling, spinning, and there was no way to stop himself from falling.

"Night," she whispered, the softness of her voice his undoing.

He pivoted towards her as if she had commanded him to look at her, as if she had absolute power over him, and tensed as he found she was closer than he had thought. Her chest pressed against his stomach and her scent invaded his lungs, her beauty fogging his mind as her heat warmed his body.

And gods, he wanted her.

Craved her.

She bewitched him.

Before he could stop himself, he slipped his hand into her dark hair and fisted it.

Dragged her closer still, tearing a gasp from her sweet lips as her free hand flew to his chest to torment him with the feel of it.

Her eyes danced between his, her heart accelerating in his ears as he bent his head towards her, as he balanced on the brink of doing something unforgivable.

Night made the mistake of lifting his gaze from her mouth.

He lost himself in her enchanting eyes, feeling like a moth drawn to a flame, aware it would end badly for him but unable to stop himself. She was too bright. Too warm. Too enticing.

He lowered his head, angling it at the same time, his breaths coming faster as his pulse rushed to match the tremulous beat of hers. Her breath washed over his lips, teasing him. Every fibre of his being sung in response, heated and vibrated with awareness of her and anticipation.

He ached right down to his soul.

Thirsted for her kiss as fiercely as he had ever thirsted for blood.

As if it could give him life and sustenance and strength more potent than that vital liquid could.

"Help me," she whispered, shattering the spell he was under, and he growled as he reared back from her, anger flaring hot in his veins as his heart roared that she was using him, twisting him against his own flesh and blood. She seized the lapels of his jacket in both hands, holding him in place, her eyes wild and brow furrowed as she desperately added, "Please? I have to get away from here. There's a house in the nearest village. My friend. I just need to go there for a while. I just need a moment away from this place. I need a moment to breathe. You can take me there if you want to keep an eye on me. I swear I'll return with you."

Night turned his cheek to her, his soul in agony as he ground his teeth and tried to weather her words, all his attempts to let them bounce off him failing. Each one struck their mark, another arrow in his heart.

"What you need to do is unhand me." His tone was cold even to his own ears, the calmness of it surprising him given the turmoil exploding within him.

He slid his gaze towards her, aware of what he looked like, how obsidian would be invading his red irises, the sign of his bloodlust staining them, and his elliptical pupils would be little more than thin slits in their centres, and how his fangs would show between his lips with each word.

A monster.

"I said, unhand me," he snarled.

She gasped and released him to stumble back a few steps as if he was one.

Her reaction pleased him, had the beast of his bloodlust rising as it realised he could frighten her. He could drive her deeper into that fear. Her blood would be sweeter then. He would show her the true face of the vampire she had mistakenly tried to turn against his own family, and once she was weak with terror, he would give her a kiss.

The bloodiest kind there was.

And when he was done with her, she would know first-hand the pain that pounded inside him with each unsteady beat of his heart.

Night gritted his teeth, his fangs slicing into his gums, and somehow found the strength to turn away from her. He stopped at the door but didn't have the strength to look back at her as what she had done ran on repeat in his head, tormenting him.

"Do not leave this room again, unless you want to learn what I do to those who disobey me."

He seized the door handle and dragged it closed behind him, but couldn't stop himself from adding another warning before it clicked shut.

"And never touch me again."

CHAPTER 5

Lilian checked her appearance in the full-length mirror hanging on the inside of her wardrobe door, smoothing her black dress and white apron and then fixing her hair. If things went to plan, she would blend in with the other servants working at the party tonight and she could escape without a hitch. Her heart pounded and she breathed slowly, calming it again as her fingertips tingled with magic. She needed to remain relaxed. If she remained relaxed, there was a chance her magic would behave itself and she wouldn't end up losing control of it in close proximity to the two-dozen-plus vampires she had watched arrive over three hours ago.

By now, the party would be in full swing, the vampires caught up in their entertainment. It was the perfect time to slip out and call a taxi and go to talk with Gillian. Night would probably be occupied until dawn, and hopefully he wouldn't check on her before she made it back.

And she was coming back.

She knew that deep in her heart. She couldn't give up on this mission. She couldn't be responsible for getting a potentially innocent vampire killed. She just wanted a few hours away from this place and the vampires, needed some space and some air. A talk with Gillian would help restore her courage and chase her doubts and fears away.

She pulled down a final steadying breath and hurried to her door. She was out of it before her nerve could fail her and hurrying along the corridor. In the time she had been at the house, she had noted there were three exits. The front door. The French doors in the main drawing room. And an exit near the kitchen in the basement. That servants' entrance was the best option. She could blend with the other servants heading back there to get more refreshments for the vampires and then slip out into the night.

The staff had set up the main drawing room and the front drawing room for the party, so the vampires would all be in those rooms. The only danger would be making it down the hallway that separated the two rooms and ran towards the entrance to the basement. She would make sure the coast was clear before passing the drawing rooms' doors.

It should be easy to slip out.

She reached the top of the staircase and stopped dead.

Or not.

Her eyes widened as she counted at least three vampires in the foyer below her and four humans. Blast. She ran through her options, which were limited. Either she gave up and returned to her room, or she braved the front door. The window in her room was out of the question, since she would need to use magic to break her fall and the vampires would sense it. Her cover would be blown. The staircase before her was the only way to reach the ground floor, so she couldn't sneak down another way and leave via a window lower down.

And giving up wasn't an option.

She needed to talk to Gillian, face to face not via a message or a phone call. She needed to see her friend and look her in the eye when she made Gillian tell her she was doing the right thing and that everything would be okay and she wasn't going to end up shackled to a vampire for the rest of her days.

The front door was her only real option.

She could do this. The vampires were all distracted, none of them paying any real attention to the servants milling around the foyer offering them glasses of blood.

She calmed herself and then started down the stairs, walking casually in an attempt to avoid drawing attention to herself. Several more vampires crossed the entrance hall, all of them beautiful women.

In fact, every woman in the foyer—vampire or human—was incredibly beautiful.

She tried not to imagine what Night was up to right that second, put it out of her head and focused on getting out of the house.

It was going well, and she had almost reached the bottom step without anyone paying her any heed, but then she looked off to her right, under the second staircase. A brunet male had a female pinned against the wall there, his back to Lilian as he openly fed from the human's vein. The woman clutched his shoulders, tugging at his black suit jacket as he bit down again, and moaned like he was sinking more than his fangs into her. Lilian told herself to keep moving as the woman writhed against the vampire, rocking her hips into his as she hooked one leg around his waist and he gripped her under her thigh, but she couldn't tear her gaze away from them.

Was the male Night?

He had the same build and same style of dress.

The vampire lifted his head and looked to his right as another female approached him.

Lilian released the breath she hadn't realised she was holding.

It wasn't Night.

She turned away, towards the exit.

And squeaked when she came face to face with a large man.

The vampire stood only inches from her, had snuck up on her without her noticing, and she wanted to curse as his crimson eyes locked with hers and she felt the familiar prodding sensation in her mind. He was trying to place her under his thrall.

This wasn't good.

"If you would excuse me." She dipped in a curtsey. "I have drinks to serve."

"The only thing you'll be serving is me," he grunted and snapped his hand around her arm in a lightning-fast move that her eyes couldn't keep up with.

She twisted her arm, trying to free herself as her fingers tingled with magic and panic spiked her veins with adrenaline, but his grip was like iron.

He yanked her from the bottom step and she landed awkwardly on her right foot. Her ankle gave out and he pulled her up onto her feet.

He grinned over his broad shoulder at her, flashing fangs. "Let's get better acquainted."

"Like hell," she muttered and kicked him in the shin. "Let me go."

Several vampires paused to stare, their whispered comments not lost on her. A human under thrall wouldn't talk back to a vampire or fight him, and an owned human would have experienced the same sharp burst of pain as the vampire groping them.

Which meant she was neither of those things.

The knowledge seemed to spur the brute on and he tugged her to him, so she crashed into his chest. Magic sparked in her veins, spells rising unbidden into her mind, and she fought to keep control. She couldn't attack this vampire with her magic. She couldn't reveal what she was.

But the thought that he wanted to bite her, that he wanted to hurt her and do things to her against her will, had control slipping through her fingers.

Electricity skittered through her veins, heading for his hand, and he grunted as she hit him with it. The second he released her, she bolted for the door.

Almost had her hand on the knob when he seized hold of her again and violently pulled her back to him.

"Leave me alone," she yelled as he tugged her towards one of the drawing rooms, a salacious grin plastered on his face that warned her that she had only whetted his appetite by trying to escape the mansion and him. "Unhand me!"

Other words rose to the tip of her tongue. A defensive spell. She moved her lips to form the first word, unwilling to let this vampire hurt her.

And then he suddenly stopped.

She looked beyond him.

To Night.

Her ears rang, all the strength flooding from her as he faced off against the vampire, his words lost on her as his expression darkened by degrees. Vampires gathered to watch, two beautiful females stopping behind Night, their gazes locked on him. Magic curled through Lilian as she glared at them, and then Night was looking at her, accusation in his pale blue eyes.

She averted her gaze, a stupid move, one that had just confirmed what the vampire had said to him.

She had been trying to leave.

She busied herself with studying the fine pale marble tiles, avoiding Night's piercing gaze.

The next thing she knew, the vampire released her and Night was seizing her arm, dragging her away from the fray and back up the stairs.

She grunted when she hit the wall at the top and bounced off it, and he was damned lucky he was saving her because otherwise she might have given him a taste of her magic.

Her arm ached where he gripped it and fear slowly morphed to anger as he roughly pulled her along behind him as if she was a ragdoll. She didn't appreciate it when he flung her into her room again. It was getting old.

"I made it very clear you were to stay in this room... but apparently you do not know how to follow orders," he barked, rage pouring off him.

He had no damned right to be angry with her and he certainly didn't have the right to accuse her of not knowing how to follow orders. Her ability to follow orders was the only reason he had met her, the only reason she had decided to return tonight after she had lifted some of the weight from her shoulders.

It was the only reason she had chosen to put her life at risk to save that of another.

Lilian turned on him and clenched her fists at her sides. "I'm not your property."

She tried to ignore the way her entire body trembled as his eyes narrowed on her.

"No. You belong to my brother," he countered.

And something crossed his handsome face, something she couldn't decipher.

She stepped up to him and tipped her head back as she snarled, "I belong to no one."

That struck a nerve. His striking eyes widened and she smiled at him, fury flowing through her veins that wasn't enough to obliterate the hurt and fear that ran through her too as she thought about what she was doing. This was going to end very badly, but she had put it out there now, and she could see in his eyes that she had surprised him, catching him off guard.

Because his brother was so perfect?

"You didn't know your brother was into taking humans against their will?" she snapped and when he said nothing, she shook her head. "I can see it, Night. You didn't know. If you had—"

"It's none of my business," he growled and pivoted away from her.

Oh no, he didn't. He wasn't getting away from her that easily.

She grabbed his arm, ignoring the hot wave of lightning that chased up hers the moment she touched him. His arm tensed beneath her grip, his shoulders going rigid, and her magic rose to protect her.

Because it felt he was a threat.

When he remained facing away from her, she inched closer to him.

"Night," she whispered, trying to get his attention.

He turned on his heel to face her and she bit back a gasp when his hard body pressed against hers. A shiver traipsed down her spine and she forgot what she had wanted to say as she looked up at him, into eyes that held so much heat and need that it stole her breath.

Night slipped his hand into her hair and twisted it around his fingers, his grip fierce and commanding, thrilling her as much as the way he dragged her closer still. She pressed her free hand to his chest, regretting it when the feel of his hard muscles sent another, sharper thrill through her that had her knees weakening and her control fraying.

Her pulse quickened as her eyes darted between his, half of her wanting him to go through with that desire she could read in his eyes and the rest fearing the fall out of it.

She had a mission to complete.

Falling for this vampire wasn't part of the plan.

He lowered his head, tilting it to one side at the same time, and his breath caressed her lips, sensitising them and flooding her with sweet anticipation, until she was spinning and losing control, aching for him to do it.

Just kiss her already.

His mouth neared hers.

Panic lanced her, images of what would happen if she let him kiss her running through her mind at a quickening pace, culminating in a terrible ending for both of them, and for Bastian too. She couldn't do this.

As glorious as his kiss might be, it wasn't worth the risk.

"Help me," she whispered and regretted it when he growled and reared back, looking as if she had struck him with those words.

Looking betrayed.

She hated that thought she could see in his eyes.

She hadn't been playing him.

She had wanted that kiss as much as he did, but there was too much at stake.

She seized the lapels of his jacket in both hands, unwilling to let him go and sure she could get through to him. He liked her. He wanted her. She didn't want to use it against him, but she needed help.

"Please? I have to get away from here. There's a house in the nearest village. My friend." She adjusted her grip on his jacket. "I just need to go there for a while. I just need a moment away from this place. I need a moment to breathe. You can take me there if you want to keep an eye on me. I swear I'll return with you."

Rather than doing what she wanted, he turned his profile to her and his expression grew calm and then cold, as if he was methodically shutting down all the feelings that had been in his touch and his eyes a moment ago.

Killing them.

And it was her fault.

She had hurt him. She could see that now. She had hurt him and he was going to make her pay for it.

"What you need to do is unhand me," he said, his tone as calm and cold as his expression.

His crimson gaze slid towards her, dark splotches around his thin elliptical pupils. They spread as she stared up into his eyes, discolouring his irises. What was wrong with him? Was this bloodlust? She had never witnessed it first-hand, but then she had never been this close to a vampire.

His huge fangs flashed from between his lips as he snarled, "I said, unhand me."

Lilian gasped and released him, stumbling back a few steps to place some distance between them as her magic shot to the fore, coming to protect her, and she almost lost control of it.

Darkness crossed his eyes, making him look like a wild beast, some vicious and bloodthirsty creature that would devour her given the chance.

And then he turned away from her and went to the door.

"Do not leave this room again, unless you want to learn what I do to those who disobey me." He pulled the door closed behind him, his words little more than a snarl. "And never touch me again."

He said that like he meant it, like this attraction she felt was one-sided.

When he had been the one to almost kiss her.

He hadn't been going for her throat like a vampire would, thirsting for her blood. No. He thirsted for her kiss. He wanted to know the feel of her lips just as she wanted to know the feel of his, and both of them were wise enough to recognise how dangerous this attraction between them was.

It hadn't been hunger for her kiss that had transformed him before her eyes though. It had to be bloodlust. The look he had turned on her had gone way beyond hunger, becoming something darker. Craving perhaps?

Starvation?

That was it.

He had looked like a man starved, one wild with hunger. Ravenous.

Dangerous.

And it had shocked her.

She had seen vampires in their true guise before, but this was different. The black that had marred his irises, corrupting them, reeked of bloodlust. It was another thing she wanted to ask Gillian and her coven about, because nothing in what she had read about Bastian or Night had mentioned bloodlust. Their brother, Grave, suffered it. Suffered was probably the wrong word.

The King of Death had harnessed it and moulded it into a terrifying weapon.

Lilian's gaze dropped to the floor. Had Night harnessed his bloodlust in the same way? Had Bastian? Maybe bloodlust was the reason he had massacred the witches of her coven in Germany. She had heard rumours that it could change a vampire into a monster, a beast who no longer thought like a man, acting on pure instinct instead to satisfy a craving for violence. If those rumours were true, then it might be the reason she didn't feel as if Bastian was capable of the crime he had been accused of committing.

She had only seen the man, not the monster.

She went to her bed, slumped onto the end of it, and stared at her hands. Night wasn't the only one with a wilder side. She had come dangerously close to losing control tonight. Hopefully the vampire she had accidentally hit with a blast of electricity wouldn't tell Night about it. Not that it mattered. Her power was running low. If she didn't escape soon, or complete her mission, then she would no longer be able to conceal that she was a witch. The spell she was using to mask her true nature was taxing, a drain on her magic as she fought to keep it in place every minute of every day.

She was growing weaker and Night had taken away the only way for her to get a boost.

If she had been able to reach Gillian, her friend would have been able to give her a potion to increase her strength. Together with the fact she would have been able to lift the spell for a few hours while away from the mansion, she would have had enough power to keep going for a few more weeks.

Lilian huffed and sank forwards to rest her right elbow on her knee. She propped her chin on her upturned palm and glared at the door.

She would curse Night for being so stubborn and loyal to his brother, and determined to carry out his duty, but being a witch with her particular talents meant that curse would be the real thing, not just a swear word or two designed to make her feel better. She needed to vent though. She needed to feel better.

So she chose one that wouldn't do him much harm. It would only irritate him a little.

"I hope you can't sleep after what you did, you bastard," she muttered.

There.

She waited, expecting to feel some sense of relief or at least less angry.

She didn't feel any better at all.

Sleeplessness was a basic spell, one she had mastered with ease as a toddler because it required little more than a thought and the power to make it happen. Human parents thought they had it bad, but their pain was nothing compared to what witch parents suffered if their babe had been born with Lilian's talent. If the crying didn't keep them awake at night, the natural magic of their offspring would. All the child had to do was think about being unable to sleep and the entire house suffered the same fate.

Lilian had mastered her powers though, which meant she could direct the accidental spell that was the result of her cursing aloud at one person.

Correction. Vampire.

If he hadn't shown up at Bastian's door that night, she would have been free.

Now, she was stuck in his house, awaiting her sentence, and her jailer was too damned handsome for his own good.

Heat flashed through her, a rush of warmth that had her biting her lip as she tried her hardest not to conjure up an image of him in her mind.

She failed.

He shimmered into being in the crimson drawing room, the candles casting a warm glow over him as he lounged in a sexy way on one of the antique gilt-framed scarlet couches that formed a horseshoe around the black marble fireplace. His piercing blue eyes held her immobile as he swirled the goblet of blood he held in one hand and stroked a line over his collarbone between the open V of his black shirt with the fingers of the other.

Lilian kicked him out of her head on a frustrated growl and focused on figuring out what to do. Escaping during the daylight hours made the most sense, but she had tossed another spanner in the works by cursing her guard to spend the next forty-eight hours without sleep, which was as long as it would take for her spell to wear off naturally. Not only that, but she suspected he was going to tell the staff to stop her if they saw her outside the room.

And she had a whole party of vampires to deal with now.

She really didn't want to get caught by one of them again.

Escaping at night was even more difficult though. She had the feeling that Night would be on his guard now and would be keeping a closer eye on his guests during the parties that were due to happen for the next few nights. He was going to be on the lookout for her.

He wouldn't be getting caught up in the human hosts and pretty vampires now.

Lilian pretended that didn't please her. Not one bit.

She saw a flash of the two females, one with raven hair and one a brunette, who had been ogling Night when he had come to save her. Eyeing him in a way that had blatantly screamed they were planning to seduce him.

They didn't irritate her at all.

She didn't want to accidentally curse them to transform into ugly old hags.

Lilian clenched her fists and pushed to her feet, and began pacing to work off some of the tension cranking her tight inside. The vampire wasn't hers. Who he seduced and who seduced him was none of her business.

But he had wanted to kiss her.

Her blood heated, becoming an inferno that scorched her anger away, turning it to cinders.

A noise outside the sash window had her roaming towards it and she frowned as she looked down at the drive.

It was worse than she had thought. Night was sending the vampires and humans away. The vampire was clever. The fewer people in the mansion, the easier it was for him to keep track of her. She huffed. Resisted the temptation to damn him.

She wasn't going to be escaping any time soon.

But that was fine.

She pulled her phone from the pocket of her dress and woke the screen. She might not be able to get away from Night, but she could still reach out to Gillian and her coven. Her thumbs danced over the screen, working as quickly as she could manage, her pulse hammering as fear rushed through her. If Night saw her with a phone, he would be angry, and he would take it from her. She eased away from the window as she finished her message and hit send.

Lilian stared at the screen and waited for the response, her pulse still pounding, anticipation making her restless. Her leg jiggled. Come on. Her message had been succinct, but also a clear distress call. She had mentioned Night and the fact Bastian had gone AWOL, and that she felt she was in danger and running low on power.

She was sure they would pull her and send someone to help her get away.

Her phone buzzed and she quickly opened the response.

And wanted to curse all over again.

She couldn't believe it. Remain where she was and stick to the plan? So much for her coven caring about her well-being. She had told them she was in danger, and they had refused to help. Mother earth. She looked out of the window at Night as he bid farewell to the last of the guests. Her heart thumped against her ribs as he smiled and waved, his whole demeanour changing in the blink of an eye and ravaging her defences.

Melting her.

Good grief, he was gorgeous when he smiled.

Lilian stared at him, the minutes rolling back to when he had been standing in this room with her, pressed deliciously close to her, and had almost kissed her. She rolled forwards from there, imagining the hard and demanding press of his lips against hers, how he would have shaken her entire world to its foundations with only a kiss.

Every inch of her ached to feel it.

Wanted to curse him for pulling away.

And herself for panicking and ruining the moment.

She lowered her gaze to her phone and the message.

She wasn't sure she could stick to the plan.

Because she wasn't sure she could resist Night for much longer.

He had told her not to touch him.
But it was all she could think about.
She wanted to know his kiss.

CHAPTER 6

Night rubbed his eyes and kicked at the sheets, pushing them down his bare body. He draped his arm over his face and sighed out his breath. Still sleep wouldn't come. His blood was running too hot, stoked by the fact that every time he closed his eyes, he saw that bastard with his hand on Lilian.

Felt her fear all over again.

And then relived how fierce she had been when he had taken her to her room.

And how close he had come to kissing her.

He groaned as his shaft stiffened at just the memory of her breath on his lips, her hands on his chest, and wanted to growl at his traitorous body. It seemed to fail to remember what had happened next. The little mortal had been luring him under her spell, attempting to turn him into putty in her hands so she could manipulate him into helping her escape his brother.

It had all been a lie.

So there was no way in hell he was going to fantasise about her.

He let his arm flop back onto the mattress beside him so they were spread out at his sides, reaching for the edges of the king-size bed, and glared at the black canopy.

Damn her.

He tugged the black sheet into his fists and growled as he clenched his teeth. Damn her for trying to use him like that, toying with him in a way that would have ended with her death had she not been the property of his brother. He had never tolerated females playing with him. He never would.

Which is why he no longer wanted her.

The spike of anger that caused that thought was quick to fade, and in the aftermath of it, he reached out with his senses, focusing them on her room to check on her.

Night grabbed the pillow from beneath his head and dragged it over his face and yelled into it, frustration getting the better of him. He had been repeating this same cycle since he had made everyone leave and had decided to go to his room. Memories of what had happened turned to anger which turned into a decision that he didn't desire her anymore, and that swiftly became a need to check on her as fear she would leave and he would never see her again got the better of him.

Weak.

He was weak.

And Lilian was the cause of it.

He couldn't go a handful of minutes without checking on her. He couldn't convince himself that he didn't care what she did or that he might never see her again. What was wrong with him? This wasn't like him. On the rare occasions a female had given him the brush off in the past, he had walked away and thought nothing of it or her again.

Why couldn't he do that with Lilian?

Why did the thought of moving from this spot, of walking away and losing his ability to sense her, come close to breaking him?

Night threw the pillow away from him on a growl, his fangs piercing his gums as he clenched his jaw. He was stronger than this. A little mortal female wasn't going to twist him into some needy, weak male. He rubbed his eyes, digging the heels of his palms into them, and snarled. If he could just get some damned sleep. He needed a moment's peace, some time away from thoughts of Lilian and replays of how close he had come to kissing her.

He let his left hand fall away from his face and turned his head in that direction. He glared at the clock on the mahogany bedside table.

It was just gone midday.

He should have been fast asleep by now. This wasn't like him either. It wasn't like him to get this worked up about anything, not in a long time. He had spent centuries honing his mind and strengthening his will. He should have been asleep hours ago, with the breaking of the dawn. Instead, he was growing increasingly tired and foggy, and increasingly frustrated.

Night rolled out of bed and paced his room, moving between the row of three mahogany wardrobes that lined one of the midnight-blue walls to the other side of the enormous bedroom. He glared at himself in the mirror above the dressing table whenever he approached that side, uncaring of the fact he was naked. Something was wrong with him.

It gnawed at him, like some vile beast nibbling away at his sanity. Something was very wrong. He was tired, so damned tired, and he wanted to sleep. So why couldn't he? He wasn't the kind of man who could go for a day or two without some solid sleep. Not anymore. Maybe when he had been younger. But age and experience had taught him the value of good sleep. It helped him keep his wits sharp. It helped him survive.

He dug the heels of his hands into his eyes again and bent his head, a low growl pealing from his lips.

Maybe he needed more blood.

He didn't think that he did and he was sure he had drunk enough at the party to satisfy his hunger, but maybe the female had messed with his head enough that he wasn't seeing things straight. He went to the dressing table and opened the small fridge next to it, took out a metal canister of blood and unscrewed the lid. Cold blood never went down well, but it was often necessary to drink it.

He brought the canister to his lips and paused, moved it away and stared at it. What if he didn't need blood?

His cousin Snow had been told to drink more blood to appease his bloodlust.

How wrong the doctor had been.

Instead of helping his cousin control it, the extra blood had fed the beast, making it crave more and giving it more control over him.

It had led to his cousin massacring everyone at the chateau. His parents. His aunts and uncles. Even the children who had been staying there.

Even Night's parents.

He focused on his body, unwilling to give his own bloodlust a chance to grow stronger. He didn't feel hungry. He'd had a canister of blood soon after arriving at the mansion and he'd had several glasses at the party. More than enough. The sleeplessness was messing with his head as badly as Lilian.

He screwed the cap back on the canister and put it back in the fridge, and turned away from it. Found himself checking on her again. She still hadn't moved.

Night swiped a pair of black trunks from the dresser and tugged them on. Maybe a walk around the house would burn off enough energy that he could sleep. Moving around the house wouldn't be a problem. He had turned the heavy automatic shutters on before his guests had arrived and they would be down now, covering each window on the ground and first floor. As long as he avoided the areas used by the servants during the day, he wouldn't be in any danger of exposing himself to sunlight.

But walking meant moving away from Lilian, to the point where he wouldn't be able to sense her. He grabbed his trousers and slipped them on, his gaze roaming to the door as he fastened them. He would walk until she was at the edge of his senses and then he would come back.

He opened the door and paused at the threshold of his room, his gaze darting to his left—to her door. An urge rolled through him, powerful and commanding, and as much as he fought it, he couldn't resist. He walked to her door and pressed his hand to the wooden panel as he focused on the other side of it.

She was very still on his senses.

Asleep?

Her heartbeat was steady and slow.

He locked onto it as thoughts of how fast it had been when he had last stood in this spot crowded his mind, and how fire had flashed in her eyes, provoking his desire and his bloodlust. He didn't want her. He shouldn't want her.

He wanted her.

He wanted her despite the dangers, despite the repercussions that would await them both if he surrendered to the attraction he felt, and despite the fact it would destroy his unbroken loyalty to his family.

He had been wrong about this feeling burning inside him.

It wasn't a case of forbidden desire. It wasn't lust. The fact his brother wanted to own her, that she was earmarked for him, wasn't what made Night want her.

He closed his eyes and tipped forwards to press his forehead to the door and dug his fingers into the wood.

She was beautiful.

Reserved but spirited.

She hid it well, but there was a wild side to her.

And she was strong.

He couldn't imagine everything she was feeling, the rollercoaster of emotion she had been riding from the moment Bastian had decided she would be his. Only an incredibly strong woman could handle what she had and still have the strength to keep fighting, to keep pushing for freedom.

And gods, he was a monster for denying her it.

The moment he had left her, he had been plagued by what he had done and the things he had said.

He had been thinking about what she had said too, and while he wanted to say that he was shocked to hear Bastian would do such a thing, he couldn't. Unfortunately, he wasn't really surprised that his brother's servants weren't all here by choice. The thought that Bastian wanted to impose a bond upon her like that, making it impossible for her to do anything but obey him, lit his blood on fire.

Made him consider dangerous things.

Like opening this door and telling her to run.

Bastian might not kill him when he discovered what he had done.

Night opened his eyes and stared at her door, his senses still locked on her. He was surprised she hadn't tried to leave sooner. He frowned. Maybe she had. Bastian had told him to keep an eye on her after all. He sighed. What was he going to do? He wasn't sure of the answer to that question.

This wasn't like him.

Lilian wasn't his business and neither was what his brother did with her.

But he couldn't stand by and let it all happen.

He just couldn't.

He pressed his emerging claws into the door and gritted his teeth, wrenched in two and feeling as if he was going to be pulled apart. His loyalty was to his family—to his brothers—and he had never interfered with Bastian's life before now. It wasn't his place, and Bastian wouldn't take it well. He had to remember those things.

If he helped her, even if he made it appear she had escaped on her own, Bastian would hold him responsible.

Might even shun him, severing ties with him as punishment for his disobedience. Bastian was too much like their father. Their father had been cold and hard, brutal when it came to family matters and acts of betrayal.

He had killed his own brother and all he had done was choose to turn a human he loved.

Night shoved away from the door. He returned to his room before he did something he would regret and ended up pacing it, thinking things over and trying to calm his mind and centre himself. Impossible. Lilian was a constant in his mind. Her every look was seared on his memory to torment him, and her every word was like a sword in his heart or a balm for his soul.

He huffed and pivoted, wearing a trench in the wooden floor, unable to rest as he thought about her. What was it about the little female that had him twisted in knots and unsure what to do?

He saw a flash of her. Long dark hair tumbling around her shoulders, feeling like silk in his grip. Caramel-coloured eyes shining with fire. Tempting lips beckoning him for a kiss, destroying his strength and tearing down his defences. She was beautiful.

And he couldn't blame his attraction to her, the desire she stirred in him, on the fact he had been alone too long.

If it was that simple, any one of the beautiful females who had been in the mansion—even Elspeth—should have inflamed him and stirred his passion. But they hadn't. He had felt nothing in their presence.

But in Lilian's...

He scrubbed a hand down his face. He couldn't let this get the better of him. His loyalty was to his family. His brother had given him a duty and he would fulfil it. He was merely swept up in her beauty, mistaking lust for something else—something dangerous—and convincing himself it was real. It was lust. Bastian would return and Night would leave, and he would find a whole line of females to satisfy his every desire, and then he would forget Lilian. He would see he was right and he had only wanted her because it had been too long since he'd had a woman.

So why did he want to throw his head back and roar at just the thought of letting Bastian have her?

He stilled. Movement. His gaze swung to his door and then the clock. The display mocked him with the hour. It was gone six now. He had lost track of time and awareness of the world for six hours and he still hadn't slept. It would be dark soon.

Night rubbed his tired eyes and stared at the door, feeling beyond it to Lilian's room. He tracked her movements around it. Or across it. She was moving at speed back and forth. Pacing. Planning her escape now her attempt to convince him to help her had failed?

His stomach twisted a little and he ignored it. He wouldn't feel guilty about what he had done.

It didn't stop him from feeling guilty about a few other things.

He found himself moving to his door and opening it, and before he could regain control of himself, he was knocking on her door.

It opened slowly and she peered up at him. The dark circles beneath her dull eyes and her mussed chocolate hair said he wasn't the only one who hadn't been able to get some rest.

Night rubbed the back of his neck, growing aware of the fact he was only half-dressed as her gaze dropped to his bare torso and then darted off to her right. His heart pounded, loud in his ears, and the pace of it only quickened as a hint of colour touched her cheeks. Maybe he should have put a shirt on before coming to see her, but then he wouldn't have evoked this telling reaction in her.

He savoured it and the way she kept her eyes off him, and how that blush on her cheeks kept darkening as he gazed at her. All the tension that had been building inside him throughout the day ebbed away as the knots inside him loosened as if her reaction had tugged at the end of the string to unravel them all. She wanted him too. He wasn't going crazy. He wasn't the only one swept up in feelings that they knew they shouldn't have. It was right there in the way she struggled to keep herself from looking at his body.

In the hint of arousal that laced her scent.

And the quickening of her pulse as it hammered a tempting rhythm in her neck.

He dragged his eyes away from her throat, sure he was going to regret this. "You can leave your room if you swear you won't leave the house."

Her caramel-coloured eyes leaped to meet his and she blinked at him as her lips parted.

"Why?" That word tumbled from her bewitching lips, shaking him from his reverie, and he lifted his gaze to lock with hers. Suspicion coloured them. "Why are you letting me leave the room? You made it quite clear last night that this was my prison cell."

He flinched but masked it by scratching his neck, pretending an itch was the reason he had suddenly moved.

"I'm not your jailer." Although he certainly felt like it, something he would never forgive Bastian for. He sighed and glanced along the cream corridor to his right, towards the stairs, as he sensed other servants moving around. "You haven't eaten all day. You must be hungry."

He returned his gaze to her and she looked more surprised now than when he had announced she was free to move around the house. Shocked that he had thought of her needs? Or maybe she was surprised that he cared.

"I'm not hungry." Her stomach growled on cue, calling her a liar.

She clutched it and glared at him, as if daring him to say something.

He would, but it wasn't going to be what she expected.

"Do not leave. Bastian will be gone for a while longer. If you can just give me time, I can… I'm not sure. Figure something out." He didn't sound confident to his own ears, so he wasn't surprised when she arched an eyebrow at him.

"Now you want to help me?" Her eyes searched his, mistrust glittering in them, and before he could defend himself and convince her that he had been torn about her situation from the moment he had met her, she continued, "Fine. I won't leave."

It was a relief to hear that, had more of the tension flowing from him. Now all he had to do was figure out a way to help her. Maybe he could speak to Bastian and convince him that he didn't really want her, and that what he was doing was wrong. Maybe he could find another pretty female or two who were willing to be his brother's servants and offer them up as an exchange.

As he had with the brute last night.

Lilian stepped closer to him, capturing the whole of his focus. Her delicate scent swirled around him and the feel of her eyes on him had his shifting to meet them. A soft look settled across her face, resembling concern, but he wasn't sure what he had done to deserve it.

She lifted her hand and stopped just short of cupping his cheek, tormenting him with the sensation of her palm close to his face and a violent need to feel it pressed to his flesh.

"Did you sleep at all today?" she murmured, a tenderness in her tone that stole his strength and made him want to sag against her and gather her into his arms so he could rest his cheek on her shoulder and find peace.

He shook his head and rubbed his eyes instead. "I could not."

Lilian inched closer still and he wanted to tell her not to, that he wasn't a strong male where she was concerned and he was dangerously close to taking hold of her and surrendering to his need of her.

Her eyes bewitched him though, holding him immobile, as if she had cast a spell on him.

They were so soft.

Held so much concern.

All of it directed at him.

He couldn't remember the last time a woman had looked at him like that. He wasn't sure it had ever happened. At least not from someone outside of his family. His mother had looked at him like that. His sister. He shut down that thought, the pain of losing her unwelcome in this moment.

Lilian's brow furrowed as her eyes darted between his, as if she could see his pain. She probably could. He had never been able to hide it well. Discovering his little Luna had walked into the sun because she had feared bloodlust might seize her as it had their cousin and make her harm her beloved family had damn near destroyed him. He had been inconsolable for months. A wretched, broken thing. He rubbed his eyes as they misted, as his heart ached and felt as if it might break.

He was too tired for this, his defences weakened by fatigue, allowing thoughts to take hold of him too easily. If he let himself think about it, those thoughts would become a nightmare when he finally slept. He didn't want to replay that day.

Lilian's palm brushing across his cheek made him tense and his hand dropped from his face as he lifted his eyes, his gaze colliding with hers.

"You should get some sleep," she whispered.

A wave of fatigue rolled over him, as if her words were magic, and something dark inside him rebelled in response, growling and snarling and driving him to lash out at her and force her away from him. He tamped down the urge. No one was casting spells on him. He was tired and he had been wanting to talk to her about her predicament, and now he had. That was the reason he now felt he could sleep.

It had nothing to do with what she had said.

His eyelids grew heavy though and he had to keep blinking to remain awake, feeling as if he would collapse if he remained standing before her much longer.

"Sleep, Night," she murmured softly. "Rest easy."

He nodded and reluctantly turned away from her, hating the moment where her hand fell from his face. He trudged to his room, fighting a yawn, and looked back at her at the threshold. She smiled.

Gods, she was beautiful.

Both inside and out.

Night tore himself away from her and stepped into his room, closing the door behind him.

He stumbled to his bed, a dark wave rolling up on him, and flopped onto the covers on his front.

Sleep swept him up in its arms and he sank into it.

Thinking of Lilian.

CHAPTER 7

Night didn't sleep long. His damned body didn't allow it. Despite how tired he was, the instinct to rise had struck him shortly after nightfall. He had tried livening himself up with a hot shower, but the effect it had was already waning as he took one of his tailored black suit jackets from the wardrobe and slipped it on.

He covered his mouth as he yawned and padded across the room to his mini-fridge. Lack of sleep meant he needed more blood to keep his strength up. He opened the door and took out the canister he had debated drinking earlier that day. He unscrewed the cap and drank a little of the cold blood. Just enough to take the edge off his hunger and give his body the sustenance it needed.

And to stop him from daydreaming about Lilian's throat beneath his lips.

He wanted to speak with her and he wasn't sure she would appreciate him staring at her neck the whole time.

Night placed the blood back in the fridge and left his room. He checked her room first, but she wasn't there, so he focused his heightened senses. They placed her in the wing beyond the staircase, so he headed that way and paused to check again when he reached it. Downstairs.

A female coming towards him bowed her head as he descended the wooden staircase, not lifting it until he had passed. After being so focused on Lilian the past few days, he had almost forgotten how servants were supposed to behave around a pureblood vampire of a noble bloodline. For some reason, the female acting submissive towards him rankled him.

He headed beneath the twin staircases and banked left, walking along the corridor towards the library. Maybe Lilian was there. He tracked her with his senses and frowned as he passed her. Before he could change course, someone knocked on the front door. His frown deepened as he pivoted to face the direction he had come and tried to sense who had come to visit.

A vampire, if he had to guess given the hour.

He started back towards the grand foyer.

Lilian appeared in view, hurrying along the corridor towards him, her dark hair bouncing against the shoulders of her short black dress with each stride.

"Is something wrong?" Adrenaline spiked his blood as he immediately prepared himself for a fight, the desire to protect her seizing him in an instant as her large amber eyes met his and he scented the fear that laced her blood.

She shook her head. "There are two vampires at the door who wish to speak with you."

"With me?" He frowned and reached out with his senses again. "Is it Laurent and Renard?"

They were the only two vampires he could think of that would want to speak with him.

Lilian gave another shake of her head and swallowed hard. "One is your brother."

She paled a little.

Night reacted on instinct, grabbing her arm and pulling her closer to him as the protective streak she roused in him demanded he make her feel safe and shield her from Bastian.

"I won't let him bind with you against your will, Lilian," he growled, his blood on fire and muscles clamping down on his bones as he sharpened his mind, readying himself.

Bastian was older and therefore stronger than him, but Night would do all in his power to make his brother see that what he was doing was wrong, even if it came down to a fight.

He frowned at his hand on her arm as he realised what he had done and said. Fool. This was Bastian's house. His brother wouldn't knock on his own door.

Which could only mean…

Her eyes widened. "It's not Bastian. It's—"

She cast a fearful glance over her shoulder.

"Grave," he murmured.

That was the reason she was afraid. Because it was his brother Grave at the door and she clearly knew of his reputation.

He tried to wrap his head around the fact that Grave had left Hell, something he rarely did. It didn't seem possible. He couldn't remember the last time Grave had set foot in the mortal world.

"Are you sure it's my brother? My cousin Antoine looks much like him." Night found it hard to believe it was Grave at the door.

Grave who hated visiting Bastian.

"He specifically asked to see his brother. Unless you have a cousin staying here, it is your brother." The bite to her tone was unnecessary, but Night let it slide, because he knew her short temper stemmed from fear.

"He won't harm you, Lilian," Night snarled and the fire in his veins burned hotter, his thoughts growing darker as the need to protect her stirred his bloodlust—something he would need if he was going to beat Grave.

He tried to calm his mind, telling himself on repeat that Grave wouldn't harm her. That his brother hadn't come here for a fight or to take her from him. She was safe. He kept telling himself that, but it wouldn't sink in. The urge to take her far away from Grave was only growing stronger as he stood there in the corridor with her, his hand on her soft flesh, her proximity wreaking havoc on him.

"Night?" she whispered, his name like a drug on her lips, addling his mind and drawing his gaze to her.

"Hmm?" he murmured as he fell into her enchanting eyes and lost himself in a pleasing fantasy of defeating his brother to protect her and her falling into his arms, grateful for what he had done.

Surrendering to him.

"Your brother is not the only guest. There is another vampire with him. He's tall... big... white hair—"

He cut her off with a growl as his fangs punched long from his gums and his bloodlust roared to the fore, provoked by what she had said.

"Go to your room and do not leave it," he snarled and when she didn't move, he bared his fangs at her.

She flinched away from him and cast him a confused look, and gods, *he* was frightening her now. He flexed his fingers around her arm. Fingers that were holding her in place, had been digging into her flesh in a bruising grip and keeping her close to him. He dragged down an unsteady breath and tried to tame his emotions, but they slipped their leashes and he knew she had seen his fear when her expression softened. He looked away from her, but still couldn't convince himself to release her. The thought that she would be unescorted in the house while his cousin was present had him tightening his grip on her rather than loosening it, had a dark voice in his heart roaring at him to keep her close.

"Night?" she whispered again, intoxicating him and pulling him back to her, luring him up from the dark abyss he had been sinking into, one filled with satisfying images of him fighting Snow and Grave.

He craved the violence. The bloodshed. The breaking of bones. He wanted to taste copper on his tongue. Wanted to feel the bruising blows.

Lilian's hand pressed to his cheek, tugging him towards the light and quietening his bloodlust.

"Should I prepare the drawing room?" She held his gaze, no trace of fear in hers now as she stood before him with her back rod-straight.

Brave little human.

She had seen his fear, had seen the darkness trying to consume him in response to that emotion, and rather than scurrying away to hide in her room as he had asked, she wanted to remain close to him.

He forced himself to nod.

"The crimson room." He went to release her and then tightened his grip again as panic lanced him. She looked from his hand to his face. He stared into her eyes, holding her gaze, needing to know she was listening and would do as he asked because it was vital that she did. "Prepare the room and serve blood. Act as a servant would. Do not look directly at my cousin and my brother. You have to play the part, Lilian. Grave will expect you to act in a manner befitting of a servant. Do you understand? I know you hate this situation you are in, but right now, I need you to do this for me."

She nodded and placed her hand over his, sending a thousand volts bolting up his arm. "I can do this. I'll prepare the room and serve you, and then I'll go to my room. You don't have to worry, Night."

He did have to worry, and not only about her performance. He needed to worry about his own too. Grave was astute and knew him too well. If he wasn't careful, his brother would see he was developing feelings for Lilian, and he would be in trouble.

Night forced himself to release her and pulled down another breath as she hurried away from him. He could do this. All he had to do was keep his eyes off Lilian for a few minutes. He could manage that, surely?

He strode along the corridor, heading back to the foyer, steeling himself as he went. The second he stepped into view, Grave was frowning at him, his pale blue eyes narrowing with it.

"Where is Bastian?" His brother's deep voice held a commanding note, one Night had heard many times in his years of service.

He knew better than not to answer his brother.

"Away." Night rubbed a hand around the back of his neck and caught himself, but not before Grave's eyes narrowed further, suspicion colouring them.

Damn it.

He was going to have to be more careful. Grave knew all his tells, could probably already see that he was nervous about something.

He looked from his brother to his cousin. The two were a contrast. Grave's brown hair was short and his clothing was neat, consisting of his standard black dress shirt and trousers. Snow's white hair was overlong and wild, and a black T-shirt and jeans hugged his muscular frame, and his heavy-soled leather boots were suited more to a biker than one of their bloodline.

Their eyes were the same though.

Icy blue. Piercing. Night felt as if both males were stripping away his layers to expose his true feelings as they stared at him.

What on earth had transpired to drag not only his brother from Hell but his cousin from the safety of his home in London? If Grave rarely left Hell, then Snow never left the theatre he owned with his brother. Snow had grown to fear his own shadow after the dreadful night the bloodlust had seized control of him, and to protect everyone from himself, and perhaps protect himself from further pain, he had holed himself up and refused to set foot outside.

Now both Grave and Snow stood before him and he could only draw one terrible conclusion.

They were in serious trouble.

All of them.

It had to be the reason Grave had wanted to speak with Bastian. They all had a target on their backs.

Lilian entered the room from the doors beneath the staircase and he couldn't stop himself from glancing at her as she approached his brother and his cousin. The urge to tell her to remain at a distance from them, where she was safer, blasted through him and he had to bite his tongue to stop himself from moving to shield her. She wasn't in any danger. Telling himself that didn't quell the need to protect her.

Part of him knew where it had come from. He didn't really view his cousin and brother as a threat to her. He could feel the unseen threat that had brought them to this place, and he wanted to protect her from that, whatever it was.

She bowed, lowering her head, acting as expected of a servant.

Night hated it.

He curled his hands into fists and clenched them, pressing his emerging claws into his palms as a new need rushed through him—he needed to get her away from this place. The thought of her becoming a slave to his brother was torture.

The thought she might end up with a target painted on her back too was sheer agony he couldn't bear.

Grave arched an eyebrow at him.

Then his brother's gaze slid back to Lilian as she straightened and Night wanted to snarl at him to take his eyes off her. Grave always had been the most handsome of them. Despite the darkness that lurked just beneath the surface, his brother drew females to him like moths to a flame and they always got burned.

He flexed his fingers, itching to snatch her away from Grave before he could charm her too.

Grave looked at him again, his gaze searing Night, filling him with a need to look at his brother. Only he couldn't tear his gaze away from Lilian as she stood before his brother and cousin, no trace of fear in her delicate scent. His brave little mortal.

"The room is ready," she said in a quiet voice, one that trembled.

Was she afraid after all?

The hint of colour that darkened her cheeks as she turned away from Grave and Snow, glancing at Night as her gaze passed him, and the subtle fragrance of desire that laced her scent hit him hard.

She had been aware of him staring at her.

And she had liked it.

Night followed her, aching to talk with her, to make her look at him and see in her eyes that he wasn't misreading things. She wanted him.

Grave's clipped steps behind him and the feel of his brother closing in on him had him shoving away his desire to close the distance between him and Lilian. He was supposed to be concealing his feelings from his brother, and so far all he had done was broadcast them for everyone to see, including Lilian.

He couldn't help it though.

His cheek was still warm from her caress.

His head still fogged by the sound of her whispering his name.

He burned for her.

Grave caught up with him just as he reached the trio of antique gilt-framed red chairs that formed a horseshoe around the black marble fireplace in the deep-crimson-walled reception room.

Night gestured to the couch that faced the fireplace as he took the armchair to the left of it, not noticing what he had done until it was too late. The position meant he could watch Lilian where she stood by the mahogany side table near the right corner of the room, beside one of the four tall French doors that framed the fireplace, two on either side of it.

Fuck.

He didn't want to look at his brother, actively avoided his piercing gaze and made things worse by ending up staring at Lilian as she began to pour blood for them.

He tore his eyes away from her and frowned as he noticed Snow hadn't moved into the room. His enormous cousin filled the doorway, wariness shining in his eyes as they followed the blood from the canister into the glass.

Crimson ringed his irises.

Night realised his mistake and cursed, was about to launch to his feet and make Lilian leave as quickly as she could when Grave barked two words.

"No blood."

Lilian snapped her head up, looked directly at Grave and then swiftly dropped her eyes back to her feet.

Grave frowned at her, a calculating edge to his eyes that Night didn't like. If his brother dared to call her on the fact she wasn't behaving as expected of a servant, he wasn't sure what he would do, but it would probably involve a vain attempt to beat his brother up that would end with himself being a bloody splat on the wooden floor instead.

Thankfully, Grave only waved her away.

Lilian bowed her head, gathered the silver tray with the goblets and canister on it, and hurried towards the exit.

Night's gaze tracked her.

And got caught on Grave.

He tried not to respond to the hard look his brother was giving him, but ended up frowning at him as Lilian moved to the edge of his senses and slipped beyond them, stirring a dark need to go after her. It was Grave's fault.

His brother's expression shifted and he looked close to rolling his eyes as Night silently threatened him, unable to stop himself from reacting to Lilian's absence and his brother's behaviour towards her.

For a vampire trying to hide his feelings, Night was doing a terrible job of things. The temptation to just throw in the towel and admit he was attracted to her was great, but he fought it and tamped it down as he schooled his features. Grave eyed him closely as he sat on the couch that faced the fireplace, picking the end nearest Night. Snow stalked into the room to ease his big frame into the armchair opposite Night.

Night still couldn't believe it was Grave sitting before him.

Grave who never left Hell anymore was here, in the mortal world, paying his family a visit.

Night was about to ask what they had done to deserve the pleasure of their company and then demand to know what was happening when Grave spoke, his deep voice sober and deadly serious, sending a chill down Night's spine.

"I need you to leave this place."

CHAPTER 8

╾∞╾

"I need you to leave this place," Grave said and Night frowned at him, a thousand questions rising to the tip of his tongue that his brother silenced by continuing, "There is a demon, one who declares himself a prince of that kind… belonging to the Devil."

Cold fear bolted through Night's blood and he shut it down in a heartbeat, his expression hardening as he waited and listened, sure his brother would arm him with more information so he could help him. It was worse than he had expected though. No wonder his brother had left Hell.

"A mission for the Preux Chevaliers that myself and Snow led should have eliminated all of his bloodline but somehow he survived, and now he is bent on killing us all in the name of revenge." Grave didn't need to say any more than that for Night to be aware of the gravity of their situation. Snow hadn't served in the Preux Chevaliers for centuries, meaning the mission had happened that long ago and this demon prince had been biding his time, building up to this moment. There was no doubt in Night's mind that the male had spent that time wisely, honing his skills, sharpening himself into a blade capable of cutting Grave and Snow down. His brother continued before Night could pledge himself to their cause, "So you have to leave."

Grave reached for Night's hand.

Night let him place his hand over it and squeeze it, even when he wanted to deny his brother the comfort of the touch because in a handful of words, Grave had made it clear he meant to send Night away and keep him from helping them.

Grave had done that before and Night had hated him for it, even when he had known his brother had only wanted to protect him. It had felt as if Grave had been questioning his strength though, believing him incapable of handling the violence and dangers of Hell.

Night resisted the desire to lift his hand and touch the scar on his throat as it burned.

"Disappear, Night." Grave tightened his grip on Night's hand.

Night looked down at their joined hands and then up into his eyes.

Grave's blue eyes slowly lowered towards Night's throat.

Night snatched his hand away and lifted it, bringing it up towards his throat as he barely leashed the urge to growl and flash fangs at his brother. He stopped before his fingers made contact with the scar tissue and averted his gaze, anger at his brother swiftly morphing into anger at the witch who had tried to take his head. He wrestled with it, trying to calm his mind and stop the memories from coming, hating the way Grave and Snow were both looking at him now.

Watching him fall apart.

He needed to be strong. If he wasn't strong, Grave would stick to his guns and refuse his help, and Night needed to help him. He cleared his throat and lowered his hand, battling the dark tide and slowly clawing back calm.

"Listen to me," Grave said and Night's gaze slid to him, and guilt flickered in his brother's eyes—because crimson ringed Night's irises. "You must disappear."

His brother wouldn't listen to a word he said. Night knew it. Grave was set on sending him away, forcing him to go somewhere safe. His vision sharpened as his pupils shifted, beginning to turn elliptical in response to the wave of anger that surged through him, driving him to seize hold of his brother and make him listen.

Make him accept his help.

He didn't need to be safe. He didn't need to be protected. Grave did. His brother was in danger and so was his cousin. They needed him. Demons of the Devil's domain were extremely powerful. Two vampires were no match for one. He wasn't even sure he could turn the tide in their favour if he joined them, but he was willing to try. It was better than being safe.

He sensed movement above him.

Lilian.

Another war erupted inside him. If he left with his brother and cousin, who would protect Lilian? If Grave was right, then the demon prince might be heading for the mansion, targeting his family. The demon would leave no one alive.

An image of Lilian lying broken and bloodied, her sightless eyes staring right through him, chilled his blood.

Grave needed him, but so did Lilian.

Maybe he could get her to safety and then find his brother and cousin and join them.

He dug his fingertips into his knee and cursed. Someone had to warn Bastian too.

"I cannot. I have to remain here and keep my promise to Bastian." Night systematically shut down his feelings, killing them one by one to clear his mind so he could focus on figuring out a solution to this problem.

A strategy.

Grave frowned at that. "What promise?"

One he probably shouldn't have brought up, but it was a good excuse for remaining here for the next day or two while he put together a plan that would see him able to help Lilian, Bastian *and* Grave.

"I told Bastian I would take care of the house while he was away on business." Night refused to look at Grave when his brother growled a warning at him.

"This is not a game, Night."

Night rolled his shoulders beneath his black suit jacket. "I can see that from your escort. How is business, Snow?"

Snow leaned back in his armchair and eyed Night, his voice as cold as the Nordic lands they all hailed from. "Going well. You should listen to your brother. This is no time to joke and be foolish."

Night knew that. Fear chilled his blood almost as much as Snow's grave tone had as he locked onto Lilian with his senses. He tracked her, wishing he could explain his reasons for wanting to remain here to Grave, but his brother wouldn't understand.

Running the Preux Chevaliers had left his brother's heart cold towards the opposite sex.

That wasn't true.

Night wasn't sure it had ever been warm when it came to females. He couldn't remember his brother ever being swept up in the same collision of emotions Night was experiencing, teetering on the verge of falling for someone.

He eased his grip on his knee and tried to relax, affecting a calmness he didn't feel at all as he thought about what he needed to do. Getting Lilian away from the house would be a good start, but what if the demon had already seen her here? What if he targeted her while she was alone and vulnerable?

No, he couldn't let her go. Until this threat had passed, he was keeping her with him.

"When Bastian returns, we will all head north," he said, his decision made.

Grave's eyebrows dipped low. "All?"

"Myself and Bastian," Night said, a little too quickly judging by the suspicious look Grave gave him.

That look became knowing.

Night silently cursed again.

This was not going well.

Even Snow looked as if he had pieced things together and was questioning his sanity.

Night tried to think of an excuse, something that sounded reasonable and would throw his brother and cousin off his scent. Grave suddenly bent forwards and clutched his chest, his lips pulling taut in a grimace as he growled.

"What's wrong?" Snow and Night said in unison.

Grave stared down at his hand.

He was still for a full minute, his expression etched with confusion and pain, and then his jaw flexed and he screwed his eyes shut as he tightly gripped the front of his black shirt.

Night jumped as Grave launched to his feet.

"Where is the nearest portal?" Grave growled.

Snow stared at Grave through wide eyes.

Night recovered more quickly, concern filling him as he looked up at Grave and sensed his fear. "Brother… what is wrong?"

"I think the demon prince might have my mate." Grave cast him a worried glance, his brow furrowing as he continued to hold the front of his shirt as if his life depended upon it.

"Then we can take my car and we will be at the nearest portal in—wait." Night's face slackened as he stared at his brother. "Mate? You have a mate?"

"I do not have time for this, Night," Grave barked.

"He has a mate. A phantom, apparently." Snow almost sounded amused, but then his tone and expression turned grave as he slid a look at Night. "Ask him about his little habit of going incorporeal."

"A phantom? Incorporeal?" Night shot to his feet now, emotions colliding and tangling inside him. Fear clashed with anger, the thought that his brother had kept him in the dark about this cutting him deeply. He had thought they were close, but Grave had a mate Night had known nothing about, and it hurt. "What the fuck is going on? How long have you had a mate?"

Who had managed to thaw Grave's icy heart? Night almost wanted to meet the female, because she had to be something special. Hell, she was a phantom. His brother must have been mad to get involved with one.

He stared at Grave, seeing the fear in his eyes—fear for this female.

Grave gritted, "I do not have time to explain myself, Night, and nor do I need to."

"I don't even know why you bother pretending to have siblings when you want nothing to do with us," Night spat and stormed away from him, regretting his words the moment they left his lips. He stopped a few strides away and looked back at his brother, his eyebrows furrowing as guilt churned in his stomach and he tried to muster an apology.

That guilt only worsened when he saw the stunned look on his brother's face.

Night dropped his gaze to the wooden floor. "You didn't deserve that."

"Perhaps I did," Grave murmured, his voice strained and low, thick with emotion Night was sure was about his mate being in danger rather than Night's outburst. His brother crossed the room to him and placed his hands on Night's shoulders. "I have not been a good brother. Neither of us have, but I can only make excuses for myself. If I keep things from you, Night, it is only because I want to protect you."

Night growled and knocked his brother's hands off him. "Like you protected me by sending me away from Hell? I didn't need you to do that, Grave. I'm strong and I can handle—"

Grave seized him by his nape and dragged him closer, cutting him off as shock swept through him.

His brother pressed their foreheads together and husked, "I know you are strong, Night. I never doubted your strength... but what happened to you... It was a moment of weakness on my part and if you hate your position that much—"

Night cut him off this time.

"Try to take it away from me and we shall really fall out, brother." He sighed and leaned into Grave's touch. "I hated it at first... but then you probably knew that."

"I did. I thought you would never talk to me again. You sent those formal reports through Asher and that was all the contact I had with you for... It felt like forever." Regret laced his brother's baritone and filled Night too.

He had lashed out at Grave in the only way he could, wanting to hurt him for questioning his strength and sending him away, shielding him and making him look weak to the other vampires in the Preux Chevaliers. It had taken a lot of work to make his subordinates respect him and view him as a strong leader.

Grave grunted and released him, shifting his hand back to his chest to clutch at it.

"I can take you to a portal," Night said and wanted to tell his brother he was coming with him, but ended up saying, "Where will you go?"

Grave didn't look sure. He drifted to the couch and sank onto it to stare at the unlit fireplace.

"I do not know." His brother shook his head and glanced at Snow.

When Snow didn't give him a direction, Grave returned to staring ahead of him.

"I need to find her, but I do not know where to look," Grave murmured and Night could sense how much that pained him, could see the strain his brother felt as tight lines bracketed his lips and he glared at the fireplace.

Night went to him and placed his hand on his brother's shoulder, gaining his attention. "Is there a place your mate might have gone, one the demon would know about? Her home, perhaps?"

Grave shrugged. "I do not know."

For a male with a mate, Grave didn't seem to know much about her.

"When I left Hell," Night said, carefully choosing his words. He had wanted to say 'when you sent me away' but Grave wouldn't take it well. Pain glittered in his brother's pale blue eyes as he stared straight through him, miles away from him. Night sighed again. "When I left Hell, you did not have a mate."

"I do not think she was ever really my mate." Grave smiled tightly and there was a world of hurt in it. "We had only a few months together... and then a century ago, she turned on me and left me. Since then, I have been trying to rid myself of her."

A century ago.

Now Night knew why Grave had changed around then, growing darker all of a sudden, his temper shortening and mood blackening—he had found his mate, had clearly fallen for her, and had lost her. The way Grave had acted since then told Night all he needed to know. This mate of Grave's had betrayed him in some way.

He wanted to demand to know what had happened, but knew in his heart that Grave wouldn't take it well, so instead Night murmured, "You could have told me. You didn't have to deal with it alone, Grave."

His brother's blue eyes held an apology, one that smoothed the sharp edges of Night's anger over being left in the dark. "It was wrong of me, Night... but I didn't want others to know."

Night could understand that, even when he didn't like it. Grave had a reputation to protect and a position to hold on to. If other vampires had learned of what had happened, they might have viewed it as a weakness, something they could exploit to overthrow him—the King of Death could be tricked and defeated.

"When my hands faded during a battle, I knew something was wrong... and then she came to me. Gods..." Grave closed his eyes.

His brother didn't need to say anything for Night to know that visit had shaken him, and awoken feelings Grave had thought were dead and buried.

Grave might not have been a true mate to her, but from where Night was standing, it looked as if she had been Grave's. Which did have one positive. It meant his brother was in no position to lecture him about Lilian. Not when he was in love with a phantom who was clearly his enemy.

Night knew all about that wretched breed. Phantoms turned men they had relations with into phantoms too, ones that eventually faded to nothing.

This woman had committed an act of revenge against his brother.

Her breed and the way his brother looked was proof enough for Night and he wanted to demand Grave let him deal with her, even when he knew his brother would shoot him down. No matter how angry Grave was, how desperate he was to hate her for what she had done, there was no doubt in Night's mind that his brother loved her.

There was also no doubt in Night's mind that Grave was in denial about his feelings.

He proved that by muttering, "Gods, I hate her."

If hate was a synonym for love, then yes, his brother really hated his mate.

"The demon is probably baiting you," Night offered as he set his mind to the task of finding where the fiend had taken his brother's beloved mate. He rubbed his thumb across his lower lip, running through all the possible scenarios, seeking the one that would fit a demon. "He will probably take her somewhere you know."

Night looked from Grave to Snow and back again.

"Somewhere you both know," he amended. "Any ideas?"

Grave glared at him, crimson bleeding into his irises. "The castle. The castle where we killed his family."

"That is a long way from a portal." Snow pushed to his feet.

"Then we best get started." Grave stood and turned to Night, his expression deadly serious. "Do not allow your attraction to the human female to cause a rift between you and Bastian."

"What attraction?" Night said, all innocence as he raised his brows and feigned shock.

Grave arched an eyebrow at him, that action calling Night on his lie.

"She's not willing." Night couldn't hold that back. It didn't justify his feelings or his desire to help her, but it might make Grave see things from his angle.

"Why doesn't that surprise me?" Grave drawled and looked at the door and then back at him. "She might not be willing, Night, but she does seem at home here. She knows how to behave around purebloods, meaning she accepted the lessons the other staff would have given her, preparing her for becoming one of them. And if she was desperate to leave and escape Bastian, she would have done so by now. Bastian is hardly holding her under lock and key."

His brother headed for the door.

Night scowled at his back and cursed him.

Because Grave was right.

Lilian wasn't exactly a prisoner, and she must have had plenty of chances to escape while Bastian was here. Her room was far from Bastian's, so his brother hadn't felt the need to keep tabs on her during the daylight hours, and Bastian hadn't given him a key for her room or instructed him to keep her locked inside it, meaning he had never bothered to do such a thing himself.

She had even had opportunities to escape when Night had been here, but she hadn't taken them. Not only that, but she had said that she would come back if he went with her to see her friend or allowed her to go alone.

So did she want to be Bastian's and gain the benefits of becoming owned by him?

Or did she want to leave?

Which was it?

He wanted to know the answer to that question.

And he wanted to know it right now.

CHAPTER 9

Lilian moved around the basement kitchen, keeping active to ward off the chill that rose from the worn stone floor. She paused briefly in front of the ancient black Aga that took up most of one wall, savouring the heat that came off it. Going to her room would have been warmer, but she also would have been closer to the vampires. Down here, surrounded by stone and the constant scent of the fuel burning in the stove, and the fire in the grate of the inglenook, she could drop the spell that concealed the fact she was a witch. It was still risky, but Night was occupied with his brother and cousin.

It had taken a lot for her not to be afraid when faced with the King of Death, a vampire with an incredible reputation for being ruthless and violent, and uncontested on the battlefield. The fear she had felt in his presence had been nothing compared to what she had felt when Night had reacted so fiercely to discovering the other vampire was his cousin.

He had looked ready to lock her away to keep her from him.

Some foolish part of her had sworn he was overreacting, but then she had seen the black in his cousin's crimson eyes as he had stared at the blood she had been pouring. Bloodlust. The whole family were afflicted with it. She had thought Night's reaction to her had been savage bloodlust, but the way he had acted was nothing compared with how the cousin had responded to just the sight of blood. She had seen Night around blood and he had been in control, looking normal. The big white-haired one had looked ready to go off.

Making her re-evaluate how dangerous Night was.

She was no expert by any means, but based on what she had seen and what she did know, on a scale of one to ten, she placed his bloodlust at an eight, Grave's at a ten, and the cousin's at one hundred.

Lilian drifted to the enormous heavy wooden table that occupied the centre of the large room and arranged the plates into neat piles, ready for putting away in the cupboards of the Welsh dressers that lined another of the stone walls. Ellen had made it very clear when she had caught her hurrying away from the crimson drawing room that she needed to finish taking care of the tasks she had been assigned that morning. Tasks that had gone undone thanks to the fact Night had ordered her to stay in her bedroom.

So far, she had checked the larders to make sure they had enough food for the next week, had put away all the cutlery that someone had just left in a pile on the table after it had been washed and dried, and she had nibbled on some crackers and cheese, because she still hadn't eaten dinner.

She had missed it thanks to Night's visitors.

She looked up at the ceiling, part of her wondering what they were discussing and tempted to eavesdrop even when she knew it was a bad idea because vampires had acute senses. She couldn't stop within hearing distance of them, and she couldn't use a spell either, because there was a chance they would sense it. The rest of her had steadily grown fixated on the fact it was Grave Van der Garde upstairs. The leader of the Preux Chevaliers. She knew all about the vampire mercenary corps of Hell.

Only vampires of the pureblood families could serve in it, and each son was required to give up four centuries of his life to it. Grave was older than Night but he was still serving. Did that mean Night had never served or had he done his years of service?

Or was her gut right and he was still serving as a mercenary?

She leaned forwards and rested her elbow on the table, propping her chin up on her hand as she thought about that, and warmed her backside on the Aga.

If Night was a mercenary, it was something they had in common.

She frowned at her own thoughts. What was she doing? Looking for things they had in common? It wasn't as if they were going to be dating and she needed to find topics of conversation, ways to make him see they were perfect for each other. He was the brother of her mark, and a man who was probably going to want her head once she carried out her mission.

If she carried out her mission.

"And that's another thing," she muttered to herself. "It's *when*, not if."

She had to do this. Her coven was counting on her. She couldn't let them down. She owed them so much for the way they had accepted her when she had feared she would be cast out. They hadn't treated her any differently after discovering her ability to read memories in blood. If anything, they had drawn her deeper into their collective embrace. They were her family. Her everything. If she could help them with something, then she would—no matter how dangerous the task was.

Lilian pushed away from the table and rounded it to the two large silver refrigerators. She opened the doors and pulled a face at the metal canisters one of them contained. She closed the door of the one with human food in it and took the canisters out of the other one. Gross. She set them down on the table and began sorting them, checking the dates someone had marked on them using little yellow stickers.

She set aside the ones that were out of date or close to it, and put the rest back in the fridge, arranging them so the oldest ones were at the front.

Lilian turned and stared at the canisters she had left out, her stomach twisting at just the thought of opening them and pouring the blood they contained down the drain. Maybe she should eat something first. She pressed her hand to her stomach as it gurgled. Or maybe not. She would probably throw up anything she ate.

Footsteps echoed along the corridor to her left and she muttered the incantation, putting her spell back in place, and busied herself with putting the plates away in the cupboard. She opened the wooden doors and grabbed several plates from the first stack and turned with them, crouching at the same time so she could put them on the low shelves without accidentally bashing them.

Or exposing her panties.

It hadn't taken her long to notice how some of the male servants in the house liked to stare whenever the females were present, gawping at their legs in a focused way that made Lilian feel they were willing the women to bend over in their short dresses.

Also gross.

She glanced to her left as the footsteps ceased and froze halfway through sliding the plates on top of the growing pile in the cupboard.

"Night," she said, shock sweeping through her. "What are you doing down here?"

He arched an eyebrow at her and she lowered her gaze, unsure whether he was irritated by how familiar she was being with him, the fact she was questioning him, or the fact she wasn't behaving in a manner *befitting* of a servant.

She hadn't called him on his oh-so-antiquated way of speaking when he had been issuing his string of warnings upstairs, but she had wanted to.

"Is it a crime for a vampire to enter this kitchen?" He leaned against the counter near the sink and folded his arms across his chest, and she wanted to curse him for frowning at her.

A man shouldn't look as good as he did when frowning.

It roused wicked heat inside her.

She liked how his blue eyes narrowed, and how a little crease formed between his dark eyebrows, and that slight downwards turn of his profane lips, and the rigid set of his square jaw. His displeasure was her pleasure.

Lilian shook herself out of it when his left eyebrow quirked and reminded herself that he wasn't a man. He was a vampire. Meaning he could sense when she was getting turned on. She was supposed to be keeping her distance from him, wasn't she? She was sure she had decided to act professional and focus on her mission, and that feeling anything for Night was a very bad idea given the fact she was intending to harm his brother.

"No, but... Bastian would never come down here." She grabbed another stack of plates and hated the way her hands shook, betraying her nerves.

Night noticed it of course, his gaze narrowing on her hands. He unfurled to his full height, coming to stand next to her, and she really wanted to curse him, because he only flustered her more.

A man—correction, vampire—shouldn't look so good in a suit either.

The tailored black jacket and slacks fit his tall, athletic frame perfectly, accentuating it and stirring that wicked heat he made her feel into a wildfire that burned up her blood. She wasn't sure when she had become a sucker for a man in a fine suit, but apparently she was. The sight of him in it, even his expensive shoes, had her belly fluttering and desire rushing to the fore, flooding her with a need to peel it off him and reveal the honed body she was sure it concealed.

So much for being focused on her mission.

Whenever Night was away from her, she set her mind on her task and was determined to do it.

Whenever he was near her, she did a one-eighty, forgetting her mission and growing determined to do him instead.

Lilian groaned and sank into a crouch to put the plates away, hiding in her work.

"Have you not eaten yet?" His tone was stern and a little demanding.

She glanced at him and caught him giving the canisters a look that was close to longing.

"Same question to you," she countered as she straightened. "Have you eaten?"

He shrugged, and even that was sexy.

She wanted to groan again. Maybe palm her face. What was wrong with her? What was it about this vampire that had every hormone in her body firing at once, craving him and willing to do whatever it took to have him? She tried to shut down her unruly desires, but his gaze collided with hers again, rousing it back to a painful level.

Unable to trust herself when she was near him, she hurried to the other side of the table and warmed her hands on the Aga.

Night was silent, his gaze on her back searing her, flooding her with an urge to look at him.

She denied it.

A strained minute passed and then another, and she could feel each second as it ticked past, growing aware that she would have to move soon or he might come to her.

"Do you want to belong to my brother?" His deep voice seemed louder than normal and she stilled and stared at the stove as she considered the answer to that question. He continued before she could figure out what to tell him. "Have you come to want it despite how things started between you?"

"No." She turned on him, close to cursing herself when that word burst from her lips, because she was supposed to be sticking to the plan, not revealing her true feelings and fears to Night.

She immediately regretted denying it when he continued.

"Have you tried to escape before last night?" He moved a step closer to her, his hard expression demanding an answer.

She shook her head and wished she hadn't when his face darkened and his jaw tensed, and she swore she saw disappointment in his eyes.

"You have been with my brother, serving in this household, for some time and you were not being held under lock and key." His tone turned colder and colder, and then he looked away from her and scowled at the dresser beside him. "You are not a prisoner here. Grave is right about that."

Lilian wanted to curse his brother. He had been putting things in Night's head, making him look more closely at her situation and now he was seeing things that might lead to him growing suspicious of her.

"I haven't been here that long." She risked a step towards him, nearing the corner of the table and snaring his attention again. His pale blue eyes were piercing. Far too calculating. She furrowed her brow. "Bastian only brought me here a week ago and I've been too afraid of him to leave."

Night moved towards her, his steps measured as he held her gaze. Sensual. A predator. Sucking the air from the kitchen.

"You are not afraid of me," he husked and her entire body trembled in response to the way he looked at her, as if he wanted to devour her, and the wicked sound of his voice.

"I did try to leave." She hurried away from him, shivering as his gaze tracked her.

When she reached the far end of the table, he pivoted to face her and leaned against a wooden post beside the Aga, folding his arms across his chest again.

Lilian tried to ignore him as she opened the first canister and poured it down the drain, but it was impossible. By the third canister, the air in the room felt too heavy, as if it was pressing down on her. She glanced at him, finding him still staring at her. Watching her.

Studying her.

She had the terrible feeling he was looking for something.

What?

"Don't you have somewhere you need to be?" she snapped and he arched an eyebrow at her, so she reeled in her nerves and tried to be polite, attempting to throw him off her scent so he wouldn't ask why she was suddenly so intent on getting rid of him. "With your brother perhaps?"

Night angled his head upwards, flashing the scar around his throat that she diligently kept her eyes away from. "My brother is gone. His mate is in trouble."

Lilian frowned at him, curiosity replacing her nerves. "Shouldn't you have gone with him?"

Night lowered his gaze to her and there wasn't even a trace of emotion in it. "My cousin will help him. Grave will only worry about me if I go with him."

"But he doesn't worry about your cousin?" She watched his eyes as she asked that question.

Not even a flicker of feeling crossed them.

He pushed off and strode to the canisters, and picked one up. When he looked as if he was going to drink it, she snatched it from him.

"It's out of date." She set it down, turned to the refrigerator and grabbed him one that was in date, and thrust it towards him. "Here."

He took it from her, his fingers brushing hers, igniting the embers of her desire, and there was that reaction she had been trying to get from him. Heat coloured his eyes, darkening them as his pupils dilated, and she felt she was on dangerous, unsteady ground. That look drew her towards him, as if he had tied a string to her ribs and was tugging on it, and she had to fight to resist the pull of him.

She drew down a steadying breath. Big mistake. Mother earth, he smelled good. Warm. Enticing.

He helped her regain control by unscrewing the lid of the canister, adding the scent of blood to the fragrance of his aftershave and ruining it.

"Stopping Snow from doing something he wants to do, especially if it involves his family, is like trying to stop the sun from rising. It's never going to happen, no matter how much you want it to." He stared into the top of the canister, frowning at it.

"Did you want to go with your brother?" she said, her voice quiet, although she wasn't sure why she feared asking that question. Because she didn't want him to go? Because just the thought of him leaving had her aching inside?

He paused with the canister halfway to his lips and lowered it again as he murmured, "I would have, but family business keeps me here."

He meant her.

"I'm sorry for being such a burden," she snapped and grabbed one of the old canisters, and then stormed to the sink and emptied it. Was she bitter or angry? She wasn't sure. She hadn't been able to stop herself from saying those words. They had risen unbidden to her lips, bringing hurt in their wake.

The reason for that hurt dawned on her, hitting her hard and freezing her in place as the last of the blood dripped from the canister into the sink.

He resented having to babysit her, as if it was a chore for him.

As if he didn't enjoy her company.

Night's gaze tracked her, so intense she knew he wanted her to look at him, so she avoided him instead, busying herself with emptying the rest of the canisters. The air thickened again, the silence weighing on her as she poured blood down the drain.

Lilian stared at it.

Blood. Human blood. What was it like to thirst for it and rely upon it for survival? She wanted to ask him that but held her tongue, clinging to her mood, but the longer he remained silent, swigging blood from the canister he gripped, the harder it became to resist voicing that question.

When the last canister was empty, she turned on the tap and watched the blood swirl and mix with the water.

"What's it like to drink blood?" She stared at the final streak of crimson as it whirled down the drain and then looked at him.

He stared at her, looking as if she had caught him off guard with that question, and then he looked down at the canister in his right hand.

"Blood is blood." His tone was far too matter of fact, giving her the impression he either didn't want to talk about it or wasn't sure what to say. "It's sustenance."

Lilian settled on it being the latter.

"I know that." She turned and rested her backside against the counter. "But… like food has different flavours to me, does blood have different flavours to you?"

She realised how dangerous her question had been as his gaze dropped to her throat, an intense quality to his eyes as crimson invaded them, ringing the aquamarine of his irises. He was thinking about her blood. About what she would taste like. A compulsion ran through her, a powerful urge to touch the spot on her neck he was staring at so intently, and she fought it. If she touched her neck, she would be in danger of finding his fangs in her throat.

She almost cursed.

And not only because she couldn't risk provoking him into biting her.

She wanted to curse the heat that rolled through her in response to his gaze drilling into her neck, and the deep yearning to know the feel of his bite and whether he would be tender with her or rough, and whether it would give her pleasure or pain. Dangerous.

She cleared her throat and turned away from him. "It was a silly question. I have other chores to do. Ellen is a bitch when it comes to dividing up the workload. If you're going to make me stay in my room, could you at least tell her I can't work? She thinks I'm slacking off."

Her poor attempt to change the subject didn't work.

Night didn't stop staring at her neck.

"Blood tastes different from different sources." His voice had gone deeper again, an almost distant quality to it now, as if he was lost in his thoughts. "Some are sweeter. Some faintly spiced. Some are sharper. There is weak blood and then there is that which gives me a boost in strength. Everyone's blood tastes different." His voice went husky, and far too thrilling, as he murmured, "I wonder what you would taste like, Lilian."

She stiffened and her hand flew to her neck, covering the spot he was staring at.

Night's crimson gaze leaped up to meet hers and then he slammed the canister down on the tabletop, startling her and making her jump, and was around the table and by the door inhumanly fast.

He paused there, his back to her. "I am sorry. I didn't mean to overstep."

He was gone in a flash.

Before the reckless part of her could tell him that he didn't need to apologise to her because that side of her wanted to know the feel of his fangs in her throat as he held her in his arms and what she would taste like to him.

Even when she knew it would be his death.

CHAPTER 10

Night was doing his damnedest to avoid Lilian. Four days had passed since Grave had visited and so far she had shown no inclination to leave. He wasn't sure what to make of that. She had settled into working around the house.

Avoiding him too.

He knew she was doing it on purpose, working hard to make sure their paths didn't cross. Several times, he had sensed her ahead of him and felt her change course and hurry away as soon as she had spotted him. He rubbed the back of his neck. Perhaps he should apologise to her again.

Staring at her neck and wondering aloud what her blood would taste like had been a foolish move, one he had known would frighten her, but he hadn't been able to stop himself.

Night finished styling his hair and padded barefoot into his bedroom, a sigh escaping him as he glanced at the window to his left. He couldn't blame her for staying away from him. She wasn't the only one actively avoiding him either.

He picked up his phone from the mahogany nightstand and checked it, bringing up a stream of one-sided messages to Bastian. Night had been sending them regularly since Grave and Snow had left, and there was still no response. The little check mark next to the messages said his brother had received them, so why the hell hadn't he come home?

He was starting to worry about him. He was worried about Grave too. Were his brothers all right? He needed to know.

He also needed to take measures to protect Bastian's staff.

And Lilian.

If Bastian wasn't going to return, then it was down to him to do it. Grave wasn't one to exaggerate an enemy. If he thought the demon prince was a threat to all of them, then he was. Night had waited long enough. He had given Bastian a chance to do the right thing and return to the mansion to deal with his staff. He couldn't wait any longer. He needed to put his plan in motion, only he couldn't shake the need to find Bastian.

He dressed quickly, donning black trousers and a dark plum shirt, and slipping his black leather shoes on. He didn't bother with his jacket this time. The tight material was restrictive and there was a chance he was going to need to fight. He couldn't risk it hindering his movements.

He left his room and went to Lilian's, only she wasn't there. Damn it.

Night checked his phone again, willing his brother to respond this time as he fired off another message, this one far sterner than the previous had been. Talking down to his older brother might provoke a reaction. Bastian hated anyone acting as if they were higher up the family hierarchy than he was.

He ignored Ellen as he passed her near the staircase and hurried down it, reaching out with his senses as he pocketed his phone. Lilian was to his right. He headed in that direction, narrowing down her location, and willing her to stay put this time. He wasn't in the mood to chase her around the house.

Night pinpointed her in the library.

The door was already ajar, so he eased it open and slipped inside, using stealth to his advantage.

She stood with her back to him, facing one of the sets of shelves that lined all the walls in the room, a book in her hand and a feather duster on the shelf beside her. Her delicate scent swirled around him and had him slipping into hunting her. All of his focus narrowed on her, the rest of the world falling away, and he eased to a halt at a distance where she wouldn't notice him. She hummed to herself, the melody soft as she leafed through the book. Her dark hair fell away from her left shoulder as she canted her head, angling it and the book at the same time, and she fell silent.

"Looking at an illustration?" Curiosity tugged that question from his lips.

"Christ Almighty!" Lilian whirled to face him, her caramel-coloured eyes enormous.

Her face darkened, shock becoming anger as she glared at him.

And then her cheeks pinkened and her gaze edged downwards to the book she clutched in both hands.

She quickly shoved it back on the shelf.

"You can read it. You can read all of them. I don't care." He gestured to the thousands of books that filled the room.

She sidestepped in front of the book she had been looking at and he frowned at her, his curiosity rising again.

"What were you reading?" He tried to see past her to the book, but she moved whenever he did, blocking his view.

When he stalked towards her, she grabbed the book and scurried away.

"Nothing," she spat, her eyes wild.

He studied her. Flustered air. Flushed cheeks. The fact she had been so startled by his presence. The way she had canted her head as if looking at an image.

He smiled slowly and advanced on her.

She backed away, keeping the distance between them even, and then her back met one of the shelves. She glared at him when he narrowed the gap between them down to nothing and moved the book behind her back.

Night leaned towards her, biting back a groan as her scent invaded his lungs—his every pore—making his soul sing and his fangs itch. He resisted the urge to drop his lips to the smooth column of her throat and focused on his mission, reaching around her. She gasped as his chest brushed hers, their cheeks close to making contact, and he took hold of the book.

He expected her to surrender it. She didn't. She clung to it, revealing she was stronger than he had thought, and he had to wrestle it out of her grip.

"Night—" She pressed her other hand to his chest and froze as he looked at her.

Gods, he had been so focused on his mission to get the book from Lilian that he hadn't realised how close he was to her.

His pulse accelerated as he gazed down at her, his lips mere inches from hers, and her eyes darkened with the desire he could sense in her. He needed to move back. He needed to leave. Only he couldn't. He stood there, looming over her, his body pressed close to hers and her breath caressing his lips, goading him into taking them.

She swallowed, and the part of him that wanted to lower his gaze to her neck and watch her pulse ticking there wasn't strong enough to win against the part of him that needed to kiss her. Tasting her lips was more important than tasting her blood, and gods, that was a revelation.

It shook him.

He wasn't sure he had ever hungered for a kiss more than he had hungered for blood, but he was aching for it, felt sure he would die if he didn't claim her lips soon. He waited for her to run, to pull away or shove him.

To stop him.

She remained where she was though, her hand branding his chest through his shirt, searing him with her touch, and her eyes locked with his, her dilated pupils beckoning him as fiercely as her lips did as they parted.

He needed to leave.

He needed to stay.

Night warred with himself and when he still couldn't move, he silently begged her to make the decision for him, willing her to show him what she wanted.

Her fingertips pressed into his chest, her hand trembling against it to betray the nerves he could already sense in her, and her head tilted up, bringing her lips closer to his.

Night swooped on them.

Groaned in time with her as he claimed her mouth.

Sure she would push him away now and steal this heaven from him. And gods, it was heaven. She tasted as sweet as she smelled as he stroked the seam of her lips with his tongue, fighting to hold himself back, afraid of pushing her too far or hurting her.

Rather than making him stop, she twisted his shirt into her fist and tugged him closer. The book fell from her hand and from his, and she wrapped her arm around him and clung to him, her body arching against his as her lips parted in invitation.

Night growled as he accepted it, angling his head and deepening the kiss, starving for more. She moaned, the sound the most wonderful thing he had ever heard, and kissed him back, her tongue brushing his and their lips clashing hard. He stepped into her, pinning her to the bookcase, and pressed his palm to her lower back, drawing her closer still, unable to get enough of her warmth and the soft feel of her body cushioning his.

"Miss Lilian." Ellen's sharp voice rang along the hall.

Lilian shoved him so hard in the chest he staggered backwards into the table in the centre of the room, striking it with his thigh and knocking it. It scraped across the wooden floor, the sound loud in the tense silence, and Lilian flinched.

Night sensed the housekeeper approaching the door and quickly moved away from Lilian, and she hurried away from him too, rushing back to the spot where she had been and picking up her duster. He grabbed the book she had dropped and seated himself at the table just as Ellen walked into the room.

"Miss Lilian, I swear if you are slacking off again—" Ellen came to an abrupt halt as she spotted him and bowed her head. "Lord Van der Garde. I do hope this servant isn't bothering you."

"No bother at all," Night said, or more accurately, squeaked. He cleared his throat and tried to sound less like he had just been caught doing something wrong. "She is no bother at all. I was just catching up on some reading."

He flashed the cover of the book at the housekeeper.

Her eyes widened and she backed out of the room. "I will leave you to it, sir."

He had wanted to tell her that he needed to speak with her about moving the staff somewhere safe, but his gaze fell to the book instead, dread chilling his blood as Ellen made a fast exit.

An intricate ink drawing of several naked people in a rather impossible-looking and compromising position greeted his eyes.

Those eyes darted to Lilian. No wonder she had been so flustered when he had come upon her and had been so desperate to hide the book. Wicked little minx.

She blushed and scurried away from him. "I should get on with my other chores."

Night was at the door, blocking her, before the book he had dropped even hit the table. "I need to speak with you."

"Oh. Um." A blush stained her cheeks and her hand drifted up, towards lips that were still red from his kiss. "I—I won't tell anyone."

He scratched his neck. "No. It's not about that. It's about my brother."

"I won't tell him either."

"I mean Grave. But I suppose it is also about Bastian. But not like that." He wasn't doing a very good job of this. "I'm worried about Bastian. I expected him to be back by now and he isn't answering the messages I've sent."

The colour drained from her face. "Oh. I see. If there's somewhere you need to be, you don't have to wait for Bastian to return. I won't go anywhere."

"No. It's not like that either." Forget not doing a very good job—he was doing a bloody terrible job of explaining himself. Now she thought he wanted to get away from her.

He grimaced as he recalled how upset she had been in the kitchen, and as he spotted the flicker of hurt and shame in her eyes. She honestly thought he was tired of looking after her? Even after he had kissed her and had wanted to do so much more with her?

So. Much. More.

He weighed up the pros and cons of telling her everything, and settled on her needing to know, and not only because it would explain his desire to find Bastian and have him come home, making her see he wasn't tired of her at all.

Quite the opposite.

He was worried that when Bastian came home, everything would change for the worse and he would lose her.

"There is a demon prince targeting my family." He tried to sound calm about that, not wanting to scare her, but inside he felt as if someone had turned loose an entire basket of snakes and they were writhing and twisting, making him feel sick as he did his best not to imagine why Bastian hadn't returned his messages or if Grave and Snow were still alive.

Lilian didn't look shocked to learn that demons existed, which led him to suspect that she knew more about his shadowy world than he had thought.

"Grave told me to leave this place and I wanted to wait for Bastian. My brother believes the demon will come after us and we're not safe here." The snakes inside him only writhed harder as one of them hissed that he should have left when Grave had told him, that waiting for Bastian to return had only placed everyone here in danger.

"And you're just telling me this now?" she said, her eyes darkening in a way he didn't like because it only made him feel more guilty about the route he had taken.

"I thought Bastian would return. I thought we could all leave together. But Bastian isn't returning my messages and I've sent dozens of them. He's reading them…" He swallowed hard as a chill skittered down his arms. "Or at least I really hope he's the one reading them."

A little furrow formed between her fine eyebrows as she looked up at him, concern glittering in her eyes, chasing away the shadows. "Night, I'm sure Bastian is safe. If this demon had him, he would have responded to the messages. He would want you to try to save your brother so he could capture you too."

Night scratched the back of his head as he thought about that and another reason presented itself. "Or the demon knows I'll come looking for my brother when he doesn't respond and is luring me into a trap… weakening me by making me worried about Bastian."

"What kind of demon is he?" Lilian moved back a step and then another, and looked around her. Her gaze settled on the chairs beside the table and she went to it, pulled two out and sat on the one to his right.

Night took the hint and went to the other, only realising once he had sat down how close it placed him to Lilian. Their knees almost touched.

"A demon of the Devil's ranks. They are powerful and dangerous, more so than—"

She cut him off. "Then he would not try to lure you into a trap. The Devil's demons don't skulk around and use traps against their enemies. There is no honour in that."

He frowned at her, and not because she apparently knew a lot about his world and he wanted to know how. The black look he couldn't stop himself from levelling on her was because she thought there wasn't any honour in slipping through the shadows and taking down enemies with stealth.

Which is exactly what he did.

She blinked and held her hands up. "I mean for demons of that breed. They value brute strength and a direct approach, one that places them in the path of danger so they can prove their prowess to their master and others of their breed."

"Nice save," he muttered and glared at his knees, still not convinced she didn't feel there was no honour in the way he operated.

"Maybe if I knew more about you, we wouldn't have misunderstandings," she grumbled back at him.

And he stared at her.

She wanted to know more about him? That had connotations, like she was looking for this thing happening between them to be more than short term, something that wouldn't be over when Bastian returned and Night somehow convinced him to let Lilian go.

Rose climbed her cheeks and she averted her gaze.

"Come with me." He reached for her hand, paused with his close to it and then took the plunge, seizing hold of hers. "I need to go to London to find my brother and make sure he's all right, and then get him to the safe house in Norway. While we're in London, we can go to my apartment and get my things."

By things, he meant his weapons.

He squeezed her hand, willing her to say yes to his proposal. He needed to keep her with him. He needed to protect her. That need ran so deep that he felt desperate as he waited to hear her response.

"I need to stay here," she said.

Night growled at her, flashing his emerging fangs, and released her hand as he narrowed his eyes on her.

She leaned towards him and grabbed his hand, holding him firm, her gaze imploring him to listen. "If what you say is true, then everyone needs to leave. Not just us. I can help the others evacuate quickly... and if Bastian returns while you're gone, I'll be here to tell him what's happening."

Night glared at her hand on his, unable to deny that her logic was sound, even when he hated the thought of leaving her unprotected at the mansion. It was only a few hours, but it would feel like an eternity to him.

"Bastian won't return now. I've been sending him messages. Grave has probably contacted him too. For all we know, he's already gone to Norway." Or he could already be dead, but Night refused to believe that. "Come with me, Lilian."

He stopped just short of telling her that he needed to know she was safe.

"Night." Her tone was soft, but commanding, and his fight left him as he heard in it that she wasn't going to do as he wanted. "Someone has to help everyone evacuate."

"Ellen can do it," he snapped, unable to keep the snarl from his voice as he thought about leaving Lilian behind, exposed to danger and vulnerable without him.

"Let me help these people," she whispered and what he heard was her asking him to let her go.

He pushed to his feet on a low growl, wrenching his hand from hers, and immediately regretted his actions as he broke contact with her. He tunnelled his fingers through his hair and huffed, turned away from her and then back to her to stare down into her eyes.

"You'll be vulnerable." He couldn't hold those words back, or the feelings that had birthed them, and he knew by the softening of her eyes that she had seen them.

"I'm stronger than you think," she whispered and reached for him, holding her hand out to him.

He wanted to take it. Gods, he wanted to take it.

But he couldn't.

If he did, he wouldn't want to let it go—to let *her* go—and maybe that was what he needed to do. Maybe she was better off away from him—away from all of them. If he left her here to help the others evacuate, she might run off once she was done, and it might be a blessing.

She didn't deserve to be put in a cage by his brother.

She didn't deserve to be placed in a cage constructed of his love either.

The need to protect her, to shield her from the world, ran too deep in him and he feared he would end up stifling her and making her hate him. The only way to stop himself from feeling a constant need to keep her safe would be to make her stronger.

The only way to make her stronger would be to turn her.

He swallowed hard.

He couldn't do that. She was light and life. Not darkness and death as he was. She didn't belong in his shadowy, dangerous world.

He backed away from her and closed his eyes against the hurt that flared in hers.

Night pivoted and paused as his mind filled with the way Grave and Snow had both looked at him, and thought about how drawn he was to Lilian and how it was getting harder by the second to control himself around her.

If he didn't go now, there was a danger he might do something he would regret. He needed space to think, to clear his head and study his feelings, and discover whether it was infatuation he felt or something far deeper.

Grave was right about something too.

Bastian would be furious with him when he discovered what he had been doing, and it really wasn't Night's place to be stealing a female who belonged to his brother. His family was everything. His loyalty was to them, not a female he had only just met, and he had to remember that.

"Evacuate the mansion," he said, his tone cold even to his ears, and walked away from her.

He had slain kings. He had massacred armies. He had courted death. He had survived its chilling embrace.

But this was the hardest thing he had ever done.

As the distance between them grew, the warmth he felt whenever he was close to Lilian faded away, leaving him hollow and cold to the bone.

But it had to be done.

The flicker of life that she had ignited inside him guttered out as he reached the drive, darkness sweeping in to sharpen his mind and empty him of feelings. His focus shifted to the demon and Bastian, to Grave and Snow, and the things that needed to be done.

If Lilian was gone by the time he returned from London, so be it.

His family needed him now.

He narrowed crimson eyes on his car and bared his fangs.

No one threatened a Van der Garde and lived to tell the tale.

CHAPTER 11

Lilian grunted as she set the case down on top of another in the foyer and straightened, pressing her hand into her lower back as it ached. So far, she had helped more than a dozen of Bastian's staff evacuate, phoning for cars and arranging places for them to stay if they didn't have a home or anyone they could stay with.

Which was most of them.

She hadn't really considered that many of Bastian's staff had been serving him for decades and hadn't aged much in that time. It wasn't as if those who still had family out there who thought they were alive could see them, not without causing serious shock, anyway.

Arranging hotels dotted around the country had seemed like a more sensible idea and she had made sure to gather a list of their phone numbers in case Bastian didn't have them. When the coast was clear and the threat was eliminated, he would be able to summon them all back to the mansion with little effort.

Ellen muttered things under her breath as she came down the stairs and Lilian turned to look at her, her eyes widening as she spotted the grey-haired woman wrestling with two red cases.

Lilian hurried up the stairs to her. "I told you to wait for me."

Ellen snapped, "I'm not an invalid. I can carry my own luggage."

Lilian tugged one from her grip anyway, refusing to get into an argument with her. They had gotten into several since Night had left. The housekeeper hadn't been happy about the fact Night had left Lilian in charge and had slowed down the evacuation by getting in the way and trying to take over, which had only ended up confusing the staff.

The silly old woman had even cancelled the first fleet of taxis Lilian had ordered, replacing them with another company that had to come from further away.

In response, Lilian had tried to get her in the first cab. Ellen had decided to scupper that attempt to get her out from under Lilian's feet by taking her sweet time about packing. In fact, it had apparently taken Ellen close to four hours to pack up her belongings.

Lilian marched her suitcase to the drive, bypassing the ones belonging to other staff that she had been setting out in order of departure in the foyer. She handed the case to the taxi driver and went back inside, reaching the bottom of the staircase just as Ellen did.

She grabbed the case the woman held.

Ellen tightened her grip on it. "I am not departing next."

"You bloody well are." Lilian yanked the luggage from her, ignoring her startled gasp. "You're slowing down this evacuation and Night gave me orders to get everyone to safety. Your ridiculous attempts to take control of this situation are placing everyone in danger and I'm done with it."

She stormed across the foyer. Ellen followed hot on her heels, trying to take the case back from her. Lilian didn't complain about her dogging her every step. It was luring her towards the taxi after all.

She rounded the back of the car, shoved the luggage into the boot, and slammed it shut.

"Take this one to London. The Langham." Lilian looked from the driver to Ellen. "Lord Van der Garde would want you comfortable. I booked you a suite."

Ellen spluttered.

Lilian opened the rear door of the car and almost pushed her into it, quickly closing it behind her so she couldn't escape.

As the car pulled away, she breathed a sigh of relief.

Only seven more staff to go.

She paused and looked at the spot where Night's pretty little sportscar had been parked all week.

Mother earth, his kiss had been electric, just as she had dreamed it would be. She wished everything that had come afterwards had never happened. She had wanted to stay in that bubble with him, the two of them the only people in the world. Nothing else had mattered in that moment. There had only been him and her, sharing a kiss that had felt as if it should be the beginning of something wonderful.

Only it had been the end.

She couldn't erase from her mind the look that had been in Night's eyes when he had left her.

That look had said he had known she would be gone by the time he got back.

It had been a goodbye.

One that wrenched at her heart still.

She wasn't sure what she was going to do once she was the only one left at the mansion. She wasn't sure whether to leave or not. Her orders were clear. Her mission was still active and her coven was expecting her to carry it out as planned.

But the thought of becoming entwined in a war between vampires and demons belonging to the Devil had her wanting to throw in the towel.

She had never been so close to being done with this mission.

The only thing stopping her was the fact it would mean she was done with her coven too.

Her family.

They wouldn't forgive her if she walked away. This mission was important to them, and it had been important to her too when she had reluctantly accepted it. They were relying on her.

Bastian was relying on her. He just didn't know it.

If she threw in the towel, her coven would hunt him down and kill him, and she had no doubt in her mind or her heart that his brothers would seek revenge.

Her coven would be next in line to face the full wrath of the King of Death and whatever the hell Night was.

She was starting to suspect he was with the Preux Chevaliers, but not as one of the rank-and-file soldiers. He had reacted badly to her damning warriors who slipped through the shadows and set traps, and she had the feeling it was because he did that.

Which would make him what?

An assassin?

It would certainly explain the reason she had been able to gather so little information on him. He was probably a master at covering his tracks, at taking down enemies using stealth so no one ever witnessed his kills.

An assassin.

Lilian shivered. In a good way.

"Who's next?" The female voice dragged her focus away from Night and her gaze to the doorway.

Polly stood there, her shadow streaming down the sandstone steps towards Lilian and her petite figure silhouetted by the warm glow of the foyer lights.

Lilian focused back on her task. "You and Alex. I'm sending you both to the same hotel."

Because she had noticed that Alex had a thing for Polly and she was meddling, trying to throw the two of them together. What better catalyst for love was there than a dire situation? Alex would naturally protect Polly and Polly would fall head over heels for her daring knight.

Lilian wished them better luck in that department than she had. Her Night had run off and left her to fend for herself. That wasn't strictly true. He had wanted to protect her and she had panicked and had ended up driving him away.

She wanted to say it was for the best, but she didn't feel it.

Alex squeezed past Polly with a bag in each hand. "Let's get out of here."

Polly followed him to the last car and Lilian checked her phone. It was another twenty minutes before the next taxis were due to show up. The petite blonde slipped into the backseat while Alex loaded their bags into the boot and closed it.

He looked at Lilian as he rounded the car and flashed her a wink. "Thanks for teeing me up."

Lilian waved him away, holding back her smile.

It wasn't difficult when she sensed a shift of power in the air and her magic rose to the fore, coming to protect her.

"Go!" she yelled at the driver.

Alex leaped into the back of the car and it peeled away, spraying gravel in its wake.

The power she could feel building in the air grew stronger and her eyes flew wide as the black car reached the tree-lined road that would take it to the gate. She could only stare in horror as two huge bare-chested demonic males appeared in black smoke there, dropping out of the air, one of them landing just in front of the vehicle.

On an ear-splitting roar, he spread his leathery onyx wings, leaned forwards and slammed his meaty fist into the bonnet. The rear of the car jacked up off the road, metal screaming as it crumpled under the force of the blow. Sparks exploded into the air, highlighting the demon's smooth black horns that curled through his wild obsidian hair and illuminating the hard planes of his face as he flashed fangs at the vehicle.

Magic rose to her fingertips and she ran towards the car, her heart drumming a sickening rhythm against her ribs.

She needed to help Alex and Polly.

Smoke billowed from the bonnet of the car as the demon eased to his full seven feet and he beat his wings, sending it swirling in the air.

Lilian chanted a protective spell, one that would form a barrier between him and the vehicle, buying the humans time to escape. She launched the glowing blue sphere at the demon.

Too late.

He grabbed the car by the wheel arches and hefted it into the air as if it weighed nothing, and she screamed in fury as he swung it at the nearest tree.

Crushing the rear of it.

No.

Lilian screamed again as he tossed it behind him and flames engulfed it. She hurled her hands forwards and that fire swept towards him, becoming an inferno as it swallowed him. He bellowed and beat his wings, twisting this way and that as the flames licked over his skin and scorched his flesh.

The demon beside him growled and turned on her, and sense kicked in as he launched in her direction, his heavy footfalls shaking the ground. She spun on her heel and ran, fear blasting through her as her rage ebbed and reality sank in. She had just attacked a demon and any moment now, he would be joining his friend in coming after her, and he was going to be furious.

Furious demons had a bad tendency to play with their prey.

Lilian cast a spell on her legs that would make her fleet-footed and lurched forwards as she suddenly sped up, her focus narrowing on the Georgian mansion ahead of her so she didn't feel sick as the world streamed past her. It didn't last long, wore off as she reached the door and went barrelling through it.

"Run!" she screamed, fear at the helm, the need to get the five remaining humans clear of the battle zone propelling her and keeping her going when all she really wanted to do was get the hell out of Dodge.

The building wasn't going to offer much protection. Not from two demons.

She stilled, cold trickling down her spine as her magic tingled in her fingertips.

Not two.

More had appeared. How many? Was the demon who wanted Night and his family dead among them? She shoved those questions aside, because she wasn't going to fight them. She was going to flee. She was getting the five servants and she was blazing a trail that would take them all far from the demons.

She sprinted through the house, heading for the smaller servants' quarters in the basement, sending up a prayer that they would be there.

They had to be there.

Her shoes were loud on the stone floor as she reached the basement and hurried along the cool corridors, checking each room she passed. She paused and backtracked as she found one of the humans. A woman.

The brunette stopped packing and looked at her, her dark eyes wide. "What? I thought we had time until the next set of cars?"

"I said to run," Lilian snapped and grabbed her arm, pulling her from the room and along the corridor.

"What's this all about?" The brunette already sounded out of breath.

Lilian found two men in the room at the end of the corridor.

"Demons," she breathed and their eyes went as round as saucers. "A whole bunch of demons just showed up and unless you want to be on their deadly dance cards, you all need to run. We're in a whole heap of shit."

As if to illustrate her point, the ceiling shook and glass smashed, and then someone shrieked.

That really wasn't good.

A demon laughed and another scream rent the air, and then a thud and a series of grunts, each one followed by another desperate cry. Lilian didn't want to think about what the demon was doing to the human he had caught. She focused on the ones she had before her. Three she could save.

"Let's go." She shoved the woman at the two men. "Stick close."

"What are you going to do against—" The man fell silent as a glow lit her palms and she summoned her strength, calling on every last shred of her power.

She was going to need it if they were going to make it out of here.

"Move." She hurried along the corridor, building a spell as she went, one that would hopefully be strong enough to shield the three humans sprinting to keep up with her.

Panic threatened to shake her as she heard crockery smashing and realised that escaping through the basement exit was a no-go. A demon was in the kitchen. No matter. They were all still escaping this hell. She drove the panic back, sharpened her mind and focused on surviving. She would survive this. She would get these humans away from danger. She raced up the stairs to the ground floor, trying to figure out the best escape route as she went. A window would be better than any of the doors.

Lilian sent out a dozen small seeker spells, ones designed to search for the demons and relay to her where they were. It was taxing to use so many, but she didn't know how many demons she was up against, and it was vital that she got a clearer picture of the odds she was facing.

The humans stopped running when glass smashed and the walls shook, and she turned back and came close to yelling at them. Only she found them cowering together close to the entrance to the basement, their faces pale and fear brightening their eyes.

"We have to keep moving. If we keep moving, we can get out of here before they close in on us." She grabbed the arm of the nearest man and looked up into his eyes. "Just shut out all the noise and focus on me."

He nodded and she glanced at the other man and the woman. They nodded too.

She kept hold of the man's hand and he linked hands with the woman, who took hold of the other man. If she had to move in a chain with them to get them all out of this, then she would. She could cast magic one handed.

Together, they ran along the corridor.

Another scream sent a chill down her spine, this one distinctly masculine, and she skidded to a halt as the butler hit the wall just ahead of her. Crimson streaked it as he slid down it to land in a mangled heap on the floor.

Not good.

A huge demon stomped into view, the black plates of armour that protected his legs clanking with each heavy step, and he grunted as he bent and grabbed the dead human. Behind her, the three other humans went very still, and she barely breathed as she willed them to remain that way. If they did, the demon might not notice them.

He sniffed the corpse and pulled a short blade from the sheath at his waist, twirled it in his grip and buried it into the dead man's stomach. He grinned, his polished black horns curling around his pointed ears to flare forwards into deadly daggers beside his temples as he gutted the butler, spilling his entrails across the floor.

The brunette behind Lilian retched.

The demon's black eyes swung her way, his golden elliptical pupils shining as bright as the sun as they narrowed.

Really not good.

She released the human's hand and quickly finished the spell she had been constructing. She shoved her hands forwards as the demon ran at her. He grunted as he struck the invisible barrier and shimmering aquamarine glyphs filled the air in front of him.

"The other way. Run!" She gritted her teeth and reinforced the spell, shoring it up as the demon rammed it.

"Witch," he grunted, his voice a thick snarl, burning with hatred.

The look in his strange eyes said her death was going to be bloody and painful when he got his hands on her.

The desire to hurl a curse at him was strong, but she was finding it hard to focus. The risk of her accidentally cursing one of the humans was too great. She had to settle this with magic.

Something that was waning fast.

Sweat beaded her brow as she kept funnelling power into the barrier, desperately trying to keep the demon at bay, fearing that at any moment the battle haze would clear and he would remember he could teleport to the other side—to her.

She sensed the humans moving away from her and stared the brute down, preparing herself for a fight.

Her heart lurched painfully as a female screamed and the sound cut off.

Lilian flicked a glance over her shoulder. Her blood chilled as she locked gazes with the brunette where she lay on the floor, ragged claw marks cutting across her chest and face. Crimson pumped from the deep gouges and Lilian slowly shook her head as fear began to get the better of her.

One of the men went flying past her and struck the barrier. It shattered under the blow, her magic failing her as panic set in.

They were all going to die here.

He bellowed as the demon she had been holding off grabbed him and dragged him around the corner, his legs kicking and flailing as he tried to break free.

Lilian stared blankly.

Mother earth, they were all going to die.

She grimaced as a sickening crunch filled the silence, the snapping of bone loud in the still air.

The one remaining human barrelled into her back, desperately grabbing her black dress. "We have to run. Right. Run?"

She snapped out of her daze and looked at him. She wasn't dying here. These demons weren't going to kill her. They weren't going to kill them.

She had failed the others, but she wouldn't fail him. She grabbed his hand and focused, channelling a spell to her fingertips, waiting for the right moment to strike. The demon who had killed the brunette lumbered towards them from behind and the human gripping her back shook her.

"We need to run," he screeched.

"Not yet." She breathed through her panic. "Not yet."

The other demon stalked around the corner before her.

"Now," she yelled and unleashed the spell.

Fire exploded in a wave around her, driving both of the demons back and blinding them. She grabbed the human and ran, pulling him through one of the drawing rooms and racing for the foyer. Her legs trembled beneath her, her head turning as her strength left her. She pushed herself to keep going, refusing to give up. She would fight until she had either spent every last drop of her power or had escaped.

They reached the entrance.

Cool, fresh air washed over her as they broke out onto the drive and her tracker spells placed most of the demons behind her.

"We can make it," she said, her gaze fixed on the woods directly ahead of her rather than the road. The trees would provide them with cover that would make it harder for the demons to find them.

Something jerked her backwards and she fell on her bottom on the golden gravel, losing her grip on the human.

She slowly turned her head as the scent of blood grew stronger, her entire body trembling as her breath stuttered and her heart felt as if it would stop.

The human hovered in the air above her, his face frozen in a stricken expression.

A squelching sound had her gaze falling to his chest.

To the claw-tipped fingers that gripped his heart as it continued to pump, spilling blood on the ground inches from her.

That hand disappeared back into the man's chest and his body dropped, hitting the threshold of the mansion.

Revealing the biggest demon she had ever seen.

Blood splattered across his handsome face and the cut muscles of his chest, and glistened on his black horns. He casually discarded the heart he had ripped from the human and lowered his gaze to her. The fire she had caused blazed brighter, devouring the wooden staircase beyond him, a fitting backdrop as he furled his wings and loomed over her.

His golden elliptical pupils narrowed in the centres of his black irises, burning as fiercely as the fire behind him.

"What do we have here?" His deep baritone rolled over her like thunder.

Shook her like a lightning strike.

She mustered her magic, but barely a spark leaped from her fingertips.

"A witch." He canted his head and studied her, and then drew down a deep breath and grinned, revealing his fangs. "A witch who smells like vampire."

Oh gods.

He reached for her.

"I shall have fun killing you."

CHAPTER 12

Night punched the entry code into the lock beside the door of Bastian's penthouse apartment in the heart of London and eased it open. He had tried knocking, but no one had answered. He peered around the door as soon as it was open enough, his senses stretching outwards to chart the entire area so no one could ambush him and his vision sharpening, brightening enough that he could see in the dark.

The dread that had been pooling in his stomach disappeared as an immaculate open-plan black kitchen and living room came into view. No sign of a struggle. He breathed a little easier and stepped into the apartment, closing the door behind him.

Now he just needed proof that his brother had been here.

He flicked the light switch near the door and the chandelier hanging in the living room above the twin black couches came on. His brother's tastes ran a little more opulent than his own. Bastian had chosen an apartment that overlooked the river and the glittering lights of London, and had filled it with the most expensive furniture there was.

Night's apartment looked basic in comparison.

The only thing their two apartments had in common was the colour scheme, and Night swore Bastian had stolen the idea to do everything in shades of gold and black from him.

He went to the onyx refrigerator and opened it.

Several canisters of blood were on the shelves, and one of them was on its side, as if someone had knocked it over. Not like his brother. For all his faults, Bastian was a neat freak. He preferred order over chaos.

Night liked a little chaos now and then.

He opened the cupboard beside the appliance, where Bastian usually kept his cooler.

It was gone.

He found a used glass in the sink and an empty canister in the rack beside it too.

His brother had been here.

Recently if Night had to guess. Bastian didn't have servants at his apartment, but he did employ a cleaning service run by and for vampires. They came every week without fail, whether Bastian was here or not, meaning Bastian had been here this week, between their scheduled visits.

He stalked through the living room, the sound of his shoes striking the wooden floor loud in his ears as he headed for the bedroom. The panorama beyond the wall of glass to his right drew his eye to it. It had taken him over an hour to get to Bastian's apartment. If he couldn't find him here, then he would have to check elsewhere for him before he could return to the mansion.

To Lilian.

In only seven hours, the sun would rise, forcing him into hiding for the day.

Gods, he couldn't bear the thought of leaving her alone that long.

The soft part of him he had shut down and killed had resurrected itself during his drive to London, coming back with a vengeance and possibly stronger than before. He had been ready to let her leave, but now he wasn't willing to allow it. He needed to find his brother and get back to her, before she disappeared forever.

He reached Bastian's bedroom, where his brother had carried the black and gold theme through from the rest of the apartment. Gold material formed the canopy of the black four-poster bed that stood against the wall to Night's left, facing another bank of windows.

For a vampire, Bastian had a lot of windows.

He froze as his eyes landed on the built-in wardrobes beyond the bed.

One of the doors was ajar.

He strode to it and opened it, and frowned.

His brother had definitely been here, and judging by the fact half of his clothes were gone, he had received Night's messages and left.

Night reached for his phone and pulled it from his pocket. He hadn't checked it since he had messaged his brother back at the mansion. He woke the screen.

And growled.

A message from Bastian stared back at him.

His brother had been in Geneva until this evening and had only just seen his messages. He had packed and left immediately, and was now asking Night to meet him at London City airport as he had the private jet fuelling up to take the two of them to Norway.

The *two* of them.

The urge to hurl his phone across the room was strong, but Night mastered it and fired back a message.

Send it back for me. Something I need to do first.

Namely, get Lilian.

He had just enough time to get to his apartment and get his things, and then return to her and drive to the airport before dawn. They would have to wait for the jet to return, but Bastian's hangar had a secure room where the sun wouldn't be a danger and they could wait out the day.

Night used all his preternatural speed to get back down to the parking garage, feeling as if he was racing against the clock now. He couldn't believe his brother had decided to just leave without making arrangements for his staff.

No, he could.

Bastian probably viewed them as expendable. As long as he and his family were safe, everything was all right.

There was nothing expendable about Lilian.

She was vital.

He unlocked his car and slipped into the driver's seat, and started the engine. He sped away from the garage, driving as fast as he could through the streets of London, uncaring of whether he got a ticket or two. If any police tried to stop him, they were in for a bad night. His mood had just taken a sharp nosedive and he didn't have time to waste on placing humans under thrall to make them let him off.

And he was getting a little peckish.

Night made it to his apartment in record time, running several lights along the way and driving on the wrong side of the road for a stretch along the river. Needs must and all that. Rather than driving his car into the garage, he left it jacked up on the curb and raced upstairs.

He was out of breath by the time he reached his own penthouse apartment, but it was better than waiting for the lift.

Night stilled, locking up tight as he looked at his door.

That didn't look good.

It hung at a jaunty angle, leaning at a diagonal into his apartment.

His senses stretched around him and he slowed his breathing, becoming silent. Nothing in the area except for him. Whoever had been here was gone. He drew in a subtle breath, scenting the air, and smelled musk and the faintest hint of smoke and ash.

Demons, if he had to guess.

His eyes slowly widened.

Demons.

"Lilian," he muttered as his heart lurched into his throat.

He raced into the apartment, leaping over the upturned couch and the broken furniture that littered the living room, heading for his bedroom. The bed lay in pieces and the mattress had been thrown aside and now rested against the wall. He crossed the room in a blur, shoved the clothes that were still on the rail aside as he reached the wardrobe and pressed his hand to a spot on the black back wall.

A faint click sounded and then mechanical whirring as the door opened.

Night stepped into his armoury as the fluorescent lights flickered on, plinking as they brightened to illuminate the three walls of weaponry.

He grabbed his favourite two swords and their holster, and then a sheath with several daggers in it.

He turned to leave and paused, pivoted back to face the way he had been and grabbed another sword.

One small and light enough that a petite female could wield it.

He hurried from his armoury and punched the panel, closing it behind him. Thankfully, his apartment was the only one on this floor and required a key in order for the lift to access it, so the authorities wouldn't get wind of what had happened and come to investigate. But he really didn't need the police finding the store of blood in his fridge, the weapons he kept in his armoury or the files he had on various immortals in his office. So just to be sure, he used his phone to fire off a message to his squad, asking them to use the spare key in his office at their HQ and retrieve the files and arrange for a replacement door, and warning them about the demon.

Night hurried downstairs to his car and threw the weapons into the passenger seat. He hit the gas and tore away from the building, weaving through the traffic at breakneck speed until he reached the outskirts of London. From there, he really put his foot down.

His heart pounded as he raced through the darkness, a vampire on a mission—one that felt critical to him. He had faced thousands of foes on the battlefield, had eliminated countless marks as an assassin, but never had he felt so sure that he would die if he failed to complete a mission.

He gripped the steering wheel, shaking off the urge to touch his throat and the scar on it.

That one didn't count. He hadn't even had a chance to start the mission before it had failed thanks to the vile witches who had intercepted his team and had taken down his commander, and had come close to taking Night down too. He pressed his emerging claws into the leather of his steering wheel as anger curled through him, as potent now as it had been back then, laced with pain as he thought about Franz.

His friend hadn't deserved to die like that.

He shook off his past and forced his focus back to the road ahead of him as it narrowed. He used his fast reaction speed to his advantage, whipping the car around each tight bend as he navigated the country lanes.

In the distance, a glow lit the sky.

Not dawn.

He frowned at it. What was it? A fire?

His blood turned to icy sludge in his veins as he thought that. His heart felt as if it might stop as he calculated where he was in comparison to where the fire was burning.

The mansion.

Night gunned the engine, flying down the lane, his pulse pounding harder and faster as he kept half his focus on the blaze as it grew brighter. Lilian. Panic sent a wave of hot needles down his body and he growled as he tightened his grip on the steering wheel and willed the car to go faster.

The second the open gate came into view, he turned and raced down the single-track road towards the mansion.

Fire blazed in the heart of it, leaping from the windows on the ground floor.

Demons.

His gut screamed that demons were responsible for what had happened and he tried to steel himself, mentally preparing himself for the fact he might already be too late to save Lilian. Humans were no match for demons from the numbered realms, let alone a demon from the Devil's horde.

Night grimaced as he looked back at the road and swerved hard, narrowly avoiding the burning wreckage of a car. He stared at it as he shot past it, his chest clenching. The demons had attacked while people had still been here.

Meaning, Lilian had still been here. He knew her well enough to know she wouldn't have left before everyone else had been safely evacuated.

"Lilian," he whispered, his brow furrowing as he stared at the mansion, willing her to be alive.

To have somehow survived the brutal attack.

A shadow danced in the entrance of the house, filling the doorway.

Night set his sights on the demon.

He was talking to someone.

Night looked down.

His heart froze in his chest as he spotted Lilian on the ground at the demon's feet.

The big male reached for her.

Night grabbed a dagger from the sheath on the seat next to him and the car hit the gravel way too fast. It slid into a spin and he growled as he fought to control it, spraying gravel in an arc behind him. As soon as it had come to a halt, he shoved the door open and leaped from the vehicle, letting the dagger fly at the same time.

It nailed the demon in his chest, hitting him with enough force that it knocked him backwards.

"Lilian!" Night yelled.

She didn't move.

She couldn't move.

Her fear hit him hard, drawing his bloodlust to the surface together with the coppery tang that filled the air. Night fought it and sprinted to her, swept her into his arms and raced back to his car. Behind him, the demon roared and ran at them.

He bundled Lilian into the passenger side of the car, pushing his weapons out of the way to make room for her, skidded over the bonnet and leaped in beside her.

He gunned the engine, the rear tyres skidding on the gravel again to spray it at the demon, forcing the brute to cover his face to protect it, and peeled away from the bastard.

Night breathed hard, his blood rushing, heart thundering as adrenaline burned through him. His hands shook against the wheel as he sped away from the mansion, not daring to slow. He glanced at Lilian. Once. Twice. A third time.

She leaned against the car door, her face streaked with blood and her eyes glassy as she stared out of the windscreen.

"Lilian." He reached over and placed his hand on her shoulder, and gave her a little shake when she didn't respond. "You're fine. I have you. You're safe. That blood... is... is it yours?"

She smelled of so many different scents that he couldn't tell whether any of it was her blood or not.

"Lilian." He palmed her shoulder and when she still didn't respond, he risked it and dropped his hand to cover hers where they rested in her lap. She tensed, the first sign of life he had gotten from her. When he stroked his thumb over her fingers, her gaze lowered to her lap. "Lilian. Is any of that your blood? Are you hurt?"

Her brow furrowed, tears misted her eyes and she shook her head.

Thank the gods.

"Alex... Polly... the car," she croaked.

Night squeezed her hand. "There was nothing you could do, Lilian."

She swallowed thickly and shook her head again. "I... the others. I tried to help them. I tried..."

Tears slipped down her cheeks and she lifted her hands, raising his left one up with them, and pressed her face to the back of his hand. Her hair tumbled forwards, brushing his arm and stealing her face from view, and he wanted to growl and turn back around to butcher the demons as she broke down.

Each sob that wracked her tore at him, slashing deep into his heart.

He couldn't bear it.

Night pulled his hand from hers, placed it on the back of her head and pulled her to him, so she was leaning across the centre console with her head against his chest. He held her as he drove, slowing his speed so he didn't have to let her go. She fisted his shirt and buried her face in his chest, the salty scent of her tears growing stronger as she cried harder rather than calmed down.

"I have you," he whispered and kept one eye on the road as he angled his head towards her and pressed a kiss to her hair. He murmured against it, "I have you. Not going to let anyone hurt you."

Never.

His heart continued to pound, replays of Lilian on the ground before that demon filling his mind and shaking him. If he had been any later, even a few seconds, she wouldn't have been alive.

He tightened his grip on her, unable to hold back the need to clutch her to him, to feel her in his arms and reassure himself that she was safe. The demons hadn't taken her from him and they wouldn't.

His brother was a different matter though.

He needed to get her to safety and the safest place he knew was in Norway.

Where Bastian was waiting.

CHAPTER 13

Lilian listened to the engines whirring, her thoughts a thousand miles away from the small private jet she was sitting in. Or at least a few hundred miles away. She didn't remember much about the last few hours other than the fact Night had somehow saved her. Facing that demon and knowing that he was going to do terrible things to her and there was nothing she could do to stop him, and watching all those people die in front of her, had shaken her.

Numbed her.

She vaguely remembered Night driving her to an airport, and him telling her that they would wait out the day there.

And that she was safe.

He had told her that so many times, whenever she had been slipping away from him, into dark thoughts that had continued events from the moment when the demon had reached for her and she had realised she was defenceless. Rather than Night saving her, the demon got his hands on her.

Lilian squeezed her eyes shut.

She was safe.

She wanted to hear Night tell her that again, she needed him to drive it home and chase the demon from her mind.

She opened her eyes and looked at him where he sat on the plump black seat opposite her, his head resting on his bent arm against the wall of the jet. Fast asleep.

He hadn't slept all day. She remembered that much despite her shock. He had helped her wash off in the hangar bathroom and had moved her to a comfortable couch, and then he had stayed awake and watched over her. And when dusk had fallen and someone had come to announce the jet was ready, he had wrapped his arm around her and helped her stand, and ushered her out onto the tarmac.

Lilian pressed her hand to her chest as her heart warmed.

It chilled a moment later, when she recalled the response she had received soon after she had sent a message to her coven. She had kept it brief, worrying that Night would wake and find her with a phone. She had told them about the demon attack and the developments that had happened, and the fact she was en route to Tromsø with Night and that Bastian was waiting for them there.

She had asked what she should do.

The answer had come back the same.

Continue with her mission.

Lilian was no longer sure she could do it, and it wasn't only because she had her doubts about Bastian's involvement in the attack. It wasn't only because part of her feared Bastian biting her and her taking his blood, something that would bind them and would mean the only way to escape the bond would be killing him or dying herself.

She couldn't do it because she was beginning to feel something for Night.

The private jet jerked and she gripped the arms of her seat, fear flashing through her as she waited for it to plunge into the ocean or smash into a mountain. She had never been on such a small plane. The damned thing juddered like it was about to fall apart whenever they hit even the tiniest turbulence, and it was unsettling. It didn't seem to bother Night though.

Night smacked his lips together and his fine eyebrows knitted slightly before relaxing again.

Lilian focused on his face, charting the sculpted planes of it, putting to memory the strong line of his square jaw, the straight slope of his nose, and the firmness of his lips. She flushed from head to toe, the shuddering of the plane forgotten as she lost herself in him.

Another little crease formed between his eyebrows and then he sighed.

"Are we there yet?" His drowsy voice was the sexiest thing she had ever heard, made her picture waking up next to him in his bed after a wild night with him.

She was about to tell him that she wasn't sure when the far-too-beautiful stewardess came over to him and leaned forwards to flash the cleavage formed by her tight black shirt.

"Lord Van der Garde, we are beginning our descent." She smiled prettily, her blue eyes sparkling with it as Night looked at her and nodded.

The woman lingered.

Lilian scowled at her. Night noticed it, of course, and looked from her to the stewardess and back again. He waved the woman away and she left without a fuss. He leaned forwards and rested his hand on Lilian's bare knee.

"How are you feeling?" His pale blue eyes searched hers, worry etched on his face that touched her.

"Better." She hated the way her voice hitched, betraying her, and glanced away from him, out of the window at the distant lights that pricked the darkness. "I can't stop thinking about it."

"The demon doesn't know about this place. Only Bastian and I know about it. You'll be safe there. Bastian is already there and—" He glared at his hand and withdrew it, easing back into his seat.

Cold chased through her when he angled his head away from her to gaze out of the window.

She wanted to scream at him that she didn't want to be Bastian's, wanted to tell him why she was with his brother in the first place, and wanted to beg him not to shut her out. She couldn't find her voice to do any of those things as she stared at him and something mechanical whined.

The plane juddered again.

"Fasten your seatbelt," Night muttered, his tone hard.

When they hit another bump, she made a snap decision, darted across the gap between them and sat beside him. He stared at her as she fastened her belt across her waist and she avoided looking at him, too afraid to find out whether he was angry with her or surprised and pleased that she had chosen to move closer to him.

The plane shook so violently she was sure something was going to vibrate loose and the whole thing would explode apart. Her hands flew to the arms of her seat and she gripped them so hard her bones ached. Mother earth, she had survived a demon prince and now this stupidly small plane was going to be the death of her.

Night placed his hand over hers, gently holding it.

She calmed the second he touched her, all of her focus darting to the point where they connected, and her gaze leaping to meet his.

He smiled softly.

Stole her heart.

She didn't feel the touchdown. Didn't notice the taxi through the airport. She lost herself in the way Night was looking at her, trying to decipher the emotions in his eyes. In fact, she was so lost in him that when the stewardess came to tell them they could depart the plane, she practically shot out of her seat only to be slammed back into it by the safety belt.

Much to Night's amusement.

He chuckled as he undid his safety belt and she fumbled with hers, and she silenced him with a scowl.

Night held his hands up and backed off, an apology in his eyes. He turned away and she wanted to apologise to him too, because she hadn't meant to make him feel he had done something wrong by being so relaxed around her. An icy gulf opened inside her as she watched him walking away from her, her body and soul growing colder with each step he took.

And then he held his left hand out behind him and rolled his fingers.

Lilian pushed to her feet and closed the distance between them, slipping her hand into his, unwilling to let his reach for her go unanswered. She wasn't the only one nervous and on edge, feeling as if everything was about to fall apart and end. She knew it the second his fingers closed around hers and he held her hand so tightly that she wanted to plead him to never let it go.

No man had ever held her hand as tightly as Night was holding hers.

"Night—" she started.

"If I could have taken you somewhere else I thought you would be safe, I would have," he cut in and his thumb brushed hers. "You'll be safe at the house. Bastian will protect you."

She frowned and stopped, forcing him to stop too. "Where will you be?"

The thought that he was going to leave her alone with Bastian had fear lacing her blood again.

Night turned his head slightly towards her and looked down rather than at her. "Grave... he needs to know what happened. I have to find him... or get a message to him."

She wanted to be angry with him for deciding to leave her with Bastian, but she couldn't be as she stared at him and realised that he wanted to help his brother. He wasn't planning on just getting a message to Grave. He was planning to find him and help him.

He was planning to fight the demon who had threatened her.

The thought of Night facing that demon had her pulling him to face her, a wild and desperate feeling flooding her.

"I don't want you to go," she bit out.

He stilled and stared at her, surprise and conflict shining in his eyes. It turned to something else as he gazed at her, something she didn't like.

"I know I said I would help you escape my brother and believe me, if I knew a place that was as safe, I would take you there," he muttered.

She shook her head. "I don't care about that... Don't fight the demon, Night. He's too powerful. I'm afraid that he'll—"

She couldn't bring herself to say it.

Night eased closer to her and feathered fingers across her cheek, his voice lowering as he murmured, "I won't. I'll stay. If I can get a message to Grave, then I'll stay. Maybe my other cousin, Antoine. Snow has gone with Grave, and Antoine always keeps an eye on Snow. He'll have a way to get in touch with him. Better?"

She nodded, barely moving her head an inch because she didn't feel better. Keeping Night with her was selfish. Not only was he strong and could help his brother and cousin in their fight against the demon, but staying with her meant that he would be in danger from her coven.

He was better off away from her.

Then he wouldn't bear witness to what she needed to do in order to fulfil her mission.

Her stomach twisted at the thought of going through with it.

Night led her out of the jet and crisp, cold air swept around her, chilling her bare legs and arms. She looked up as she reached the tarmac. Two black cars awaited them. A Bentley that was out of place given their remote location, and a Volvo that looked far more suited to handling the terrain.

The driver of the Bentley stepped out of it.

Night immediately waved him away. "You are not needed. You may return. I already arranged transport."

She looked at the Volvo he pulled her towards. "Are we using this because it's less conspicuous?"

Night opened the passenger door and held it for her. "No. I just don't like being driven around like some entitled prick."

He smiled for her, but this time it was strained and quickly faded.

Lilian got in the car and watched him as he rounded the front of it. The fact Night didn't like being driven didn't surprise her. He was right and he was different to Bastian.

Bastian.

She pressed her hand to her stomach as it squirmed. The thought that she was going to see him again had her falling silent as Night started the engine and they pulled away.

Lilian's gaze roamed to him as they departed the airport and cut through the town, watching the way the lights flickered over his handsome face as he glared at the road as if he wanted to kill it.

Everything that had happened at the mansion still felt as if it had happened to someone else. She couldn't really get over the way Night had come rushing in to save her from the demon, like some dark knight, protecting her and saving her life. Would he feel so protective of her if he knew why she had met his brother and what her plan had been for him?

Still was.

What her plan still was for him.

The air between them seemed to grow colder the longer they sat in silence, and she struggled to find a way to break it, to make him talk to her again. She didn't like this oppressive atmosphere between them. It had her dangerously close to making him take her somewhere else, even if it wasn't as safe for her. A rash decision like that would probably get them both killed.

Bastian was expecting them now. Night couldn't take her somewhere else without it looking suspicious or worrying his entire family. Her coven was expecting her to be with Bastian too, carrying out her mission.

She couldn't do it.

She wished she could be as calm and collected as Night as he pulled off the main road and the car rumbled along a narrow lane that wound through a forest, heading uphill.

Lilian flexed her fingers in her lap and then clenched them, focusing on her magic. She had managed to get the concealment spell back in place as soon as her power had moved off the red slash, and it was holding so far. Her magic was gradually growing stronger and as it did, she felt braver, her fear of the demon growing weaker.

Her fear of Bastian and what her coven wanted her to do remained as strong as ever though.

Night pulled the car to a stop outside an unassuming wooden house someone had painted in blood red and white.

Lilian pulled down a breath, suddenly feeling as if she couldn't get enough air.

He looked across at her, a softness in his blue eyes that warmed her because it told her that he could sense her panic and her fear. She wasn't alone. She would be as soon as Night discovered her reason for being with his brother, but right now, she wasn't alone. He was here with her and he had said he wouldn't leave.

Rather than hurrying her from the car, he sat with her. She breathed a little easier, gathering her courage and trying to vanquish her fears as she stared at the illuminated façade of the house. Night sighed and she glanced at him, catching the way he was looking at the house. Maybe she wasn't the only one afraid of what would happen if they went inside that building—a building where Bastian was waiting for them.

Night looked as reluctant to see his brother as she was.

Minutes ticked past and neither of them moved.

Eventually, the door opened, revealing Bastian. How had she ever thought the two of them looked alike? Bastian was nothing like Night. The cold look on his face as he frowned at the car made Night in his worst mood with her look like a gentle kitten.

Bastian folded his arms across his chest, causing his thick black sweater to pull tight across his arms.

Night huffed and reached for the door, and she barely stopped herself from grabbing him and yelling at him to drive. He exited the car and said something she didn't hear to his brother. Bastian spoke and gestured at her.

Lilian eased the door open and stepped out of the car.

"I will send a message to Antoine." Bastian pulled his phone from his pocket and gazed down at it as he turned away from them and went inside. "It was good of you to bring her to me, Night. We may continue where we left off now."

Night glared at him as he slammed the car door and followed his brother, but she saw the flicker of shock in his eyes and it rippled through her too. They were running from powerful demons and all Bastian could think about was claiming her as his servant. She shut the door and went after Night, wanting to catch him before he could reach Bastian.

She wasn't sure what she would do if she managed it.

Make him take her away from his brother?

She curled her hands into fists. If she did that, her mission would be a failure. What she wanted wasn't as important as what her coven needed. They needed to know who had attacked them. They needed vengeance.

And she had sworn to help them.

Night was already in the living room with Bastian when she reached him.

"I won't let you have her," Night growled.

Bastian swung towards him, shock flooding his eyes as he looked at his brother, his hands dropping to his sides and his phone forgotten.

He recovered a heartbeat later, his face darkening as crimson ringed his irises. "What did you say?"

Night took a hard step towards him. "I said I won't let you have her. I know she isn't willing, Bastian. I know she doesn't want to be owned by you."

Crimson invaded Night's eyes as he narrowed them on his brother and his pupils transformed into thin elliptical slits.

"Really?" Bastian snarled and then looked at her and she tensed. "That is not the impression she has given me."

"Well, it's what she's told me. She tried to leave you, Bastian. She doesn't want to be yours and you cannot force her. It isn't right." Night squared up to his brother and she feared that at any moment, they were going to come to blows.

Suspicion coloured Bastian's crimson eyes. "It sounds to me as if you want her for yourself, Night. Tread very carefully, brother. You are on dangerous ground."

Night bared his fangs at Bastian and didn't back down.

He didn't deny that he wanted her for himself though.

"As noble purebloods, surely we should do as society expects of us and uphold our good name by letting humans decide whether or not they want to be owned by us," Night snarled, darkness washing across his features as his eyebrows knitted hard. "If society learned that you have a habit of owning humans against their will… Imagine the fallout, Bastian. Imagine how it would tarnish the Van der Garde name. We are supposed to set an example for all to follow. Or do you no longer believe that? Are the Van der Gardes now no better than common elite?"

Bastian's face had been slowly darkening throughout Night's tirade, but the moment Night mentioned elite, the name given to vampire bloodlines with turned humans in their ranks, he looked ready to murder his own brother.

Bastian wasn't lying. Night was on dangerous ground, and she had the feeling he knew it and was intentionally provoking his brother. Why? To cover the fact he desired her or to force his brother's hand and make him release her?

Bastian drew down a breath, the darkness lifting from his face as his shoulders relaxed and his appearance changed, becoming unreadable. He was up to something. Every instinct she possessed said that.

"I will give her a choice then." Bastian's tone was calm as his gaze slid to her. "Do you want to be mine?"

Night's head swivelled towards her.

Lilian stared at Bastian, mind spinning, thoughts whirling together as duty and desire ripped her in two directions. She knew what she had to do. Bastian was right in front of her and she could fulfil her mission, could give the coven the peace of mind they needed and the vengeance they desired if she discovered through his blood that he was responsible for the attack.

She looked at Night.

But letting Bastian claim her would destroy what they had, and would turn him against her. Whether Bastian was innocent or not, her blood would be the death of him without her coven here to remove the poison from him if he wasn't guilty. Not only that, but Bastian was making it sound as if she was choosing between them. She didn't want Night to think she had picked his brother over him. She didn't want to ruin what they had.

Yet she couldn't bring herself to say no to Bastian. Her sense of duty wouldn't allow it. Her coven was everything to her and she feared stepping into a world without them in it. She wasn't brave enough to turn her back on them. Especially when things between her and Night were so uncertain. What if she took the leap and he grew bored with her and discarded her?

She pressed her hand to her chest, over her heart as it warred with her head. Her head said to stick to the plan and say yes to Bastian. Her heart said to scream no and seize Night and run far from Bastian.

Far from her coven.

She frowned as something struck her. She didn't have only two choices. There was a third option. The mission was falling apart, the plan nowhere near on track, and her coven wasn't here to guide her. She was on her own.

Meaning she could do things her way.

"I need your blood," she said to Bastian.

Before she could explain why, Night pivoted on a growl and was gone.

She leashed the urge to curse. It hadn't come out right. He hadn't given her a chance to explain things. He had assumed she was giving his brother the green light to own her and had left. Bastian grinned at her, showing her that Night wasn't the only vampire making assumptions and solidifying a feeling she had—one that said he wouldn't be interested in giving her blood to clear his name. He wanted her as his servant.

She really hadn't thought her new plan through.

Bastian probably wouldn't feel inclined to reveal whether or not he had been the one to attack the coven. He viewed her as an inferior being after all. A vampire as lofty as Bastian didn't answer to someone lowly like her. She could threaten him with magic or her coven coming after him, but he was old and powerful and fast enough that he could probably kill her before she could cast a spell.

And it wasn't as if she could put him off trying to make her his servant by telling him that her blood was poisoned and he would die if he drank it.

Revealing that to the vampires would be a death sentence.

Bastian would want to kill her, and Night would be furious with her for wanting to kill his brother and probably wouldn't stop him.

She huffed. This was why she needed to master her bad habit of making rash decisions. She wished she could be as calm and collected as Night, thinking things through and picking the best course of action after calculating every possible outcome.

She wasn't going to master it any time soon though.

In fact, she was about to make another one.

And this one might cost her everything.

She was tempted to slap the smile off Bastian's pompous face, but instead spun on her heel and ran after Night.

She couldn't let him leave. If she did, she would never see him again. He would go after Grave and Snow, and would fight the demons, and he would get himself killed. She raced from the house, desperate to reach the driveway before Night could turn the car around and leave.

She needn't have rushed.

The Volvo was still parked where it had been.

Night was just sitting there in it, clutching the steering wheel and glaring daggers at the bonnet.

He didn't want to leave her.

He didn't want to leave her and he was fighting with himself, locked in a silent battle between departing and staying.

She decided the outcome of that battle for him, running down the steps to the car and opening the passenger door. He tensed and whirled towards her as she slid into the seat beside him, and then blinked, a stunned look crossing his face. Surprised to see her? She was surprised she was sitting here too, going against her coven and disobeying their orders.

Apparently, her desire for Night was stronger than her sense of duty to her family and she was going to take the leap.

And maybe hope that her coven didn't disown her.

"What are you doing?" Night went to turn towards her, one hand leaving the steering wheel.

She grabbed it and shoved it back onto the wheel. "Drive. Please, just drive."

Before she changed her mind and did the right thing rather than the reckless one.

She was going to get into serious trouble for this.

The heated look Night gave her said it might be worth it.

CHAPTER 14

Night's blood was running hot, and not only because of his argument with Bastian—an argument that had made him realise how badly he wanted Lilian. He didn't just want her for now, to entertain himself with for a while. He needed her for longer than that.

Lilian was his.

And she had chosen to leave with him.

That was the real reason he was on edge, barely able to concentrate on the road as he drove them back into the heart of the town. She had left with him, and now he felt as if he was in danger of losing control.

He felt wild.

Hungry.

Night parked the car in a garage a short distance from a hotel that overlooked the waterfront and stepped out. He breathed deep of the crisp air, using it to cool his blood and tame his hunger. Lilian exited the car and her scent mingled with the air, cranking his temperature back up.

"What I said back there," she whispered and avoided looking at him. "It didn't come out right."

She was nervous. Why?

"Let's just find somewhere to sleep and we can talk about it then." Night closed the car door and rounded the back of it, opened the boot and grabbed the black holdall that contained his weapons.

She shut her door and came to him. He slammed the boot, locked the car and slung his bag over his shoulder. When they had settled in, he was going to teach her how to use a sword. He needed to know she could defend herself if the demons came after them. He was sure that they wouldn't find them in such a remote place, and he intended to keep moving to cover their trail as soon as night fell again, but the desire to make sure she could at least effectively stab and slash to drive demons away from her if things went wrong was strong.

Undeniable.

He pocketed the keys. "Ready?"

She surprised him all over again by slipping her hand into his. Good gods, he liked the feel of her hand in his. It calmed the part of him that was still wild with a need to protect her, assuaging that urge as he sensed how close she was to him and felt her hand in his. She was safe. Maybe he didn't need to train her in the art of the sword. Maybe just holding her hand during any fight they ended up in would be enough to calm his instinct to protect her.

He looked down at her. Or not. The urge to make sure she could fight was still strong, had the bag in his hand feeling heavy. Would she prove better with the sword or the daggers? He hoped it was the sword. A dagger was a far more close-quarters weapon than a sword, and he didn't want her getting within arm's reach of a demon. He would focus on teaching her how to use the sword and would do such a good job that he wouldn't have to teach her how to use daggers. A solid plan.

Night led her back through the parking garage and out into the waning darkness. The hotel he had spotted beckoned him and he struggled against his hunger. Not a hunger for blood. He hungered for Lilian. For her kiss. For more than that.

He focused on her, sensing her fatigue and using the fact she needed to rest to keep his urges in check.

The staff in the hotel gave him the usual looks humans did when he showed up in the small hours with a female in tow. Not that he had done that in a while, but it had happened frequently enough in the past that the judging way the men and women looked at him didn't bother him anymore.

"I need a suite," he said in Norwegian as he pulled his wallet from his pocket and slapped his Coutts Silk Card down on the counter.

The woman serving him didn't look impressed, but the blond man with the manager name badge was quick to hurry her out of the way.

The human male fawned over him as he arranged their room and Night spoke to him in fluent Norwegian.

"I am sorry we arrived so late. It's our anniversary and this is a surprise trip for my wife, and the jet was delayed in London. I honestly thought I would have to call the whole thing off." Night squeezed Lilian's hand and smiled at the manager. "She was so surprised when I picked her up from work, and then angry that I forgot the bags I had packed. I said I would make it up to her by letting her shop to her heart's content. She's always wanted to see the aurora. I hear they're putting on a good show this year."

Lilian's look grew more and more curious as she gazed up at Night.

The manager wished her a happy anniversary and shopping trip, and she stared at him, confusion filling her eyes.

"The manager wanted to wish you a happy anniversary and he hopes you'll put a good dent in my credit card," Night said to her in English and she looked even more confused. When she opened her mouth to speak, he smiled tightly. "This surprise trip isn't going well though, is it?"

She blinked and then caught up and shook her head.

She looked at the manager. "It's going terribly, but I think it's about to get better."

Night's gaze whipped back to her and he wanted to ask her what she meant by that when she gave him a heated look.

The manager chuckled and slid a piece of paper across the counter to him. "Sign here."

Night struggled to drag himself away from Lilian, managing it for just long enough to scrawl his name on the slip and take his card back, together with the access card for the suite.

Lilian's smile was wicked as she took it from him and tugged on his hand, leading him towards the lifts. What was she up to?

His heart drummed faster, blood pumping harder and growing hotter as she glanced over her shoulder at him, wicked heat in her eyes. Gods. He swallowed to wet his throat and told himself that things weren't leading where his body thought they were. It didn't stop his cock from reacting.

He stepped into the lift beside Lilian and she pressed the button.

And then glanced down.

Right at his hips.

Her cheeks heated.

Night glanced there and grimaced. His stiffening cock pressed against his black slacks, tightening the material across it. A painfully visible erection.

He cleared his throat. "You should get some rest. The bed—"

He didn't get a chance to finish that sentence.

Her mouth was on his, her hands clutching his shoulders to drag him down to her, and he groaned as he dropped his bag, swept her into his arms and pressed her back into the metal wall of the lift. *Really* groaned when she hopped up and wrapped her legs around his waist.

Pressing against his hard-on.

Night stole control of the kiss, deepening it. Lilian moaned as his tongue brushed hers, her fingers digging into his shoulders.

The lift pinged.

Godsdammit.

No way he was going to release her.

He eased down into a crouch, still kissing her, and fumbled for his bag, found the strap and straightened. Lilian's grip on him tightened further as he turned with her and carried her along the corridor, opening his eyes occasionally to check the numbers of the rooms they passed. When they reached the right one, he took the card from her and swiped it, opened the door and walked inside.

Still kissing her.

The door swung shut behind them and Lilian pushed from his arms. He growled and tugged her to him, not letting her get away. Her fingers worked at the buttons of his shirt, frantically opening them. Night backed her towards the bedroom, his lips clashing fiercely with hers, and dropped his bag near the door.

Just as she finished with his shirt.

He let her strip it off him and reached for her dress. A moan pealed from his lips as she skimmed her palms down his chest and stomach, the brief caress a torment that only made him want her more. He yanked her dress up over her head and threw it aside, as desperate as she was now.

Taking his time with her went out of the window as she tugged at his belt, hurriedly undoing it and then his trousers. He kicked his shoes off and kissed her again, harder this time, bending her to his will as she shoved at his trousers, making them fall down his legs. Night kicked them away too and seized hold of her, pulling her to him as he backed her towards the bed, his pulse hammering and blood burning.

He needed her.

Right now.

Lilian toed her shoes off, leaving them in the middle of the floor, and then unfastened her bra. He groaned and pulled back, not wanting to miss the sight of her breasts being freed, eager for his first glimpse. Dark pink buds tipped them, growing pert as he gazed at them, his mouth watering.

Night grabbed her backside and pulled her up his body, wrapped his mouth around one nipple and groaned as he sucked it. Her hands flew to his shoulders, fingertips pressing into his bare flesh, and she moaned with him, the scent of her arousal growing stronger.

Intoxicating him.

He couldn't get enough of her as he alternated between her breasts, as her nails scored his back and she clung to him. One hand shifted to his hair and she gripped it and pulled his head back. Her mouth was hot and wicked as it claimed his, her tongue thrusting against his, battling him for dominance.

Rousing an urge to make her submit to him.

Night strode to the bed and fell onto it with her, landing on top of her.

Between her thighs.

She moaned and trembled as he rubbed between them, grinding his caged cock against her hot flesh, but she didn't submit. Her kiss grew fiercer, rougher, delighting him and sending a shiver down his spine. His cock hardened painfully and he groaned as he rocked against her, losing control as need built inside him.

"Night." She fisted his hair, tugging at it as she pressed her nails into his shoulders.

She needed more.

So did he.

Night eased back and reached for her panties. Her hands were there in an instant, swiftly pushing them down her legs, her eagerness stoking his own. He groaned as she raised her feet, flashing heaven at him, and his shaft kicked, demanding freedom. Night shoved his trunks down, obeying it.

Lilian's gaze seared him.

He glanced at her and the hunger that shone in her eyes as she stared at his steel-hard length arrested him and had him kneeling on the bed staring at her.

Her tongue poked out and swept across her lips.

Night growled and lunged for her, grabbing her knees and pushing them apart so he could seat himself between them as he covered her. She giggled and then groaned as he pressed her back onto the bed and kissed her, pouring his passion into it.

It wasn't enough.

He reached between them, as frantic as she was as she rocked against him, rubbing her slick heat up and down his cock to torment him. He gripped it and pressed her down onto the bed, pinning her there with one hand as he fed his cock into her with the other. Her eyes widened and then grew hooded, her reddened lips parting on a moan as he slid into her, refusing to rush this moment.

Gods, she was hot and slick around him, gloving him perfectly.

Driving him wild.

He groaned and covered her, drove the last few inches into her and set a hard pace that wouldn't hurt her but was just enough to have her tightly gripping his shoulders. She kissed him fiercely, her passion matching his, showing him how perfect they were for each other. Her hips rocked to meet his, her moans driving him on as he seized her hip and raised it, sliding deeper into her with each thrust.

"More," she whispered against his lips and gripped his nape.

Night curled his hips to plunge deeper, ripping a sweet cry from her lips. He devoured it in a kiss, seizing control even as he lost it. Hunger took over, the need to find release stealing control from him and her judging by how she desperately tried to ride him, her hips jerking against his, and how she nibbled at his lower lip between kisses, biting so hard he feared she might break the skin.

The thought of her drawing blood had him rising above her to gaze at her throat.

Her pulse hammered a fast, tempting rhythm in her arteries.

His fangs dropped and his thrusts grew savage as he imagined taking her vein.

"Night." Her soft voice pulled him back to her and his gaze leaped to hers.

The fear in it was unmistakable.

"I won't," he muttered between plunges, shaking off the urge to bite her. "I don't... want to... make you... my servant. Don't... want to... own you."

He groaned as she flexed around him, her look softening to tell him that he had touched her with that declaration. It was hard, but he resisted her vein and dropped his head to kiss her instead, softer now so he didn't cut her with his fangs.

She arched towards him, her head pressing back into the mattress and mouth leaving his as she cried out. Her body trembled around his, her thighs quivering against his hips, and her hands clutched him as she came undone. He tried to keep going, wanting to push her to another release, but the sight of her climaxing and the feel of her gripping him, body tightly squeezing him as it grew slicker, was too much.

He drove deep into her heat and shuddered as release wracked him, pleasure blasting through every inch of him to steal his breath as he spilled. He groaned with each throb of his cock, each jet of seed, and she moaned with him, her body twitching in response to each one.

Night lowered his head and pressed it to her collarbone as he held her beneath him, keeping her in place as he slowly came down. He tensed as she wrapped her arms around him, and then relaxed as she smoothed her fingers through his hair and held him to her. Gods. Lilian was his undoing. His weakness. She made him feel things he never had before.

He wanted to stay like this forever.

With her.

He rolled onto his side and gathered her to him, stroked his fingers down her spine and clung to the moment.

Lilian didn't try to end it. She nestled closer to him instead and tipped her head up, beckoning him. Night kissed her. Softly. Slowly. Savouring it now. He brushed his hand down her arm and frowned at how cool her skin was. She was getting cold.

He knew exactly how to warm her up.

She squeaked in surprise as he scooped her up into his arms and stood, and looped her arms around his neck as he carried her.

"Where are we going?" Her gaze lifted to his face.

"Shower. Get you clean and warmed up." He carried her into the bathroom and set her down inside the cubicle, turned on the water and waited for it to get warm.

Lilian pulled him down for another searing kiss.

Night backed her under the spray and tried to focus on washing her.

He failed dismally.

Cleaning turned into making love against the wet tiles, and he wrung two more releases from her before the water grew cooler. They took it in turns to quickly wash each other before it went cold.

Lilian giggled as she hopped out of the shower, her eyes bright and cheeks flushed.

And gods, Night wanted to add a third session to their tally.

He reined in the urge and his out-of-control body, and dried himself off, watching her as she did the same. She went to wrap the towel around her body, took a look at him and then shrugged and let it fall to the floor. He groaned and rubbed a hand over his mouth as she walked naked from the bathroom. She glanced over her shoulder as she reached the door, a slight smile curling her lips and telling him she knew what she was doing to him, and then she disappeared around the corner.

Wicked female.

Night stalked after her.

Lilian giggled and ran the second he had her in his sights.

He easily caught her before she reached the bed, snagging her around the waist. She moaned and rubbed her bottom against him, getting him going again and wiping the smile off his face.

Night growled and pushed her forwards, so her front landed on the bed. He grabbed his hardening cock and ran it down the cleft of her ass to her damp folds, and watched as he eased it into her heat, joining them again. She moaned and pressed back against him and he gripped her hips, holding her in place as he took her, rocking her forwards into the bed with each powerful thrust.

He leaned over her and lowered one hand to her stomach, and skimmed it down to her mound. He delved between her petals and stroked and squeezed her pert bead as he plunged into her. She buried her face into the covers and cried out, her body spasming around him a split-second later.

Night roared his release, burying himself to the hilt inside as he spilled. He held her on him, gazing down at her, his head hazy and fatigue rolling up on him.

She moaned and angled her head to her right, resting her cheek on the mattress. "I think I'm really done now. Mercy."

He chuckled and pulled out of her, and pulled her up into his arms to kiss her. She moaned and kissed him back for a few seconds before she pressed her hands to his chest.

"Don't get me started again," she murmured against his lips.

As tempted as he was, she wasn't the only one feeling tired.

She released him and moved past him, and he jolted when she smacked his backside. "We'll pick this back up this evening."

Night fought the urge to pick it up right that moment and watched her wobbling towards the bathroom. He would have found her inability to walk straight amusing but his legs were weak beneath him. He moved around the room, closing all the curtains and blinds and making sure there weren't any cracks where sunlight could enter.

"That's a fine sight," Lilian murmured as she entered the room and walked towards the bed.

He flexed his backside for her, gaining an appreciative noise as his reward.

She slipped under the covers and drew the ones on his side back. Luring him again. Night finished checking the last curtain and went to her. The moment he was under the covers, she was settling against his side and resting her head on his chest.

Gods, this was nice.

He definitely couldn't remember ever sharing a bed with someone like this, all cuddled together like a couple.

His eyes slipped shut and he relished the feel of her fingers as she stroked his chest.

"Night?" she murmured. "Are you worried about Grave?"

He frowned and husked, "A little. How much do you know about my world?"

"I'm well-versed in it. I've known about vampires a long time. I know there's many other species who share this world with me. I even know your brother runs a mercenary corps."

He opened his eyes and looked down at her. "Do you know Bastian once served in it?"

She nodded, rubbing her cheek against his skin.

"Did he tell you?" He was surprised when she shook her head. Bastian loved to tell people how wonderful he was. "How do you know then?"

She smiled up at him. "I read it in his library. Bastian has handwritten accounts of his life in service."

Night rolled his eyes. "Now that doesn't surprise me. Do any of them mention that Grave surpassed him? I doubt they do. Bastian strives for power… to live up to our hallowed family name… and demands the same of me and my brother. When Grave seized control of the Preux Chevaliers, becoming the leader of the entire organisation, Bastian hadn't been pleased. Not like Grave had expected."

Night had felt for his brother that day. He had seen how disappointed Grave had been before he had covered it and had witnessed for himself how part of Grave was still striving to get his brother's approval and praise. Gods, Bastian was a poor substitute for the father who should have been the one to drive them towards greatness. Out of the father he had had and Bastian, he wasn't sure which of them was worse. Neither were the father he and Grave had deserved. Neither had a supportive bone in their body.

"Bastian doesn't sound like a nice vampire." She idly traced the underside of his left pectoral.

"Bastian has his reasons." He left it at that.

"Are you more like Bastian or Grave?" she said and he frowned at her. "Just trying to get a clearer picture of you."

"Then you're going the wrong way about it by trying to compare me to my brothers." He turned his cheek to her and stared at the ceiling as he mulled over her question. His answer wasn't going to satisfy her. "Neither. I'm not as ruthless and cold as Grave or Bastian. Both are that way in different respects. Grave on the battlefield. Bastian in the boardroom."

She rolled onto her front, pressing her breasts to his chest, and looked into his eyes as he shifted them to meet hers. Genuine curiosity filled their caramel depths.

"Where does that leave you then? Do you serve in the vampire army?"

Night toyed with a strand of her dark hair, his gaze remaining fixed on hers as he nodded. "I'm a commander of a unit here in the mortal world. An assassin… for want of a better term."

"That is very different from your brothers… and it explains a lot about you."

"What does that mean?" His eyebrows knitted and he hoped it wasn't a bad thing.

She smiled.

"The way you move. The way you act. You have this calculating look sometimes…" She reached up and lightly rubbed her thumb between his eyebrows, smoothing away his frown. "You always seem to be weighing up the odds and finding the best course of action. When I first saw you at the mansion, you were so mysterious. I couldn't figure you out."

"And now?" He lowered his hand and stroked it down her spine beneath the covers.

"Now I know I was right about you. I thought maybe you were like an assassin. I could easily imagine you stealing into somewhere in the dark and dispatching foes without a sound, taking down a whole gang of bad people before any of them noticed and then leaving without a trace."

She made him sound rather epic.

The reality of his work was often quite the opposite. Fewer enemies. More bloodshed. Silent takedowns were his favourite method of killing, but usually things didn't go quite as planned. He was dealing with immortals after all. Most of his foes were as strong as he was or had sharp senses that allowed them to detect him before he was within striking distance.

She stared at him, or rather through him, and he sensed panic in her.

"What's wrong?" He brushed his fingers down her arm.

She tensed and blinked, and she was back with him. She shook her head and the pain that flashed in her eyes told him where she had gone. She had been thinking about the mansion and what had happened.

"I should have made you come with me. I never should have placed you in danger like that." He gathered her to him, cupping her cheek and making her rest her head on his chest again. "I swear, Lilian, I won't place you in danger like that again."

The air charged with the unmistakable feel of magic and his senses blared a warning.

Witches.

Five of them.

And they were closing in fast.

CHAPTER 15

Night rolled from the bed and hurried around it. "Get dressed."

He grabbed Lilian's shoes as he reached them, tossing them at her, and followed them with her dress.

"What's this all about?" She bundled the clothes into her arms, her fear hitting him hard.

"Witches," he growled, rage burning up his blood, and she paled, her eyes growing enormous. He grabbed his black trousers and pulled them on. "We have to leave. Now."

He had lived long enough to know the witches were heading his way for a reason. He wasn't sure how they had found him or why they were after him, and he wasn't hanging around to find out. Under different circumstances, he would have stayed and fought them. He glanced at Lilian. He couldn't risk her though. He needed to get her out of here before the witches reached them.

"Move. Now!" he barked and she tensed, her shoulders going rigid, and he thought she was going to remain where she was, sitting in the bed, looking confused and stunned.

But then she pulled her black dress on, threw the covers aside, and popped to her feet as he strode away from her and dropped to his haunches in front of the holdall.

"Night—" She went silent as he unzipped the bag, grabbed the sword he had picked for her and thrust it towards her. "What do you expect me to do with that?"

"It's so you can defend yourself." He gripped the sheath near the point and held the hilt out towards her. "Take it."

She hesitated and then did as he instructed, and he noticed her hands were shaking. He checked the witches. They were closer. Any second now, they would be at the door. The night was against them too. It would be dawn in only a few hours. He could make it work. He would drive until the sun threatened to break the horizon and then he would find the nearest house and make it his own.

"Don't worry." He pulled his twin swords from the bag and rose to his feet, coming to face the door as he realised that they wouldn't be escaping without a fight. "I won't let them near you."

"Wait. Night, there's something you need to—"

The door burst open, cutting her off.

Night launched at the fair-haired female in a black dress who entered at the front of the group, catching her off guard as he narrowed the distance between them in a flash. He brought his blade down and growled as one of the witches behind her grabbed her and pulled her back, and another swept her hand out.

His sword bounced off an invisible barrier just in front of the witch.

Night flashed his fangs. So that was how they wanted to play it. Fine. He backed off, closing the gap between him and Lilian, his fingers flexing around the hilts of his swords as the five witches entered the suite. His gaze darted over them, cataloguing everything about their physical appearances and how they moved, his mind swiftly calculating which ones could handle themselves in a fight and which had been brought to provide protection for the warriors.

His senses charted how strong they were, and which were the biggest threats to him and Lilian.

The fair-haired female and the brunette who came to stand beside her were the two most liable to do some damage. The other three who remained at the rear seemed more like the backup, witches brought to defend the ones who stared him down, their eyes glittering with stars and malice.

That feeling went both ways.

Night bared his fangs at them and growled as he backed off a step, trying to gain more room in the cramped space. The suite had only one exit, which meant if he wanted to get Lilian away from danger, he had to go through five witches.

So be it.

He embraced the hunger that rose within him as he stared the witches down. *Witches.* Dark memories crowded his mind and sharpened his focus, and the scar across his throat tingled and burned. He readied his swords as he let his bloodlust rise, stoked it with thoughts of cutting down these witches, removing another five of their vile kind from this planet.

"What do you want?" He added a hint of fear to his voice as he mentally prepared himself.

His feint worked.

The fair-haired witch stepped forwards, the silver stars in her grey eyes fading as she opened her mouth to answer him. The sense of power in the air weakened as she relaxed, foolishly believing he wasn't a threat to her.

When he was Death himself.

Night crossed the distance between them in a flash, using all of his speed this time, and was behind her in an instant, one sword against her throat and the other arm around her waist, the blade he gripped in that hand aimed at the other warrior witch when he twisted the one he held towards her.

"We're leaving," he snarled. "Try to stop us and I'll kill you all."

The witch in his grip went deathly still. None of the others looked inclined to do anything reckless.

"Move." He glanced at Lilian.

A mistake.

The brunette witch launched at her and he snarled as he shoved the one he held away from him and lunged to intercept her. He took a hard blow to his back as a spell hit him, and bellowed as lightning arced through his bones, but refused to go down. He stumbled into the brunette witch, knocking her off course, and caught the stricken look on Lilian's face as he went down with her, landing on top of the female.

He snarled and shook off the electricity coursing through him as it ebbed, stabbed his left blade into the floor and pushed up. His head turned and his throat burned hotter, stinging now. He tried to swallow and panic lit his veins when he felt he couldn't.

Night brought his right sword down, fury burning up his blood as he swung it at the brunette witch. She shoved her hands towards him and hit him with a blast of magic that sent him crashing into the ceiling. He grunted as he dropped and hit the floor again.

"Lilian," he gritted and his vision wobbled. Whatever spell the bitch had hit him with was messing with his senses and twisting them into a mangled mass that had him tasting his words. "Run."

That word tasted like ash.

Night grimaced as he staggered to his feet again, cursing Lilian when she didn't move. He stumbled in front of her, blocking the path of the witches, refusing to let them get to her. If she was too afraid to run, then he would just have to protect her.

He would have to find a way to kill these witches before they could kill him.

He set his sights on the brunette. Attempting to attack Lilian had separated her from her group, making her more vulnerable. A little at least. He could make it work. He waited for the spell to fade enough that he could sense the positions of all the witches again and then launched at the brunette. Magic laced the air and he threw himself into a slide, narrowly dodging the spell. The window to his left exploded and he slammed his feet into the brunette's ankles.

Taking her down.

Night grinned and plunged the tip of his sword into her left shoulder, pinning her to the wooden floor. She screamed and he rolled to his knees and gripped his remaining sword in both hands. He brought it down hard, aimed at her neck.

Electricity lit him up again, ripping a bellow from him as it coursed through him, zinging up and down his body, growing stronger and stronger. His arms shook as he tried to keep hold of his sword, as he fought to regain control of his body and master the pain so he could finish the witch off. This wouldn't stop him from claiming her head.

A red veil descended as memories darkened his mind, as his throat blazed and he tasted blood.

Bloodlust seized him in crimson talons and he roared as he inched his blade down, pain searing him as the spell continued to ravage his body. He narrowed his scarlet eyes on the witch below him as she frantically pulled at the sword pinning her. She would die.

Lilian lunged for him.

The fair-haired witch seized her and pulled her back.

The distress that shone in Lilian's eyes as she desperately fought the witch, the fear he could sense in her, had him forgetting the brunette and surging to his feet despite the spell that still poured electricity through his bones.

On a feral roar, he kicked off, his focus locked on the one hurting his Lilian.

He raised his blade above his shoulder, holding it in both hands and twisting it to aim the point at the witch. He would paint the cream wall of this suite with her blood.

Pain blasted across his left side and the room twirled around him as he was thrown across it, spinning from the force of the blow a witch had delivered. Cold swept down his side, sapping his strength as it spread through him, and he grunted as he hit the wall near the broken window. He landed hard on his knees and blood burst from his lips.

He tried to look at Lilian, battling the cold that was slowly freezing his muscles, desperate to see her. A different sort of cold chilled his heart as his gaze found her and the stricken look on her face hit him hard, together with the deep fear he could see in her eyes as the three defensive witches approached him, murmuring words that charged the air with the vile scent of magic.

It was over.

He had failed to protect her.

No. He pushed his hands against the wooden floor and fought to get up, to stand and fight.

"You just don't quit, do you?" The fair-haired female holding Lilian back narrowed her sparkling eyes on him.

Night weakly bared his fangs at her and gritted his teeth against the pain that ripped through his chilled muscles as he reached for the wall, intending to use it to pull himself up.

The brunette pressed her heeled black boot into his spine and shoved him back against the floor. "Stay down, vampire."

"No," he growled and summoned all of his strength, which wasn't much. His head fogged as he tried to push onto his hands and knees despite the force the witch stepping on him applied to his back.

He couldn't give up. He couldn't stay down. Lilian needed him.

His vision tunnelled, everything going black and white and then shades of crimson. Someone grabbed his wrists and yanked them behind his bare back, locking them together, and he struggled, making a pathetic attempt to break the bonds that now held him.

He managed a growl as they hauled him onto his feet. His knees buckled and he hit the floor hard on them, and Lilian broke free of the fair-haired witch and ran to him, a beautiful look of concern on her face.

One of the other witches caught her and held her arm in a bruising grip as Lilian stared at him, her brow furrowing and an apology shining in her caramel eyes. He wasn't sure why she was looking at him like that. He was the one who should be apologising. He had been the one to fail her after all.

The witches succeeded in pulling him onto his feet this time. Two of them held him upright and he seethed as he watched a third gathering his things. Leaving him alive had been their greatest mistake. He would break free of his bonds, and then he would kill them.

All witches must die.

His throat burned and he gagged on the memory of blood filling his airways, choking him as his life had poured from him. He fought the encroaching darkness, refusing to succumb to oblivion, but when one of the witches opened a portal before him, charging the air with magic again, it was too much for him.

He slumped in their grip and blacked out.

Night groaned and shuddered, rolling to his left to escape the frigid cold that chilled his right side. It was no better there. The hard bed—ground?—beneath him was icy. A shiver wracked him and he curled up, tucking his knees to his chest, and sleep tried to claim him again. A noise had his ears twitching. Metallic.

His senses fought the haze in his mind and the aching fatigue that inhabited every inch of his body, attempting to sharpen to locate the source of that sound. He managed a deeper breath and caught strange scents, ones that didn't match his last memories.

He smelled water and rusted iron, and mould. A lot of mould. And excrement.

This place smelled like death.

Night had wrought enough of that to know the smell of it.

He stilled his body and slowly pieced together his strength, driving back the darkness that ebbed and flowed through him, mastering it again and regaining control. As it waned, his senses grew clearer. It wasn't a bed beneath him. It was stone. He was no longer in the suite. He was in a cell.

Night looked down at his wrists. Unbound. He rubbed at them and then his bare arms, trying to warm his chilled muscles. The witches had taken him somewhere.

If he was here, where was Lilian? Was she in another cell nearby? She wasn't in the same one as he was. He tried to sense her, but he couldn't feel anything beyond the four stone walls that surrounded him.

He rolled onto his back and grimaced as he continued onto his front and his hands and knees. His muscles protested as he staggered to his feet and ached as he rolled his shoulders and began moving around the cell, attempting to warm up. He didn't feel the cold as badly as humans did, thanks to his vampire genetics, but the spell had done a number on him. He swore he could still feel it now, freezing his muscles whenever he managed to get them warmed up.

Night kept working his arms and his legs, rubbed his chest and refused to let the spell win. Eventually, his muscles no longer chilled whenever he warmed them, and he grinned. A small victory, but a victory nonetheless. He flexed his fingers and curled them into fists, and narrowed his eyes on the wall. If he couldn't sense Lilian, maybe he could find a way to see if she was on the other side.

He was strong and healed quickly. He could probably punch a hole in the wall given enough time. There were downsides to such a reckless plan though.

Injuring himself would mean he would use up precious strength as his body healed, and he would need blood to restore it and continue healing.

He also had his doubts about the wall.

To test a theory and see if his suspicions were correct, he went to the wall and pressed his palm to it.

And went flying backwards into the centre of the cell.

He landed hard on his backside and glared at the wall as blue, red and green glyphs shimmered outwards across the stones from the point he had touched. If he had punched it, he probably would have been hurled across the room with enough force to trigger the containment spell on the other wall. Good thing he had decided to practice caution instead. He didn't want to be a vampire pinball.

A panel on the door to his right slid back, the scraping of metal on metal loud in the silence.

Night locked gazes with a woman and then she closed the panel again.

He picked himself up and went to the door. "Is Lilian all right?"

No answer.

He growled and wanted to press his hands to the iron, to hammer it with his fists, but the image of being ricocheted around the room by the spell was enough to keep his hands at his sides.

"Answer me. I demand to know if Lilian is all right!" He snarled those words, his bloodlust rising as the stricken way she had looked at him filled his mind.

He was sure she was in danger and that it was his fault. These witches had been after him. Anger at himself flooded his veins, twisting together with fear for Lilian, and rage directed at the witches, blending into an explosive mixture that had him pacing away from the door and back again.

The urge to bash his fists against the door was strong and he had a hard time resisting it as he stopped before the flush iron panel.

"Answer me!" He raised his hands and held them before him, tempted to lash out even when he knew he would only end up hurting himself.

Fear rose to grip him, filling his mind with images of Lilian being tormented by these witches. His precious Lilian. He sagged to his knees as his strength left him, his hands falling to his lap as he stared at the door.

"Lilian," he murmured, despair swift to flood him, to see the opening in his strength and slip inside to tear it down. He lifted his head, his brow furrowing as he looked at the peephole, his voice low and weak. "Please. I need to see her. I need to know she's all right."

The witch still didn't answer him.

Night fought the rising tide of his anger, refusing to let it cloud his mind and colour his actions. As much as he wanted to rip apart every witch in this coven, he couldn't. Attacking them would only get him killed, and if he was dead, he couldn't save Lilian.

"Think," he muttered to himself, low enough that the witch wouldn't hear through the door. "There has to be a way."

He straightened his back and closed his eyes as he rested his palms on his thighs and steadied his breathing, conserving his strength as he focused his mind, shutting everything out.

He centred himself, allowing all of his feelings to fall away and logic to rise to take its place, and drawing on his knowledge of witches and his past battles with them.

A solution would present itself.

It always did when he meditated like this.

He would bide his time, and he would form a plan.

He willed Lilian to hold on and wait for him. He wouldn't fail her again.

He would save her from these vile witches.

CHAPTER 16

"You've done well, Lilian," Beatrice said as she seated herself behind her desk in her pale violet office.

The arched windows on either side of her black leather wingback chair allowed light to stream into the room and had Lilian's thoughts drifting to Night. She hoped he was somewhere dark, safe from the sun.

Normally, Beatrice's soft voice inspired calm in Lilian, but not this time. As she looked at the fair-haired elder of her coven, she felt only fear.

"When I contacted you, I was told to continue with the mission. What changed?" Lilian remained with her back rod-straight and her hands folded in front of her hips, as was expected of someone of her position when she was speaking with the leader of their coven.

It didn't stop the two elders seated to the left and right of Beatrice from eyeing her as if she was out of line by asking that and questioning the coven's head witch. The brunette, Maryon, looked borderline suspicious and Lilian had to fight to rein in the urge to glare at her as she recalled the way the witch had stood on Night's back to pin him down.

"It was not me who responded to the message. The handler responsible has been reprimanded for not bringing the message to me. As soon as I heard you were in danger, I used the tracking spell to find you." Beatrice leaned forwards, her grey eyes sincere, and Lilian wanted to mention that she had been in danger the entire operation.

This witch before her had ordered her to become a slave to a vampire. What about that wasn't dangerous? It was certainly life-altering. She'd only had her sense of duty and vague promises of finding a way to break the bond to keep her going throughout her mission, and in the end, it hadn't been enough.

She had run, and she feared Beatrice knew that and it was the reason she had come to get her at last.

Petra brushed her silver hair over her shoulders, her blue eyes bright and her German accent lending a hard edge to her words as she said, "But you have succeeded in your mission in a roundabout sort of way."

Lilian frowned at her. "Pardon me?"

Beatrice leaned back in her chair and steepled her fingers. "The vampire. Bastian. You have helped us capture him, and now we will be able to take his blood and you can see whether he was responsible for the attack—"

"That's not Bastian. It's his brother, Night," she blurted and immediately regretted it when Beatrice's eyes narrowed and Petra perked up, sitting forwards in her chair.

"Night Van der Garde," Petra murmured, her gaze sharpening in a way that rang alarm bells in Lilian's head.

Those alarm bells grew louder when Petra looked at Beatrice and the coven leader said, "You *have* done well."

She barely leashed the desire to say something. Not that she was sure what to say. The way the three women looked at each other had her feeling desperate though. They were plotting something.

Did they intend to use Night to lure Bastian to his doom?

"You will question Night Van der Garde for us." Beatrice's tone brooked no argument. "You are close to him and he has been asking for you. He is concerned about your welfare and wishes to see you. When he does, he will be relieved and you will have your opportunity to question him."

Night was worried about her? That warmed her, but it left her cold at the same time. She had gone from one mission involving a Van der Garde to another, and this time there was more at stake. If she asked Night about his brother and family, and whatever Beatrice wanted her to ask him, and then Night discovered she was with these witches, he would be hurt. He would feel as if she had used him.

And she would have.

She didn't want to hurt him like that.

"You seem reluctant." Maryon stared at her, quietly studying her, and Lilian knew from the cold edge her dark eyes gained that she had seen straight through her and knew the reason she didn't want to comply with their new orders. Her lips tilted into a ghost of a smile, one that was chilling. "Shall we tell you a story about your vampire, Lilian?"

Lilian frowned at her. They knew about Night? She wanted to know what they knew, but at the same time, she feared it. The look in Maryon's eyes said that whatever she knew about Night, it would change the way Lilian looked at him, and the witch liked the idea of that.

Maryon wanted to hurt her.

To destroy her feelings for Night.

She waited, aware that she wasn't going to be given a choice. They were going to tell her whatever damning tale of Night they knew and she was going to be forced to listen to it.

It was Beatrice who spoke.

"Night Van der Garde," she murmured thoughtfully, her eyes ice-cold. "That vampire once rampaged through the seat of power of our sister coven, back when we had allies. He was ruthless and left the halls drenched with blood. He cut down any who stood in his way. He slaughtered all who tried to stand in his path and many who were fleeing the horror. The elders. The adults. The children."

A chill skated down Lilian's spine and she stared at Beatrice, her ears ringing and mind numb. He wouldn't. Night was a warrior, but Beatrice made him sound heartless. She couldn't believe the one who had done such a terrible thing was the same vampire who had tried to defend her last night, who had been so desperate to protect her, not knowing she wasn't in danger.

"We must know if he is the one responsible for what happened in Germany." Petra pushed to her feet. "You will take his blood and see if he is… or I will be the one to question him next time, and I will not be gentle."

Lilian swallowed and her gaze leaped to the silver-haired German witch. She didn't want to question him or use his blood to see his memories, but she couldn't let Petra near him. The witch liked to torture her prisoners, was sadistic and cruel, and the thought of letting Night fall into her hands turned her stomach and made her want to vomit. The look in Petra's eyes said she would be particularly brutal with Night, and Lilian could understand why. The witch had lost many close friends in the attack on the coven in Germany. She had grown up there and had lived there before coming to join the house in England as one of Beatrice's commanders. This attack had affected them all, but it had deeply affected Petra. She was out for blood.

So as much as she feared discovering that Night was responsible for the attack that sounded far too much like the one he had carried out on another coven in the past, she would do as her superiors demanded.

"You… you said question him *next time*. You've already spoken to him?" Lilian looked between the three witches.

They had mentioned that he had asked about Lilian but she had presumed he had been speaking to the guard, not one of the elders.

Beatrice's tone was measured, no trace of emotion in it.

"He was not very talkative. He kept asking about you. He even told me he wouldn't tell me anything until he had proof that you were alive." Beatrice eyed her closely and Lilian wasn't surprised to hear it. "He seems very attached to you."

Lilian's blood ran cold again. "He kept watch on me for Bastian when Bastian was called away on business and saved me from the demons."

"And you thought you'd fuck him as a thank you." Petra sank back onto her seat, as calm as anything as Lilian's gaze flew to her.

"No. We were in Norway to meet with his brother. It was late and Night thought it best to sleep before we drove there and—"

"Spare me the bullshit." Petra held her hand up, cutting Lilian off. "Beatrice and Maryon filled me in on all the juicy details. That room reeked of sex. You two must have been quite busy before your sisters came to *rescue* you from this *danger* you were in."

Lilian snapped her mouth closed.

"Where does your loyalty lie, Lilian?" Beatrice said.

Lilian's eyes darted to her and she didn't hesitate. "With my coven."

"Then, as leader of that coven, I order you to question the vampire and determine whether he was responsible for the attack in Germany."

They were testing her.

She looked at each of them in turn and steeled herself. They were right. This was her family and a vampire had committed a terrible crime against them. If there was a chance Night was that vampire, she had to question him.

She just wasn't sure what she would do if she found out he was guilty.

Lilian bowed her head and backed towards the door, turned as she reached it and opened it. She strode along the corridors of the ancient castle, the floorboards creaking under her booted feet and the witches in the paintings that lined the green papered walls staring at her. Judging her. She glanced at a few of them. Each was a coven elder, a witch of immense power who had been responsible for steering their family towards greatness or protecting it from harm.

She felt the weight of responsibility resting on her shoulders more and more with each step she took, each one that carried her down through the building to the basement. Whatever her feelings for Night were, she had to protect her coven from further harm as the elders before her had. She needed to do all in her power to defend it, as she had sworn to do when she had joined the ranks of the witches who served as the mercenaries in their coven.

Her stomach somersaulted as she reached the basement and she paused for a moment, around the corner where no one would see her. She pressed her hand to her stomach and drew down a breath, one deep enough to calm her rising nerves but not so deep that she smelled the disgusting scents that filled the air.

All she had to do was question Night and ask him to prove his innocence by letting her take his blood. She could probably skip the questioning part, but it was risky. Her attachment to Night and fear of him being responsible might cloud her gift, making her omit details as she dreamed his memories.

When she felt steady again, she tilted her head up and rounded the corner, and marched along the damp corridor. The stones beneath her feet were uneven, worn in places by water and far too much scrubbing. How much blood had been spilled in this place? She had never questioned anyone before, had only been here once or twice, but she knew the witches who dealt with the prisoners enjoyed making them talk.

Witches like Petra.

Lilian spotted two guards outside a door ahead of her and drew down another breath, a sudden desire to turn around and leave rushing through her. Forget fearing discovering Night was responsible for the attack. She feared discovering what the elders had done to him while trying to make him talk.

She wasn't sure she could handle this.

Each step she took towards the guards was a struggle, a monumental feat when every part of her wanted to walk in the other direction. One of the women looked at her and Lilian forced herself to keep moving, the scrutinising look the witch gave her enough to have her steps coming easier. She didn't want these guards to know how afraid she was or how reluctant. They would report it to Beatrice.

Lilian stopped when she reached the two witches and waited as one opened the iron door for her.

"Extract the information." The other witch slid her a cold look, one that had unease sliding through Lilian for some reason.

She frowned at the woman and stepped into the cell, her eyes struggling to adjust to the pitch darkness. A light above her flickered on and Night stepped forwards, emerging from the shadows.

"Mother earth," she whispered, her eyes widening at the sight of him, shock sweeping through her to shake her and deepen the doubts she had been trying to keep at bay.

They hadn't just questioned him. They had worked him over.

A vicious slash cut across the bridge of his nose and another intersected his right eyebrow. The skin around that eye was dark, mottled with bruising, and his lip had been split. Blood still tracked over his chin and reddened his nose, and drops of it had dried on his dirty bare chest too. She ran her gaze down his battered and bruised torso to his filthy black trousers and his bloodied, grimy hands.

They had been treating him like an animal.

She took a step towards him, unable to stop herself.

Night bared his fangs at her and snarled like a beast. "You're a witch?"

Lilian nodded slowly, some part of her aware of the danger she was placing herself in by admitting that, but she didn't want to lie to him. His elliptical pupils narrowed in the centre of his crimson irises as he glared at her, and she realised that this time the mistrust went both ways. Witches rarely trusted vampires.

Night looked as if he hated her breed with a passion.

He eased back and his demeanour changed, his expression growing calm and his posture relaxed. She could read his eyes now though, knew him well enough to see that despite his collected air, emotions still existed inside him.

And the dominant one was betrayal.

He felt as if she had betrayed him.

Or perhaps it was her own guilt making her see that in his eyes as he stared at her.

"I'm sorry," she started and his expression remained placid.

He didn't even twitch.

She glanced at the witches behind her, part of her needing to know they were still there and that she could get out if she needed to, and then she stepped into the cell. The door closed behind her with a deafening bang and she tensed, her shoulders hiking up.

Night still didn't react.

She wished she could be as composed as he was. She began fidgeting with the front of her dress and then stopped, smoothed it down and looked him in the eye.

"I never meant to hurt you, and I'm sorry other witches did. If you answer my questions, you'll be released." She didn't miss the brief iciness that crossed his eyes. It made her feel that releasing him would be a terrible mistake and that he was already plotting his revenge.

He tipped his chin up and looked down at her.

"I have nothing to hide. Unlike some." His bitterly cold tone cut at her and she flinched, unable to stop the reaction in time to hide how much he could wound her with only words and the distance it created between them. "Ask what you will, but I want to know something and I will not answer a damned thing until you tell me. Why did you want Bastian's blood?"

Lilian looked down at her feet and considered how much to tell him. The elders hadn't told her to keep Night in the dark. They wanted answers and telling him why they wanted his brother might help her get those answers. She lifted her gaze to meet his crimson one.

"This place... it's only half our coven. We have—*had*—another house in Germany... in the Black Forest. It was attacked recently. It was destroyed and we know a vampire did it." She struggled to hold his gaze as his eyes narrowed on her, anger flaring in them. "The vampire who attacked was brutal and left none alive as witnesses. We only have the word of another coven to go on. There was talk of a vampire being seen in the area before the attack and someone recognised him as Bastian Van der Garde."

His eyes grew cold and calculating as he went very still, sending a chill through her. His stony expression gave none of his feelings away.

Here was the assassin he claimed to be and she had been the one to bring him out.

"Do you intend to bring harm to my brother?" His tone was calm and measured, but as cold as a blade as he studied her closely, and she felt a lot rested on the answer to that question.

"He brought harm to us first," she countered, the wrong response judging by the barest twitch of his fingers that had her tensing and bracing, preparing herself for his wrath. Only he didn't move. He remained where he was, the ten feet between them feeling like a vast, frigid ocean. She didn't miss that his claws were out though.

"You are mistaken about my brother."

She was beginning to feel that too.

"Who attacked my coven then?" She risked another step towards Night and he still didn't react.

He just stood there, cold and aloof, distant from her. "I will answer that when you answer my question. Why did you want Bastian's blood?"

She held his gaze, seeing deep in his that the answer to this question was important to him. She didn't want him to believe that she desired anything from his brother, especially not a servant bond, so she answered him truthfully—almost.

"I have a power. I can see memories in blood. I dream them. The plan was to take Bastian's blood during the process of me becoming his servant and I would dream his memories. They would either clear his name or prove him guilty. We didn't believe he would give up his blood if he was asked for it directly, so the best plan was to become his servant. He would have to give me his blood then. In Norway, I decided to skip the exchanging blood and becoming a servant part and asked for his blood instead. I was hoping he would be compliant." She omitted the part about how her blood would have fatally poisoned his brother if she had gone with the original plan of becoming his servant.

"I know my brother," Night said, his face an unreadable mask. "Bastian isn't violent. His bloodlust is kept in check and he has no reason to attack witches. He's a businessman, Lilian."

Which was the exact same vibe she had gotten from Bastian in their time together.

"Myself, on the other hand." Night shrugged.

Deepening that feeling that her elders had been telling her the truth about him and he really had attacked a coven and come close to wiping them out. She stared at him, not finding it difficult to imagine he was capable of slaughtering so many witches under the right conditions, but finding it hard to believe he would be so heartless at the same time.

"Do you know where Bastian was last month, on the seventh?" Her eyes darted between his and she hesitated, not strong enough to ask him to give his blood to her. He wouldn't. She knew it in her gut. He didn't want her to see his memories.

Part of her didn't want to see them either.

"I'm not his keeper," Night drawled, unwittingly forcing her hand.

She stared him in the eye and told herself that she could do this, that she didn't really have a choice. Her coven wanted her to prove her loyalty to them and this was the best way to do that.

"Then will you give me your blood?"

He tensed, his right eyebrow quirking. A reaction at last, but the flash of heat in his gaze wasn't quite what she had expected. She had thought he would be furious with her for wanting it, not aroused by the thought of it.

Still, he shot her down with a firm shake of his head.

"Someone believed to be Bastian Van der Garde was seen in an area where a coven was attacked." She eased another step closer to him, capturing his attention. "My mission is to discover who was responsible."

"It wasn't Bastian. You can accuse him all you want, but it won't change the truth." Night stared her down. "Bastian would never do such a thing."

Lilian gazed up into his scarlet eyes and felt certain he was speaking the truth about his brother. What reason would Bastian have had for attacking witches? The only thing that got Bastian's blood pumping was money, whether it was made by his business or trading on the stock markets. Her coven wasn't involved in anything that might be in direct competition with him or provoke him into wanting to take them out. They hadn't been a threat to his fortune.

So either someone was setting Bastian up, or he hadn't been the vampire witnessed near the scene of the crime.

"Would you do such a thing?" she said, despising herself for asking him that but needing to know the answer. Bastian and Night looked alike, similar enough that one could easily be mistaken for the other.

He didn't answer her.

When he looked away, turning his cheek to her, it was answer enough. Her elders had been right about Night. He had slaughtered an entire coven.

Her gaze lowered to his throat.

And she had the feeling it had something to do with that scar.

CHAPTER 17

Night twisted his hands and grimaced as his wrists throbbed in response and his shoulders ached. Gods, he was tired. And angry. Rage kept his blood at a boil as his mind churned over everything Lilian had told him and how she had looked at him.

The accusation in her eyes, tempered by fear and unfounded hope, had revealed that she knew.

She knew the things he had done in his past, and she wished that she didn't. He wished he could have given her the answer she had wanted to hear—that he would never slaughter a coven of witches in a brutal attack like the one her coven had suffered—but lying to her was something he didn't want to do.

Although apparently it was something she was perfectly willing to do to him.

All the time he had known her, she had felt human to him. It must have been a spell. If he had sensed the faintest trace of magic in her, he would have kept his distance from her, and he would have driven her away from his brother. Her nefarious plans for Bastian would never come to fruition now, and that was a comfort.

Not quite enough to get him through his current predicament, but it gave him strength.

The other thing that kept him going?

The knowledge that he would make these witches pay for targeting his family.

For harming him.

He gritted his teeth and grunted as the guard struck him again, the short metal baton the male gripped hitting him in the ribs with enough force that he feared another of them might break.

Night stared beyond the bald-headed brute to the closed iron door. It wobbled in his vision and he swallowed thickly as he struggled to blink to clear his sight. Crimson discoloured his left eye almost immediately. His own blood. The cut on his forehead was healing, but not rapidly enough, thanks to this male working him over.

It had been hours since Lilian had walked out of that door and he wasn't sure he could take much more of this. He had been at his limit for the last hour maybe, teetering on the verge of collapse. Sheer will alone kept his feet planted firmly to the ground and his knees locked to keep him standing.

He refused to give the male witch the satisfaction of breaking him.

The fiend struck him hard in the stomach this time.

Night grunted and leaned forwards to spit blood on the flagstones. He hung from his bound wrists, staring at the crimson glistening beneath his bare feet—all of it his.

Gods, he was so thirsty.

His mouth was like a desert and his fangs constantly itched to rip into the guard's carotid. He would gorge himself on this male's blood if only the bastard would get close enough to him, and then maybe he would be strong enough to break free of the chains that held him in place against the icy stone wall.

When the guard had first entered the cell to work him over, Night had had the strength to fight back and had even come close to biting the man a few times, but the witch's savage assault had quickly put an end to that. Now, he barely had the strength to remain on his feet, and soon he wouldn't even have that.

"If you want to kill me," he drawled, slurring some of the words, "just do it already."

The guard struck him again, hitting him hard in the gut. Night's left knee gave out as pain ricocheted through him and he struggled to get air into his battered lungs, each breath sheer agony. He trembled as he forced himself to stand again, refusing to let this guard steal his dignity.

He wouldn't die on his knees.

He was a Van der Garde.

"You want blood," he murmured at the pool beneath him and chuckled mirthlessly. "There's your blood. Give it to that little bitch. Let her see for herself the pain I'm going to bring when I get out of these chains."

He launched towards the guard, making him tense and lash out, and grunted as the male struck him hard on the left temple. Fire and lightning spiderwebbed across his skull.

And Night laughed.

The guard gave him a look that said there was something seriously wrong with him.

There was nothing wrong with him. There was everything wrong with Lilian.

"Want to ask me some questions?" Night drawled as he fought to remain on his feet and blinked rapidly to clear his hazy vision. Much more of this and he would pass out. His body was burning through energy at an accelerated rate, trying to heal him, and if he didn't black out from the pain, he would black out from hunger.

Gods help anyone who untied him then.

He wouldn't be able to stop himself from biting them. He wouldn't even be aware of it until after his fangs had pierced their vein and he had drunk his fill of their blood, restoring his strength and his sanity. His vampire instincts would have taken over, driving him to survive.

Part of Night hoped the guard was the one to unchain him if he passed out.

A little payback would be nice.

Part of Night feared it might be Lilian.

He shut that part down, killing all the soft emotions that tried to surface as she filled his mind. His heart chilled again and his blood burned with rage. Better. He stared at the guard, silently goading him.

"Tell me your involvement in the attack on my coven." The male repeated a demand he had issued several times before.

This time, Night responded. "I wasn't involved. Neither was my brother."

"Lies." The guard hit him again, swinging the baton hard into his gut and making Night double over.

He spat blood onto the floor, hitting the male's boots this time, earning himself a hard blow to the head. His vision tunnelled. Not good. Another blow like that and it would be lights out.

Night shook it off and glared at the guard, seething with a need to break his shackles and drink the bastard dry. "You want to blame one of us. Fine. Go ahead. It won't change the fact we weren't involved."

He slid a dark look at the door beyond the guard, replaying that moment Lilian had stood there and he had realised something.

She was a witch.

Had she been targeting him from the moment Bastian had left her with him? He chuckled again, the sound maniacal even to his own ears. Maybe he had been her target all along. Accusing Bastian of butchering a coven was so laughable after all.

And the way Lilian had looked at him was seared on his mind.

She knew about his past.

Had she always known?

He wasn't sure of the answer to that question, his mind too sluggish to piece things together from the way she had acted around him and the way she had looked at him in this cell.

He had wanted to lash out at her.

Gods, he had wanted to hurt her.

He saw a vision of his hand closed around her delicate throat, squeezing the life from her as she looked at him through wild eyes.

Shut it down in an instant when his heart ached, unable to bear it.

But still, he wanted to hurt her. He wanted to wound her as she had wounded him. Whatever soft, foolish feelings he'd had for her, they were dead now. She was dead to him. He wouldn't give her anything. He wouldn't give these witches anything.

They could all rot in Hell.

He glared at the guard, holding his gaze, the darkness he had been trying to hold back rushing to the fore as his strength waned. Pleasing images of tearing through this coven flooded his mind, the taste of blood on his tongue becoming that of a dozen witches. He would gorge himself on them, feeding his bloodlust until it transformed him as it had then. He would leave no one alive.

All of them would pay for daring to target his family.

Him.

He laughed again as he realised how much like Grave he was, the harsh sound bursting from his lips, and the guard moved back a step, looking uneasy now.

He had been wrong. He was like one of his brothers after all.

Night barked out another laugh, sanity slipping through his fingers as the darkness welled up inside him, severing the part of himself that had been coming to care for Lilian.

For a witch.

He had been an idiot for worrying about her. A fool for falling for her.

She had played him well.

All those smiles and secret looks, the softness of her touch and the feelings that had shone in her eyes had been lies. She had been manipulating him the entire time.

Her coven in Germany had been brutally attacked.

Had she lied about that too?

Was it possible this coven was the same family as the one he had attacked all those years ago and this was their revenge? They were punishing him for what he had done to them.

It had to be.

The guard struck him again, the metal bar doing its job this time, cracking Night's ribs and weakening him further, driving Lilian from his mind and hardening his heart once more. Pain came in the wake of the blow as his body desperately tried to heal.

This was what they wanted.

This guard had never been here to question him.

He had been sent to deal enough damage that Night's body would be constantly forced to heal, devouring what little strength he had and making him ravenous for blood.

Foolish witches.

It wouldn't make him comply with their demands or give them whatever information they wanted. It would only hasten their deaths.

Bloodlust gnawed at the edges of his sanity, coaxing him into surrendering to it, and he wasn't sure why he was still holding it back. He stared at the floor, wheezing with each breath as his ribs burned, and contemplated embracing it, despite the danger of him not coming back from transforming into little more than a beast.

The guard turned away from him.

The iron door opened to let him through and closed with a bang behind him, and the cuffs holding Night upright opened. He slumped unceremoniously to the flagstones and keeled over, clutching his broken ribs. Gods, he was so hungry. He fingered his ribs, gently feeling them to figure out how badly they were broken, and grimaced as white-hot fire blazed across his chest.

Night held them and sank onto his backside, grunting as even that action caused pain to rush through him and his vision to blur. He focused on breathing, drawing down slow, shallow breaths that didn't hurt his ribs, and tried to calm his turbulent mind to fend off the bloodlust.

He had been tortured before.

He knew what came next.

They would try to make him talk by offering the one thing he needed.

Blood.

The door opened again and he smiled coldly, saliva pooling in his mouth at the thought of blood.

He opened that mouth to say they had moved to the next step quicker than he had thought they would as he lifted his head.

Those words died on his lips as he stared at the person standing in the doorway. His stomach dropped and hunger roared up on him to swamp his mind with crimson and shattered his hold on his bloodlust. The momentary spike in fear he felt was swift to fade, the thirst and craving that consumed him obliterating it.

He cursed the witches.

They knew what he really needed, because he was staring right at her.

Lilian.

CHAPTER 18

Lilian stood on the threshold of Night's cell, unable to believe her eyes as she stared at him. She didn't recognise the vampire before her. As he stared right back at her, his crimson gaze held a feral light that made him look wild. His bare chest rose and fell with his rapid breaths and his fingers constantly twitched, his claws darkened with blood and dirt. His handsome face, now beaten and bloodstained, had a sharpness to it.

Hunger.

The guard—her coven—had beaten him black and blue, raising his thirst by forcing his body to heal grievous wounds, and she wanted to look away from him but forced herself to keep her eyes locked on him.

She had done this.

She was responsible for his condition as much as the guard who had tortured him and the elders who had ordered it.

The desire to tell him that she was sorry was strong, but awareness of the two female witches behind her had her holding her tongue. They were watching her. Scrutinising her. This was another test. How she reacted here would likely determine what happened to her and her punishment would be severe if she showed kindness towards Night.

But the sight of him tore at her strength and had her fighting the urge to go to him and help him.

The man she had passed on her way to this cell had been covered in splatters of blood and she had feared they didn't belong to him, and now that she could see Night, her worst fears had been confirmed. She couldn't believe her coven had done this to him, and at the same time she could. In their eyes, Night was an enemy, and potentially responsible for the massacre that had happened.

In her eyes?

She couldn't bring herself to believe he had done it. She wasn't naïve. She knew the reason she couldn't believe he had slaughtered dozens of witches was because she didn't want him to be the one who had done it. She wanted him to be the vampire she had been falling in love with, the one who had been strong but kind to her, who had smiled at her and moved mountains in order to protect her. She didn't want him to be a cold, heartless murderer.

But by his own admission he was.

Her gaze lowered to the silver scar that cut across his throat.

No. He wasn't. Deep in her heart, she knew he'd had his reasons for rampaging through a coven, killing anyone who stood in his path. He had been seeking vengeance.

Her own coven wanted a taste of that too and she was to be the tool that carried it out.

She was no better than him. If he was a cold, heartless murderer for carrying out his revenge, then she was a cold, heartless murderer too.

Or she would have been had Night not walked into her life to change the course of it.

She felt the two guards close in behind her, a reminder that the course of her life hadn't changed that much. Her coven still wanted her to fulfil her mission. There was still time for her to end up being a tool for vengeance.

"Continue your mission." One of the guards shoved her shoulder, pushing her into the cell.

A bad feeling washed over her as the door closed with an ominous boom behind her and everything grew darker.

She wasn't sure how she was supposed to continue her mission. Did they want her to question him? Take his blood and dream his memories? The thought of trying to get close to him as he was now had her opting for the former.

"Night," she started and his eyes narrowed slightly. "Um... I need you to tell me more about your brother. Anything you can think of that might help clear his name. Are you sure you don't remember him mentioning anything about a trip or where he might have been on the seventh?"

Night just stared at her, his bare chest heaving with each hard breath he pulled down. She glanced at the darkness that marred his skin on one side of his torso and looked away, guilt churning her stomach. The guard must have broken his ribs. She couldn't imagine how much pain he was in or how hungry he was.

She stared at the stones beneath him, at the blood that glistened on them, and then lifted her head and looked at the chains that hung from the ceiling and the crimson that coated the sharp edges of the manacles. Her gaze lowered again, settling on his chafed wrists and the dried streaks of blood that tracked up his arms from them.

Her brow furrowed, her heart aching as images of him with his hands bound above his head, being beaten by the man she had seen, filled her mind.

Her gaze collided with his, the apology on her lips fading as his scarlet gaze seared her, the hunger in it frightening her a little. She wanted to go to him and do something to help him, to make him see that she hadn't known what had been happening to him and she would have tried to stop it if she had, but she feared what he would do.

His fingers twitched and curled into fists, his muscles flexing and his entire body tensing as he stared at her. Lines bracketed his mouth as the set of his jaw hardened, and his hands shook as a war erupted in his eyes. He was holding himself back. Fighting his hunger.

How long would it be before it got the better of him?

Lilian looked over her shoulder at the door, at the slot that was open to reveal one of the women. "He's in no fit state to talk. What do you expect me to get out of him? He already told us that his brother didn't attack the coven."

"The elders wish to know if he did."

She swallowed, sick to her stomach at the thought of finding out the answer to that question, and looked at Night.

He glared at her, a savage twist to his expression as his lips peeled back off his enormous fangs and his elliptical pupils narrowed to thin slits in the centres of his crimson irises. He could still understand what they were saying, and she took that as a good sign. If he could understand, then there was a chance he might do as she needed.

"If you answer my questions, I will get you blood, Night." She softened her tone as she said his name. Whenever she had used it before, he had reacted as if she wielded power over him by speaking it. She drew down a fortifying breath and exhaled, centring herself and seeking the strength to do this—to ask him this. "Did you really attack a coven a long time ago and slaughter everyone?"

In response to that, he growled and flashed his fangs.

"Answer the question, Night. Please? Did you do that?"

He snapped his fangs this time, jerking forwards as he did so, and then grimaced and eased back. He drew down a shuddering, shallow breath and shifted his hand to his side.

Clutching his bruised ribs.

Lilian turned to the door. "Give me some blood! He can't talk when he's like this. He needs to heal. Just give me enough to help him take the edge off his hunger."

"No." The woman's cold eyes backed up that word, telling Lilian that she didn't care that Night was suffering.

That bad feeling she had grew worse.

She turned back to Night, desperate to get something out of him and painfully aware that if she didn't then things were probably going to get very bad for her.

And for him.

"Did you really attack a coven of witches, Night?" She kept her tone even and soft, warm despite the chilling fear she felt.

Instead of answering her, he lumbered onto his feet and prowled around her, his gaze locked on her. Lilian swallowed and backed towards the door. When her spine met the cold metal, she banged her fist against it, not taking her eyes off Night.

"Let me out. This is dangerous." She kept banging, her fear cranking up a notch as Night made another pass, pacing back across the cell, closer this time.

"That's the reason you're in there," the woman said. "You fraternised with the vampire. That wasn't part of the mission. You let him get under your skin and now you believe he's been telling you the truth about his brother and himself. You believe in this vampire more than you do your coven."

Lilian whirled to face the door and pressed her palms to it, her eyes flying wide as she shook her head. "No. That's not true! You're wrong. I'm loyal to my coven—my family! I would never turn against it like that. Please. Let me out. I'm loyal to my coven."

She dug her fingertips into the door.

"Prove it." The guard's cold eyes slid towards Night. "Take his blood and see his past."

Lilian frantically shook her head, an icy chill slithering down her spine as her heart skipped a beat and she breathed, "That's suicide."

She stared into the woman's eyes and saw in them that she knew that.

She wasn't here to prove her loyalty.

She was here to die for her perceived betrayal.

And they wanted her to take Night down with her.

The elders had already decided that he was responsible for the atrocity committed against their coven, even though they had no proof and she wouldn't be able to give it to them. They didn't want her to. They wanted her to die and they would let Night die with her, keeping him in this cell as her blood slowly killed him.

They would take pleasure in watching him wither and die.

Lilian banged her palms against the door. "Let me out! I need to talk to the elders. They're wrong about this. They're wrong about me. They're wrong about him!"

The guard looked beyond her to Night, who was still pacing but was keeping his distance, and then at the other guard. She nodded. For a moment, Lilian thought they would do as she asked, but then they both began muttering as one.

An incantation.

The hairs on her nape rose and dread pooled in her stomach, and she frantically beat the door with her fists. "Let me out!"

Night loosed a long, low growl that had her spine stiffening.

And then his arm snapped around her waist and he dragged her back against him.

And sank his fangs into her throat.

Pleasure blasted through her, hot and intense, blinding as he caged her against the wall, one hand pressed against it and the other clutching her waist.

Cold replaced it a moment later as the reality of what he had done hit her.

"No. No. No!" She tried to wrench free before it was too late and her blood hit his tongue, but he snarled and bit down harder, the pain-pleasure combo fogging her mind for a second as he drew on her blood.

Night growled against her throat and it turned to a groan as his grip on her tightened, his hand splaying against her side and palming it as he pressed his front against her back.

Fear for him had her fighting the effect of his bite, made her desperate enough that she did something she knew would anger him.

She muttered a protection spell and cried out as his fangs sliced through her flesh as it hit him, hurling him away from her. She pivoted to face him, bracing herself at the same time, sure he would be on her again before she could convince him not to bite her. He picked himself up on another low, threatening growl, and she held her hands out before her.

"Night, listen to me. You're under a spell. Give me a moment and I'll be able to figure out what it is and cast the counter-spell." She backed off when he advanced on her, his gaze locked on her throat. Blood trickled over her skin there, the hot slide of it making her hyper-aware of the wound and how much of that precious liquid she was losing. Her head turned and she shook it, unsure whether she was trying to clear it or tell him to stop.

She tried to focus as he stared at the wound and somehow managed to summon the spell that would tell her which one they had used on him. She didn't get a chance to cast it before he was on her again, sucking greedily on her throat, making her head spin and blood burn. He grasped her bottom in both hands as he fed deeply and she pressed her hands to his shoulders.

Not to push him back, but to funnel the spell into him.

It went to work, rapidly running through his body to reveal the spell the guards had used. She heard one of them mutter to the other, and then they began chanting again. Lilian cried out as Night bit her again and held on to consciousness, refusing to succumb to the encroaching darkness. If she did, she was as good as dead, and Night would follow her to the grave.

The second she knew which spell the witches had used, she built a counter-spell and chanted the incantation as she shifted her hands to the sides of Night's head. She clutched it and channelled the spell into him as it built, untangling his instincts from the spell the witches had used and freeing him of it.

As the last thread gave way, he released her and staggered backwards, a vicious snarl pealing from his lips. His crimson gaze narrowed on her, a hunger for violence or maybe just more blood shining in it, and she feared her spell hadn't worked and then it struck her that it had, but Night was too far gone. His bloodlust was in control now.

They were doomed.

She sagged against the wall, the last of her strength leaving her.

It was over.

Night's demeanour changed in the blink of an eye, the shift from vicious to vulnerable happening so quickly she couldn't keep up as his gaze dropped to her neck. His brow furrowed and he approached her, but halted and edged back a step when she managed to lift her hand and touch her throat. The wound was ragged and the feel of blood pulsing from it made her want to be sick. She flinched.

He flinched too.

His scarlet gaze fell to the floor and then edged back to her, and then lowered to the damp flagstones again. He edged towards her, keeping his gaze away from her, and she would have found his behaviour fascinating if it wasn't for the fact she was so tired. Maybe she would sleep for a while.

Her eyes slipped shut.

Night roared and was on her, and she didn't have the strength to fight him as he wrapped his arms around her. She sagged in his embrace, ready to welcome the long sleep.

Only Night didn't sink his fangs into her to finish the job.

He gently swiped his tongue over the wound on her throat, his actions tender as he held her to him, one hand cradling the back of her head while the other supported her back. The pain eased as he licked the ragged holes his fangs had made, the fog in her head clearing slowly and a sliver of her strength returning.

When he pulled back, looking as if his heart was about to break, she drowsily patted his arm, trying to show him that she wasn't done for yet. Whatever he had done, it had stemmed the bleeding and had stolen away the pain.

His brow furrowed and his gaze lowered to her throat again, and he leaned in and licked it some more, each sweep of his tongue over her flesh sending a ripple of pleasure through her, a faint echo of how she had felt when he had first bitten her.

Just as she was about to clutch his arms and hold on to him, he drew back again and looked down at her, his soft eyes darting between hers. His handsome face hardened and he stepped back, and she wanted to tell him to stay with her, to keep holding on to her because she needed his strength right now, needed him to chase her fears away by being close to her. She was too tired to speak though, and she needn't have worried because he didn't release her. He kept hold of her with his right hand and lifted his left to his mouth.

She flinched as he sank his fangs into his forearm.

What was he doing?

He eased his arm away from his lips and offered it to her.

Lilian stared at the blood as it welled up to fill the two puncture marks, her magic rising to the fore to rouse a fierce need to take what Night was offering. Her magic wanted it, and she knew why. His blood would trigger her ability to see his memories. With it, she could prove his innocence.

But by taking it, she would also bind them. He would become her master, and she would become his servant. He didn't want that.

So she closed her eyes to shut out the sight of it and shook her head.

Night growled, and she thought he was angry with her, but when she opened her eyes, she found him kneeling on the cold stone floor, bent over and clutching his stomach.

The poison.

She needed to get him the cure and fast, but she wouldn't find it here. Her coven wouldn't give him the antidote. They wanted him dead. She would need to find it elsewhere and that meant she had to get him out of this place.

How?

The door creaked open and sickness rolled through her as she got the answer to her question. She knew what she had to do.

Lilian stared at the two witches as she moved on unsteady legs to the centre of the room, coming to stand before them with Night behind her, shielding him. She stared the guards down, her heart rushing so fast she felt dizzy and her palms damp. She could do this. It was her and Night or them. This was the only way.

She narrowed her focus down to the witches, careful to shut Night out of her mind, and growled two words.

"Drop dead."

Both women sank to the ground, falling onto their sides, and she closed her eyes and turned her face away from what she had done. Tears stung her eyes and she fought them back. They hadn't given her a choice. She hadn't turned against her coven. They had turned against her. They had tried to kill her.

She grew aware of Night's gaze on her back and slowly came to face him, opening her eyes at the same time. He looked paler than before and there were shadows around his eyes. How long did she have?

She wasn't going to stick around to discover the answer to that question.

Lilian stooped and took hold of Night's arm, guiding it around her shoulders. She helped him onto his feet, bearing his weight for him, and guided him out into the corridor. It was slow going as they inched past the cells, heading for the stairs.

The hour was late, so few witches would be moving around upstairs, but she went to a large black box near the bottom of the staircase anyway. The more cover they had, the better. She opened the box, keeping Night's arm around her shoulders with her other hand, and stared at the array of switches and wires.

She wasn't sure which switch did what, so she opted for the safer route of taking it all out. She held her hand out in front of it and summoned her magic, and hit the panel with a blast of lightning. White jagged bolts leaped between the wires and the switches, the strange plasticky scent of an electric fire filled her nostrils, and she snatched her hand back as smoke rose from several of the fuses.

"That should do it." She tensed when all the lights went out.

Night growled and gathered her closer. Still trying to protect her? What could he sense? She imagined that any witches on the floor above them were now using spells to light their way and grimaced as a flaw in her plan hit her.

Any one of them might know where the fuse box was and could be coming down to check on it.

She didn't want to kill any more of her friends and sisters, so she forgot about heading upstairs to escape.

"Come on." She stroked his arm with her free hand to calm him as he continued to snarl low in his throat.

It worked. His growling subsided and he relaxed again, allowing her to turn him around. She dragged him back along the corridor in the direction they had come, each step harder than the last as he placed more and more weight on her shoulders. The poison was working too quickly. Much faster than she had expected.

Time was against her.

When she reached the end of the corridor, she backtracked and leaned Night against the left wall a short distance from the end and made sure he wasn't going to fall in a heap on the floor. Satisfied that he would remain upright, she made her way to the end wall and pressed both hands to it. This was going to drain her, if she could manage it, but it would be worth it.

Lilian focused, building the spell in her mind. The stone beneath her palms vibrated, gently at first, but it built rapidly, becoming a violent juddering that shook her entire body too as she kept at it. Her hands numbed and she stared at the mortar, watching chunks of it fall from between the stones. Some of it turned to sand under the assault, and some of the stones even cracked. She squeaked and leaped to her left to avoid one as it fell, striking the ground where her foot had been.

She studied the wall, hoping it was weak enough now. Maybe she should hit it with a little more of the tremor spell she had been using.

Voices sounded along the corridor behind her.

Maybe not.

She grabbed Night with her right hand, twisting beneath his arm and clutching his wrist to keep it around her, and threw her left one out in front of her, aiming her palm at the wall. A violet orb shot from her hand and struck it. The ground bucked and dust exploded in a cloud to enshroud them and choke her. She pulled Night deeper into it, squinting as she tried to see where they were going, and grimaced as she stubbed her foot on one of the fallen stones. She guided Night over them, her ankles wobbling at times as she navigated the uneven terrain, and her pulse jacking up as the voices closed in on them.

She didn't breathe a sigh of relief when they hit the cool, clear night air on the other side.

She dragged Night forwards as quickly as she could manage, heading down the sloping green that surrounded the castle, towards the lane that cut through the forest. When Night slowed further, his feet barely moving, she risked expending a little more power and cast a spell on him to make him float.

It certainly woke him up.

He growled and kicked at the air, frantically trying to touch the ground.

"Shh, you're fine, Night. Just a little spell." She weathered his glare, hoping he didn't carry out the threat that shone in it. She was well aware she was a witch and that she deserved his wrath, but she was also helping him. She was saving him for a change. Surely that went some way towards making amends with him and proving not all witches were evil and deserved to die? She petted his hand and pulled him along with her. "I need to get you to an old friend. She'll be able to help you."

Lilian thought Night might have growled 'witch' at her, but she wasn't sure.

She kept hold of him despite his struggles and attempts to touch the grass, and began running, pulling him towards the portal in the forest.

One that she would use to get him to Elissa.

Elissa was a witch, one who had left Lilian's coven a long time ago to strike out on her own, but she had also recently become mated to a man who was half-vampire and half-incubus. That made her the ideal candidate to help Lilian. Elissa might not have her magic anymore because she had taken demon seed—incubus seed—into her body, severing the connection between her and the earth, but she was still exceptionally knowledgeable, and she had been living with vampires at the theatre for some time now. She probably knew a lot about that breed and Lilian hoped it meant she would be able to help her buy Night some time while they worked on removing the poison from his blood.

And if Elissa couldn't help her, maybe the vampires could.

It was a great plan.

CHAPTER 19

It was not a great plan.

Lilian knew it the moment the darkened glass front door of the Vampirerotique theatre slid open and the sandy-haired vampire on the other side took one look at Night and growled.

"Cristo." The man's dark brown eyes darted from Night to her and narrowed, a crimson corona emerging to ring his irises and his Spanish accent growing more pronounced as his expression darkened. "What the hell happened to Night?"

Lilian looked at Night, her stomach somersaulting and not only because he looked paler than the last time she had checked on him and there were shadows in the hollows of his cheeks. The vampire who had answered her frantic knocking knew him.

She was doomed.

Coming here had been a terrible mistake.

She could see it in the now fully crimson irises of the vampire opposite her as he stared at Night, fury mounting in his eyes.

"Tell me what happened," he snarled and advanced on her, his hands flexing and causing the sleeves of his fine black suit to tighten across his muscles as they flexed. He looked ready to rip her apart if she didn't tell him everything.

Not good.

Lilian struggled to keep hold of Night as he slumped, his knees giving out, and fear lanced her, spearing her heart and making it feel as if it was about to break. She looked at the vampire.

But she didn't get a chance to answer him.

Apparently, fate had decided that things *could* get worse for her.

An unholy roar rolled out of the open door on the right of the elegant red and gold foyer, close to the curving steps that led up to the second floor, and suddenly there was a dark-haired vampire right in front of her, his bright scarlet gaze searing her.

She tensed and gasped, and wasn't quick enough to stop him.

He wrenched Night from her grasp and bared his fangs as he pulled him away from her, deeper into the foyer.

"Night." Lilian lunged for him, her heartbeat going wild as adrenaline surged through her and the tattered shreds of her magic rose to her fingertips, coming to her aid as a desperate need to get Night away from the vampire blasted through her. He was in no condition to be handled so roughly.

The vampire who had taken him from her snarled and lashed out at her with his free hand, easily supporting Night's weight with his other, doing a better job of keeping him upright than she had been. Lilian dodged backwards, narrowly avoiding the brunet's claws, and focused on her magic, trying to calm her mind and stop herself from reacting.

Because lashing out with a spell would place Night in danger.

She needed to get him away from this vampire though.

Said vampire took one long look at Night, and a growl pealed from his lips, low and feral, and then he was pushing Night at the other vampire and coming at her as the sandy-haired male caught Night.

Her eyes widened and she backed off, heart pounding so fast that she was sure it would stop. Her head spun, thoughts blurring as blood loss, using her magic too much, and fear for Night combined to crush her strength.

Lilian chanted a spell anyway, willing to risk passing out in order to stop the vampire from harming her. She was no good to Night dead and he needed her help.

The brunet vampire roared and swung at her.

Night was suddenly in front of her, blocking the vampire's blow with his forearm, and the male was quick to leap away from him, a stunned look on his face.

"Night," she yelled as he dropped to his knees, hitting the floor hard on them, and she fell to hers beside him.

She gripped his bare shoulders, needing to check him over, but he snarled like a beast and wrapped his arms around her. She grimaced as he squeezed her against his chest, his body curling defensively around her, and growled over his shoulder at the brunet.

The brunet stared back at him, shock written in every line of his handsome face, and it was then she noticed something.

He looked an awful lot like Night and Bastian.

She groaned as it hit her, Night's words when Grave had visited the mansion coming back to haunt her.

His cousin Antoine looked much like Grave.

Meaning, he looked like Night and Bastian too.

Meaning, the vampire who looked ready to murder her and was so protective of Night was his cousin.

Mother earth, her good plan might have been her worst one yet.

Tense seconds ticked past as the two vampires remained locked in a silent battle, and then the brunet backed off another step and relaxed.

Night instantly sagged against her, as if his cousin standing down had stolen all of his strength. Her heart ached, fear squeezing it hard as he didn't only slump in her arms. His breathing was too rapid. She pressed her palm to his clammy forehead and swallowed hard, barely stopping herself from cursing him and his cousin. He had overexerted himself by protecting her, and as much as she appreciated it because he had probably saved her life, she wanted to scold him.

She gently twisted Night in her arms so he was resting with his back on her thighs and stroked his sweat-slicked brow as she gazed down at him, willing him to fight the poison. He just needed to fight a little longer. She would save him.

"What is wrong with my cousin?" The brunet confirmed her suspicion as he took a hard step towards her, worry shining in his crimson eyes. He didn't only look like Night, but he sounded like him too, his regal English accent making her ache to hear Night's voice again. "How did this happen?"

She wanted to explain everything later, when the brunet vampire couldn't kill her, which she was sure he would try to do when he heard how Night had come to be in his current condition, but the hard look he levelled on her demanded an answer right that moment.

She feared he wouldn't let her search for Elissa until she told him, so she lined up the words. She gently stroked Night's brow as he struggled to breathe, using all the magic she could spare in another healing spell. The last one she had tried hadn't worked, but maybe this one would. Fear of his cousin's retribution stole her voice, so she angled her head and gazed at Night, narrowing the world down to only them and pretending she was talking to him to make the words come.

"Last month, one of the houses of my coven was attacked… in Germany. No witnesses were left alive. Someone placed Bastian Van der Garde in the area, close to the scene. I was sent on a mission to determine whether he was guilty." She fought the flicker of nerves that ran through her blood and kept her gaze locked on Night's face, bracing herself for his cousin's wrath. "I was supposed to become his servant. It would have given me access to his blood and I could have used one of my gifts to dream his memories. It also would have…" She blew out her breath. "There was a spell in my blood. Whoever took it would be poisoned. My coven meant to remove the poison if I saw Bastian was innocent… but Bastian was called away and ordered Night to take care of me… and then demons attacked and we fled to Norway… and he got into a fight with Bastian and I left with him… and then my coven found us."

Her vision blurred and she blinked to clear it, needing to see Night's ashen face. She stroked his cheek, willing him to keep fighting, and her brow furrowed as her heart felt as if it was on the verge of breaking. She couldn't lose Night.

"They wanted to blame him for what happened. I didn't know they were torturing him. If I had— It doesn't matter. They…" Her voice grew hollow as what had happened carved a hole in her chest all over again. "They used a spell on him to make him bite me. They wanted to kill us both."

The two vampires in the room with her growled at that and she sagged a little as she looked down at Night, her chest feeling as if someone had scraped everything out of it. She had never been so tired. She stroked his cheek and her head dipped towards him when it became too heavy to hold up. She rested her forehead against his, feeling as if they might be doomed to die together after all.

"There is only one Lord Van der Garde who would do the things your coven has laid at Bastian's feet, and I do not recommend setting your sights on Grave." The brunet's deep voice rolled around her, like thunder echoing off cliffs, distant one moment and loud the next.

Night mumbled, "Brother. Stay away. Won't let you. No one. Hurts Grave."

Lilian pushed herself up and caressed his damp brow as his broken words gave fear a tighter grip on her. His condition was worsening. Her heart clenched and she managed to lift her head and look at his cousin.

"Elissa," she murmured, silently beseeching him to not kill her nor turn her away and make her leave like she could see he wanted to in his eyes. "Elissa can help him."

The male came to her and nudged her aside, easily dislodging her despite her attempt to keep hold of Night. She wanted to curse her weakness, but cursing herself would get her nowhere. She reached for Night instead, her hand missing his by less than an inch as his cousin lifted him into his arms and turned away from her.

"We shall take it from here." His tone was cold, emotionless, clearly conveying another message to her.

He wanted her to leave.

"No." She pushed onto her feet and staggered a few steps. "Elissa. Elissa can save him. Need to save him."

He stopped her by turning on her with a snarl, his pale blue eyes as hard as steel, freezing her in place. "You've done enough damage. Night would not want a witch near him when he is weak."

Lilian glanced at the scar around Night's neck, that feeling she had whenever she saw it growing stronger. A witch was responsible for what had happened to him and that was why he hated her kind. She reached for him anyway, unwilling to let the vampire take him from her. He could strike her if he wanted, could lash out at her with his full strength, but the only way of stopping her from going with Night would be killing her.

A woman stepped into her path, her hand landing on Lilian's shoulder, a silent order to stay where she was. She felt magic in that touch, felt strength trickle into her as the weak threads of her power tangled with that of this woman, slowly restoring some of her strength.

Watching the brunet vampire carrying Night away from her was the hardest thing she had ever done. The most terrifying. She shook with a need to follow him and when he disappeared into the gloom on the other side of the door, the sandy-haired vampire following him, it felt as if there was a string that tied her to Night and it had reached its limit, tugging her in that direction.

The woman held her back.

She flicked a look at her.

Familiar silver-grey eyes held hers.

"Dish the dirt. All of it," Elissa said and Lilian stared at her, struggling to believe it was really her.

She looked as she had before she had been exiled from their coven, but different at the same time. Her long flowing hair was now a stunning shade of silver that almost matched her eyes.

The mark of a tainted witch?

The tales of what happened to a witch when she took demon seed into her body were wrong though. The proof of that was right in front of her, in the magic Lilian could feel seeping into her to strengthen hers. Elissa hadn't lost her connection to the earth and magic when she had become tainted. If anything, Elissa felt stronger to Lilian now.

As embarrassing as it was, Lilian opened the floodgates and told Elissa everything. She held nothing back, not even how she was coming to feel something for Night and how afraid she was. When she was done, Elissa's soft features were set in a hard line.

"Come on." Elissa grabbed her hand and dragged her towards the door. "We have work to do."

"The vampire—"

"Antoine can growl all he wants, but he can't save Night. We can." Elissa pulled her down a dark corridor and through a huge double-height black room that had a staircase against the opposite wall. Beneath that staircase there were four crimson couches set around a coffee table. Elissa tugged her past them to the stairs and stomped up them. "I know where to find him."

Lilian stared at her back and frowned. Elissa wasn't wearing a black dress. Rather than the traditional garb of a witch, she wore tight blue jeans and a violet halter-top. They suited her.

"If my mate was here," Elissa grumbled.

Lilian wanted to ask her to finish that sentence because she was curious about Elissa's mate, but climbing the stairs was already taking its toll on her. She was breathless and panting as they reached the first turn, and was struggling to keep going when they reached the second, passing another floor.

She was close to making Elissa stop when they finally reached the top floor.

"I know a way to save your vampire." Elissa pivoted to face her, the grimness of her expression making Lilian uneasy. "It involves another spell on your blood though and getting Night to drink it to cleanse his. Are you strong enough?"

She nodded. "I don't think his cousin is going to let that happen though."

Elissa huffed. "You might be right about that. Antoine can be a little stubborn at times, especially when it comes to his family, but I'll make him see sense."

Lilian wasn't sure that she would, but she didn't know these vampires like Elissa did. If her old friend was confident that she could get past Night's guard, then she would manage it.

She followed Elissa to the first door on the right and tensed when Elissa knocked and someone answered her with a growl. The silver-haired witch banged her fist against the door again.

"Come on, Antoine. Don't be a dick. I know a way to help Night. I'm guessing right now you're trying to make him drink his weight in blood, but you know that won't get the poison out of his system... *if* you can make him drink it even." Elissa leaned against the doorframe. "I know how to get him to feed. You have to offer him something he wants to bite. A juicy morsel he can't resist."

"Juicy morsel?" Lilian hissed at her as she frowned. "I'm not a juicy morsel."

"You were tempting enough that he did that to your neck." Elissa waggled a finger at the wound and Lilian's hand flew to it.

She grimaced at the lumpy feel of it. It was healing, but still sore and felt disgusting beneath her fingertips.

"Leave," Antoine snarled.

The door opposite opened and a beautiful green-eyed blonde poked her head out. "What's happening?"

"Antoine won't let us save Night because we're witches and witches are pure evil, apparently." Elissa pointed at Lilian. "This is Lilian. She's a member of my old coven and Night's lover. She's trying to save him, but your husband is determined to kill him with a blood overdose or something stupid like it."

The blonde sighed melodically and stepped out into the hallway, and it was then Lilian noticed the black bundle in her arms. She rocked it gently as she crossed to the door and banged her fist against it. The baby wriggled and mewled, and the woman gazed down at it adoringly and gently tapped her fingertip against its nose. Lilian assumed it was meant to soothe the baby, but it kicked harder instead and began to cry.

The woman pouted down at her child. "Is Daddy upsetting you? He's upsetting everyone. It's not just you, my beautiful little Helena."

"I am not upsetting her, Sera." The door flew open to reveal a black-walled room and the brunet vampire. He glared at the blonde and then softened before Lilian's eyes as his gaze dropped to the squirming bundle of black. He peered down at the baby. "Shh, little one. All is well. Daddy is here."

Sera held Helena out to him. "Take her for a while? I'm starving."

He gave her a black look, one that said he knew she was palming the baby off onto him on purpose so he couldn't protect Night.

"They don't mean him harm, Antoine," Sera murmured. "Look at her. She clearly loves him."

Lilian had been lost in looking at Night, aching with a need to go to him and help him as he writhed on the black covers of the grim steel four-poster bed before her, but the moment Sera's words registered, her head whipped towards the couple and her eyes widened. The looks the two vampires and Elissa gave her said there was no point in denying it.

"I do love him." She glanced back at Night, warmth blooming inside her to chase the cold away for a moment before it crept back in. "I love him and I'm going to save him, and if you try to stand in my way—"

"I won't," Antoine interjected and slid a look at Night. "But I'm not leaving him. His history with witches… I can't leave him alone with two of them."

She squirmed a little at that, heat climbing her cheeks as she thought about Night biting her in front of others.

The thought of him biting her in front of Elissa was bad enough, but the thought of Antoine being in the room at the time too had her wrestling with the desire to call the whole thing off. Being bitten by a vampire seemed so intimate. She didn't want an audience for it.

But neither Antoine nor Elissa looked as if they were going to listen to a word she had to say if she attempted to convince them to let her be alone with Night.

Lilian mustered her courage and looked at Night. She could do this.

"Once his fangs are in you, I'll hit you with a spell and hopefully he'll be so into feeding that he won't notice the magic." Elissa palmed her shoulder. "You can do this. Just keep him focused on you. If you feel faint, hit the mattress and we'll pull you out, okay?"

She nodded, already feeling faint at just the thought of mounting the bed. Why did it have to be on a bed? It made what she was about to do feel even more intimate and made her blush harder.

"I'll give you another little boost. Your blood seems clear of the original spell, so that's good." Elissa's magic entwined with hers.

Lilian wanted to moan as strength flowed into her.

"It left my blood the moment Night had taken enough of it to trigger it in his veins instead." She patted Elissa's hand. "I'm ready. Let's do this."

Elissa released her and Lilian marched to the bed and clambered onto the mattress beside Night, nerves threatening to get the better of her. This wasn't sexual. This was about healing him.

Saving him.

She focused on that.

She leaned over Night, bringing her throat to his lips. They parted and his fangs brushed her skin, sending a shiver down her spine and fogging her mind.

She needn't have worried about being aware of her audience.

As Night's fangs gently pierced her throat, the whole world fell away.

CHAPTER 20

Night had never tasted anything like the blood pouring down his throat. He drank greedily, unable to get enough of the spiced liquid, ravenous for more. The flavour changed as he sucked harder, becoming laced with subtle hints of bluebells and sunshine, summoning imagined glades like ones he had seen in pictures, where sunlight filtered through silver birches to illuminate a sea of delicate flowers. He needed more. More. He drank deeper still, a groan rolling up his throat as he clutched the source of the delicious and addictive blood to him.

In the wake of the bewitching taste came strength. If the taste was soft and subtle, a gentle wave that swept over him, then the strength was fierce and intense, hitting him like a tsunami.

He craved more.

Awareness steadily built inside him as the blood worked to heal him, driving out the chilling cold and flooding him with warmth. Scents mingled with that of the blood. Sounds followed. And as his senses came back online, he pinpointed two other people near him and his host.

And snarled against the throat of his victim.

This blood belonged to him and him alone. He would let no other taste it. He would let no other have her.

Her?

A need to hold on to his host clashed with a desire to hurl her away from him, and his drinking slowed as he struggled to piece things together and make sense of the dual opposing reactions.

The scents grew clearer. Familiar.

Antoine.

And *magic*.

Night growled as all the warmth that had been flowing through him turned to icy cold. The female in his arms shifted her hands against his bare chest, rousing rage in his blood, and he tore his fangs from her throat, swiped his tongue over the puncture marks and shoved her away from him. She hit the end of the bed and rolled off it, landing on the floor with a grunt.

The silver-haired witch in the room with him scowled at him as she stooped and helped Lilian onto her feet, but Night kept his glare locked on Lilian.

His blood boiled at just the sight of her as she stood with her gaze downcast, guilt written in every line of her dirty face.

He still couldn't believe that she was a witch. His scar burned and he resisted the temptation to touch it. Her hand shook as she lifted it and brushed her fingertips over the fresh set of marks on her throat. His marks. Giving him blood wasn't going to make up for what she had done or what he had been through.

Night looked down at his bare chest.

At all the blood on it.

His blood.

Antoine came to him and pressed a hand to his forehead. "Are you well?"

"As I'll ever be," he snarled in response, keeping his glare fixed on Lilian.

His cousin looked from him to her, and back again. "I will drop off some clothes for you later. For now, we will give you some privacy."

Night was about to thank him.

But then his cousin tacked on, "You look as if you need to talk."

His head swivelled towards his cousin. Before he could stop him, Antoine had walked out of the room and the silver-haired female had followed him. The door closed.

Leaving him alone with Lilian.

Talk? He wasn't sure he wanted to talk with her, and he definitely wasn't sure it was wise for him to be alone with her.

He stared at his chest and pulled down an experimental breath, steeling himself against the pain he was sure he would feel. Only he felt nothing. He felt normal. His ribs no longer burned and ached, and his lungs no longer felt battered and bruised. He touched his side and drew down another breath, and stilled when he caught her scent on him.

The scent of her blood.

It wasn't only his blood dried on his skin.

His gaze leaped to her, to the ragged marks on the side of her throat, and the memory of what he had done hit him hard, knocking him off balance. He had savaged her throat in a fit of bloodlust that had come upon him out of nowhere and then he had offered his in return.

He had been wild with a desperate need to heal her and make her stronger.

Night stared at her, some of his anger abating. "I'm glad you refused my blood. I don't want to be bound to you."

Tears filled her caramel-coloured eyes.

Guilt tore at his chest, ripping through his ribs to his heart. Worry replaced his anger, that damned heart softening as he watched her fighting her tears and was sure he was the cause of them. He hadn't meant his words in the way she had taken them. He had meant only that he didn't want to bind her to him as his servant.

Not that he didn't want her anymore.

Gods, he shouldn't—she was a witch after all—but he wanted her as fiercely now as he had before he had discovered what she was and had found himself in a cell, held by her coven.

"Did I hurt you?" He reached for her as his brow furrowed, the need to touch her compelling him to make her come to him together with a desire to check the wound he had inflicted and make sure she would be all right.

Rather than coming to him as he wanted, she distanced herself, turning away from him and pacing across the black-walled room.

Night curled his hand and drew it back to his chest, his rage completely deflating as he stared at the distance between them and realised how badly he needed her to come to him, and how cold this space between them made him feel. He was sure a female had never made him feel like this, so torn and confused, desperate and wild, and afraid.

He feared that this distance that separated them would never go away, not even if she paced closer to him. It wasn't a physical space between them. It was an emotional void, a perilous crevasse that had him feeling as if every hope he'd had of a brighter future was gradually crumbling into it as the void grew.

Devouring him from the inside.

"I deserve your anger after what I did to you in that cell…" Before he could continue, she shook her head.

Making her tears fall.

He ached to go to her as they slipped down her cheeks, diamond drops that trembled on her jaw as she cast him a bleak look.

"It's not that." She sucked down a shuddering breath and scrubbed her eyes with the heels of her hands.

He could sense her pain. It ran deep. Fathomless. It echoed inside him and tore at him. He frowned at the black bedclothes beneath him, trying to remember everything that had happened, but it was hazy. Things came and went. He recalled biting her in that cell. He recalled not wanting to bite her, even though he had been drawn to her. He remembered the bastard who had tortured him. He remembered the way his blood had burned when he had realised she was a witch.

Night focused harder, sure the reason she was so upset was hidden somewhere in his memories. The haziest patches came after the guard had left. Had they thrust Lilian into his cell? Yes. Yes, they had. He lowered his hands to the bedsheets and clutched them as he inched forwards from there, wracking his brain and piecing together fragmented moments.

The answer hit him.

Her coven had turned on her because they believed she had betrayed them.

He had been resisting his urge to bite her, fighting the need for her blood, and she had been desperately trying to get away from him. The guards had refused to let her out and they had said something to her, and then he had scented magic and it had been a blur after that.

He growled as he realised why.

They had cast a spell on him.

They had pushed her into his cell intending for him to kill her and when he hadn't, they had used magic to make him do it.

Gods, he couldn't imagine what she was going through. He couldn't imagine what it would be like to suddenly lose his family in the way she had or have them try to kill him.

Lilian rubbed her dirty arm and stared at the floor. She looked small like that. Vulnerable. Roused a fierce and undeniable need to gather her into his arms and shield her from the cruelty of this world.

He despised her coven.

He despised witches.

He frowned. That wasn't quite true. Not anymore. He didn't despise all witches. As much as he hated them, he couldn't bring himself to hate her.

"I'm sorry they did that to you." He tracked her with his gaze as she began to pace again, her expression drawn and gaze still downcast.

Her pain grew stronger and he wanted to apologise to her again, because he hadn't intended to make her feel worse. He had been hoping to make her feel better. He scrubbed a hand over his matted hair and sank back against the pillows, searching for something he could say that would ease her pain. Maybe admitting he wasn't angry with her anymore would be a start.

"You should rest," she whispered, the softness of her voice enchanting him, making him aware of how tired he was.

Not a spell. Just an effect she somehow had on him. Her words were magic. Anything she said in that soft, tender tone had him wanting to obey her, because she always sounded as if his doing it would mean the world to her and would ease her mind.

"I know," he murmured, gaze still following her even as his eyelids grew heavier. Sleep urged him into her waiting arms, but he resisted, needing to know that Lilian would be safe before he closed his eyes and allowed it to take him. "I don't want you wandering around the theatre. I saw how Antoine looked at you. Did my cousin scare you?"

Her cheeks paled and her eyes slipped shut, and he had never seen her looking so tired. His fault. He had taken too much blood from her.

She gave a small nod and her voice was quiet as she said, "If I had known your cousin owned this place, I might have asked Elissa to meet me elsewhere."

"Elissa?" He canted his head to his right as his eyebrows knitted.

"The witch who was here. She used to be with my coven. When the guards... When you... I didn't know who else to take you to and I didn't know how to remove the poison myself. Elissa was the only witch I knew I could trust and who might be able to help me save you."

"Poison?" He swallowed thickly. "I was poisoned?"

It would certainly explain the chilling cold and how he had been constantly losing strength despite having fed from Lilian, and the bizarre and surreal things he had seen. How out of his head had he been? Maybe that fire-breathing dragon he vaguely recalled saving Lilian from had been a hallucination after all. He had wondered at the time how a dragon had come to be in the mortal world without perishing.

She twisted her hands in front of her hips and then jerked her head up and looked him in the eye. "I wasn't completely honest about my plan regarding Bastian. It wasn't my idea. The elders put a spell in my blood so that when Bastian bit me, he would have been the one poisoned, and if I had seen in his memories that he was innocent, the elders were going to give him the antidote."

"And if he had been guilty, he would have died as punishment for his crime." Night folded his arms over his chest, sleep forgotten as his instinct to protect his family rose to the fore and had him glaring at Lilian. "And rather than my brother being poisoned, you poisoned me instead."

All his anger leached from him to leave him cold and shaken as something else dawned on him. He had been in so much danger and he hadn't even realised it. Worse, Lilian had been and still was in phenomenal danger. Memories bombarded him, a rush of every moment that had led up to him being in this bed.

Antoine had tried to attack her.

His cousin wanted her dead and had tried to kill her, and Night had stopped him.

Good gods, she was lucky his other cousin, Snow, wasn't at the theatre. Snow would have gone straight through him to get to her, would have ended her there in the foyer, cutting her down without mercy.

"I don't want you leaving this room," he snapped. "Not without me."

The way she looked at him cut him like a blade, the dark edge to her eyes so far from what he had wanted to see in them. He knew he was being overbearing, that once again he was ordering her around and shutting her in a room, and that it was becoming a very bad habit for him. She didn't need to point that all out to him with that look in her eyes.

"I just want to protect you." Night held his hand out to her. "I can't do that if you're out there. If you stay here, I'll be able to sense anyone who comes into the room and can wake to make sure they don't hurt you."

Her look morphed into one of concern and she cast a nervous glance at the door. "You think I'm still in danger?"

He nodded.

Lilian's fine eyebrows furrowed slightly and she looked torn as her eyes darted between him and the door.

Finally, they settled on him. "I'll stay if you answer a question for me."

Night nodded again.

"Did you really kill an entire coven?"

He almost flinched as she asked that. Not quite the question he had expected. He busied himself with looking at the sheets, avoiding her gaze as it drilled into him. If he didn't answer her, she would leave. If he did answer her, well, she would probably also leave.

"Back at my coven, when I first came to your cell, you looked as if I had betrayed you." Lilian's eyes darted between his as he lifted his head to look at her and she slowly approached him. "You hadn't felt betrayed because I wasn't a captive like you. You had felt betrayed because I was a witch, and I wasn't sure why until I looked at your scar. Tell me how you got it. Does it have something to do with what you did to that coven? Was it revenge?"

He hated talking about it, but the soft look she gave his throat as she sat on the bed beside him, so close to him, made him want to talk to someone about it for the first time in what felt like a very long time.

And when she leaned towards him and gently stroked her fingers along the line of the scar, her gaze tender and brow furrowed, he couldn't stop himself.

He wanted her to know the truth.

To know him.

He settled his gaze on the ceiling between the four thick steel posts of the bed and then his eyes strayed to the plate that secured one of them to the ceiling. Snow's bed. He was in Snow's room. The sturdy bolts that held the posts in place were a dead giveaway. Snow was prone to rages when his bloodlust took him and needed to be chained.

Night wished he had still been chained when they had pushed Lilian into his cell and used a spell to force him to bite her. He glanced at her throat and away again before she noticed, shame eating away at him.

"I've served in the Preux Chevaliers for six hundred years." Those words were easy for him to say, a gateway to the more difficult ones. If he was doing this, he needed to build up to it slowly, and it wouldn't hurt to give her some backstory so she could see why he had done the things he had. "Grave was against it, of course. I was… too soft."

"Too soft?" She looked as if she might laugh when he glanced at her again, but her expression remained serious when their eyes locked. "It changed you."

He nodded. "Little by little. I was insistent. All Van der Garde sons had served and Grave showed no inclination to leave the corps, so I submitted myself for consideration. It was my duty to serve. I had to uphold my family's name and maintain our reputation."

"You make being a Van der Garde sound like a chore."

He almost smiled. "I suppose it is in a way. Things are expected of me. There is a name to live up to and constant pressure to do it. Serving was difficult at first. Grave was right and I wasn't cut out for it. I bounced around from one legion to the next, passed between them as someone tried to find a use for a Van der Garde with a little too much heart. I began to feel like… perhaps… I was too much like our sister."

"Sister?"

"Her name was Luna." He stared at the far wall, a faint image of her forming in his mind.

"Was? She's—"

He nodded, cutting her off, not ready to tell her about his sister yet. "I eventually settled in the Second Legion and the commander took me under his wing. Franz was stern, but fair too, and taught me well. He took the time to train me and others in his legion. He liked to call it sharpening his weapons. I began working in the field... and experiencing the darker side of our world... and it changed me, but it gave me the purpose I had badly needed."

Her little sigh and wistful look said she knew all about needing a purpose.

"What is your coven like?" He wanted to know more about her, and it didn't hurt to know more about her family too. He had the feeling they hadn't seen the last of them.

"We're mercenaries too. When I joined the field operatives... It was all I had dreamed about as a young witch. I studied hard to learn all the spells I needed to master in order to be selected, but it still wasn't guaranteed that I would be chosen." She tucked her knees up against her chest and picked at the dirt on his trousers with her right hand, her eyes on her fingers and a solemn look settling on her face. "I was so excited when I was chosen... even though I knew in part it was because I possessed two useful talents."

"Two?" He arched an eyebrow at her. "You mentioned you can dream memories. Is that one?"

She nodded and hiked her shoulders in a small shrug. "I also curse people when I... well... curse. Even if I don't mean to. Or sometimes when I do mean to."

His eyes widened slightly as he vaguely recalled her telling the two guards to drop dead and that they had. "That's one hell of a power. I'm not sure I could master that one. Aren't you afraid of accidentally cursing someone?"

"All the time." The sorrowful edge to her eyes as they shifted to meet his said it had happened in the past.

He edged his hand towards hers and she tensed as their fingers touched and then relaxed, her gaze falling to her hand and softening again.

"When I was with the Second Legion, I was part of a small advance team. We were scouting a coven of witches someone wanted the Preux Chevaliers to take down. Franz was a cautious man and knew the dangers of a direct confrontation with witches. I was second in command and suggested our small party stay at a local inn, acting as travelling traders." He skimmed his hand over hers and held it, needing the contact as memories roared up on him and his pulse raced, the fear he always felt when he remembered that night clamouring in his veins and shortening his breath. Lilian turned her hand in his and held it, tangling their fingers together, and he looked up into her eyes, silently thanking her for lending him her strength. "We thought we were blending well. The blood was flowing—in tankards—and the locals were accepting our presence well, those who ran the inn pleased to have guests for a change rather than just locals who wanted ale and food."

He could see every second of that night as if he was still there. He could hear the locals singing as they grew more inebriated. Could smell the fire and the food, and the perfume the females who had drifted to his group had been wearing.

"What happened?" Lilian stroked her thumb over the back of his hand, drawing him back to her.

"Franz followed a female who had been talking to him out into the night and when he didn't return, I got a bad feeling. The other three men in our team told me he was probably taking more than blood from the female, and I tried to believe them, but in the end, I needed to see with my own eyes that he was fine." Night clutched her hand a little tighter as his chest constricted and his throat burned. "I set aside the female who had been fawning over me. She tried to make me stay… charmed me and wanted me to come to a quiet corner with her instead—"

He grimaced as Lilian squeezed his hand hard enough that it hurt and met her gaze.

The black look in her eyes disappeared and they dropped to his hand, and her death grip on it eased as horror flitted across her face. "Sorry."

She didn't need to apologise. If she had been telling him a story about a man who had been trying to seduce her, he probably would have reacted the same. Or worse. Most likely worse. Demanding to know the name and location of the man, and dispatching his team to eliminate him sounded like the sort of reaction she would have gotten from him.

Night would lead the team of course.

And the kill would be his.

He cleared his throat, pushing aside the pleasing images of taking down the faceless male.

"When I ignored her and went in search of Franz, she insisted on coming with me, so we could be alone together once I realised my friend was fine. I should have known she was up to something but she was rather… distracting." It seemed like the best way of describing the blonde female's appearance and behaviour, without mentioning her low-cut corseted dress or the way she had been looking at him with desire darkening her hazel eyes and the scent of it rolling off her. Everything about her had made him want to forget finding his commander and instead pull her into a shadowy recess where no one would see them as he took his fill of her. "She kept palming my hand, the contact between us teasing me into wanting more. I should have known it was a trick. A spell."

"When did you figure it out?" Lilian shuffled a little closer, twisting her knees towards him so they brushed his hip as she tucked her feet in beside her bottom.

"When I thought I heard her saying something to someone else. I snapped out of it and spotted her friend bent over Franz, her hand glowing as she pressed it to his chest. I tried to stop her, but it was too late and the blonde witch I had been with turned on me and attacked." He lifted his free hand to his throat and rubbed it as he tasted blood. He told himself it was Lilian's blood, not his own. He wasn't back there, and this witch wouldn't hurt him. She cared about him. It was right there in her eyes as she looked at him, a soft quality to them that warmed even the coldest, darkest reaches of his heart. He swallowed, his Adam's apple rubbing his palm. "I reacted quickly, but not quite quickly enough. If I had been slower, her blow would have taken my head clean off. As I fell... I was sure it was the end and that she would finish me off. She looked as if she wanted that... but then my team came rushing out and drove them off."

"How did you survive?" She caressed the start of the scar below his ear, making his skin tingle.

He swallowed again, trying to move the lump from his throat as he felt sure he was going to gag. It wasn't blood. He wasn't back there. He was here, with Lilian. Safe.

Alive.

"One of the innkeepers was a breed that could heal. They did some work on me, enough to stop me from bleeding out. I don't really remember too much about that time." He did, but he refused to let those memories come, kept them locked away. "I only remember a hunger for revenge. It kept me going. It kept me fighting. I wanted to find the witches and end them. I wanted to make them pay in blood for what they had done."

And he still did.

"It took me over five months to recover, first healing the wound and then my voice box. I was bedbound for all of it... on Grave's orders. The doctors worked tirelessly to help me... but gods... the pain." He pushed the memories back down inside. The pain had been immeasurable, and learning to speak again had been humiliating. Some part of him had wished he had been slower, that he had died, and the rest had burned with the fire of a thousand suns, driven to live and hunt down the witches. "By the time I was strong enough to leave the infirmary, the coven had disappeared."

"Night." Lilian squeezed his hand, lightly this time, and she sighed softly as she shook her head. "I don't blame you for going after them. If someone had done such a terrible thing to me…"

Stars emerged in her irises, sparkling brightly. A sign of her magic, stoked by the anger he could sense in her. She looked awfully like she wanted to hunt down the ones who had hurt him and deal with them herself. Perhaps she could help him. He had never imagined he would team up with a witch, but he couldn't think of anyone he wanted by his side more than Lilian.

"I spent thirty years trying to track down the witches… unable to let it go. Grave reassigned me to the position I'm in now, and I know he did it to get me out of Hell… away from my mission of revenge." Night smiled slowly. "By sending me to the mortal world, my brother unwittingly placed me in a position to fulfil that mission. I chanced upon a lead that brought me to the coven."

"And you attacked it." There was no judgement in her eyes as she said that, no anger or resentment, or fear and hatred.

"Only because I discovered the witch who had tried to take my head still lived there with the one who killed Franz… my commander… my mentor… my closest friend." Night toyed with her fingers, avoiding her gaze, soul-deep aware this would change how she looked at him even when he didn't want it to. "My attack on the coven was calculated and carried out carefully. I slipped in unnoticed and managed to reach the two responsible for what had happened. I injured one, but the other raised the alarm, and in the ensuing confusion both escaped. When I realised they had slipped through my grasp… my bloodlust. I fell into a rage. I was so furious that they had escaped again, after so long of trying to find them and being so convinced I would have my revenge… It was too much. Bloodlust seized me and it was all a nightmarish blur, and then I came around and… I saw what I had done."

The halls of the house had been drenched in blood.

It had saturated every inch of his clothes and stained his skin.

"I won't apologise for what I did… but there is a part of me that regrets it. I killed so many that night and for what? I never got my revenge."

He lifted his gaze to meet hers.

"The witch who almost killed me is still out there."

CHAPTER 21

Lilian finished the last scrap of the omelette she had made and pushed the empty plate away from her. She leaned her left elbow on the table, propping her chin up on her palm, and dragged the book she had set aside in front of her, and then her coffee. She sipped it as she flicked through the pages, pausing whenever she found a spell that intrigued her.

For most of the night and half the day, she had buried herself in the books Elissa had brought for her to read. That was a lie. For most of that time, she had been lost in thought, running over everything Night had told her. His emotions had been so evident as he had recounted the tale of how he had come to get the scar that ringed his neck, and despite his best efforts to hide it, she had seen how afraid just remembering what had happened made him. She couldn't imagine the depth of the terror he had felt when he had almost lost his head, how afraid he had been of dying, and how desperate he must have been to live in order to survive the wound.

It was clear to her now that it had affected him deeply, setting him on a dark path that had consumed him and had coloured his view of all witches. He didn't trust any of them. She hadn't missed the way he had kept a wary eye on Elissa when she had delivered the stack of old spell books.

Lilian supposed that was another lie.

He did trust *her*.

Maybe he hadn't back in the cell, when he had felt she had betrayed him, but she couldn't really blame him for making presumptions and lashing out at her like that, even when it had hurt her. If a vampire had almost taken her head, she probably would have despised and not trusted any of his breed too.

He trusted her now though. Again. Her proof was the fact he had fallen asleep while she had been in his temporary quarters, leaving himself vulnerable to attack. If she had wanted to harm him, she could have done it.

She stared at the book in front of her, mulling over what he had told her. Her elders had told her the truth and he had attacked a coven, but it hadn't been a cold, baseless act of violence, and she found it hard to blame him for what he had done. If someone had killed her beloved friend and tried to kill her, she would want revenge too, and she probably wouldn't have stopped until she had gotten it either.

But he hadn't gotten his revenge.

Did that gnaw at him? Was he still looking for the witches?

She idly sipped her coffee as she frowned at the page, something gnawing at her. What if someone was setting Night up and that was the reason her coven's house in Germany had been attacked? But if they were, why would someone have told them Bastian had been seen in the area? Surely, if this whole thing had been a kind of trap, they would have told her elders that it was Night who had been there?

Lilian eased to her right, lifting her chin from her palm, and toyed with her lower lip as she thought about that. Her gaze locked on the stove opposite her and it blurred as she lost herself in thought.

"It really shouldn't surprise me that you wandered off despite my request that you stay in the room with me."

Lilian jumped and twisted on the chair, looking over her shoulder as that lush baritone invaded her thoughts.

Night leaned in the doorway, his arms folded across his chest, causing the dark silver-grey shirt to pull tight across his shoulders and biceps. He didn't look impressed with her.

She huffed and went back to her coffee.

"I dozed off in the armchair and woke hungry. No one else is awake and you really shouldn't be either." She scowled at him as he rounded the table on her left, coming into view again. "You were supposed to be resting."

"And I was… and then I skimmed the surface of waking and sensed you were gone." His ice-blue eyes darted between hers, the worry in them hitting her hard.

"Sorry. I was careful." Something she really felt she needed to be.

Antoine's attitude towards her hadn't changed one bit since she had helped Night recover from the poison. When Elissa had brought her the books, Antoine had come too, and had glared daggers at Lilian while helping Night into the shower. While Night had been showering, Antoine had issued a warning—if she hurt Night, he would deal with her.

His fangs had been down and crimson had ringed his irises.

By *deal*, she had imagined Antoine meant *killing* her. He would kill her if she hurt his cousin again.

That had set her on edge and when Night had come out of the shower, she had been too afraid of his cousin's wrath to look at him. She had hidden in her books, staying tucked up on the armchair even when Night had looked at her.

For five solid minutes.

She knew he had wanted her to look at him, but fear had gotten the better of her. Fear of Antoine's retribution. Fear that if she went to Night and tried to curl up beside him to sleep that he would reject her. Fear that some part of him was still angry with her and blamed her for what had happened to him.

Fear that he hated her now because she was a witch.

It had all been too much for her tired mind and wounded heart to handle. Her emotions had run amok, and she hadn't had the strength to put her foot down and scream at herself that Night didn't hate her. He wasn't angry with her. He didn't blame her.

He wanted her close to him.

It had been easier to drown in despair.

She had dozed off in the armchair, succumbing to sleep, and had woken with a cricked neck and a slightly more positive attitude. Only slightly. She still worried what Night thought of her now.

Night went to the refrigerator, opened it and took out a canister. He unscrewed the lid and downed the contents, grimacing the entire time. Was drinking cold blood the equivalent to eating cold leftovers? Not nearly as satisfying as eating the meal when it was fresh and hot.

He set the empty metal container down on the counter beside his left hip. She stared at it as she searched for something to say, needing to break the ice between them.

"Are you healing well?" She glanced at him and found him staring off into the distance above her head, looking a thousand miles away from her.

Maybe he hadn't come here to talk to her. Maybe he was only here because he had been hungry when he had awoken, like her. He probably hadn't expected to find her here and now he didn't know what to say to her. He didn't want to be around her. She tried to silence that voice of her deepest fears, but found yet again that she didn't have the strength.

Her feelings for Night stripped it from her.

She loved him.

It had taken Sera saying it to make her see that she was way past falling for Night. She loved him and now Sera and Elissa, and Antoine, knew it and Night didn't and she feared Antoine would say something and then Night would know and she wasn't ready for him to know. Not yet. Not until she knew how he felt about her.

"I should probably get out of your way. Give you some peace." She pushed the chair back and stood.

Night's gaze snapped down to her, his eyes narrowed briefly and then he ran a hand over his mussed dark hair. "I'm just a little tired."

He was lying to her.

"It's fine. You don't have to pretend things are the same between us, Night. I know they've changed. Maybe it would be best if I... if I stayed somewhere—" Before she could finish her sentence, Night was before her, the dark slashes of his eyebrows meeting hard above his crimson-ringed eyes.

"No." He moved around her and blocked the exit.

"No?" She stared up into his eyes, unsure what was happening, caught up in a maelstrom all over again and afraid of misinterpreting him and getting hurt.

"No." His tone softened and the hard edge to his expression faded into a tender look. "I'm sorry. If I made you feel you did something wrong... I'm sorry. It isn't you, Lilian. Gods, I don't want you to leave. Don't leave."

He reached for her and she remained where she was and let him stroke her cheek, savouring the comforting touch and the way his eyes became pure aquamarine as he gave her a look that made her feel as if she was the most beautiful woman in the world.

As if he adored her.

Loved her.

"What's wrong then?" She lifted her hand and covered his with it, holding his palm to her cheek because she was afraid he would steal his touch away from her before she was ready. She needed him to keep touching her, to chase the darkness from her heart and her mind, to fill her with light and warmth again and reassure her that nothing between them had changed.

"I'm worried about my brothers." The earnest look in his eyes as he said that revealed how deeply he loved his family, and the edge of fear in their depths told her that he was genuinely afraid for his brothers. "I'm sorry I upset you."

"I'm sorry I got you caught up in all this. I'm sorry my coven hurt you like that... I'm sorry that I hurt you too." She leaned into his palm as a weight settled on her heart. "This last month... I don't know. Things have been so different in my life and I'm not really... I don't really know..." She didn't know how to speak, apparently.

Night brushed his thumb across her cheek.

"I'm quite familiar with the complex and often infuriating conundrum of no longer really knowing where you stand on something or how you feel. One of the few perks of being fourteen hundred years old." He smiled softly and she wanted to tease him about his age, but she liked that look on his face, loved how gorgeous he was when he let that smile come out to play. "You'll figure things out. Don't force it."

It was hard though. She was no longer sure where her loyalties rested or whether her coven was going to come after her to kill her or whether she even wanted to go back to them if they didn't. Her coven—her family—had been her home for her entire life. The thought of no longer being a part of it was frightening, even when she knew they had wanted Night to kill her. She still clung to the hope she could make them see they had been wrong about her.

She still believed she could make them take her back.

A foolish endeavour? Try as she might, she couldn't convince herself to let them go. Her family meant too much to her.

"Come here." Night gathered her into his arms, slipping his hand on her cheek around her nape, and angled her head back.

He dipped his head and captured her lips, his kiss soft and tender, warming her and chasing the chill from her heart. She pressed her hands to his chest and tiptoed, craving more of this sweet kiss that told her things he wouldn't put into words—things she needed to know.

When he drew back and gazed down at her, there was more than affection in his eyes. There was fatigue too.

"You need more rest." She stroked her hands over his chest.

"I know." He gently combed his fingers through her hair. "I was too worried about you to go back to sleep. You'll just have to come to bed with me. Nurse me back to health."

She arched an eyebrow at him and he smiled wickedly, not even trying to hide that he was angling for more than sleeping together. If she set foot near his bed, she would be naked and under him in less than a minute. It sounded tempting.

His heated gaze took on a shrewd edge that had her wondering what he was plotting.

Or what he knew.

"What's that look for?" She pushed her palms up his chest to his shoulders and looped her arms around his neck, tempted to pull him down for another kiss.

He shot down that urge. "What did your coven say in response to your message?"

She came dangerously close to cursing him. Apparently, he could see straight through her. Or read her like a book. Or maybe he just knew her better than she had thought.

"I didn't tell them where I was." She quickly put that out there, not wanting him to get any wrong ideas about what she had done or that she was a danger to the vampires here. "I was careful. I know Elissa got into a lot of trouble with our coven and I'd never place her or anyone here in danger. I just... I want to clear your name... and mine too. I don't want them coming after you."

"I take it their response wasn't a favourable one." His eyebrows knitted as he swept his knuckles across her cheek and searched her eyes, concern glittering in his pale blue ones. "We will find a way to make them see neither of us did what they believe we did. I promise, Lilian."

She nodded, warmed by how he wanted to help her even as she chilled at the same time. Because there was a way he could help her, but he would never go for it. The only way to clear his name was to take his blood and dream his memories, and capture them with a spell so her coven could see what she had.

"I'll stay with you this time if you sleep. I won't go anywhere." She slipped her hand into his and eased past him, tugging him around to face the door.

He didn't look as if he believed that, but the flicker of heat in his eyes said that he was more than happy to follow her upstairs to bed. Wicked vampire. She glanced back at him from time to time as she led him up through the theatre to the bedroom he had been given, the heat that built in his eyes stirring in her too, until the desire to sleep beside him became a fierce need to sleep with him again.

By the time she crossed the threshold of the room, she was aching for him, her mind filled with the last time they had been together and how incredible it had been. Her vampire was insatiable and she wanted to bring out that side of him again, but knew she couldn't. Not yet.

He was still healing and recouping his strength.

So she needed to make sure he didn't overexert himself.

She smiled wickedly as an idea hit her.

CHAPTER 22

Lilian closed the door behind Night and led him to the four-poster bed, the fire in her veins burning hotter as she thought about what she was going to do. When they reached it, she pushed him down to sit on the black covers, and he cast her a curious look.

His lips parted.

Before he could ask her what she was up to, Lilian crawled onto the bed beside him and kissed him. He groaned and tunnelled his fingers into her hair, clutching her to him as his tongue tangled with hers, and she kept moving forwards, forcing him to lie back. She swept her lips over his and then broke away from them, kissing a path down the straight line of his jaw to his throat.

She lingered there, peppering it with kisses as he slowly tilted his head back, his grip on the back of her head tightening as she teased him. She stroked her tongue over his vein, feeling the point where his scar intersected it, and did it again as her mood shifted, desire becoming laced with something akin to sorrow.

"Lilian," Night murmured and she shook that sorrow away, aware that he could sense it.

She didn't want this moment to be tinged with sadness over something that had never happened. He hadn't been hers when he had received this wound she traced with her lips, but the thought it might have taken him from her still weighed heavily on her heart. She loved this vampire. She loved him with every drop of blood in her body. With all her heart and her soul.

Lilian gazed at his throat, an urge rushing through her, one that stole control and had her lightly biting down on his flesh. He groaned hotly and bucked against her, his fingertips pressing into her scalp as his other hand flew to her lower back to pin her to him.

"Gods, Lilian. Don't." He pulled her away from his throat and she stared down at him, wanting to know why he had stopped her and why he sounded so strained. Crimson eyes stared back at her and his fangs flashed between his lips as he uttered, "I'll want to bite you."

The way he lowered his gaze from hers told her all she needed to know. He wanted to bite her and he thought she would stop him. He didn't know her as well as she had thought after all.

Lilian gathered her dark hair, pulling it away from her face and her throat, revealing it to him. She used a simple spell to produce a pin and twisted her hair around it and fastened it in place. Night stared at her throat the whole time, gazing at it like a man starved, the heat in his eyes blistering and making her shiver.

She lightly traced her fingers down it to tease him, keeping his eyes locked on it, and then dropped her hands to his chest. He didn't stop her as she began unbuttoning his shirt, revealing his honed body inch by delicious inch. His gaze remained rooted on her neck.

Until she opened his shirt and stroked her palms over the hard slabs of his pectorals and down the defined ropes of his stomach. He drew in a sharp breath, the action causing his muscles to flex, and she wanted to purr at the sight of him. Pale skin. Firm muscles. His build was slight—athletic—but it pushed all the right buttons in her. She didn't like overly large men or grossly muscular ones. She liked them exactly like Night.

Lilian dropped her head and kissed a trail down his chest, savouring him this time, exploring every inch of him as she worked her way downwards. Night's hands slipped from her and she glanced up at him, looking up the length of his gorgeous body to his face as he draped his arms across the mattress above his head.

Surrendering control to her.

She shivered and heated, let out a small moan as she dipped her head and kissed lower still. He sucked in another breath as she circled the sensual dip of his navel with her tongue and she looked down, a groan escaping her as the blunt crown of his cock poked out from the waist of his trousers.

Lilian had them open in a handful of seconds, a hunger to know the taste of him at the helm. She moaned in time with him as she stroked her fingers down the rigid length, admiring it and deciding where to start. It kicked against her hand and she wrapped her fingers around it and lowered her head, took him into her mouth and rubbed her thighs together as heat pooled there, her desire soaring higher. She fluttered her tongue around the head and Night arched, his hips coming up off the mattress as he groaned.

He liked that.

She set to work, torturing him with soft licks and harder flicks of her tongue, sucking him and stroking him, whipping him into a frenzy. When his groans deepened and he reached for her, she pulled back, the need to push him over the edge with her mouth transforming into a need to feel him inside her. She wanted to feel him coming inside her.

Lilian pulled her black dress off and tossed it aside, and Night stared at her, hunger blazing in his eyes as he took in her naked curves.

"Where's your damned underwear?" he growled.

She looked down at herself. "I didn't bother putting it on after my shower. The dress Elissa gave me was long enough to go without it."

His eyes widened, a flicker of disappointment in them. "You showered here... in this room?"

She nodded and it dawned on her.

"You were sleeping." She dropped to all fours and crawled up his body, giving him her best sultry look, one that worked like a charm on him because his eyes darkened and his anger became desire. "Next time, we'll shower together."

"Next time," he echoed, his voice sounding distant as he gazed at her breasts.

She was about to roll her eyes when he captured her left breast in his hand, drew her up to him, and wrapped his lips around her nipple. She moaned instead, her eyes falling shut as he teased her, having his revenge. His free hand skimmed over her backside and she shivered as he teased her damp folds.

"I want to taste you too," he husked against her breast.

"Next time," Lilian parroted, too lost in the wicked feel of his fingers teasing her flesh to want to move from her current position.

Night lowered his hand and caught her inner thigh, pulling her legs further apart so she was forced to sink lower over his body. He groaned as he gripped his shaft and she followed him as he stroked it through her folds.

She eased back as he reached her entrance, taking him into her, and he lifted his head from her breast. She captured his lips as she sank onto him and set a slow pace, kissing him as she rode him, a different sort of heat building inside her as he held her to him. She had never made love before.

Was this what it felt like?

Every inch of her felt full and warm, and she lost awareness of where she ended and he began. It was as if they had blended together as they moved in perfect symphony, not even a trace of a dark emotion in her as Night filled her with light. With love. It was all she could feel as he kissed her, as he rocked inside her with slow, long strokes that had her soaring higher.

And higher.

"Lilian," Night breathed against her lips and kissed her, his fangs brushing her lower one, and she knew what he wanted.

She needed it too.

Lilian angled her head away from him, baring her neck.

Night swept his lips over it and then eased his fangs into her, tearing a gasp from her throat that quickly gave way to a moan as the sting of them piercing her became incredible pleasure.

His first pull on her blood tipped her over the edge.

She cried out as a warm wave crashed over her, as she quivered around his cock, her breath leaving her in a rush. Night groaned into her throat and joined her, plunging as deep as she could take him as he spilled. He pulled on her blood in time with each throb of his length, and gods, it made her feel incredible. Pleasure hit her with each wave, rocking her, the intensity of it building as Night continued to feed from her.

Oh gods.

She covered her mouth and muffled a cry as she climaxed again, the feel of him feeding triggering a second release. Her cheeks burned.

Night withdrew his fangs, quickly swiped his tongue over her throat, and leaned back, his gaze on her face only making her blush harder. She couldn't look at him. It was too embarrassing.

"Don't you dare say anything," she muttered.

Risked a glance at him.

His cocksure smile was far too enchanting.

It became a full-blown grin as he rolled her over, coming to rest on top of her. She was tempted to find a way to wipe it off his face, but he was gorgeous when he smiled like that. She savoured this rare glimpse of his other side instead, sure it wouldn't last, not while everything with his brothers and the demons and her coven was still hanging over them.

Lilian lured him down to her, her fingers gently cupping his nape.

He took the hint and kissed her. Soft. Slow. Reverent. Did he love her?

This kiss made her feel as if he did.

"You should get some more sleep," she whispered against his lips between kisses, before he got himself and her fired up again.

He stilled and sighed, and even though he clearly didn't want to, he rolled off her.

Lilian scooted to the edge of the bed. "I'll just go use the bathroom and then I'll be back."

She hurried to the bathroom, quickly took care of cleaning herself up, and then came back to him.

He was sound asleep beneath the covers.

Lilian's gaze shifted to his neck.

She needed to know if he had been telling her the truth and he'd had nothing to do with the attack on her coven. She could capture his memories with a spell while she slept, one that would allow her to show her coven they were wrong about him. She needed to clear his name. Her coven wouldn't stop coming after him. They wanted revenge. Until they had it, they wouldn't stop.

One part of her heart argued that she should ask him for his blood.

The rest argued that he would refuse her.

Because taking blood from him would bind them.

She didn't care that it would make her his servant. It was the only way to clear his name, and she needed to do that. She needed to protect him from her coven. Nothing other than proof that he was innocent would stop them from coming after him and trying to kill him. She didn't want to lose him, so she was going to risk his wrath and do this.

Lilian stroked her fingers across his brow. Maybe being owned by him wouldn't be so bad.

She swept her fingers across his lower lip, revealing his fangs were still down, and steadied her pounding heart. He was going to be angry with her. She gently pressed his lower lip to the tip of his fang and he flinched in his sleep as it pierced it. She released his lip and stared at it, watching the bead of blood bloom. She would find a way to make him forgive her.

Lilian lowered her head and kissed him.

Capturing that drop of blood with her tongue.

She rolled onto her back and Night pulled her to him, tugging her like a ragdoll into his arms as he turned onto his side. He nestled against her back, his breath fanning her neck as he sighed, and she pieced together the spell to record her memories.

Cast it.

And then closed her eyes.

Images emerged from the darkness, dim at first, but they grew brighter as they sped past her, flickering before her eyes. A hundred thousand moments swept around her, scenes building and falling away at a dizzying pace. As time passed, the stream slowed, allowing her to see moments in Night's life.

Through his eyes, she saw the attack on his commander and on him, and felt his pain and how close it had come to destroying him. She studied the faces of the two witches, hoping she might recognise them so she could help him have his revenge. Only she didn't recognise either female.

Time skipped forwards and she saw how desperately he had tried to find the ones responsible, his almost constant search for them. She witnessed what he had done to the coven and how a black rage had consumed him when the witches had escaped him.

She felt how driven he was to hunt them down and have his revenge.

He couldn't let it go.

She let the next few decades rush past her and slowed when she felt she was nearing the end of his memories, catching up with the present.

A paper with a date of two months ago flashed before her, followed by memories of what appeared to be an office, and conversations with vampires, and a mission he had carried out.

And then her.

Lilian stopped there, denying the desire that rose within her. She wanted to know how Night felt about her, but she didn't want to discover it this way, by snooping at his memories. She wanted to hear it from him.

She jerked awake and stared at the pillow before her.

Night hadn't attacked her coven.

But someone had made it look an awful lot as if he had and had pointed her coven at his brother. Why? To draw Night out into the open?

She carefully extricated herself from Night's arms and hurried to her dress, picked it up off the floor and found her phone. She fired off a message to her coven, telling them that Bastian wasn't to blame and neither was Night, and that she had proof and wanted to meet them to clear his name.

A message came back almost instantly this time.

A time and a place.

She swallowed her racing heart as her hands trembled.

They wanted to meet.

CHAPTER 23

Lilian was avoiding him. Again.

She had been gone when Night had awoken and Antoine had kept him busy until close to midnight, talking to him and introducing him to his daughter, Helena. *Helena.* That had been Night's mother's name and the baby resembled her, with a shock of pale hair and large eyes, and the way she laughed. Night had somehow ended up holding the squirming bundle and staring at her.

Unable to believe his cousin had a family now.

With a turned human of all things.

That and the fact Grave had mated with a phantom gave Night hope that his family might accept Lilian. He wasn't sure Bastian would, felt certain his brother would never let him hear the end of it, but he didn't care. If only part of his family accepted her, that was enough for Night. He wasn't giving her up. She was his now. His forever.

Finally, Antoine had left, but only after issuing a request. He wanted Night and Lilian to move into one of the guest rooms on the floor below now that Night was starting to feel stronger. Antoine had taken great pains to explain how comfortable the guest quarters were and Night had stopped him by telling him it wasn't a problem.

The room was Snow's after all, and Antoine wasn't the only one hoping that their sibling would come home soon.

Night set the final stack of books from Snow's room on the dressing table next to the rest and arranged them neatly. Spell books. Lilian had a glow to her whenever she looked at them, one that made it clear she was excited about reading them. Would she find any new spells in them?

Maybe she already had.

He decided to ask her about that when he found her. He wanted to show her that her being a witch wasn't a barrier between them or something he needed to overcome. Just in case she felt it was and that was the reason she was avoiding him.

Where had she gone? She had returned briefly when he had been moving their things and had made her excuses and left just as quickly once he had told her which room they were in now. He was sure she had muttered something about Elissa.

Night went in search for the witch's mate, Payne. The part incubus vampire had a room on the same floor as Night's new one and it wasn't hard to find him. He simply followed the sound of a child giggling. He had learned from Antoine that Helena wasn't the only youngster in the theatre now. Callum had twins with his werewolf mate, Kristina, and Elissa had brought a young incubus boy with her when Payne had brought her to the theatre. According to Antoine, Luca was her nephew and she had saved him after her sister had passed away.

And the child incubus was also Payne's uncle.

But the half-breed was raising him like a son with Elissa.

Night poked his head around the door and peered in at the sandy-haired boy where he sat on the floor with Payne, playing with a wooden train set and laughing whenever Payne derailed it with his own engine and made a noise like the collision had caused them to explode.

"Is Lilian here?" Night said.

Payne lifted his head and shook it. He ran a hand over the dirty-blond spikes of his hair, flashing the line of markings that tracked up the underside of his forearm to disappear beneath the rolled-up sleeves of his dark pinstripe shirt.

"She said something about Elissa." Night smiled at the boy when he stared up at him.

"Play?" Luca offered the train and blinked big eyes at him.

"Ah… not right now. Maybe later. I'm looking for Lilian." Night awkwardly held his hands up in front of him, hoping the boy wouldn't get upset.

He wasn't really sure how to handle children—holding Helena had made that painfully clear to him. At least Helena could only kick, giggle or cry. Luca talked, walked and played, and was looking at him as if he was the biggest disappointment on the planet because he had refused to take the train. He waited, holding his breath and hoping that the boy didn't burst into tears.

Luca shrugged and then beamed at him, his demeanour changing in an instant. "Aunty Lilian is very pretty. I told Mum that I'm going to marry her when I grow up."

Night glared at the little imp. "She's not on the market."

Luca looked at Payne, his fair eyebrows pinned high on his head. "What does that mean, Daddy?"

Payne rubbed his neck now and patted Luca on his shoulder. "Um… it means that she's spoken for… like how Mummy can't be someone else's bride because she's mine."

Apparently, Night wasn't the only one who was clumsy with children.

Luca's head swivelled towards Night and his eyes narrowed, a flicker of incubus blue and gold emerging in them as he pouted. "I don't think Aunty Lilian would want to marry you. I think she wants to marry me."

"Well, we'll let her decide that." Night stared the kid down, admiring how much gumption he had but finding it irritating at the same time.

"Are you the one who bit her and made her cry?" Luca glared at him.

Night's eyes widened.

Before he could say anything, Payne was shaking his head. "You got it all wrong, kid. Night did bite her, but that was yesterday, and she didn't cry then."

"She had red eyes earlier. I heard Mummy say she was crying."

"She was crying?" Night stared at the boy, needing to know the answer to that question as a thousand other ones filled his mind. Why had she been crying? Who had made her cry? Was it something to do with her coven? With him? Had he done something wrong?

Or had she been upset because she intended to leave?

She had threatened to do so earlier, when he had found her in the kitchen.

He didn't wait for Luca to answer him. The need to find her had him racing through the building, using all the speed he could muster to cover every inch of it. She had to be here somewhere. She couldn't have left.

He sped across the black-walled double-height room and froze as he sensed her.

His head whipped to his left, towards the ring of couches.

She sat there with a book on her lap, staring at him, surprise etched on her face. "Night. What's wrong?"

She pushed to her feet, causing her book to fall onto the coffee table, and her fear laced the air, tainting her sweet scent.

"What's wrong?" Her caramel-coloured eyes searched his as she hurried to him.

He looked down at her hand when she gripped the front of his grey shirt, his blood rushing in his ears, and his breath leaked from him.

"I thought you were gone. I was trying to find you and Luca said you had been crying, and I was afraid you had been upset because you had decided to leave… me. I thought you had left me." His brow furrowed as he wrapped his arms around her and tugged her to him. He held her to his chest, his fingers tangled in her dark hair, and lowered his head, pressing his lips to the top of her head and breathing her in. She was here, in his arms. Not gone. She was here.

She wrapped her arms around him and held him. "I'm not going to leave you."

He ached for her to tack a 'never' onto that sentence.

He reluctantly eased her away from him and gazed down at her. "You've been avoiding me."

The way she averted her gaze said he was right and she had been.

"Why?" He framed her face with his hands and angled it towards his, making her look at him. "Did I do something wrong?"

"No." She shook her head, moving his hands, and then heaved a sigh. "I have. I did something wrong. Oh, Night. I know you're going to be mad at me, but I needed to know, and now I do. I have proof. I can show my coven and they'll leave you alone."

He frowned, a feeling building inside him as she spoke, one he focused on to make it clearer—stronger.

"You're mad at me. I knew you would be." She placed her hands over his. "Please, don't be."

"All day I've been trying to put my finger on why I feel different." He tried to keep his tone soft, but it was hard as he thought about what she had done. She had taken his blood without his permission, binding them together as master and servant. He focused on the connection he could feel linking them, and murmured, "I thought it was just because I love you."

Her mouth gaped open.

"You love me?" She blinked up at him.

Night nodded. "I love you."

"You're sure?"

He frowned at her again. "Of course I'm sure. I've never been more certain of anything. Do you want me to *not* love you?"

She was quick to shake her head, causing her fall of dark hair to brush across the shoulders of her plain black dress. "No. It's just… I love you too, and I was worried that you didn't feel the same way and I could have taken a peek at your feelings in your memories, but I resisted and now all day I've been fretting over whether or not you love me as much as I love you."

The fact that she had resisted finding out his feelings from his memories warmed his heart. If he'd had the talent she possessed, he wasn't sure he would have been able to resist taking a look at the times they had been together to discover how they had made her feel and how she felt about him.

He would have been greedy, wanting to know her innermost desires and how deep her love for him ran.

"You are right. I do not love you as much as you love me." He tucked a rogue wave of hair behind her ear as he banded his other arm around her and she stared at him, horror shining in her eyes now. "I love you more."

She slapped his chest and pouted. "You do not."

Night feathered his fingers across her cheek, the softness of her skin stealing his focus for a moment before he thought of another way to tease her and couldn't resist it. This lightness between them was too bewitching. He wanted more of it.

"Alas… I cannot wed you." He set her away from him. "For you are already spoken for."

A little crinkle formed between her eyebrows. "By who?"

"Luca."

She slapped his chest again, hard enough that it stung this time.

"I'm not marrying Luca." She twirled away from him when he tried to seize hold of her and shot him a naughty smile. "I'm not marrying you, either."

Night would see about that.

She hurried towards the stairs.

Night beat her to them, coming to a halt in front of her and blocking her path.

Her laughter as she collided with him died suddenly and she looked up at him, worry creasing her brow. "Are you mad at me? There might be a way to undo the master-servant bond."

"I'm not." He shook his head, a small part of him feeling he should be but the rest overruling it. He stooped and gathered her into his arms, and straightened, lifting her feet from the floor and holding her under her backside so she was taller than he was. He gazed up at her, warmed from head to toe by just the sight of her and the feel of her in his arms. He husked, "Part of me likes the bond, because now I know no vampire can touch you. Now I know you're all mine."

She stroked his shoulders, her caramel-coloured eyes soft. "I was always yours, Night."

He groaned and lowered her, and as soon as she was close enough, he captured her lips in a kiss.

It ended on a sigh.

"I know I'm being selfish." He leaned back and looked at her. "I know we have to break this bond."

"Why?" She looked hurt, and she felt it too, as if he was breaking her heart by saying that.

"I'm worried that another vampire might touch you, even accidentally, and it will hurt you too. I don't want you to have to live in constant fear of a vampire other than me touching you. I can't do that to you." He gathered her to him and kissed her again, a brief one that held all the love he had for her in it. "We'll talk to Elissa and see if she knows a spell that can undo this or can help you find one... but... even when it's gone, you're still mine. You'll always be mine, Lilian."

She rested her forehead against his. "And you'll always be mine."

Gods, that warmed his heart.

He kissed her again, unable to resist her lips and the need to let her know how much her words had meant to him. She smiled against his mouth and nipped his lower lip, threatening to get him going again and filling his head with a vision of twisting and pinning her to the wall and pulling her ankle-length black dress up so she could wrap her legs around his waist.

She stiffened.

Night sensed it too.

He broke away from her lips and looked at the silver-haired witch to his left. "Just the woman we were looking for."

Elissa pointed at herself, right at the cleavage made by her starry blue halter-top, which Night diligently kept his eyes away from as Lilian's gaze seared his profile. He didn't want anyone other than her. He glanced at her and caught her blushing hard as she stared at him. She had no reason to be embarrassed. They had only been kissing. This theatre showed a hell of a lot more than that on the stage most nights of the week, and he could almost guarantee that Payne liked watching the performers practicing and that his little witch accompanied him.

Elissa had probably seen all manner of wicked things in her time here.

A couple kissing was hardly going to shock her.

Lilian pushed out of his arms, her blush fading as she smoothed her dress down, fixing her appearance. "I took Night's blood. I needed to see his memories so I could clear his name. The problem is, by taking it, I bound us as master and servant. I'm not worried, but Night is. Do you think there's any way to break this bond?"

Elissa pulled a thoughtful face. "Maybe. We can get to work on it. It might take some time. You should probably warn the others so they don't touch you."

Night made a mental note to do that as soon as possible.

"Come with me and we can get started." Elissa held her hand out to Lilian.

Lilian hesitated. "You go on ahead. I have to talk to Night about something else."

That didn't sound good.

What else did she need to tell him?

Elissa slipped past them to head upstairs and Lilian fidgeted, drawing out his agony until the witch was well beyond the sphere of Night's senses.

"Spit it out." He wasn't sure he could wait any longer. Her fear hit him hard and he reached for her, and she didn't pull away. She seized his hand instead, clutching it tightly, and every instinct he possessed said something was wrong. Something had shaken her up. There was only one thing he knew that could have done that. "Your coven contacted you."

"I told them I have proof and... they want to meet."

Night shook his head. "No, Lilian. It's too dangerous. They tried to kill you. There has to be another way."

"There isn't. I need them to see the memories I saw in your blood and the only way to do that is to cast another spell, one that will transfer the captured memories from me to another." She toyed with his fingers, her gaze dropping to them. "I have proof that you're innocent. I can stop them from coming after you."

"What about you? What if they try to kill you?" he barked, refusing to back down. This was madness. Her coven wanted her dead. They wanted him dead.

She closed her eyes and then opened them and tipped her head up, staring right into his. "They won't. I'll be careful and use protective spells. I know they'll understand this was all a big mistake."

He could see how important this was to her, and how desperate she was to prove both her innocence and his, but he couldn't bring himself to trust her coven.

"What if it's a trap?" he said.

Her face fell, sorrow washing across it, and her voice was small as she said, "It won't be."

She didn't believe that. She was afraid that it would be a trap and just the thought it might be was hurting her.

"They tried to kill you, Lilian. They wanted you dead. They want me dead." His tone hardened as anger got the better of him, the memories of what her coven had done and what they might be planning stoking it until it was an inferno in his veins. "You can't trust them."

She had been shrinking away from him, but as he hurled the last four words at her, she stiffened and straightened, tipping her chin up as she squared her shoulders.

"I need to meet them, Night." She looked up into his eyes again, her voice stronger and tone firmer now. "I need to try. I can't rest knowing that they're out there, believing a lie, unaware of the truth about you. I can't rest knowing they will come after you again. You can be mad at me all you want, but I'm doing this. I *need* to do this."

He sighed. This wasn't a battle he was going to win. He had been in love with this witch for barely a handful of days and she already had him wrapped around her finger, willing to do anything for her.

"If you are going, then I am going too." He gave her a look that said he wouldn't hear any arguments on this matter either. She had made up her mind and so had he. They would do this together.

And if it was a trap, he would slaughter them.

He would do whatever it took to protect her.

"What time is the meeting?" His breath fogged in front of his face as he asked that, and he frowned as he looked at Lilian and saw her breath misting the air too.

She cast a worried look around them and closed ranks with him. "Why is it so cold all of a sudden?"

The answer to that question drifted into the room across the way from them.

Two phantoms.

One was a striking white-haired woman he didn't recognise.

And the other was his brother, Grave.

CHAPTER 24

The fact that Night's brother was now a see-through pale echo of himself was disturbing as hell.

But it was nothing compared with the fact Grave was looking at Lilian as if *she* was the ghost as Payne and Elissa appeared, and other occupants of the theatre came down to see what was happening.

Lilian stood beside Night, struggling to hold Grave's gaze as his brother stared at her. Night closed ranks with her, narrowing the small distance between them down to nothing, hoping to allay her fears and show her that his brother wasn't a threat to her. Even if Grave did find out what had happened since they had last seen each other, even if his brother lost himself to his bloodlust, Night wouldn't let him get to her.

He edged his hand towards hers and brushed his fingers across the backs of her knuckles.

Grave slanted him a look.

One that made it perfectly clear how unimpressed he was with Night and how he was fighting the urge to bring up what he had said back at Bastian's mansion, when he had accused Night of being attracted to Lilian.

And Night had denied it.

"Does Bastian know?" Grave bit out.

Night glanced down at his black leather shoes and then squared his shoulders, tipped his chin up and looked his brother in the eye. Grave despised weakness in any form. His brother would only grow angrier with him if he didn't stand his ground.

"He knows." Night held his gaze, refusing to look away, showing his brother that he wouldn't let him shame him, or scold him for what he had done. "After the fact."

Grave shook his head and huffed, and then sighed as he admitted, "I probably would have done it the same way."

Bastian was a cold, greedy bastard, and Night and Grave had quickly learned that it was better to ask forgiveness than permission when it came to their brother and his perceived belongings. Asking for permission normally resulted in being turned down. Asking for forgiveness never failed. Their oldest brother always ended up letting them off the hook.

Eventually.

Night shoved his fingers through his hair as a wave of fatigue rolled over him and denied the urge to look at Lilian. He wanted to take her to their room, curl up on the bed with her and sleep with her in his arms, only this time, he wanted to wake to find her still there.

Grave looked him over, his expression slowly darkening as he took in Night's clothing and then studied his face. When his older brother looked ready to commit bloody murder, Night held his gaze and silently pleaded him not to ask. Lilian was afraid enough as it was. If Grave asked what had happened to him to make him look so tired and why he was wearing Antoine's clothes, she would probably panic and dig her own grave by attempting to explain things.

Night's gaze shifted to Lilian and he looked down into her eyes as he tangled his fingers with hers and clutched her hand. Eventually, Grave would demand to know what had happened, but when he did, Night would be the one filling his brother in. It was better things came from him. Whatever happened after that, he was here for her and he wouldn't let his brother hurt her.

He looked back at Grave and caught him gazing at the other phantom in the room with a lovesick look in his pale blue eyes that Night also found highly disturbing, but at the same time, it made him happy. He was glad his brother had found love and had a mate he obviously adored.

But he wasn't glad it had turned his brother into a ghost.

The white-haired female looked down at the strip of pale material that had been tied across her chest, over her freakishly flowing white dress. The ends of that dress were ragged and drifted ethereally, as if they were fluttering in a breeze no one could feel, and as he watched them, he noticed something.

She was floating.

Her feet weren't touching the floor.

He looked at Grave's shoes and frowned as he saw his brother was floating too.

If Grave wanted him to answer some questions, then Night was going to be asking some of his own too.

He looked to his brother for an explanation, but it was Snow who stepped forwards. The big white-haired vampire looked like a shadow compared with the paleness of Grave and the phantom, his muscular body clad in a skin-tight black T-shirt and jeans and heavy boots.

"We have books from a phantom mage... and we need one spell in particular." Snow's deep voice rolled through the room, drawing everyone's focus to him. "One that will turn Isla corporeal, and hitting Grave with the same spell probably wouldn't hurt."

Grave slanted their cousin a warning glare, probably because Snow was obviously amused by Grave's predicament. Snow just smiled and shrugged his broad shoulders.

Isla?

Was that the name of Grave's mate?

Night would be asking about her later, when he and Grave were alone, and Grave was no longer a ghost. He wanted to know about Grave's mate. She was a new addition to his family, and a welcome one at that. Grave was hiding it well, but Night knew him well enough to spot the tells.

His brother was happy.

For the last century, Grave had been a miserable bastard—or at least more gloomy and dark than usual—and now Night knew why.

Isla had broken his heart.

But now it looked as if she had pieced it back together.

So Night forgave her for hurting his brother and wouldn't hurt her in return. Instead, he would do his best to ensure she remained with Grave and became part of their family.

And he hoped that Grave would be as welcoming to Lilian.

"We'll take a look." Elissa stepped towards Snow and took the sack of books from him.

She jerked forwards when he released them. The sack hit the hard floor with a boom that echoed around the double-height room. Payne chuckled until she shot him a black look, stars sparkling in her grey irises. He schooled his features and hurried to help her, easily lifting the heavy sack and swinging it over his right shoulder, flashing the line of markings that tracked down the underside of his forearm. They were dark, muted colours. Night guessed it was a sign of not fear, but something akin to it. Uneasiness? He clearly didn't want his mate to be angry with him.

Grave's jaw tensed and he glared at a point beyond Night, and Night was about to ask him what was wrong when the sack his brother had been holding suddenly became solid and dropped right through him. Grave shuddered.

Isla casually turned completely solid in order to set her own sack of books down at her feet, cerulean blue leather trousers and a matching corset and boots replacing her white dress for a heartbeat before she turned phantom again.

Snow took one of the bags of books and Night went for the other. He carried it over to the small area of couches near the stairs, Lilian trailing after him. She settled herself on one of the red sofas and Night sat beside her, keeping a watchful eye on his brother as he talked with Isla.

He didn't like the way Grave's expression slowly blackened as he spoke with her, or how both of them grew animated, but he resisted the temptation to use his heightened hearing to listen in on their conversation and focused on helping Lilian with the books instead. He wouldn't like it if Grave eavesdropped on an argument he was having with Lilian after all.

She sighed and flicked through the first book, pausing only to hook the glossy waves of her dark hair behind her ear. Revealing one of his bite marks. She bore several now, and as he stared at the mark on her throat, he wanted to add another. He couldn't get enough of her blood, or how intimate biting her felt. It had never been like that for him before.

Isla drifting over to them had him focusing back on the room, and he frowned as Grave remained at a distance, floating back and forth between the stairs and the corridor that led to the foyer. Isla must have angered him. His brother always paced whenever he was worked up about something.

Night slid her a black look.

She kept her head bent, her eyes locked on the pages of the tome resting on her lap, avoiding him.

Minutes ticked past and eventually Grave drifted to Isla and looked down at her, and Night couldn't remember the last time his brother had looked as if he was lost for words. She looked up at Grave, but he just stood there, mute. His brother's pale eyes dropped to the book on her lap and his eyebrows knitted hard, and then he sighed and another look crossed his face.

Making his feelings clear to Night.

Grave was a male used to having purpose and a direction, much like Night. He was used to leading others. Right now, his brother wasn't sure what to do with himself. It was a feeling Night knew well as he glanced at the book Lilian was flicking through. He didn't know magic. He didn't know what they were supposed to be looking for, not like Isla apparently did, and Elissa and Lilian.

His brother looked as if he felt he was a fifth wheel, and honestly, Night felt that way a little too. All he could do was pass Lilian books and sit there, watching her work. As much as he enjoyed her company, the inaction grated on him.

And yet again, it struck him that he was more like Grave than he had thought.

Snow rose from one of the couches as the pretty raven-haired angel Antoine had introduced as Aurora appeared on the stairs, her white dress flowing around her legs as she hurried down them. His cousin met her at the bottom, scooped her up into his arms and kissed her as he carried her up the stairs.

Gods, Night wanted to do that with Lilian.

He stared after them, a deep feeling of longing filling him.

And when he glanced at Grave, his brother looked as if he wanted to do the same with Isla.

Night leaned back in his seat beside Lilian and yawned as fatigue rolled over him again. Grave arched an eyebrow at him. Night gave him an unapologetic look and sneakily rested his arm along the back of the couch behind Lilian.

He was about to draw her back against it, so he could hold her, when she looked across at him.

"It's gone dawn. You should get some rest." The concern in her soft voice touched him, but he didn't want to go to bed without her.

He huffed and considered refusing her order, but then he pushed onto his feet and dropped a kiss on her brow. "Don't fall asleep on the books… Come sleep in my arms… It's way better."

Lilian smiled and leaned her head back. Night took the invitation, pressing his lips to hers in a slow, soft kiss that had everyone staring at them when they finally broke apart. He placed his hand on her shoulder and gave it a squeeze, and then walked around the couch, trailing his fingers off her and doing his damnedest to tempt her into coming with him, even when he knew she wouldn't.

Because she was happy Elissa wanted her help with the spell. She was happy she was being included as a witch. He hoped that being with Elissa, someone who was from her coven, soothed the hurt she felt and tamed her need to return to them. He didn't want to lose her, and he knew he would if she went back to her family.

He wanted her to be part of his family now instead.

He glanced back at her from the bottom of the stairs and her soft smile hit him hard.

Gods, she was beautiful.

"Don't expect such sweetness from me," Payne murmured against Elissa's neck and she giggled, her shoulders coming up to lift the hem of her starry blue halter-top away from her dark jeans.

He growled and playfully nipped her bare shoulder. She pushed at his arm.

"Go to bed... Luca is probably still up waiting for his story." Elissa nuzzled Payne's cheek and whispered words into his ear that had the urge to go back to Lilian, grab her and take her to their room growing so strong inside Night that he almost surrendered to it.

Payne flashed Elissa a wink and disappeared.

Night forced himself to head upstairs to their room. Each step that took him away from Lilian was harder than the last and he hated it when she slipped beyond the boundary of his senses. He trudged onwards, another wave of fatigue crashing over him, and blinked to ward off sleep. Maybe if he waited up, she wouldn't be too far behind him.

They could kiss a little at the very least.

He opened the door of their room, closed it behind him and went to the bed. He sat on it and twisted so he was laying with his head on the pillow, rested his hands on his stomach and stared at the ceiling. Waiting.

His eyelids grew heavy.

Waiting.

His eyes slipped shut.

He woke with Lilian in his arms as darkness fell. She was fully clothed like he was, her head nestled close to his chest and her breathing soft. He gazed down at her and stroked his fingers through her hair, watching her sleep. His beautiful Lilian. He had never thought he could feel anything other than hatred for a witch, but he loved her.

A sound like thunder boomed overhead.

The entire building shook and dark power spread like an oily tide down through the layers of it, and Night froze as he recognised the feeling that bloomed inside him.

The demon prince.

Night focused on the space above him, sure the male was there, had come to this place to attack it. The bastard was about to learn it was unwise to target his family. He growled, causing Lilian to stir, and rage burned up his blood.

It chilled a moment later.

When a baby wailed and a woman screamed.

"Helena!"

CHAPTER 25

Lilian's eyes snapped open, silver stars sparkling amongst the rich caramel of her irises, and the tinny scent of magic laced the air around Night. He launched from the bed and seized her wrist, pulling her from it. She hit the ground running, following close on his heels as he exited the bedroom and ran along the corridor, heading for the stairs.

They weren't the only ones on the move.

Night sensed Grave and Isla high above him, and footsteps rang out in all directions, most of them coming from the top floor. The whole theatre was heading to the rooftop. He charged up the stairs, a need to reach Grave driving him to go faster, to use all of his preternatural speed to get to his brother before the demon prince could hurt him or the baby. He couldn't. Lilian wouldn't be able to keep up with him and he needed to keep her by his side, where he knew she was safe.

She muttered something and magic charged the air, and then she was matching his speed, coming up beside him on the staircase. He looked down at her feet and then up into her eyes, and she nodded.

Night wasn't sure what she had done, and he didn't have time to question her. He could only trust that she could keep up with him now. He sprinted hard, the world blurring around him, and sure enough, Lilian remained by his side, her feet moving as quickly as his were.

They weren't the first to reach the moonlit rooftop.

A crowd had gathered there, blocking his view, and he pulled Lilian forwards, into the throng, needing to see his brother was all right.

Grave stood beyond the group, facing the demon prince as Isla slowly manoeuvred herself around the black-haired male, and just behind Grave was Sera. Her short red dress fluttered around her thighs and her blonde hair shifted in the breeze as she stood with her back to Night, her fear palpable as she stared at the demon.

The towering male stood a short distance beyond Grave, his black leathery wings stretched out behind him and his head bent towards his bare chest as his polished onyx horns curled around to resemble those of a ram.

Night looked down, curious about what the demon was looking at, and darkness poured through him as he spotted Helena. The bastard held her in his black gauntleted hands, his razor-sharp talons close to her delicate flesh as she wailed and kicked, clearly terrified.

He went to join his brother and Lilian's grip on his hand tightened, her fear hitting him hard. He glanced at her. She stared at the demon, her eyes enormous now, fear written in every line of her beautiful face, tearing him in two. He wanted to stay with her, but he needed to help his brother too.

Night wasn't the only one who wanted to fight the demon. Antoine's crimson eyes were fixed on the male as he leaned forwards, Snow's fierce grip on his arm the only thing that was stopping him from attacking as he bared fangs. His cousin glared at Snow's hand and then looked at Sera, his face crumpling for a moment as a war erupted in his eyes. Night could name the desires that were tearing him in two. He wanted to fight the demon and save his baby, but he also wanted to protect his female by getting her away from the male, and he wasn't sure which to do first.

He didn't get a chance to make a decision as he wrenched free of Snow's grip.

"I will kill you for what you did." Isla launched her hands forwards.

The demon prince reared back. Grave disappeared. Night was about to bellow his name as his heart jolted into his throat, but suddenly his brother was there again, standing right in front of Helena.

And turning solid.

Grave snatched her from the demon's hands and was speeding away from the male before he had noticed that Isla's attack had been nothing but a charade to gain his attention.

The demon prince looked down at his empty arms and then his gaze shot to Grave as he stopped beside Sera. The demon roared, the sound deafening as it rolled across London like thunder.

"You have taken enough family from us... I will not allow you to take any more," Grave snarled at the demon prince and then quickly checked on the squalling bundle in his arms.

Helena's blue eyes opened and fixed on Grave. She calmed in an instant and his brother had never looked so relieved. That feeling washed through

Night too as Grave handed the baby to Sera, who immediately bundled Helena up into her arms and backed away towards the roof exit. Antoine was waiting for her there and pulled her into his arms as soon as she was close enough, wrapping both her and Helena in the shelter of his embrace.

Snow stood beside him, a picture of wrath as he stared down the demon prince.

The demon stared right back at him, calm and cool, but Night had faced enough enemies to see through his façade. The sight of so many powerful adversaries had rattled him.

If the demon wanted a fight, he would have one. Every person on the rooftop with Night and Lilian were family. Not by blood, but by a powerful bond of friendship that he had discovered existed in this theatre. The people he had met in his time here were as close as a family could be, always watched out for each other and took care of each other, and they had faced enemies far more powerful than this demon in their time.

They had faced an angel incursion—a war the vampires, fae, wolf shifter and angel of Vampirerotique had won.

Aurora's green-to-blue eyes glowed in the low light as she narrowed them on the demon prince, the petite angel looking ready to cut him down—a look that didn't suit the normally gentle female.

The bare-chested demon flexed the onyx talons of his gauntlets as he shifted his focus back to Grave, his pupils nothing more than thin vertical slits in the centres of his black irises, blazing gold in the darkness.

Grave looked at Night and shook his head, issuing a silent command that had Night wanting to growl and bare fangs at him. The worry that shone in Grave's blue eyes was enough to have Night staying put, even though it was a struggle to stop himself from pushing through the crowd to reach his brother and tell him that he wasn't going to stand by and let him do this alone.

It really became a struggle when Snow stepped forwards, the grim look on the white-haired vampire's face making it clear it wouldn't be wise of his brother to try to stop him from fighting. Snow wanted to protect his family too.

When Grave nodded, Night really wanted to growl. He scowled at his brother, hurt arrowing through him, even when he knew Grave was only trying to protect him. Grave wasn't questioning his strength or his abilities. He was just trying to keep him safe. Lilian squeezed his hand and he turned his head towards her, gazed down into her eyes and heard the silent words they held. He stole the comfort she offered with that gesture and look.

Snow and Grave faced the demon.

The onyx-haired male growled through sharp teeth and held his hand out before him, and the pommel of a black blade rose out of the flat roof. The huge broadsword slowly travelled upwards, the blade seeming to go on forever as it materialised, and then it finally tapered to a point. The demon twisted his hand, took hold of the black-and-red hilt, and snarled as he hefted it in front of him, pointing it at Grave and Snow.

And Isla.

She drifted closer to them, her twin curved blades drawn and clutched tightly in her hands.

A war cry left her lips. "Nulla Misericordia!"

The motto of the Preux Chevaliers.

No Mercy.

The demon turned on her with a roar.

The phantom launched herself at him, turning solid as her twin blades clashed with his sword, blocking it and driving it back. She lashed out with her blades, catching him across his armoured thigh with one and just above his hip with the other. A thin ribbon of red formed where she had cut him, and the male twisted, planted his left foot behind him and swept his blade upwards, slicing through the air.

Snow was there before it could reach Isla, his own sword striking the black blade, sending it back the way it had come and filling the night with the ring of metal clashing with metal.

The demon shifted his focus to Snow.

Grave launched his own attack, drawing his katana and rushing around behind the demon. He went from ghostly to solid and snarled as he slashed up the demon's back, catching one wing and ripping the leathery membrane.

The male flapped those huge wings, battering Grave with them and driving him back.

Each second that ticked past, Night found it harder to stop himself from entering the fray. He had to do something useful. Something that could help those who weren't included in the fight. He had to protect them in his own way.

He turned to the others.

"Antoine, get everyone out of the theatre." Snow didn't take his eyes off the demon as he issued that command.

"I am not leaving," Antoine snapped.

Snow grimaced, huffed and then sighed as he readied his blade and the demon turned on him. "Please. I need to know you are all safe. Think of Helena."

Night looked at Antoine, and then Sera where she nestled close to her mate, her hand closed protectively over Helena's head as she clutched the baby to her chest.

Snow was right. Night needed to get the rest of them away from the theatre. It was the only way to protect them. He had already contacted Bastian about sending the jet so everyone could leave the theatre and go to various safe houses across Europe, a plan he had been putting together with Antoine, before Grave had shown up. Maybe everyone could reach the airport and take it in turns to use it? It wasn't large enough to evacuate everyone at once, but they could probably get everyone to safety in two trips. One if Antoine got the theatre's private jet ready too.

"Take the females and children, Antoine. It is your duty to protect them now." Grave held the demon prince's gaze as he circled him. "Payne... you can teleport. Take them all somewhere remote. Somewhere safe."

The demon's glowing gaze slowly inched towards Payne, and Night readied himself. If the demon tried to target him, Night would protect him. Grave was right. Payne could teleport everyone to safety. That would be far quicker and safer than driving across London to the airport and waiting for the jet.

"The cabin," Payne said and Snow grunted in agreement as he launched at the demon.

Night tuned the battle out as he focused on his task. "We have to get the most vulnerable out first. Are you the only one in the theatre who can teleport?"

He growled as Aurora left the group, joining the battle, and wanted to make her come back. He reined in that need. Aurora was powerful, more than strong enough to battle a demon and win. It was better she fought with his brother and the others. With her on their side, they could turn the tide of the battle in their favour.

He looked at Payne again. "Well? Are you the only one here who can teleport?"

"I will help," an unfamiliar female voice put in as she pushed through the crowd, laced with a Russian accent and a slightly disappointed edge that didn't quite dampen the teasing lightness of it when she continued, "Although, helping out the incupire isn't normally my style... so you know I still hate you, and I'm just doing this to keep me in the lead on the 'who's awesomest' scoreboard, right?"

Payne chuckled, the sound out of place in the thick night air. "I still hate you too, succubus, but this time you're going down."

Night stared at the newcomer. A succubus. She certainly looked the part in her black leather corset and mini-skirt and thigh-high stiletto boots.

She fluffed her black bob, the blue that ringed her pupils in her dark eyes growing brighter. "I like going down… but I also really hate missing a good fight, so let's make this quick and then we can come back and kick arse. Race you!"

The female grabbed hold of Antoine, and he, Sera, and Helena disappeared with her.

Payne muttered something and seized hold of Night and Lilian, and darkness swallowed them.

"Not the plan," Night growled as they landed in the deep snow outside a small cabin at the edge of a frigid, desolate valley surrounded by towering, jagged mountains. "You were meant to take those most in danger first."

"I'm not dumb," Payne shot back. "Grave wanted you out of there and I'm not about to argue with a vampire whose nickname is the King of Death. I like being alive."

The half-breed squared up to him.

Night bared his fangs. "Take me back. Leave Lilian here, but take me back."

"No." Lilian tightened her grip on his arm. "Take us both back. I can help. I'm a witch. I know spells that can slow the demon down or weaken him."

"Listen, lady, taking you back is the same as taking Night back. A death sentence. I get you want to fight. I want to fight too. We all do. Look at us." Payne nodded towards the others.

Night looked at Antoine and found him staring across the valley, fear etched on his features as he looked south, towards London.

"After Grave and Snow, you were the two priorities on that demon's list. He would have targeted you to weaken them. Grave and Snow both needed you and Antoine away from there." Payne's tone was soft, but Night still growled at him, because he knew that.

He knew Payne had done the right thing, that staying in London would have made him a distraction that might have gotten his brother or cousin killed, but it didn't mean he liked it.

Payne clapped a hand down on his shoulder, squeezed it as he gave him a sympathetic look, and then disappeared.

And all Night could do was wait.

And pray.

Hoping his brother and the others survived.

CHAPTER 26

Lilian stifled a yawn, hiding it from Night. He had been nagging her to rest since she had finished helping Elissa with the spell that had made Isla corporeal again, and in turn had made his brother solid once more. She put his sour mood down to the fact Grave and the others had dealt with the demon prince without his help, and she could understand why it had upset him. He wanted Grave to rely on him, to see him as someone strong who could help him, and Grave insisted on protecting him.

While she was thankful the King of Death had a deeply protective streak when it came to Night, she also wished the vampire had at least given Night something he could do. The fact that Aurora had been sent by Snow to snatch Lilian and Elissa from the cabin because they had been needed really hadn't helped matters.

Night had been in a terrible mood with her for hours and had given his brother the cold shoulder. She wasn't sure whether the two of them had spoken since Night had returned from the cabin.

She glanced at his hand and gently brushed the backs of her fingers across his. His head swivelled towards her and his scowl melted away, his expression softening as the hard edge left his eyes. He looked down at their hands and then back at the dark park that surrounded them.

"You should have rearranged this meeting," he grumbled and that was the tenth time he had told her that.

"I tried. They insisted we meet tonight." She wanted to reach for his hand again, but knew he would move it away this time, evading her touch. "I could have come alone. It would have been safer."

He scoffed. "Safer? These witches tried to kill you, Lilian. They tried to kill me. If you think I would let you come here alone, without my protection, then you really don't know how much I love you."

"I know," she whispered and risked it, stretching her hand towards his to brush his fingers again. He didn't move his hand away, and some of the tension knotting her chest unravelled as he shifted his hand instead and took hold of hers. He held it tightly, silently telling her how much he cared about her and wanted to keep her safe. She squeezed his hand. "I have to try, Night."

He didn't understand that, and that was fine. As far as he was concerned, her coven was now their enemy, and he wished she could think that way too. But her coven was her family. They were all she had ever known. They had raised her and taken care of her, had been there for her through so many difficult times. It was hard to shake the love she felt for them or how deeply she needed them in her life.

Maybe she could make him understand her need to heal the rift between her and her family.

"Night..." She gazed down at their joined hands, avoiding his gaze as she gathered her strength, finding the courage to open her heart and let him in as he had with her. "My coven has been my family for over one hundred and fifty years. I know what they did—what they tried to do—but I can't just turn my back on them... because they never turned their back on me."

"What do you mean?" He paused and pulled her around to face him, and when she still didn't have the courage to look at him, he cupped her cheek with his free hand and tilted her head up, forcing her to lock gazes with him. His eyebrows furrowed as he looked down at her, his gaze soft and filled with yearning—a need for her to tell him.

She swallowed her nerves and said, "My mother passed away two decades ago. I never knew my father. My mother didn't speak about him much, but the other witches who were around at the time I was conceived told me that she never reached out to him to tell him that she was pregnant."

"Why not?" He stepped closer to her, curiosity brightening his striking ice-blue eyes.

"None of them knew, until... until I accidentally discovered my talent for reading memories in blood." She tightened her grip on his hand, needing to feel he was there for her and that he wouldn't pull away. He wasn't a witch. He wouldn't view this as a black mark. Not like so many others had. She held his gaze, needing to see it for herself though. "That talent only runs in dark magic bloodlines. My father... he was of the dark. That was why my mother never contacted him. Our coven is of the light. Dark magic is forbidden. She must have feared he would come for me and want to be a family, and that she would be exiled from the one that had raised her and had always been there for her."

Night's expression hardened. "They didn't exile you?"

She shook her head. "No. I feared they would, but Beatrice, our coven leader, summoned me to her office and she was... *nice*... to me. I went in there braced for something awful, expecting it to happen, that I was going to lose my family just as my mother had feared losing it, but Beatrice told me that I was part of the coven, that I was as important to it and loved by it as any other member, and maybe even more so because of my newfound talent."

And it had felt good to hear that.

"She gave you a purpose," he murmured and his gaze lowered, turning pensive.

Lilian nodded. Beatrice had given her purpose and a direction, just as Night had been given one when he had begun working in the field for the Preux Chevaliers.

"You must see why I have to do this, Night. We're not so different. What would you do if the Preux Chevaliers kicked you out and there was something you could do that might clear your name with them—with your brother—and allow you to return to them?"

He looked as if he was chewing on a wasp now, upset that she had found a way to make him see how important this was to her and how desperate she was. She was well aware of what they had done to her, and to him, and part of her felt she shouldn't forgive them. The rest of her wanted to try. She knew it was foolish, but she had to try. Even if they didn't take her back, if she could clear his name and stop them from coming after him, it would be worth it.

Her hand fell to the pocket in her black dress and the glass bottle in it had never felt so heavy. A lot rested on the potion it contained. Elissa had helped her harvest her memories and distil them into liquid form so Beatrice could see them with her own eyes. Pure, unfiltered memories. Beatrice would see everything she had, which made her doubly glad she had left Night's memories before she had shown up in them.

He sighed. "I would try."

She tiptoed and kissed him for that, stealing a little comfort and reassurance at the same time. When she pulled back, he still didn't look impressed, but at least he knew why this was important to her now. Sharing a little about her past with him had felt good, and when they were done with this meeting, she was going to tell him more things about when she had been growing up and all the mischief she had caused. She was sure he would like to hear it.

Plus, she wanted to hear if he had been naughty at all while growing up.

Night led the way through the park to the fountain where she had agreed to meet Beatrice. Her nerves rose with each step she took that brought her closer to that point and she struggled to tamp them down. She could do this. She wouldn't be alone. Despite her protests, Night had insisted on remaining at her side during the meeting. She had tried to convince him to hide in the shadows of the trees that lined the open patch of green, but he had refused. She could understand that too. He wanted to protect her and he didn't trust her coven—or witches in general—so he wouldn't cower and hide from them.

They reached the fountain, an elegant circular one that filled the night with the sound of rushing water, and she drew down a breath. Night glanced at her and squeezed her hand before releasing it. He reached beneath his black suit jacket.

Checking his weapons?

He had gone to speak with Snow before they had left, and had returned with two short swords, and had fashioned a holster for them so he could wear them under his jacket, hidden from mortal eyes.

And witch ones.

He didn't want Beatrice to know he was armed.

"There won't be a fight," Lilian said and Night cast her a glance that told her he didn't believe that for a second.

That part of her that didn't want to forgive her coven didn't believe it either.

Lilian glanced around the dimly lit park as she waited, every minute feeling like an hour. Where was Beatrice?

She was about to ask Night what time it was when she felt the familiar caress of magic sliding over her skin. Her head whipped to her left, gaze locking onto a point on the other side of the fountain, and her pulse picked up when she spotted Beatrice.

And eleven other witches.

"I don't like those odds," Night muttered.

She wanted to tell him it would be fine, but she couldn't bring herself to lie to him. It didn't feel as if it was going to be fine. It felt as if her coven was about to prove Night right about them.

This was a trap.

Lilian tried to be reasonable. Beatrice had said that she would meet her in the park. She hadn't said she would be coming alone. Lilian had just presumed that was the case. And really, it made sense for the coven leader to come with backup. Beatrice hadn't known what she was walking into and Lilian might have been the one setting a trap for her.

She looked at the older, fair-haired woman who stood front and centre in the group, flanked by Petra and Maryon.

"I have a potion." Lilian reached into her pocket and stepped forwards, moving in front of Night. She held the small black bottle out to Beatrice. "I distilled the memories into it. If you drink it, you'll see that Night didn't attack our coven."

Her hand shook as she waited for Beatrice to say or do something.

Finally, the witch angled her head towards Maryon and nodded.

Maryon crossed the short span of pavement to Lilian, her dark eyes cold and unreadable. Lilian swallowed as Maryon took the bottle from her and stared at it, and then at Night. She willed Night not to react. If he did, he would give her coven a reason to attack him.

Thankfully, Night remained still and silent behind her.

Maryon turned away from her, her fall of dark hair swirling away from the shoulders of her black dress with the sharp motion, and returned to Beatrice. She placed the bottle into the coven leader's hand and moved back into place beside her. Beatrice didn't even look at the bottle as she slipped it into the pocket of her black dress. Her grey eyes remained fixed on Lilian.

"Now, if you will hand the vampire over to us until we have had time to check what you have given me." Beatrice held her hand out to Lilian, her tone gentle and her expression soft, warm almost. "He won't be harmed."

Lilian looked over her shoulder at Night, her heart pounding faster as she met his cold gaze and a shiver bolted down her spine. Not caused by him, but by what Beatrice wanted her to do. She looked back at her coven leader, a woman who had been like a second mother to her for her entire life, and for the first time, she felt she couldn't trust her.

And that this was another test.

Beatrice wanted her to choose between Night and the coven. Beatrice knew what would happen if she let the witches take Night. Her vampire would turn against her, would be wounded and furious, and it would destroy his love for her.

His eyes softened, warmed, and a war erupted inside her. She didn't want this to be the last time he looked at her like that, as if he loved her. As if she was the centre of his universe.

But if she didn't do as her coven wanted, then she would lose her family.

A family that was important to her.

"Hand the vampire over or we will be forced to take him from you." Beatrice's harsh tone had ice forming in Lilian's veins and she looked at the witch, no longer recognising her.

This wasn't the witch who had helped raise her, who had shown her compassion when she had feared she would be exiled because of her tainted blood. This wasn't the witch who had given her kind smiles in the hallways and had gently encouraged her to pick herself up and keep striding forwards whenever she had stumbled on her path to becoming a useful, powerful member of the coven. This wasn't the witch who had guided her to her calling, helping her find the position that had made her feel fulfilled and often happy.

She was seeing another side to Beatrice, had witnessed the lengths the woman would go to in order to get what she wanted, and how ruthless she could be in pursuit of that. The coven wanted someone to blame for what had happened to their house in Germany, and all Beatrice cared about was giving them what they wanted.

She didn't care that Night wasn't to blame.

She was going to haul him up before the coven and kill him to appease them.

If Lilian did as Beatrice asked, Night would die and Grave or Bastian, or all of his family would come after her coven. They would kill them all and then what? One of their sister covens rose up to seek revenge?

She couldn't let that happen. She couldn't let her coven have Night or any of his brothers. She wouldn't let this turn into a cycle of revenge.

She looked back at Night and made her decision, one she hoped would be worth it as she gazed into his eyes.

Lilian turned to Beatrice—to her coven—her heart breaking and tears misting her eyes as magic rose to her fingertips.

"If you want Night, you'll have to go through me."

CHAPTER 27

Night drew his twin swords as Lilian's words registered, together with her pain. He sensed the hurt in her, the fear, and he wanted to growl and curse at the same time. He had put her in this position by insisting on coming with her. If he hadn't, she could have spoken with her coven safely. By accompanying her, he had given them what they wanted.

An opportunity to get their hands on him.

He was old enough to know when someone was setting him up as a martyr, and he wasn't willing to be the sacrifice this fair-haired witch wanted in order to appease her bloodthirsty followers.

Lilian threw her hands forwards and several glowing violet orbs exploded from her palms, rocketing towards the group. She didn't pause to see if they hit their marks. She pivoted on her heel and seized Night's arm, tugging him around with her.

Night stood his ground, refusing to run, and she cast a pained look over her shoulder at him. The fear in her eyes struck him hard, but he couldn't do as she wanted. He was sorry, let her see that in his eyes, but he wasn't going to run from these witches.

If he did, they wouldn't stop coming after Lilian.

The only way to keep her safe was to take these witches down, even when he knew that would hurt her. They were her family. She looked beyond him to the woman she had been speaking with and for a moment, she looked as if she would try to make him run again rather than fight, but then her jaw set in a hard line and her caramel-coloured eyes sparkled with bright silver stars. The magic he could sense coming off her grew in intensity, rolling over him in powerful waves, and she released his arm.

Lilian turned back to face the witches, her eyes narrowing on them, intense concentration etched on her beautiful face.

"Why don't you all drop dead?" she bit out.

And surprise washed across her features.

It struck him that she had tried cursing them and it hadn't worked.

The fair-haired witch smiled slowly.

Beside her, one with long silver hair and cold blue eyes laughed. "It won't work. We've taken measures to ensure you can't affect us with your powers. You can thank me and Maryon for that."

The witch's German accent lent a hard edge to her words that only made her sound crueller than Night already knew she was. This was the witch who had ordered the male guard to beat him and question him, and who had wanted to stick around to watch the show. The guard had called her Petra. Although Night had been in pain at the time, he recalled she had been bitterly disappointed when she had been called away from his cell.

Night set her as his first target, and the brunette, Maryon, as his second. The dark-haired witch had been the one to stand on him back in Norway, keeping him pinned to the floor when it hadn't been necessary. He had been too weak and tired to fight back.

Not this time.

As he came to stand beside Lilian, he felt as if someone had supercharged him. He felt invincible. Whatever he needed to do in order to emerge the victor from this battle, he would and could do it. Nothing would stop him from protecting Lilian.

She attacked again, sweeping her arm out to launch three blue spears made of crackling light at the witches. They dodged them with ease, but ended up scattered by doing so, giving Night an opening. He grinned and kicked off, shooting into the midst of them, aiming for Petra.

The silver-haired witch slammed a hand into his chest and sent him flying backwards. He grunted as he hit something soft and took them down with him, and rolled heels over head to land on his feet in a crouch beside the fallen witch. He stabbed her through the heart with his right sword, not giving her a chance to retaliate, and launched upwards, springing back into action.

Two of the other witches saw what he had done and one screamed a name while the other attacked. He ducked beneath the twisting violet orb she launched at him and threw himself forwards into another roll, coming onto his feet behind her. He raised his sword to cut her down and growled as he spotted the orb swerving to track him.

Another orb struck it, and the two detonated. The explosion hurled Night and the witches away from each other, sending him sailing through the air. He twisted and tried to right himself, and braced when he realised he didn't have time. He released his swords a split-second before hitting the grass hard and grunted as he rolled across it. The moment he came to a halt, he was back on his feet and sprinting towards his blades. He scooped them up and roared as he ran at one of the witches who had been thrown by the blast.

To his right, bright, colourful flashes of light drove the darkness back, dampening his vision on that side. He kept his senses fixed on Lilian, making sure she was safe, and crossed his arms as he closed in on the witch who was picking herself up off the grass, looking dazed.

Night reached her and uncrossed his arms at speed, and his twin blades cut through her head, severing it. He followed through, bringing his swords down to his sides, the swiftness of the action ridding them of blood. It splattered across the grass, the scent of it filling the air, mingling with the coppery tang of magic.

Making his mouth water.

Two down, ten to go.

He turned his sights on Petra.

She hurled a spiralling whip of fire at him and he nimbly dodged it, landing several feet to his right. The grass sizzled as the whip struck it and he felt the heat of it despite the distance between him and it. He growled and shot towards Petra. She brought the whip back and struck again, and he leaped to his left this time, and then his right as she struck again, zigzagging towards her.

The second he was close enough he lashed out with both blades.

And growled as they hit a barrier.

Vibrations rang up his arms as the swords he gripped hit it and bounced back, and he staggered backwards.

Into another witch.

Petra lashed at him with the whip again. Night grabbed the witch behind him and hurled her into the path of it. She screamed as the fiery whip struck her, wrapping around her chest, and Petra didn't even react. Her eyes remained cold and expression placid, even as the witch burst into flames and turned to ashes before Night's eyes.

The whip unravelled and Petra drew it back again.

Night decided that allowing it to touch him, even for a second, would be a very bad idea. One that would probably result in his death.

He pivoted and ran, leaping when the tip struck the ground so it didn't hit him. A wave of fire rolled forwards from the point it had hit, almost catching another witch.

"Petra!" the fair-haired one snapped.

"I'm sorry, Beatrice." Petra didn't look as if she was sorry, and clearly, she wasn't going to stop because she readied the whip again.

Night needed to get the damned thing off her.

Or put it out.

He glanced at Lilian and she sent Maryon flying away from her and looked at him. Her gaze shifted to Petra and narrowed, and ice formed on her fingers. Rather than leading Petra away from his little witch, Night turned in Lilian's direction and led the woman towards her.

Night could feel how focused Petra was on him. It would be her undoing. Focus was key on the battlefield, but losing awareness of your surroundings by focusing on one enemy was a sure-fire way of losing your head.

Franz had taught him that.

Night looked back over his shoulder as he passed Lilian.

Saw the shock ripple across Petra's face as Lilian launched the spell at her.

Petra tried to pull her whip back, but it was too late. The one Lilian had cast hit it and ice spread outwards from the point it had struck, moving rapidly along the length of the whip, extinguishing the fire as it went. The weight of it had Petra lunging forwards as it dropped to the ground, and her expression shifted from surprise to fury as she narrowed her eyes on Lilian.

Lilian hit her again, striking her with two blasts of light that knocked her away from the whip and sent her crashing into the fountain. Stone exploded outwards as Petra hit it, chunks of it flying through the air to rain down on the witches, knocking several of them down.

Night was quick to take advantage of the opening, moved through the witches like a shadow, cutting down several of them. His senses blared a warning and he sped up, narrowly avoiding being struck by a white spear that left a huge impact crater in the ground.

Beatrice's starlit eyes narrowed on him as he glanced at her, and another white spear appeared in her hand. She hurled it at him, aiming at where he was about to be, and he twisted to face the way he had come, trying to stop it from hitting him.

And grimaced as the spear cut through his calf.

The scent of his own blood spilling had him growling and his mood darkening, his bloodlust rising to the fore. A hunger for violence spread like an oily black tide through him and he focused, refusing to give it control. He wouldn't risk Lilian. There was no knowing whether or not he would hurt her if he surrendered to his bloodlust.

He would use it as Grave did.

As a weapon.

Night focused harder, sharpening his bloodlust, stoking it but holding it back at the same time. He snarled and bared his fangs as he sprinted at Beatrice, on a collision course with her. She summoned another white spear.

He swept his blades down at his sides and flexed his fingers around the hilts, tightened his grip on them and kicked off, launching into the air above her and catching her off guard. He spun in the air, bringing his blades up at the same time, and roared as he brought them down as he twisted towards her, putting all his strength into the blow.

His swords struck the white spear as she hastily held it aloft, and he grinned as it shattered under the force of the strike, splintering into a thousand pieces. He had her now. He followed through, hitting the ground in a crouch and kicking off, thrusting his right blade towards her at the same time.

And bellowed as something struck him in his right shoulder, knocking it backwards, and icy cold instantly spread over his chest and down his arm.

Night staggered backwards, breathing hard as he looked at his shoulder and saw the shard of glowing blue ice protruding from it. He growled through his clenched teeth as he stabbed his left sword into the earth, gripped the icy blade and yanked it free of his flesh. Fiery pain throbbed in his shoulder as he cast the shard away from him and he struggled to focus through it.

"Night," Lilian breathed and a wall of shimmering glyphs appeared before him, between him and the witches.

She sounded strained, as tired as she felt on his senses, but there was something else in her voice too.

Shock? Fear?

He swallowed hard and pressed his left hand to his shoulder, and looked for the witch who had hurled the ice spear at him, stopping him from claiming his prize.

He stilled right down to his breathing.

Perhaps it was both of those emotions he had heard in Lilian's voice, feelings that flowed through him as he stared at the blonde witch before him.

He stared into the witch's hazel eyes, unable to believe his.

Jana.

The witch who had tried to claim his head as *her* prize.

CHAPTER 28

Lilian recognised the two new witches. Not because she had met them before, but because she had seen them in Night's memories.

The blonde with the hazel eyes had been the one to almost kill him. Lilian thought her name was Jana. She definitely remembered the name of the other witch. It had been clear in Night's memories, as if the pain and grief of the moment, and the eternal fire of his rage had seared it on his mind.

Karlotta stood beside Jana, looking exactly as she had the night she had killed Franz, only her black hair was shorter now, barely reaching her jaw.

Night grabbed his second sword and gripped the hilts so hard his knuckles burned white, and Lilian closed ranks with him. She gently touched his arm and focused, using some of her remaining strength to summon a healing spell and funnel it into him. His eyebrows knitted and his jaw flexed, and she wanted to apologise for hurting him. It was necessary. The spell would knit the worst of his wounds back together. She wasn't strong enough to fully heal him, had to hold back and not use all of her magic, but she could take away the worst of his pain for him, so it wouldn't be a distraction in the fight ahead.

The sculpted planes of his face hardened as he stared the two witches down, his shock subsiding at the same rate as it did in Lilian. Rage burned through her too as she pieced together what he probably had.

Jana and Karlotta had been the witches who had 'witnessed' his brother near Lilian's coven's house in Germany.

They had turned another coven against him.

They had set him up.

She could only think of one reason why. They wanted revenge for what he had done, wanted to stop him from constantly hunting them, and they weren't strong enough to face him alone, so they had killed all the witches in the house in Germany and had then pretended Bastian had been there, all so her coven would target him.

And Night.

Apparently, Grave wasn't the only vampire in their family who had made a powerful enemy who now wanted to wipe out his bloodline and everyone he cared about.

The two witches hadn't only set Night and his family up. They had set her up too in a way. She had come dangerously close to being owned by Bastian because of them and had almost been killed by her own coven.

Jana didn't look pleased as she stared at her.

Why?

Lilian guessed this hadn't been part of the plan.

Jana had wanted Night to end up alone, at the mercy of witches, but he wasn't. She might not be as powerful as Beatrice or Petra and Maryon. She probably wasn't as powerful as Jana and Karlotta. But she was going to fight.

This wasn't going to go anything like how Jana had envisaged.

Lilian wasn't going to let these witches take Night from her.

She was going to give him the revenge he needed instead.

"Beatrice. The potion. Drink it. You'll not only see that Night is innocent, but that these two bitches set him up. They set us all up." Lilian quickly cast a protection spell as a long shard of ice came flying at her.

It hit the barrier and breached it, just the razor-sharp tip breaking through the invisible wall.

Pointed right at her head.

She was growing weaker.

Soon, she wouldn't even be able to cast a barrier. This wasn't good. If she couldn't convince Beatrice that Night was innocent and these two witches were responsible for everything, then she would have to fight and she wouldn't stand a chance against so many powerful witches.

"Drink it," Night growled and Beatrice cast him a withering look.

"You do not tell me what to do, vampire." Beatrice pulled the bottle from her pocket and looked as if she might do it though.

Karlotta stared at it, her dark eyes widening as she looked from it to Lilian. "You dark little minx. You can read memories."

"Do not listen to her. It is probably poisoned," Jana said and approached Beatrice. "She is a liar and a traitor. She sides with the vampire over her own coven. She will say anything to buy herself the time to help him escape. The vampire murdered our sisters. He must pay."

When Beatrice looked as if she might drink the potion, Jana's eyes brightened and narrowed on her profile, and her fingers subtly flexed. Lilian looked at her hand and her gut clenched. Ice glittered on her fingers, gathering in her palm. She was going to hurt Beatrice.

Lilian reacted on instinct, driven to protect her. She lunged forwards, grabbed the spear of ice that still protruded from the barrier, letting that spell shatter at the same time, and hurled it at Jana.

It clipped the blonde's shoulder and a thin line of blood bloomed on her bare skin.

Jana turned murderous eyes on Lilian and threw the spear that formed in her hand at her instead, and Night struck it with one of his blades, shattering it as he moved in front of Lilian. Before she could try to convince Beatrice to listen to her and believe her, the witches attacked.

Lilian cast another protection spell, stopping the fiery whip that cut through the air towards Night, and hurling a spell after him as he kicked off. It would boost his speed and strength, but it came at a price. Her head turned, vision wavering for a moment before it sharpened again. She was expending too much energy. Her tank was almost empty.

Night cut through the witches, dodging most of their spells as he tried to get to Jana and Karlotta. Maryon raised her hand towards the sky and swiftly brought it down, and a dozen bolts of lightning struck the ground, shaking it beneath Lilian's boots and charging the air. Night bellowed as one caught him and a witch screamed as another hit her and she was thrown clear of the battle, landing close to the trees.

Lilian ran into the fray, muttering an incantation as she closed the distance between her and Night. She waved her hand in Maryon's direction as the dark-haired witch raised her arm to strike Night with another bolt of lightning and hit her with one instead, giving her a taste of her own medicine. Maryon cried out, juddering violently, and Lilian almost tripped over her own feet as her legs weakened beneath her.

Night shook off the blow and growled as he ran at Karlotta.

Lilian breathed harder, struggling to keep going, and chanted another incantation in her mind. She grimaced and gritted her teeth as she cast both hands forwards, towards Karlotta, and blue fire burst from her palms, becoming a spiralling funnel that snaked through the air to strike her. Karlotta screamed as she was knocked sideways, the skin of her left side blistering as the flames burned her, and the black material of her corseted dress glowing with blue embers as she landed.

The fire would not only burn her, but it would drain her strength too.

Night took the opening Lilian had given him, closing the distance between him and Karlotta down to nothing, and bared his fangs as he attacked. His eyes blazed crimson, the hunger in them unmistakable as he clashed with the witch, driving her backwards as she struggled to use magic to defend herself. Any offensive spell would be dangerous at such close quarters, liable to hurt her as well as Night.

Lilian's head turned and she dropped to one knee. Her heart thundered against her ribs so fast she felt dizzy, and she blinked to clear her vision. Night had been right. She should have rested rather than coming to the meeting tonight. She had been so desperate to clear his name and show her coven that she wasn't a traitor though, had only been able to think about making that happen.

And now she regretted it with all her heart.

Night roared as he thrust his twin blades towards the witch.

Karlotta bellowed as they sliced through her chest and Night lifted her with them.

"Karlotta!" Jana turned on Night, her hazel eyes enormous as she stared at Karlotta as Night lifted her above his head on the swords.

He roared again, the sound echoing around them, and pivoted with Karlotta, hurling her at Jana. Jana desperately tried to catch her, but Karlotta hit the grass and rolled across it, landing close to the fountain. Jana dropped to her knees beside the fallen witch, pulled her over onto her back and stared at her.

Karlotta stared back at her.

Unblinking.

Petra shot past Jana, heading for Night, and Maryon flanked her.

Lilian had to do something.

Her gaze darted to Beatrice. "The potion! Drink the potion! Night isn't our enemy. Jana is!"

Jana's head slowly swivelled towards Beatrice.

Beatrice looked from the blonde to Lilian and unscrewed the cap on the bottle. Jana launched at her as Beatrice tipped the contents into her mouth, and Lilian surged to her feet and ran at her.

She barrelled into Jana's chest, knocking her backwards, and the witch grabbed her by her hair and yanked her head back.

Lilian grunted as Jana head-butted her and her vision tunnelled. Not good. She fought the witch, wrestling with her to hold her back long enough that Beatrice could see she had been telling the truth.

Night was innocent.

Jana and Karlotta had set him up.

She was sure they had been the ones to kill the witches in her coven's house in Germany too, an attack that replicated the one Night had carried out on their coven as revenge.

Jana fought harder, slamming a fist into Lilian's gut, and Lilian gripped her nape and struck her hard across the face. Her knuckles burned as flesh met flesh, and fire blazed up her arm. This close to Jana, she could feel how powerful the witch was. Lilian was no match for her. Not even Beatrice would be.

But together, there was a chance they could take her down and avenge their coven.

And Night.

Lilian looked over her shoulder, unable to resist the urge to see if Beatrice had witnessed Night's memories, desperate to know whether the witch would be fighting with her or against her.

Beatrice held her hand up and Petra and Maryon, and the remaining six witches, leaped away from Night. He breathed hard and leaned forwards, looking as exhausted as Lilian felt as his swords lowered to his sides and he kept a wary eye on the witches.

Beatrice stared at Jana, her eyes darkening as her eyebrows knitted hard and her lips thinned. "You."

Jana viciously twisted Lilian around so her back was to Jana's front.

And pressed the sharp tip of a shard of ice against Lilian's throat.

"Lay down your weapons, vampire, or I will kill her."

CHAPTER 29

Night's heart couldn't beat any faster. It hammered a fierce rhythm as he stared at the ice dagger poised to pierce Lilian's vein, his mind racing to calculate the outcome of every possible move he could make.

Jana had already taken one person he loved from him, her integral role in Karlotta's plan making her as much responsible for Franz's death as her friend. He couldn't let her take Lilian too.

But what could he do?

If he dropped his swords, then Jana would kill him and then she would probably kill Lilian too. If he didn't, she would kill Lilian. He wasn't fast enough right now to reach Lilian and get her clear before Jana made her move.

Lilian stared at him, both hands locked around Jana's arm to keep the shard from jabbing into her throat. Her caramel eyes brightened, silver stars emerging in them.

"Drop dead!" she gritted.

Jana laughed, the high mocking sound rankling Night as much as it evidently did Lilian. Lilian's lips flattened and her eyebrows drew down as the witch behind her continued to chuckle.

"Your power won't work on me." Jana lowered her mouth to Lilian's ear and stared right at Night. "I took precautions, but you're so weak right now I probably didn't need to worry. You're like a kitten, witch. Feebly clutching at life."

Lilian's eyes darkened and Night shook his head, silently warning her not to provoke Jana.

He could see and scent how desperate Jana was now that she was outnumbered, and that only made her more dangerous. He had faced many foes in her position, and all of them had been willing to do anything to escape, had been wild and unpredictable. He couldn't let her escape though. Not again.

He needed to do something.

Jana closed her free hand around Lilian's neck and squeezed. Night's heart jerked into his throat as Lilian gasped, her eyes flying wide and desperation filling them as she tried to breathe. He cast a glance at Beatrice and then the other witches, and all of them looked ready to fight on his side now.

It was enough for him.

For once, he was going to trust witches.

He couldn't reach Lilian without Jana harming her, but maybe they could, if he gave them an opening they could use.

Night's grip on his swords loosened and the hilts slipped towards his fingers, and Jana's expression turned triumphant as she watched him surrender to her.

And then he noticed something.

He tightened his grip again, clutching his weapons.

Watching as Lilian's breath turned to mist in front of her face.

Night smiled slowly.

Jana looked unsettled as she stared at him, and then her eyes darted around, taking in the other witches. Trying to see what he had. Victory. He had seen his victory.

Jana would die this night.

Maryon blew out her breath, watching it fog in the air, and whispered, "What's happening?"

Night grinned at Jana now. "You messed with the wrong family."

Jana locked up tight, her hazel eyes widening as she paled, and Lilian stiffened too.

Behind them, Isla appeared, her long white hair flowing in an unfelt breeze as she rose up to loom over Jana, the distant buildings still visible through her phantom form.

The blonde witch twisted towards her and hurled her free hand towards Isla, unleashing a spear of ice that went straight through the phantom, and giving Night her back. Big mistake.

Isla clucked her tongue at the witch.

Night kicked off, his gaze fixed on Jana's back, and he readied his swords. He needed to be careful. Jana still had hold of Lilian. If his aim was even slightly off, then he would harm his witch.

He didn't get a chance to land a blow.

Jana turned and shoved Lilian at him to stop him, sweeping her other hand out at the same time. A wave of ice daggers shot outwards in a fan, hitting several of the witches, including Maryon. The green orbs that had been building above the brunette's upturned palms rocketed in all directions as the shard of ice punctured her left side.

Night dropped his swords and caught Lilian, twisting so his back was to the orbs as he curled his body over her to shield her. One of the orbs shot straight past them, narrowly missing them, and he growled.

Maryon grunted and dropped to her knees off to his left, and several witches screamed as they were struck by the haywire spell and hit the ground, shuddering as green lightning arced over their bodies.

"Maryon!" Petra yelled and raced to her side.

The brunette witch flopped onto her back, breathing hard as she stared at the shard of ice, her hands shaking as she reached for it.

Petra sank to her knees beside her and took hold of her hands, stopping her. "You'll lose too much blood if we remove it."

Night guided Lilian behind him and turned to face Jana.

She was gone.

He snarled, flashing his fangs as his senses reached outwards and he located her a short distance away. Running. She suddenly stopped. Why?

The answer became apparent when a bright red flash lit up the park, silhouetting not one but two figures.

Grave.

His brother kicked off, sweeping his katana up in a fast arc, and blue light detonated as it struck a barrier. Night checked Lilian was all right, smoothing his palms over her cheeks as she stared in the direction of Jana and Grave, her skin ashen and eyes dull. He could feel how tired she was, but he could sense something else too. She still wanted to fight.

He slanted a look at Beatrice.

The fair-haired witch nodded.

Satisfied that she would take care of Lilian, and that the witch was no longer a threat to either of them, he dropped a kiss on Lilian's brow and then pivoted, picked up his swords and sprinted into the darkness.

Isla came up beside him, her feet floating above the grass, her face a picture of determination as her white hair streamed behind her together with the flowing hem of her pale dress.

Jana hit Grave with a spell that sent him flying towards them.

Isla's blue boots hit the ground as she turned corporeal, her cerulean leathers instantly replacing her white dress, and she grunted as Grave slammed into her, knocking her backwards.

His brother huffed. "You did not need to do that."

She pushed him off her. "You would have flown clear into the trees if I hadn't."

Night had the feeling this was going to turn into an argument if he let it, so he said, "She's getting away."

"Do not get me started on you." Grave scowled at him, his crimson eyes flashing with a warning that Night felt all the way to his soul.

He was in for an earful once this battle was done.

Isla disappeared in a white blur.

Jana shrieked and turned, breaking right as Isla appeared before her. Night charted an intercept course and ran, pushing himself past his limit. His legs ached with each stride that carried him swiftly across the grass, fatigue rolling up on him. So much so that Grave overtook him. Night glared at his brother's back as Grave passed him with ease.

Grave's silver blade was a bright flash in the darkness as he swept it upwards. It didn't hit its target. Jana struck it with a spear of ice, knocking it off course, and then thrust the tip of it at Grave. His brother dodged backwards, the razor-sharp point of the spear coming close to gutting him. Too close.

Night sprinted around behind Jana and bellowed as he lashed out at her with his right blade. The witch turned, her speed surprising him and catching him off guard. His blade hit her spear and she rotated it, swirling it around as she lunged towards him. He tried to keep hold of his weapon, but his shoulder burned as he tightened his grip, and he wasn't strong enough. She knocked the sword from his grip. He growled and thrust his second blade at her, and she dropped low, his sword cutting through the air above her head as she swept her spear across his thigh.

Fire blazed a trail over it in the wake of the spear and the scent of his blood hung heavily in the air.

Grave roared and jabbed his blade at her back as he appeared behind her, and the witch rolled to her left, leaving his brother coming right at Night instead. Grave's eyes widened and Night used his remaining blade to knock his brother's blow off course before it could skewer his one good leg.

"You are hurt." Grave's crimson gaze took in his leg and then his shoulder.

"Spare me the lecture." Night pressed his hand to his injured shoulder. "Berate me all you want later. Right now, we have a witch to kill. She's the one who almost took my head."

His brother's eyes darkened dangerously, black invading the scarlet, and his gaze swung towards Jana as she picked herself up and started running again.

There would be no escape for her. Not because his brother was harnessing his bloodlust now, but because Lilian and the other witches had formed a circle around them. They were up to something.

It became apparent as Jana reached the middle of the circle.

Pale violet light burst from each witch in the circle, including Lilian, and fell to the ground to fill the space between them at the same time as it shot up into the sky.

Forming a great dome.

Magic filled the air inside it, making the hairs on his nape stand on end, and he readied his swords. The soft sound of chanting reached his sensitive ears. A spell. The witches were keeping the barrier in place. Jana twisted this way and that, her eyes widening and her fear hitting him, rousing his bloodlust.

This ended now.

The scar on his throat burned and he lifted his right hand and touched it.

His ears twitched as he singled out Lilian's voice. She was chanting a different spell. He looked for her and found her moving away from the wall of the dome, heading towards Jana. The witches beyond her sidestepped a few paces, reducing the gap she had left. Stopping the barrier from being weak at that point, Night guessed.

What he couldn't guess was what Lilian was up to.

Jana's eyes glowed pure silver and she unleashed a battle cry as she came at him and Grave. Isla intercepted her before she could reach them, striking the witch hard across her face with the back of her hand and sending her sailing towards the fountain. The witch stopped in mid-air before she could hit it and held her right hand out.

In front of it, a dozen ice daggers appeared.

They shot towards Night, and he, Grave and Isla broke apart, heading in different directions. Four of the shards shot towards him and he moved as quickly as he could as his thigh burned. He leaped right when he sensed one coming at him, dodging it, and then darted left and put on a burst of speed to evade the next two.

Jana unleashed another dozen shards as she lowered to the ground.

And then another as Night, his brother and Isla finished dodging them.

Night glared at the witch as he leaped over one of the daggers and it buried itself into the grass where his foot had been. He couldn't get close to her when she was throwing the shards at this rate, and she didn't look as if she was going to tire any time soon. He glanced at his brother as they crossed paths and then froze as a female screamed.

"Isla!" Grave bellowed and shot in a straight line towards his mate.

Night looked over his shoulder in her direction and he growled as she pulled an ice dagger from her thigh. Grave reached her, but before he could check on her, she had transformed into a ghost again, her eyes glowing ethereal blue as she narrowed them on Jana.

"Can you teleport?" Grave said, his face awash with concern as he looked Isla over.

She subtly shook her head. "Not right now. There is something in the spell the witches are using."

Jana raised her hand above her head and a spear formed there. She threw it at Grave with such force that his brother barely dodged it. It struck the ground and shattered, and Jana followed it with another wave of ice daggers.

This time, three dozen of them.

Grave wouldn't be able to dodge them all.

Night's chest constricted and he kicked off, racing towards his brother, sending up a silent prayer he would make it in time as Grave readied his blade and stared the threat down. His brother was insane. There was no way he could cut down that many daggers. He was fast, but not that fast.

Grave's sword and hands turned ghostly, and his brother's eyes narrowed, concentration shining in them as his jaw flexed. He was trying to turn into a phantom. Trying and failing by the looks of it.

Night ran harder, his heart feeling ready to stop as the ice daggers neared Grave.

They were going to hit him.

A wall of flames burst from the ground, shooting high into the air, and the daggers hit it. They melted on contact, causing steam to billow from the flames, and Night looked over his shoulder.

Lilian kneeled on the ground a short distance away, her right hand outstretched and the other one pressed against the grass to support her as she leaned over, breathing hard. Her lips peeled back off her clenched teeth as she slowly moved her hand towards Jana, her arm shaking violently. Night looked back at the flames, unable to believe his eyes as they bent towards the blonde, gathering into a fiery vortex.

Lilian screamed and the vortex suddenly shot towards Jana.

The blonde dodged it, all her focus on evading the fire that snapped at her.

Giving Night the opening he needed.

He summoned all his remaining strength, shut down the pain that wracked him and flexed his fingers around the hilt of his remaining blade. He launched at Jana, speeding towards her while she fought the fire with her ice. Each spear that struck the flames destroyed them, causing the fire to dwindle and weaken.

But not quickly enough to save her.

Night roared as he kicked off, sailed through the air and brought his blade around, putting everything he had into one final blow.

Jana looked up, her gaze colliding with his, and she raised her hand as ice formed above her palm.

Too slow.

Night's sword cut clean through her neck and he landed in a crouch with his side to her, his free hand pressing to the dirt to support him as the pain of his injuries caught up with him and his body shook from the exertion.

Jana wobbled and then toppled, her head rolling away from her.

A fitting death.

She had tried to take his once, and in the end, he had been the one to take hers.

"Night!" Lilian stumbled towards him and he sensed the others closing in on him.

He sagged back to rest on his heels, his shoulders slumping as he stared at Jana and a strange feeling swept through him. Lightness. Relief. It was over.

Lilian wrapped her arms around his neck, pressing her forehead against his cheek, and he dropped his sword and banded his arms around her. That sense of relief grew stronger as he held her in his arms, growing aware that she was safe now.

Or at least he hoped she was.

He looked over her head at Beatrice as the fair-haired witch approached him. Behind her, Petra helped Maryon walk, supporting her weight.

Beatrice dipped her head. "We owe you both an apology."

Lilian emerged from his arms and looked at the witch, and he could sense her nerves, and hope.

"You have done well, Lilian. I never should have doubted you. For that, I am eternally sorry, and I can only hope you will forgive me." Beatrice shook her head slightly. "What we did was inexcusable, and I will understand if you no longer want anything to do with us, but if you need us, we will be there to help you. It is the least we can do."

The least Beatrice could do was get on her knees and beg Night not to decapitate her too, but Lilian wouldn't want that, so he held himself back. Her coven was important to her, and although he knew that it would take her a long time to overcome what they had done, he also knew that she would eventually choose to become a part of her family again.

She nodded and nestled closer to Night.

"Where's my fancy apology?" Night drawled and sensed Grave and Isla come to a halt behind him.

His brother's fury was palpable, stoking Night's rage.

"I would apologise, witch," Grave growled. "And make it a good one or I will have the First Legion pay a visit to your coven."

Lilian cast Night a worried look and he stroked her side as he held her gaze, trying to show her that her coven would be safe from him and his brother, while not ruining their show of force.

Beatrice bowed. "To you, Night Van der Garde, I can only offer my sincerest apologies and a promise that should the Preux Chevaliers ever need the assistance of witches, they can call upon our mercenaries. If you would accept it, we can discuss terms of an alliance."

Night muttered, "Shrewd female. An alliance would offer you protection from my wrath, as long as you continue to please my brother."

Isla put in, "Grave is not easy to please."

Night could practically feel Grave scowling at her as he grumbled, "I am quite easy to please. You are the difficult one in this relationship."

Isla huffed and the air chilled.

Night grimaced as his shoulder ached in response to the cold and he shivered.

"Are we quite done here?" Lilian said and placed her hand on his chest, her eyes filled with concern as she looked at his shoulder. She shifted her gaze to Beatrice. "You will repay us for what you did by serving the Preux Chevaliers for… two decades… three?"

She looked up at Grave now.

"Five," he growled. "Five decades of devoted service. By then I will be ready to forgive you for what you did to my brother and Lilian."

Night arched an eyebrow up at Grave as he came to stand beside him. His brother was getting soft now he had a mate. Part of Night had expected to have to fight his brother on Lilian, to make him see that he loved her and that he didn't care about what she had done, because he wanted to be with her.

He needed to be with her.

And here was Grave talking about not forgiving the witches for what they had done to her too.

The witches bowed their heads and moved away to attend to their fallen.

Grave held a hand out to Night.

Night took it and Grave hauled him onto his feet, and he pulled Lilian onto hers.

"All those rumours are true." Night shook his head as he looked into Grave's eyes.

They narrowed on him, a crease forming between his brother's eyebrows as he muttered, "What rumours?"

Night grinned. "You do have a heart."

"Shut up." Grave scowled at him and held his hand out to Isla.

It didn't stop Night from grinning as he reached for Lilian and wrapped her in his arms.

Grave started across the park with Isla, his voice grim in the darkness, sending a chill down Night's spine.

"It is a long walk back to the theatre, and I am going to use every second of it to make it painfully clear how angry I am with you for not telling me your foolish plan to get yourself killed."

Night bit back a groan.

This was going to be the longest walk of his life.

CHAPTER 30

∞

As threatened, Grave had scolded Night all the way back to the theatre, not allowing him to get a word in to explain himself. His brother stood over him in the back room of the theatre as Lilian helped him remove his shirt and Elissa moved around him to get a look at his shoulder.

Anger rolled off Grave in powerful waves. His brother scowled and waved Elissa away as she looked at him.

The silver-haired witch huffed. "I wasn't going to tend to your wounds, anyway. I just wanted to know if Isla needed healing too."

Grave grunted, "She is resting. Her wound will heal by itself soon enough."

He folded his arms across his chest, tightening his dark shirt across his shoulders, and stared at Night.

Night snapped, "I didn't tell you because I knew this was how you would react. You would have tried to stop me from going, and I needed to go. Lilian needed me there and she would have gone without me."

"Perhaps I might have reacted a little better. Perhaps I might have surprised you," Grave barked, the air around him chilling as a blue glow lit his aquamarine eyes.

Night looked at his brother and admitted to himself that Grave might have, because his brother was different now that Isla was back in his life.

Grave kicked one of the crimson couches, knocking it towards Aurora as she carried a pitcher of water and some rags towards him, and earning himself a scowl from Snow.

But not that different.

His brother growled, baring his fangs at everyone, and pivoted away from Night. He strode to the middle of the double-height room and began frantically pacing, taking swift strides between the corridor that led to the foyer and the stairs that led to the staff quarters. Night winced as Elissa pressed her fingers to the wound on his shoulder and pain bloomed in it, a fiery sort of stinging that made him turn his head away from it and focus on Grave, because he didn't want to see his flesh knitting back together.

Lilian sat beside him and placed her hand on his thigh, drawing his gaze there. He looked from her hand to her face, right into her eyes, and smiled as he saw the concern in them. He was fine. She didn't need to worry. He had survived worse injuries.

He was worried about her though. She was still too pale.

"How long will it be before you're fully recovered?" He wanted to reach for her and stroke her cheek, but moving his arm would be a mistake. He knew what happened when witches lost their connection to healing spells, had witnessed it for himself once. The spell would go haywire inside him, causing him more pain and injuring him.

Lilian shrugged. "A few days. As long as I don't do any spells. My... my connection to my coven is still intact. Their power is trickling into me to recharge my battery."

She looked relieved by that. He placed his left hand over hers on his thigh and gently squeezed it. As much as he hated her coven for what they had done to both of them, he was glad they hadn't severed ties with her and that if she wanted to one day, she could work with them again.

As a freelance witch.

No way he was going to let her go and live with them.

She was his now, part of his family, and sooner or later he would find the courage to broach that subject. Right now, the crushing nerves he felt whenever he thought about asking her whether she wanted to stay with him, and the fear she might say she preferred to be with her coven, had him leaning towards it being later. Much later.

Grave paced back into view, scowling at his boots as he muttered, "Some might call it insubordination. A fitting punishment might be relieving him of his position."

Night shot to his feet and grimaced, biting back a bellow as Elissa lost her connection to him and the spell tore through him.

"Bloody idiot," Elissa muttered and grabbed his wrist, and the pain lessened and faded to nothing. She released him, but still scowled up at him.

Night paid her no heed as he stalked towards his brother. "You are not relieving me of my position. I earned that position. I won't give it up."

Grave shot him a glare. "You wouldn't get a say in the matter."

Night stared him down. "I would have told you, but you were recovering from your battle against the demon prince and being made corporeal again. I didn't want to risk you."

He grimaced as Grave looked less than impressed and he realised that his actions might have come across as payback for Grave not allowing Night to help him with that battle. They hadn't been, but he could see why his brother thought they had.

Night scrubbed his nape and sighed at his shoes, and then looked his brother in the eye. "I love you too much to risk you like that."

Grave huffed and folded his arms across his chest again, his look stern, but then he mumbled, "I love you too."

Night knew that. It was the reason Grave had been so worried, and so angry with him.

"Don't you have a phantom to take care of?" Elissa snapped and went to Grave, pushing his back, shoving him towards the stairs. "Scram. You're disturbing my patients. I'm taking them to their room and they're not to be disturbed until I say so."

Grave glared at her, but obeyed her order, heading up the stairs.

"Come on, you two." Elissa jerked her chin towards the stairs. "Up you go."

"Your witch is bossy," Night muttered to Payne as he passed the half-breed, and Payne shot him a look that said he was well aware of that.

Elissa grumbled, "I heard that. I was going to help you too."

"Help me?" Night frowned at her back as Lilian joined him and he took hold of her hand. He clutched it as they followed the witch up the stairs. "With what?"

"I'll tell you once you're resting." Elissa looked over her shoulder at him and winked.

Night arched an eyebrow at her, trying to figure out what problem he had that she could possibly help him with. When they reached his temporary quarters, she waved him towards the bed. Curious to know what she was going to help him with, and assuming it was his other injuries, he toed his shoes off and sat on the bed. Lilian sat beside him.

Elissa closed the door, turned to them and planted her hands on her hips, ruffling the hem of her black flowing camisole where it met her dark jeans. "I found a spell… in the books Grave and Isla brought with them. It's risky, but it might work… or undoing this bond might kill you. One or the other."

Night shook his head.

"No. I can't risk that." He looked at Lilian, aware this decision wasn't only his to make. She was the one most affected by the bond they shared, the one who would experience pain if another vampire tried to touch her without his permission. It was more her decision than his and whatever she decided, he would abide by it. "What do you want to do?"

It strangely felt as if a lot hinged on her answer to that question, as if he was asking her more than what she wanted to do in regards to the bond. He was asking her what she wanted to do about them too.

Did she want to be his?

He searched her eyes, trying to find the answer to that question as she pursed her lips and frowned.

She looked at Elissa and his stomach felt heavy as he braced himself for her answer.

"I thought of something else," Lilian said and leaned towards Elissa. "Might there be a way to alter the bond rather than undo it?"

Elissa's look shifted towards pensive. "What do you have in mind?"

Lilian glanced at him and a hint of colour touched her cheeks. She hesitated, a flicker of nerves in her eyes and her scent, and lowered her gaze to her knees and then lifted it back to lock with his as she tipped her chin up. She was learning. The best way to deal with a Van der Garde was to look them in the eye and not be weak.

"Elves are the forebears of vampires. Could this bond be transformed into something akin to what elves share with their mates? Think about it... We exchanged blood as an elf and their mate would." She sighed and fidgeted with her skirt, her confidence waning as she added, "I know vampires are different to elves... but they're the same in many ways too. You share DNA. It might be possible."

Night wasn't sure it was, but then what did he know? He couldn't imagine a vampire had ever tried to find out whether their species had retained enough elven DNA to allow them to bond with someone as elves did. Vampires could be fated mates of other species though. It was entirely possible that someone could be the fated mate of a vampire.

He certainly felt protective and possessive enough of Lilian to be her fated one.

"It might take a long time for us to figure out of it's possible," Elissa put in.

Night glanced at Lilian. "Are you willing to put up with the bond as it is for that long?"

Lilian nodded. "I want to keep our bond. I like it."

He could read in her eyes what she wouldn't say. She wanted to be his mate. It was right there, shining in them as she looked at him. Maybe his fears were unfounded after all. Maybe she wanted to stay with him and that was the reason she had hesitated to accept Beatrice's offer to return to her coven.

"Leave." Night didn't look at Elissa as he issued that command, putting force behind that one word.

He wanted to be alone with Lilian.

Right now.

The second Elissa closed the door behind her, Night pounced on Lilian, capturing her lips in a soft kiss as he pulled her beneath him. Her lips danced across his, teasing him and wrecking his control, threatening to get him going and make him forget what he wanted to say. He forced himself to break away from her mouth and rose off her.

Night gazed down into her eyes and husked, "Say it."

She blinked. "Say what?"

It was no use playing innocent with him.

"Say what you really want," he growled, hungry to hear it.

Her cheeks pinkened, but she framed his face with her hands and held his gaze. "I want to be your mate."

Night growled again and kissed her, harder this time, unable to hold himself back as he thought about the fact she wanted to be his, that she wasn't going anywhere, and that she was choosing him over her coven. He drifted away from her lips, peppering her cheek and her throat with kisses, and then drew back and looked down at her again.

"I want to be your mate too, Lilian. I love you. I love you so damned much." His brow furrowed and he stroked her cheek, resting his weight on one elbow as he drank his fill of her beauty and the soft look in her warm eyes. "I need you with me. Always. I don't want to be apart from you for a second… even when I know I will have to be."

His mood faltered as he thought about the team he led and he almost wished Grave had followed through with his threat and removed him from his position. Almost. He loved his job, but he loved Lilian too, and he didn't want to leave her for weeks on end.

"I could come with you," she said and before he could say a word, she continued with a little frown marring her brow. "Grave might be amenable to it. My coven is meant to serve with the Preux Chevaliers for fifty years after all. Your team would simply have one witch mercenary assigned to its ranks."

He wanted to argue against it, but the thought of keeping her close to him all the time and the thought of having a powerful witch on his team's side in any fights, was far too tempting and he couldn't deny her.

"I'll speak with him… but I'm afraid you won't be the first female serving in the Preux Chevaliers." He feathered his fingers down to her jaw and her brow crinkled. "Isla already decided she was joining the First Legion. I don't think Grave got a say in it."

Lilian smiled.

"I'm not surprised. You Van der Gardes growl and snap your fangs, but in here…" She pressed a hand to his chest. "There's a heart that loves deeply… and is easily commanded by the woman that steals it."

He mock-scowled at her, but didn't bother to deny it. He kissed her instead, pouring his love into it, letting her feel that she was right and he did love her deeply, and he would do whatever she wanted.

Even accept her as a member of his team.

Fighting beside her had been exhilarating, like nothing he had ever experienced before, and in time they would learn to read each other's moves and would become a formidable team. No enemy would be able to stand against him and his witch.

Lilian stroked her hands over his bare shoulders, her touch light as she reached his injured one. "How would a mating work if your vampire blood still possessed the ability to have a bond with a fated mate?"

Night hated comparing himself to elves as much as the next vampire, but he thought about it anyway.

"I believe we would exchange blood. Much like we already have. Only we would do it while I was inside you." He groaned as her eyes darkened, desire glittering in them as they lowered to his throat and he realised it wasn't sex that had her arousal soaring.

It was the thought of taking his blood.

She wanted it.

He had been asleep the last time she had taken it. He wanted to know what it would feel like. No one had ever bitten him.

She couldn't bite him, but she could feed from his vein.

Night looked down as she tugged at his trousers and groaned again, his shaft stiffening as it dawned on him where this was going. He wanted to be inside her too. Ached for her. He pushed her dress up and she raised her arms, allowing him to pull it off over her head. She flopped back onto the bed as he cast it aside and tackled his trousers as he unfastened her bra and shredded her panties with his claws.

She scowled at him for that one.

He wiped it off her face by spreading her thighs and guiding his cock into her.

She moaned and clutched his left shoulder as he inched into her, joining them, and her eyes fluttered closed as he withdrew and plunged back in, setting a slow rhythm.

"Look at me, Lilian," he husked.

Her eyes opened, sparkling with silver stars and hunger as she tracked his hand as he brought it up to his throat. He drew a line on the arch of it with his claw, tempting her. Her tongue poked out, driving him wild as she flicked it over her lips, and then she was on him. Her mouth closed over the tiny wound and he groaned and shuddered as she sucked on it, drawing his blood to her.

Pleasure crashed over him, exquisite bliss that was almost as startling as the connection he felt to her as his blood flowed into her, nourishing her. She moaned against his throat and he groaned with her, every inch of him as hard as stone as hunger pounded inside him.

A need to mark her too.

Night dropped his head and sank his fangs into her throat.

She cried out, the sound muffled as she refused to release his neck. She sucked harder as he made his first pull on her blood. Good gods. He shuddered, the pleasure so intense he spilled as he rocked into her, craving more even when he felt sure it would kill him. She cried again, her body throbbing around his, greedily pulling him deeper, and he moaned in time with her as his entire body trembled and shook.

Lilian released his neck and licked it, the tenderness of the action warming his soul, but not as much as the single word she softly whispered in his ear.

"Mine."

Night groaned and released her, swiped his tongue over the puncture marks and looked at them, and then into her eyes.

He pressed his forehead to hers and then kissed her, silently thanking fate for placing her in his path and bringing them together.

A witch had killed him once. She had failed to take his head, but she had left him so cold and dark it was as if he was dead.

And now a witch had brought him back to life.

He would thank the gods for the gift of her every day of the years he intended to share with her.

And one day, they would find the way to grant her wish, because he wanted it with all his heart too—a heart that was now hers.

She would officially be his mate.

But until then, he would make sure she knew he belonged to her and she belonged to him, and he was never letting her go.

He brushed his lips across hers and breathed against them.

A single word that he felt to the very depths of his soul.

"Mine."

The End

ABOUT THE AUTHOR

Felicity Heaton is a New York Times and USA Today best-selling author who writes passionate paranormal romance books. In her books she creates detailed worlds, twisting plots, mind-blowing action, intense emotion and heart-stopping romances with leading men that vary from dark deadly vampires to sexy shape-shifters and wicked werewolves, to sinful angels and hot demons!

If you're a fan of paranormal romance authors Lara Adrian, J R Ward, Sherrilyn Kenyon, Kresley Cole, Gena Showalter, Larissa Ione and Christine Feehan then you will enjoy her books too.

If you love your angels a little dark and wicked, her best-selling Her Angel romance series is for you. If you like strong, powerful, and dark vampires then try the Vampires Realm romance series or any of her stand alone vampire romance books. If you're looking for vampire romances that are sinful, passionate and erotic then try her London Vampires romance series. Or if you like hot-blooded alpha heroes who will let nothing stand in the way of them claiming their destined woman then try her Eternal Mates series. It's packed with sexy heroes in a world populated by elves, vampires, fae, demons, shifters, and more. If sexy Greek gods with incredible powers battling to save our world and their home in the Underworld are more your thing, then be sure to step into the world of Guardians of Hades.

If you have enjoyed this story, please take a moment to contact the author at author@felicityheaton.com or to post a review of the book online

Connect with Felicity:
Website – http://www.felicityheaton.com
Blog – http://www.felicityheaton.com/blog/
Twitter – http://twitter.com/felicityheaton
Facebook – http://www.facebook.com/felicityheaton
Goodreads – http://www.goodreads.com/felicityheaton
Mailing List – http://www.felicityheaton.com/newsletter.php

FIND OUT MORE ABOUT HER BOOKS AT:
http://www.felicityheaton.com

Printed in Great Britain
by Amazon